BAREFOOT IN THE DARK

Lynne Barrett-Lee

Published by Accent Press Ltd – 2006
ISBN 1905170378
Copyright © Lynne Barrett-Lee 2006

The right of Lynne Barrett-Lee to be identified as the author of
this work has been asserted by her in accordance with the Copyright,
Designs and Patents Act 1988.

Printed and bound in the UK by
Cox and Wyman Ltd, Reading

Cover Design by Anna Torborg

The publisher acknowledges the financial support
of the Welsh Books Council

With thanks to everyone at the
Children's Hospital for Wales,
Cardiff

Chapter I

January

People will tell you that there is no essential difference between Monday and any other day of the week. The sun rises and sets just as it does on, say, Thursday. The meteorological patterns that govern the weather do not lay on any special horrors at Monday's behest. It is not possessed by a malevolent alien life-force, nor is it occupied by evil spirits or gremlins.

For Hope Shepherd, however, this was plainly so much tosh. When you were newly divorced, and all-at-odds with the world, Monday was a day like any other only in the same way that a rottweiler was like a poodle, or a self-assessment tax return was like a hair-appointment card. Thus, as she jogged the last fifty yards to Cefn Melin Station with a box-file under her arm and a thumping headache, she knew there was only one sure route to defeating the beast that was Monday and that was, simply, by getting better organised to deal with it: in particular, by remembering all those things that should never be *done* on a Monday. Like taking Friday's lunchboxes out of school bags. Like being forced to acknowledge that you cannot put a tin of beans in a sandwich. Like taking the school uniform you have remembered to wash on Sunday evening out of the washing machine. Like noticing that you do not have twenty pence for your son's bus fare. Like remembering you have failed to set the alarm again.

Of course, you could just cancel Monday altogether. Or designate it a non-contact day, like teachers have from time to time. A day in which hopelessly disorganised people could pause, take stock and, well... get organised.

Except Hope knew that if you did that, Tuesday would simply become The New Monday, which was why one of her New Year's resolutions this year was to stop trying to re-schedule the Gregorian calendar and to simply lick herself into shape. It would be a challenge, however, because getting organised was not something that came easily to her. Getting organised was

1

something her ex-husband used to do. And still did, no doubt. And would do in perpetuity. Hope didn't do organised. Organised was boring. She used to do spontaneity and optimism, didn't she? Yes. *So* much better. And optimism did work, in a roundabout way. Why fuss, for example, with the bother of remembering an umbrella if you knew perfectly well it wasn't going to rain?

Except now it was. Which struck Hope as unfair, and a metaphor for the state of her life generally. She shunted her bag higher on her shoulder and broke into a run. Missing the train was an absolute no-no, because the next wasn't due for twenty minutes. She'd no business aiding and abetting a day that was already intent on frustrating her. This, she thought, as she scuttled down the ridiculously long flight of steps – the station was in a cutting – was what making all those New Year's resolutions was really all about. Greeting every new day with a smile. Yeah, right. She bared her teeth, her breath whistling as it tried to keep up with her, and jumped the last two steps before sprinting towards the platform.

Hope didn't get the train often – she generally drove to work – but today she was off to the printers in town and had to bite the fetid bullet that was rush-hour commuting. She ran faster. The train, she saw, was already at the station.

She braced her shoulders, quarterback style, in preparation for pressing her way into the fuggy interior. Even from outside, her nose prickled under the assault of anti-perspirant and perfume, of jackets smoked overnight in essence of chip fat, of cloying post-weekend early morning breath.

The doors on the eight-forty-two from Cefn Melin to Queen Street were of the concertina variety. There was a well – a deep step – between door frame and carriage, which had to be kept clear for the doors to sweep shut. She needed to get her hand round a pole and pull herself up before they did. But even as she made one last heave out of no man's land, some sixth sense told Hope her day was about to get worse. And it did. As she moved fully on board and the doors began hissing, she felt the crush of someone else trying to squeeze in behind her and an unlikely resistance as she lifted her right foot. Hope had not, up to now, been aware of her laces. Which was why she had no reason to know that the one on the right was undone. But plainly it was, for as she tried to lift her foot from the doorwell, she felt it begin to slip out of its trainer,

2

like a resolute trout trying to escape from a net. She scrunched her toes up and swivelled to see, but before she could do anything else, she was shunted hard from behind and felt the chill wind of the morning – and it just became chillier – now playfully caressing her besocked right foot. And then something else. Something infinitely more worrying. The plump-plump of an item of unattached footwear, as it fell the short distance between carriage and well. And, although she couldn't see through the Narnian coatscape, her ears didn't deceive her. The doors had shut.

And if the doors had shut...

'Er, excuse me,' she panted at no one in particular. 'Do you mind if I just... er... oomph... excuse me... I'm sorry... um, it's just that my trainer's come off.'

The body closest to her, which was wide and smelled of bacon, was attached to a smiling female face topped off with an arrestingly-hued rain-hood. She shuffled a little to make room. Hope peered at the floor. She couldn't see her trainer.

'Come off, lovely?' asked the woman, even though it must have been completely obvious. Because she too was now looking down at Hope's sock.

'Yes,' said Hope, dipping to scour the doorwell itself. She still couldn't see her trainer. 'Er. Oh *God* –' The train began gliding slowly, but oh-so-surely, out of the station. A small explosion of panic whumped in her stomach. Heads turned. 'Oh God! Where's my trainer gone?'

Feet began to move. Eyes peered downwards. Everyone around her was now looking at the floor. Hope banged heads with a man in a suit. It was at this point that she realised there were worse things than your trainer falling off. Immeasurably worse. Like your trainer falling off as you were boarding a train, and then – the realisation leapt up and bear-hugged her – failing to board the train with you. 'Oh my God!' she cried now. ' It must still be on the platform!'

A ripple of mild interest began to eddy around her.

'Er, can someone press the alarm or something, please? My trainer – '

'I can't see it,' said another female voice, which belonged to a stout lady with a stiff conker-brown coiff and an ivory pashmina, who was wedged against the window behind her. Was it she who

3

had pushed her? Was it this hateful woman who had trodden on her lace? The woman in the rain-hood peered through the perspex and shook her bagged head. 'I can't see it on the platform, lovely.'

The platform which was fast disappearing beside them. 'But it must be!' Hope gasped.

The woman shook her head sorrowfully. 'I don't think it was.'

A glimmer of hope surfaced. 'It must still be here, then!'

The wodge of legs shuffled some more.

'I can't see it,' said a voice.

'Me neither,' said another.

Because it wasn't there. Because it was under the train.

'You've got to laugh,' quipped the woman in the rain hood, patting her.

Yeah, right, thought Hope, miserably. Or you'd cry.

At the offices of Heartbeat, a little after eleven, there was a tangible *joie de vivre* in the air, of the kind that only an entertaining misfortune happening to someone else on a wet Monday morning could bring.

Kayleigh, who did reception plus the filing and photocopying, had picked up Hope's left trainer and was clutching it to her chest as she gaped.

'What?' she said. 'You mean you got off the train and walked all the way from the station to the shoe shop with one trainer missing?'

'Well, no, as it happens,' corrected Hope, dumping her box-file on her desk and reflecting that having spent nineteen pounds ninety-nine on another (rather nasty) pair of trainers meant she would now have to forego the Eva Cassidy CD she wanted. 'Have you tried walking any distance in one shoe?'

Kayleigh shook her head.

'So I took the other one off as well.'

'So you walked there in your *socks*? God, wasn't everyone looking at you?'

'Yes.'

'God, that's dire! I'd be mortified.'

'Oh, but it gets worse.'

'Worse?'

'Yes,' she said. 'Because I stepped in something unspeakable outside Benetton. Sick, to be precise. So then I had to take my socks off as well.'

'What? You mean you walked all the way to the shoe shop barefoot?'

'Barefoot.'

'In *January*?'

'In January. God, I'm so wild.'

'I don't doubt it,' said Simon, with habitual tenderness. He was sitting opposite Hope wearing a pea-green sleeveless sweater. 'Oh dear,' he added. 'You must have felt such a prat.'

Hope irritably pulled a pen from her pen pot. 'Oh, it's not that,' she said, though this was entirely untrue. On alighting at Queen Street station, her most compelling thought was that as she had never been so excruciatingly embarrassed in her life she might as well do the thing she most wanted to at that moment. Which was to sit down on a bench on the platform and burst into tears. But she hadn't done it, and for very sound reasons. One being that if she had burst into tears her embarrassment would have leapt, at a stroke, to unimaginable proportions, and the other being that she wasn't allowed to anyway, another major New Year's resolution being that she wasn't going to burst into tears over nothing any more.

And she had made the shoe shop and the memory was fading. As her mother would say, *Darling, nobody died.'*

'Well, it was a bit,' she conceded now, reflecting that listening to Eva Cassidy might not be an altogether uplifting pastime anyway, what with her having died. 'But mainly it's the money. Fifty-five quid I paid for those trainers! And it's been raining all morning. So even if it's still there it'll be fit for nothing.'

'It'll be fine,' soothed Madeleine, who had come in from a meeting of her own, and who thought nothing of spending that amount of money on lunch. 'I used to have my au pair put all my kids' trainers in the washing machine. They come up a treat.'

'And that's assuming it hasn't already been mangled by fifteen trains,' Hope added. 'Or zapped by four million volts. Or –'

'But someone will have seen it and handed it in, surely?' Simon gently persisted. He persisted gently in all things. He was that kind of man.

Hope shot him a look of frustration. 'That's just the point! There's no-one there to hand it in to. There's no-one there, period. The station's unmanned. And besides, who's even going to see it if it's down on the line?'

'You never know,' Simon said. 'Someone might have seen it.'

Hope lifted her foot and peeled down one of her new socks. There was a blister the size of a sprout on her heel.

'Oh, come on,' she said irritably. 'And pigs might fly. Besides, even if someone did see it, Simon, who in their right mind would pick the bloody thing up?'

Before he could utter another platitude, she stood up and took herself off to the toilets. Because quite without warning, the tears, ever threatening, had welled in her eyes in treacherous floods. Bloody hell. Bloody *hell*. What a start to the week. What a start to the year. She chewed on her lip and railed at her frailty. When would this stuff ever stop?

Chapter 2

Some five miles distance from the Heartbeat office, Jack Valentine was sitting in the studio six cubicle at the BBC, swivelling on a chair while he went through his script. He glanced up as his co-presenter bounced in.

Patti pulled a face and gestured with a finger at an object on the filing cabinet. 'Jack, what is that, exactly?'

Jack looked on appreciatively as she plopped herself down on another chair. She was wearing a sapphire-coloured stone in her belly-button today. Patti's stomach was as familiar a presence to Jack as was her round, rather cherubic face. He felt certain he would be able to pick her out in a police line-up on the strength of it. Jack was rather fond of Patti's belly. It wasn't so much sexual as sensual (he'd decided), but he liked the caramel-brown softness and rotundity of it. The way it swelled so unashamedly whenever Patti sat down. And it was smooth. Hairless. His ex-wife's belly-button had had a row of little hairs growing down from it, which had sprung forth in pregnancy and never quite gone away. She would, he remembered, pluck them out irritably on occasion, but never, to his knowledge, in the last year or two. Probably the sort of thing her half-arsed womens' group disapproved of as being too submissive and spiritually-draining an act. Jack wondered idly whether Patti's belly would at some point sprout hairs as well, but he'd not scrutinised enough post-partum bellies to know. Come to think of it, there'd only been Lydia's, hadn't there? He hoped not. Patti's belly had such a youthful exuberance.

He tore his gaze from her navel.

'It's a potato,' he said. 'I'm leaving it there to seed.'

Patti's jewel winked at him as she tutted. 'You never can do it, can you?'

'Do what?'

'Give a straightforward answer to a straightforward question,' she said equably. She waved her pen in the air. 'You know what I mean. What's it doing on the filing cabinet?'

Jack plucked the trainer from the top of the cabinet and turned it over thoughtfully in his hands.

'I found it,' he said, 'while I was waiting for the train this morning. Size four. Very new. I've been wondering who it belongs to. Look –' he lifted it to show her. 'There's even a clue. It has a purple drawing-pin stuck in the heel.'

Unlike Hope Shepherd, Jack Valentine was not a man given to last-minute panics. Not because he was particularly well-organised, but because years of working to broadcasting schedules had taught him that the only sure way to minimise disaster and dyspepsia was to be half an hour early for everything you did. A strategy that involved a lot of waiting around, but one that had stood him in good stead. He had got through almost the entire canon of Penguin Classics, digested impressive chunks of Stephen Hawking, and travelled much of the developed world with Bill Bryson. He was thus never lost for dinner party conversation. Though this particular skill (oh, happy thought) was one without much practical application now.

Getting the train, on the other hand, was a wholly new experience. One that would have been one of Jack's New Year's resolutions, had it not been one of his après-divorce resolutions, and therefore something he should already have been doing for three months. But he hadn't, and not being fully up-to-date with the train timetables – where did one get them? – he had arrived at Cefn Melin station a good twenty minutes before his train was due in. He watched the nine-ten wheeze away as he started down the steps. It had been bitterly cold first thing, spiky with hoar frost, but by then rain had rumbled over and was falling in quantity, scooping up icy shards from the trees as it came. A damp sort of day. A dull sort of day. A day that lent itself to introspection, and this morning, this second Monday of a new and (he fervently hoped) better year in his life, was well-suited to the almost ceaseless motivational dialogue that he had begun with himself on January 1st. He'd flipped up his collar and made his way across to the platform, pulling his paperback from his jacket pocket as he did so. He was reading *Captain Corelli's Mandolin*, a Christmas gift from his cousin Sally in Kent. Since discovering Amazon, Sally had taken to dealing with Christmas by simply having book parcels dispatched to everyone on her list. Jack didn't mind. He liked getting parcels. Would that stop, he wondered? Lydia had always been the one to do presents and his own efforts this year had been patchy, at best.

He was just folding back the corner of page fifty-one when he sensed something odd at the edge of his vision. He took three steps along the platform. There was something teetering on the edge, a little further along.

He slipped the book in his pocket and strode towards it, seeing very quickly what it was. How curious. A lone trainer, on its side, at the very edge of the platform. He looked all around him, but the station was deserted. Whoever had lost it had obviously gone. Intrigued, he picked it up. It was small, almost brand new – there was still the faded remains of a price sticker in the heel – and decorated with two glittering silver flashes. How long had it been here? He peered in, then eased a hand gingerly inside it. It was stone cold. He wondered briefly about the foot that had vacated it. Had it meant to do so, he wondered? Was it even now hobbling around Cardiff unshod?

'So you brought it to work. Are you *on* something, Jack?'

Patti left her chair and peered idly through the window. In the studio, Dave Parfitt ('Dave's Daily' – nine till eleven) was cocking an arm and winking at her. She poked up a finger and turned back to Jack.

'No,' he said, idly twizzling the laces round his finger. 'I just didn't know what else to do with it.'

'Er… leave it there?' Patti suggested. 'Bet you were popular when its owner came limping back for it and found it had disappeared.'

'Ah, but I figured they wouldn't,' he said. 'It had obviously been there a while. And a Northbound train came in while I was waiting for mine, so they clearly weren't going to, either. Would you, in the rain? I thought I'd take it down to Central Station and hand it in at the lost property office.'

Patti crossed the cubicle again and reached behind him for mugs. 'But you didn't.'

'No. I schlepped all the way down there and it was shut.' He placed the trainer back on the filing cabinet and smiled fondly at it.

For reasons he couldn't fathom exactly, the absurdity of finding this pristine little trainer had brought an unexpected lift to his day. A good deed done. A resolution adhered to. 'I'll drop it by tomorrow,' he said, gathering up his script. Patti was poised by the coffee machine, waiting. Jack nodded. 'Make mine a large one, will you? Oh, and no sugar.'

'No sugar?' she asked incredulously, teaspoon arrested mid-plunge.

'New Year's resolution number thirty,' said Jack.

Jack's show, which was (to his mind at least) rather unimaginatively called 'Valentine's Day', had been running from eleven till one, Mondays to Fridays for well over three and a half years. Almost an institution, as Hilary, their most recent producer, had not long ago pointed out. This comment, with its scary Jimmy Young-ish connotations, had alarmed Jack. His contract was due for renewal in a few months, and he wondered, as he was apt to recently, how they'd take it if he didn't want to renew, if – no, no, *when* – he was offered the job at ITV Wales.

He slipped the cans from his ears and sat back for a breather while they went to the 'Daily Audio Diary' – a regular they ran before the twelve-thirty news. For reasons best known to herself, Hilary had thought it would be interesting to give the job this week to a retired clam digger from Tenby, a man in his eighties with a fearsome cough. This, the first of five three-minute shorts was, even with some fairly brutal editing, not so much a diary as a montage of alarming respiratory symptoms, punctuated with violent expulsions of phlegm. Patti pulled the cans from her own head and winced.

'Jesus Christ,' she observed. 'That is *so* not nice. Anyway. Good weekend?'

Jack, who knew Patti spent the bulk of her weekend hopping from bar to club to all-night rave to bar again (between intervals spent shopping for her peculiar handbags), wondered whether now would be a good moment to admit that his principal post-divorce occupation was not the procurement of young women, as Patti imagined, but the sharing of one too many pints of Fosters with Danny in the Dog and Trouserleg. He needed to get out more. He needed to get *in* more, in fact.

'I emulsioned my bedroom,' he confessed. 'I bought a new toaster. I had a row with a man in B and Q about a light bulb. Oh, and I found an abandoned trainer at the station this morning. Does that count as a high spot?'

Patti smiled indulgently. 'Ahhh. Hey, but I'm sure Prince Charming would have thought so. Except the owner of that –' she nodded her head towards the adjacent cubicle, '– is probably not so much gorgeous blonde in ball gown as irritating pubescent with tongue-stud and scowl.' She began flicking idly through the next two pages of her script. 'A nice thought, though.'

'What is?' said Jack, who had lost the thread, having moved on from contemplation of his risible social life to the contemplation of his impending transformation from successful young broadcaster (he had been that once, hadn't he?) to irritable old git who lived on Pot Noodles and shouted at cars.

'That trainer. The thought that it might belong to a latterday Cinderella. Be rather karmic, wouldn't it? If you tracked her down. I mean, what with you being such a dead ringer for Prince Charming and all… '

He glanced at her now. She was winding him up.

There was a crackle in his cans. Hilary, who sounded as though she was eating a crustacean of some sort, waved at him through the glass.

'You can do me a favour, Jack, actually,' she mumbled at him through it. 'We've got five minutes to fill at one thirty-five because that MP we'd arranged on the sewage story has had to go and have an abscess drained. Have a prattle about it then, why don't you? You're good at that. It'll save me trawling around for something else for you to go to.'

Patti grinned. Then slapped a hand down on her script. 'Now there's a thought! Hil? We should make it a comp. We should offer a prize to whoever comes to claim it. That would be a laugh, wouldn't it?'

Laugh? Competitions were the bane of Jack's life. Constantly bombarded with freebies from publicists – here's three copies of our latest bestseller, now if you could just manage a brief interview… and maybe a teensy mention of the title… there was a constant flow of stuff to be won and shipped out. They spent ridiculous amounts of time sifting through emails and postcards and even more packaging up parcels of tat. Back when he'd been working at Red Dragon FM and they'd come by a (sweaty, frankly) Craig James tour T-shirt, they'd had enough emails and phone calls almost to jam the national grid.

And what would be the point? Quite apart from the fact that he knew he was being teased (so why the hell had he picked the trainer up, anyway?), the chances of anyone listening actually owning it were about as likely as Wales winning the next World Cup. The nearest the average 'Valentine's Day' listener got to leisure footwear was the sort of crepe soled shoe you could buy in Clarks and fold in half. The notion depressed him. He was forty years old. In radio terms, almost out to pasture. Almost in the hinterland of light chat and muzak. In life terms almost out to pasture, come to that. How long before he would start feeling drawn to beige clothes? And just when he had so much to give. He really needed to step up his TV encroachment campaign. Perhaps he would call Allegra after he'd finished up here, and see how things were shaping up with the new show. Perhaps he'd finally ask her out for that drink. Or perhaps not. She might say yes. No. Let's face it. *Would* say yes. And there was football on Sky. Shouldn't risk it. Yes, he should. This was not the right attitude. He would ring Allegra. He *must*.

'Yeah,' he said, flicking through his own script. It would at least save him another trip to Central Station. He took a final gulp of his coffee and grimaced. He would have to dump resolution number thirty, for certain. 'Whatever,' he said. 'Yeah, OK. I'll fill with the trainer. Have we got a prize of some sort knocking around?'

Chapter 3

'Be of good cheer!' announced Simon. 'Because I have found your trainer!'

Hope, who was only of fair to middling cheer most days at the moment, was sitting in the staff room repairing the seam on a suede cushion. She looked up now to see Simon in the doorway, a refill pad clutched to his chest.

She smiled nevertheless. Because that was what you did. 'I beg your pardon?'

'Your trainer,' he went on, crossing the room and plonking himself down opposite her. 'It's turned up! Who'd have believed it?'

'Not me, for one. Who's found it? Did someone hand it in or something?' This was patently impossible. Who would know it was hers?

Simon shook his head. 'Nope!' he said happily. 'It's turned up on the radio.'

Hope stopped stitching. 'The *radio*?'

He gestured back towards the office. 'Just then. I wasn't really listening, but then they mentioned Cefn Melin Station – it's some sort of competition they've got going.'

'You've lost me.'

'I'm not sure what it's all about, but the gist was that someone there found the trainer a few days back and they've been asking the listeners to help find its owner.' He consulted his pad. 'Reebok. Size four. It has to be yours.'

Hope filed the information that he had noted this information and fretted about it. 'Sounds a bit daft.'

'Oh, it's some sort of spoof. It's that kind of show. They've called it Operation Cinderella. From what I could make out, they've been asking people to ring in. Anyway, I made a note of the number for you.'

Hope finished the knot and bit the end off the cotton. She wasn't sure whether to be amused – it *was* funny – or, more pressingly, alarmed at the little swirly doodles she could see Simon had drawn next to her name on his pad. His quiet devotion, which had been burgeoning steadily since her divorce, was becoming almost palpable. And the longer he went on without doing anything about it the worse her inevitable rejection would be. Perhaps she should invent a lover to dissuade him. Perhaps she should invent one anyway. So much less stressful than a real one.

'Well, if it's true, that's incredible. I mean, what are the chances of that happening?'

'I know,' he said happily. 'So I got the number –'

She stabbed the needle back into the spool of cotton. 'Thank you.'

'– so you can ring and fix up when you're going on.'

'Going on? What, on the radio?'

'Of course.'

'God, I don't have to do that, do I?'

'Oh, I think you probably do. So you can claim your prize.'

'There's a prize?'

'Oh, yes. Apparently. Champagne, I think.'

'Really? God, how embarrassing.'

'What's embarrassing?'

This was Madeleine, who had spent the morning in discussion with a big supermarket sponsor and who had returned with a melon under one arm. She put it down and crossed her arms, while Simon repeated his news.

'And no-one else has come to claim it, apparently. So he said, anyway.'

'So who said?' asked Madeleine.

'Jack Valentine.'

'Jack Valentine? What, the presenter, Jack Valentine? Really?' Madeleine clearly knew who he was. Which was more than Hope did.

'So have you called them?' Madeleine asked, turning to her.

Hope grimaced. 'Not yet. I'm just trying to tot up all the reasons why not, but I can think of any. Give me a minute.'

'Don't be daft, Hope. Call them!' urged Simon.

Madeleine, who always thought on her feet, clicked her fingers. 'Hey, hey hey!' she said suddenly. 'Hey hey *hey!*'

'Hey hey what?' asked Hope, picking up the cotton and the cushion, and not liking the sound of things at all.

'Hey hey hey,' Madeleine said again, fifteen minutes later, and this time on a rising note. 'This is good. This is double good, in fact. Tell me, Simon,' she went on, turning to train her beam upon him. 'Just how big is this radio show anyway? Prime time?'

'Lunchtime,' he said. 'It's just finished.'

'Hmm,' she said. 'That's a little disappointing. I thought he was on in the mornings. But nevertheless… never-the-less… '

'Nevertheless what?' Hope asked her.

'You know what I'm thinking, don't you?' she said, grinning. 'I'm thinking the fun run.'

'You are?'

'I am.'

'Er, *why?*'

'Trainers, of course! Serendipity! The happy correlation that you surely cannot fail to see which exists between between a lost trainer and a charity fun run! You can see it, can't you? We can make something out of this. I'm thinking the P word. I'm thinking the C word. I'm – God, yes – thinking the S word, in fact.'

As manager of the Heartbeat fundraising department Hope knew all about the P word and the S word, of course. Together they comprised her mission statement. Her *raison d'etre*. Publicity and Sponsorship. Or, more accurately, ways and means of prising cash from the wallets of the financially well-placed. Which in the case of putting on an event of this magnitude – which was what they were trying to do right now – was no small feat, as the heaps of polite rejections on Hope's desk bore witness to. It wasn't, she thought, great for her psyche, this job.

Madeleine slipped her backside on to the corner of Simon's desk, scattering his carefully stacked piles of receipts. And then splayed her fingers.

'We have a misplaced trainer, right?'

'Right.'

'And now we also have access to a celebrity.'

Ah. That would be the C word, then. 'Right,' agreed Hope.

'Which means we have a chance of some publicity.'

'Right.'

'So what does that add up to? Hmm?'

15

'Sponsorship,' announced Simon with the oily beam of a clever-dick school boy.

'Exactly,' beamed Madeleine. 'Precisely, Simon. We have, in short, a serious fundraising opportunity here.'

She trained her eyes upon Hope.

'You, in fact,' she said, stabbing the air in front of her. '*You* have a serious fundraising opportunity here, Hope. Or should I say Cinderella?' She threw her head back and laughed her big laugh. 'Because, sweetie, you are going to the ball.'

'Export this time?'

Jack took a long look at the half pint of beer that was beginning to swim in front of him. This was becoming too much of a habit. He and Danny had been here less than an hour and a half, but already they had got through three pints each. Well, two and a half in his case. He wasn't sure whether to be relieved or concerned that he was a good half pint behind.

'Christ, mate,' he said, pretending a midweek *joie de vivre* that was entirely at odds with the whining of his gut. It was becoming tiring, this façade of buckish blokedom he felt obliged to veneer himself with whenever he was with Danny in the pub. But it was required. He was wifeless and carefree and potent. And he had wasted no time in broadcasting the fact. Which was another good reason for not upending the Export with such fervour. Because doing so made him believe everything Danny said, including the notion that women would be queuing round the block for him. (Twenty-seven-year-olds, blonde and leggy, they'd agreed.) The sober him knew this was not about to happen, because for it to happen you first had to be there. On the block. Out there. Ready for action. Yet he wasn't even sure where 'there' actually was. He shook his head. 'You're a bit ferocious on the beer tonight, aren't you?'

Danny had stood up and was ferreting in his jeans pocket for money.

'Bah! What's the matter with you? It's – oh. Hey. Almost forgot. He pulled something else from his pocket and handed it to Jack. It was a pink post-it note with a website address scribbled on it.

'What's this?'

'Dave gave it to me. Thought you might like it too. Don't worry. It's all straight stuff,' he added. 'College girls. Cheerleaders. That sort of thing. Check it out.'

Jack read it. *www.shaggalicious.com*.

God. It wouldn't, it *couldn't*, come to that.

He sat back. He would have to knock this on the head. This was the second Wednesday running that he had drunk one too many in the Dog and Trouserleg. And would, as a consequence, be the second Thursday running that he surfaced for work as if from a particularly noisome and gloopy swamp, with a number of large mammals playing keepy-uppy on his head. He was too old for midweek drinking. It had been all right when he was young but now a hangover was becoming a two-day event, the love affair between his stomach and lager having gone the same way as his marriage to Lydia. Dyspeptic and altogether sour.

Forgetting to eat. That was the thing. That was why he felt as if his duodenum was trying to make a forced entry through the back of his tonsils. Gastric irritation. Drinking on an empty stomach. He could almost hear Lydia droning on about it now. But it was true. He had not eaten since eleven-thirty and that had only been a doughnut. The consequences of this oversight, which were becoming more apparent by the moment, lowered his mood further. So wimpish. So girly.

'So go on, then,' Danny urged, flapping a damp ten-pound note in the face of the barmaid. She was new, and called Emma. Jack didn't know how Danny had garnered so much information about her, but she was apparently nineteen, and in her gap year before starting a degree in European Studies at college. But she was mainly, everyone agreed (and Jack wasn't about to contradict them), a bit-of-a-serious-babe. She was also busy serving someone else, so she ignored Danny. He turned back to Jack. 'Go on then,' he said again. 'Give us the low-down. Did your mystery Cinderella turn out to be a stunner, or what? I hear she got in touch.'

Jack suppressed a sigh. Danny, whose current grounding was in the shape of three kids in five years (one only weeks old) and a wife with a hands-on approach to fighting off hands-on activities, was apt to regular flights of carnal speculation. Jack sometimes wondered if Danny was having less sex than he was. Which would have been difficult.

'Haven't a clue,' he replied. He had, if he was honest, entirely lost interest in the subject. No. More than that. The trainer nonsense was beginning to fill him with an ill-defined but distinct unease. He was beginning to find the whole spectrum of nonsensical things he was obliged to do in the name of listener numbers embarrassing. When he'd got his MA in Broadcast Journalism, was this the kind of thing he'd had in mind? This puerile quasi game-show presenter he was turning into? It was not. He had nothing against game-show hosting as a career choice. It was just that it had never been his.

'I haven't met her yet,' he said dully, reconsidering the alarming volume of beer still in his glass. 'I didn't even speak to her. Hil did. She's coming in Friday.' It was of little consequence. All he knew of the trainer's owner was that she was thirty-nine and that she worked for some charity or other. The word 'cardigan' had lodged itself in his mind. As had 'worthy' and 'well-scrubbed'. Why 'scrubbed', particularly? It just seemed to fit. He wasn't holding his breath.

Danny drained the glass in his hand and sighed extravagantly. 'God, I envy you,' he said, as if he'd only just thought about it. 'My whole life right now is just one long round of crap and sick and Jules having a face on. What I wouldn't give to be you, mate.'

Jack privately conjectured that Danny could do a lot worse than go home and make an effort to help out a bit, but feeling ill-placed to give anyone a lecture about the secrets of a happy marriage, he swallowed another tepid mouthful and shook his head. To be him. Danny was way off-beam. There was nothing more spicy in his life right now than the microwaveable chicken jalfrezi that was waiting for him at home. Like a lone iceberg in a sea of empty fridge. And no milk. Or was it no Frosties? It was always one or the other, anyway, no matter how hard he tried to get things together domestically. Perhaps, if he left now, he'd be in time for the mini-market. He checked his watch. Or perhaps not. It was such a little thing, remembering to have proper food in the house. Why couldn't he get the hang of it? He'd been so good at first. The day after he'd moved into the flat he was like a child in a toy shop, going round Sainsburys. A libertine let loose among an abundance of sensual delights. He'd bought speciality beers, a pineapple, lots of different types of biscuits, a selection pack of pesto sauces and bags of pasta with names like tropical diseases. He'd even bought an apron. Navy with stripes. And a pleasing little perspex mill that did salt one end and pepper at the other (Lydia having retained possession of their poncey Philippe Starck ones, because they'd been a present from her womb awareness group or something). But it had been a novelty thing. Now it was just plain boring. And with that thought came a sudden sense of humility that women did this thing day in, day out, all their lives. Guilt nagged at him. Guilt for all the mornings when he'd been brusque with Lydia. There'd been so many.

'*Any thoughts on dinner?*'

'*God, I don't know! Anything! How can I think about food straight after breakfast?*'

But she'd had to. Because someone had to, and it hadn't been him. Not just make dinner, but think about dinner. Think about what she would need to make dinner. Consult the inventory that was lodged in her brain and know, with some cognitive skill that entirely eluded him, which ingredients she already had in the house. He could readily see, now, what a burden that was. Another failure to add to his list.

'Not for me, mate,' he said, as Emma ambled up again. Danny paused to flop his mouth open and emit a low and appreciative moan. Which she also ignored. 'Oh, go on. Put a half in there for him, Em,' he told her, gesturing to Jack's glass. 'It's only half ten.'

'It's only Wednesday,' Jack countered. It's only January, he thought. A mere fortnight into his new health and fitness regime and already he was at sea. OK, he was walking to the station intermittently, but he was also eating erratically, drinking excessively, and failing to sign up for any sort of gym, despite there being two within guilt-inducing distance, both sporting huge neon signs that were tricked out with some sort of invisible beam that pawed at his conscience every time he drove past.

Danny, who had no doubt augmented his calorie intake with a shepherd's pie or a chicken casserole at teatime (Julie being rigorous in the matter of proper family mealtimes) offered him a pork scratching.

'What's the matter with you? Here – get that – oh shit.'

'What?'

'My mobile.' He fished around in his other jeans pocket for it.

'Shit. It's Julie.' He arranged his face into one of compliance and humility. 'Hello, my lovely – just –'

There was a lengthy silence punctuated by more facial contortions.

'OK. On my way.'

Jack forestalled Emma's hand on his glass, much relieved. Thank goodness for Julie.

It was a clear night, frosty. And very, very cold. So cold, in fact, that every intake of breath was like inhaling spicules of ice. The puddles that had been loitering outside the pub earlier were now crystal dinner plates, and the pavements themselves were whitewashed with glitter. It was nights like this (in conjunction with the lager, admittedly) that always made Jack feel melancholy. So much beautiful stuff in the world and yet here he was, beginning his fifth decade (the thought almost made him stumble) and all he had to show for it was a maintenance agreement of terrifying proportions, a rented flat in Cefn Melin (courtesy of Julie's mother, who played bridge with the man who owned the house), an increasingly part-time relationship with his son, a job he was beginning to feel was turning him into a comedy representation of himself – Prince Charming! Christ! What nonsense was that, for God's sake? A question mark hanging over his entire career, and… What else? Oh yes. That was it. No milk.

He got the key into the lock at the fifth attempt, and lurched foward into the gloom. The flat smelled faintly floury, like a long-closed-down bakery. Legacy, no doubt, of his hurried breakfast Pop Tart, which he hadn't been able to eat on account of having nuked it, on account of not bothering to read the instructions, on account of thinking – misguidedly, as it turned out – that as Pop Tarts were marketed for dumb adolescents, that they would be foolproof in the same way McCain's Microchips were. He shuffled into the kitchen and opened the fridge door. A new smell – chilled socks? – prickled his nostrils. He pulled the curry from the shelf and spent some moments contemplating the icons and tables that were printed on the back. Perhaps not. Perhaps he'd just have a cup of tea. Ah. But black. Perhaps he'd just have a biscuit, then. He bent to grope in the cupboard under the work top, but the action of rising with the plastic biscuit box made the silence around him crash and boom in his ears so unpleasantly that it was some moments before he dared focus on anything for fear he might be violently sick. His reflection scowled at him from the kitchen window.

Shit, he hadn't finished the piece for the *Mail* yet. Or phoned Allegra back. Perhaps he'd better just go to bed.

Chapter 4

It was ironic, thought Hope, the domestic set up she had right now. Which was basically that she worked till the usual time – five, five thirty-ish, depending on workload – and her mum, who looked after Tom (fourteen) and Chloe (nine) after school three afternoons a week, was there to greet her when she got in, like a genetically modified version of herself. They'd had this arrangement in place since the autumn term. And though she was grateful, though it was workable and sensible, though it had been, OK, a Godsend, it felt all wrong. Because it *was* all wrong. Because her mother was doing what she used to do, and she was now doing what Iain used to do. Right down to the details. Her tutting about shoes and abandoned school bags in the hallway. Her mum bustling about in the kitchen making tea. She even pecked Hope on the cheek like Hope used to peck Iain on the cheek. Though, thought Hope ruefully, as the familiar rush of irritation washed over her, had she known then what she should have known then, she would have ditched all the pecking and tea-making duties and clamped his scrotum in her garlic press instead.

'He's very handsome,' her mother said now.

'Who is?'

'That DJ, of course! Jack Valentine.'

'How would you know?'

'Because I've seen him on 'Wales this Week'.'

'Have you? I thought he was on the radio.'

'He is. Only he was on there the other week talking about the stadium or something. He's got a lovely head of hair.'

'That sounds rather alarming. So has Dave Lee Travis.'

'Now there's someone you never hear about any more. I think he's dead, isn't he?'

'Of course he's not dead, Mum.'

'And not like that. I mean, it's not bushy or anything. Just lush.'

'Lush?'

22

'Dense. You know. Nice and thick. Healthy-looking. And he's got a very handsome face. Puts me a little in mind of Paul Newman in that film. What was it called? *Cool Hand Luke*, that was it. No, it wasn't. That was the egg one. He had it cropped in that, didn't he? No, it must have been *Hud*. You know.'

'I don't.'

'Yes you *do*. That one with Patricia Neal.'

'What time did you put the fish fingers in?'

'And that black shirt. I've always liked a man in a black shirt.'

'Mum? What time?'

'Oh, ten past. They'll be done by now, I should think. I put them on two-twenty because your oven's so cold. I don't know what possessed you to get electric. You'd have been so much better with gas. You know where you are with gas.'

She had known where she was with being married to Iain. Or so she'd thought. Electricity was different from what she was used to. And so better, by default.

'*Twelve?*' she said now, pulling the baking tray from the oven.

'What?'

'Mum, why have you cooked twelve fish fingers, for goodness sake?'

'What? Oh. I just did what was left in the packet. I had to make space for Suze's bolognaise sauce. Did I tell you she'd popped in with it?' Hope rolled her eyes. 'And there's no point in putting two fish fingers back in the freezer now, is there? Besides, Tom's a growing boy. You never seem to give him any proper food these days. Now, shall I mash these, or what?'

It was silly. But there was no telling Madeleine that. And she got to be reunited with her trainer, which was an unexpected bonus. Thank God she hadn't thrown the other one away. But speaking on the radio. Now that *was* a scary concept.

'So that's the plan then, is it?' her mother asked now, while doling out beans on to plates for the children and reminding Hope to ring her sister-in-law to thank her for the bolognaise sauce. That she hadn't asked for in the first place. That she didn't even want. 'Friday? I'll need to know when it is you're going to be on, exactly, because I've promised your Aunty Doris I'll tape it for her.'

Hope pulled the almost empty ketchup bottle from the fridge and started banging it upside down against the table top.

'Half-past twelve, I think. Or just after. That's when they've told me to get there, anyway. God. I'm going to feel such a prat. But Madeleine seems to think there might be something in it for us – what with the fun run and everything – and she does have a point. And I get my trainer back. But, ugh. I can't imagine anything more silly. Prince Charming, indeed. I mean, how sad is that?'

'But he is.'

'What?'

'Charming.'

'Who is?'

'Jack Valentine!'

'We'll see. He's got a very silly name.'

Hope had never been to the BBC before but, even so, she hadn't expected to be so nervous. Or find that she was the sort of person who'd try on eight different combinations of tops and bottoms before seven in the morning. Her stomach was lurching unpleasantly. Going to the BBC was something other people did. People with aggressively styled hair and all-over tans. People who could open their mouths in front of microphones and be confident that long strings of sensible words would come out. People not like her, in fact.

She negotiated the last roundabout and tried to slow the anxious thumps in her chest. The buildings, which were of a late-sixties persuasion and many in number, reared imposingly at the intersection of two roads, surrounded by towering Scots pines. She pulled in at the entrance to find a man staring balefully out at her from the doorway of a Portakabin.

'I think I've got a space reserved,' she told him.

He nodded with the gravitas of a person for whom the parking space shortfall was the bane of his existence. Which, Hope reasoned, it probably was. 'Just as well, my lovely.' He shook his head. 'Just as well.' He directed her up to the front of the biggest building, and, just as the girl on the phone had promised, there was a space ready and waiting for her, with a board on a stick beside it. Reserved for Hope Sheppard, someone had written in felt pen. It wasn't the biggest space in the world, and she spent some minutes shunting the car back and forth before getting into it, under the scrutiny of a young man who was hovering with a cigarette just outside the entrance, and whose incurious yet somehow still critical presence made her pulse thump all the more.

Once inside the reception, which was bare save for glass cabinets containing various awards, and six televisions with pictures but no sound, she was greeted by an elderly man in a navy-blue uniform. She wrote down her name, and her organisation, and the time she'd arrived, and then went and sat on a low leather couch, a little visitor sticker now attached to her chest.

There was nothing to read apart from a glossy book full of accounts and montages of smiling celebrity faces, and having established that Jack Valentine's was probably not among them, she looked out of the window instead. Eventually a pretty girl with freckles, who introduced herself as Ffion, shook her hand limply and took her off through a low glass security gate and then on though some heavy double doors.

Hope followed her up a flight of stairs, along a short corridor and then through a door that said 'Cubicle' on it, which seemed rather strange. Everything seemed to be covered in hessian.

'Plonk your bits down,' the girl urged as they entered. 'Water? Wee? Anything?'

Hope dithered about the wee, before accepting some water and sitting down on the chair in the corner that the girl indicated. The room she was in was full of wires and huge consoles. Enough buttons and knobs to direct a small jumbo jet, presided over by a kindly-looking woman in a hand-knitted sweater. She smiled up at Hope but didn't speak. Instead, her fingers clattered over the keyboard in front of her, and the words 'Hope Shepherd – Heartbeat – is here' appeared on a screen to her right. Beyond her, a long plate-glass window looked through to what Hope assumed was the studio. It was bigger than the cubicle – which figured – and housed a large circular table with a hole in the centre, the surface of which was dotted with monitors and microphones. There were two people in there. The man, who she assumed must be Jack Valentine, was seated at the far side of it wearing oversized headphones and looked not in the least like Paul Newman, and the young blonde adjacent to him was similarly attired. Their voices were issuing from some part of the equipment.

'Still raining out?' asked the lady at the console now, turning to her. Hope nodded. 'Couple of minutes and I'll take you through to the studio, lovely.' The atmosphere was informal. Classroom-ish, even. An oversized clock dominated the small room.

The man – this would be Jack Valentine, then – stuck his hand in the air and curled his fingers to form a thumbs up sign. He pushed the headphones back from his head so that they sat looped around his neck. Music – *Steps*? – began to usher from the equipment.

The lady at the console pushed a button.

'Yep,' she said. 'Right ho.' Hope could see the man talking, but his voice had now gone. 'OK,' the woman said now. 'That'll work. Uh huh. Go to the bus shelter straight after the weather then I'll bring Hope in and we'll do the Cinderella piece after that.'

She turned back to Hope.

'Still raining out?' she asked her.

Hope nodded a second time. 'Still raining,' she said.

'You are *so* not what I expected,' observed the girl in the studio, whose name, it turned out, was Patti. Hope, who had now been bustled into the studio and plonked down on the opposite side of the table in front of one of the big, spongy microphones, was fearful to so much as exhale. But Patti was talking, wasn't she? So it must be OK.

'My fairy godmother didn't show up,' she responded, wondering quite what it was that the girl *had* been expecting. 'So I had to come in this. Sorry.' But Patti didn't seem to get the joke.

But the whole thing was a joke. Clearly. The man – Jack Valentine – spoke for a while about some ongoing drama about groundwater in a basement somewhere, about the fact that there was an outbreak of Japanese knotweed somewhere else, and then, seemingly without pause, or indeed, reason, about the fact that pretty much everywhere in Cardiff, the men, it had been revealed in some survey, had turned out to be the least romantic in the UK. He then pressed a switch and more music started playing. It was a Disney theme of some sort, – oh, God, it was Cinderella – over which he began speaking, this time with some feeling, recounting his encounter with a small abandoned trainer and his quest to track down the maiden to whom it belonged. Hope was wincing along so comprehensively to this that she was completely unprepared when he pointed his pen at her and said, 'So, Cinderella. The nation needs to be told. What happened to you on the way home from the ball?'

He was smiling right at her, and nodding his head minutely, to indicate, she assumed, that she should say something back. Hope swallowed. Her tongue had become glued to her teeth.

Hope wasn't sure what it was that she did say, only that for what felt like about half a day she twittered on about who she was and where she worked and how she'd come to lose her trainer and that she'd had to walk all the way to the shoe shop with nothing on her feet and how someone in the office had heard the announcement on the radio and how funny it had been that she should lose her trainer of all things because her charity was doing, well, a charity fun run, and wasn't that a coincidence? And he'd smilingly agreed that it was.

And then it was over. Just three minutes had passed.

Someone else shuffled in then, a young boy with a lip stud, wearing jeans with a crotch that hung down between his kneecaps, three T-shirts and an expression of mild dissent on his face. And suddenly Jack Valentine was saying something about the weather and the boy started talking about low pressure and fronts. Hope realised, somewhat shocked, that this mellifluous voice was the very same she'd heard read the weather when she'd been on the way here. These radio people were so odd.

He went. Someone else came. A plate of biscuits arrived with him. Jack Valentine chatted to someone in the cubicle, and Patti – was it Patti? – scribbled furiously on a pad. Hope really wasn't sure what she was supposed to do. So she sat stone still and silent, in case the nation should hear her, while a red light burned steadily and the clock hands marched round.

'Way to go!' said Jack Valentine suddenly, startling her.

'Oh,' Hope whispered. 'Is it all right to speak now?'

There was a further moment's hesitation as Jack Valentine listened to something that was being said to him in his headphones, then he pulled them off and nodded at her.

'You were great,' he said heartily. 'Just great.'

27

'Great,' agreed Patti. Hope thought they probably said this to everyone. She hadn't been great in the least.

'It's just, well, you know I was talking about Heartbeat,' she went on. 'Well, I was wondering if I could have a chat to you about it. You see, the fun run –'

'Isn't fun run an oxymoron?' asked Patti, looking pleased with herself.

'Not necessarily,' said Jack, smiling at Hope politely. He had friendly eyes. The palest of pale turquoise. Not green. Not blue. 'Well, it's just that we were rather hoping we might be able to –'

'Hold up.' He looked beyond her and pulled one half of the headphones over his head again. Her mother had been right. He did have a good head of hair. Short, but indeed dense, and the colour of wet sand. He started nodding.

'I can't imagine why anyone would want to run for pleasure,' Patti continued. 'I mean –'

'I do,' said Hope, feeling old and sad. She could then think of nothing useful or intelligent to add. Jack Valentine took the headphones off again.

'So,' he said. 'You wanted to talk to me about your fun run.' He looked enquiringly at her.

'Well, it's publicity, basically. We're hoping to… well, I was hoping I might have an opportunity to have a chat to you about it sometime. You see, we're… well, I was wondering if perhaps I could buy you lunch sometime soon and discuss it.'

She really didn't feel it remotely necessary to waste money on buying lunch for some swanky danky DJ, but Madeleine had been insistent on that point. Chat him up. Charm him. Buy him lunch.

'Lunch, eh?' said Patti, winking at Jack Valentine.

'Hem hem,' said Jack Valentine, on a rising note.

'They don't feed us much here,' said Patti to Hope. 'Do they, Jack?'

Jack Valentine winked back at her. 'You're on,' he said to Hope. 'Call me here later. OK?' Then his put his headphones back on and the woman in the sweater came in to escort Hope out of the studio, leaving her with the impression that she'd missed some in-joke. These radio people were really very odd.

28

Chapter 5

It was apparent to Jack as soon as he got to the Hilton that to agree to meet Hope Shepherd there was a singularly bad move. Would she now assume that they'd be having lunch there? Or worse – he pulled back his cuff to take a look at his watch – be already in the lobby waiting for him? It was a distinct possibility.

Perhaps he should have been less firm in the matter of who was buying who lunch in the first place. When she'd called him, which she'd done that very same afternoon, she had been insistent that the meal would be on her, for the very sensible reason that it was she who wanted something from him and not vice versa. But he had countered with the less obvious but (to his mind) laudably honest point that if an attractive woman from a strapped-for-cash charity were to buy him lunch he would feel very uncomfortable about turning her down, should her proposal not be to his liking. Besides, he had added with what was turning out to be a possibly misjudged flourish, he would *like* to buy her lunch. Which had effectively ended the debate.

He had started the day in an unexpected and pleasingly buoyant mood. It had caressed him along with the sun-shaft that had tracked his little bedroom, and hauled him steadily from the mire of his early morning stupor, with the promise of spring, and new beginnings, and hopefulness, and the feeling that his new and better life was surely due to start. Until he stood up, at least, and found he had a headache. But only a two-can affair – very minor. All in all an excellent start to the day.

He had breakfasted on the one remaining Pop Tart (pausing only to make a note on the little wipeable memo on his fridge to get more before Ollie arrived later) and had toastered it to perfection. No bubbling brown scorch stripes raked down the front. No incendiary effect on his tongue as he bit into it. Jack knew Pop Tarts could not become a fixture in his life, but this small charge-taking exercise had pleased him no end.

As had the prospect of taking someone out for lunch. Despite Patti's endless ribbing about shagging fairy princesses, he'd found himself rather pleased that Hope Shepherd was not a cardigan-clad worthy. That she had all the right bits and in all the right places. That she was normal and friendly and, well, so *nice*. But now he was all anxious again. It occurred to him that he could still, if he was quick, whiz into the Hilton and see if they had a table in the Razzi, but Hope Shepherd's appearance, as a slim blur of charcoal hurrying across the concourse, effectively scotched that one.

'Hello!' she said, while she was still fifteen yards away, waving a gloved hand around as if she'd just picked him out at an airport arrivals hall. She was wearing a strange knitted grey duffel-coat thing that he wasn't altogether sure what to make of, and knee-length high-heeled black suede boots, of which he approved unreservedly. A knitted black polo neck burgeoned from the top of the coat-thing, almost exactly the same colour as her hair.

'Hello,' he said back, altogether less explosively.

She drew level with him, plunging her hands back into the pockets of the coat. 'Chilly, isn't it?'

'Very,' he said. 'But then it is January.' He smiled. 'So.'

'So,' she said back. 'Where are we off to, then?'

She didn't make any gestures towards the hotel, which made Jack surer still that he should have booked a table at the Razzi restaurant, despite its ridiculous name. She looked like she would sit well in their window, but he also decided that if he said McDonalds at this point, she would not bat so much as one of her thickly-lashed eyelids. She had no make-up on at all, as far as he could tell. He liked that.

'I thought we'd go to Beano's,' he said, proffering an arm to guide the small of her back in the right direction.

'Oooh, lovely,' she said, moving off before his arm made contact. He dropped it self-consciously and fell into step.

'You know it, then, do you?'

'I went there for my divorce party,' she said, turning to grin at him. 'Got comprehensively wasted and took out an urn. I hope they'll let me in.'

Jack had not had a divorce party. He'd just got comprehensively wasted at home.

Beano's was the kind of restaurant that Cardiff was sprouting all over the place these days. Achingly trendy, full of braying office workers. The kind of restaurant that tried to sell you onion marmalade and shrink-wrapped biscottis, and alarming-sounding mustards full of bits of twig. But the guy who ran the place knew him and could be relied upon to gush. Hope, who looked agreeably impressed by all this, studied her menu enthusiastically, going 'hmmm' a lot and nodding.

'So,' he said again, noticing with some alarm that the word had become a pre-cursor to many of his conversational openers of late. As if he were on *Question Time* or trying to organise a group of cub scouts. 'Your fun run.'

She smiled at him over the top of her menu.

'Our fun run,' she said, nodding. 'In actual fact, I'm not sure 'fun run' is quite the word we should be using. It's five kilometres, and there's a bitch of a hill half way through. We don't really want to encourage any cardiac arrests, do we?' She giggled delightfully. 'But yes. That's what it is.'

The waiter, a brisk antipodean in a long leather apron, brought glasses of iced water. Jack picked his up and took a long swallow. 'So,' he said. 'What's it in aid of, exactly?'

She hugged her menu and leaned forwards.

'Well, you know what we're about, presumably.'

'Er… heart disease?'

'Exactly. Though in its broadest sense. I mean, we are about raising money for heart disease – well, not *for* heart disease, of course. We don't organise food drops of saturated fats or anything. Ha ha. But more for the support of families whose lives have been touched by heart disease, which is slightly different.'

'Sort of "if you or a member of your family has been affected by any of the issues raised in this programme" type of thing, then.'

She picked up her glass and sipped from it, nodding.

'Exactly. I mean, we do give a lot for research, but our more high-profile activities are all about one-on-one support. We handle a lot of individual cases. You know, support for families when, oh, I don't know, someone has to have bypass surgery or something. Financial support. Respite care. That sort of thing. It's a very broad remit. But that's not my area really. I'm in fundraising, of course.'

'Of course. And this is a fairly ambitious fundraiser, by the sound of it. And your baby, I take it?'

She beamed at him. '*Exactly*,' she said again. Jack was enjoying the novelty of being in the company of someone who leapt on everything he said with such enthusiasm instead of saying 'well, no', or 'not quite' or 'hmm'.

'So, Cinderella,' he said. 'Where do I fit in?'

Her handbag did not look like the kind that would house anything more bulky than a purse and a lipstick, but it clearly did.

'Excuse the scrawl,' she said, unfolding several creased sheets of A4 and simultaneously shunting various condiments out of the way. 'And ignore the back. They're old scripts from *Pobol Y Cwm*. One of the girls in the office gets them for scrap.' The waiter returned and wanted to know, though clearly not desperately, what they wanted to have for their lunch.

'I'll have the – oh, sorry. Are we having starters?' she asked. Jack nodded. 'Right. The goujons with the chilli jam to start and for my main course I'll have the goat's cheese and caramelised onion tart. It's a starter as well,' she added, presumably just in case the waiter wasn't fully conversant with the contents of his own employer's menu, which Jack had to concede was a possibility, 'but I'll have it for my main course – oh, in fact, thinking about it, instead of the chilli jam do you think I could just have some mayonnaise? That's with the starter, OK? Thanks.'

Jack hoped the waiter did shorthand. 'Tortillas and dips and double egg and chips, please,' he said.

'Fat chips or skinny chips?' asked the waiter, still scribbling.

'Fat chips.'

'Good choice,' observed Hope. 'Cutting down the surface area, that's the thing.' She grinned again. For someone so immersed in the less palatable end of the healthcare spectrum she seemed a very jolly person. She seemed to be perpetually on the verge of emitting a big, throaty laugh.

'Anyway,' she went on, sliding a finger over her notes. Her nails were not coloured but very shiny. 'You probably already worked out that having taken on such an ambitious project – and it is ambitious for us, I can tell you, because we're only a very small charity – what we really need to secure, to get it off the ground, is some serious backing from a nice well-heeled corporation and a big name, of course, to get us noticed.'

'A "big name", eh?' He raised his fingers to put it in quote marks. 'But no luck as yet?'

She shook her head.

'But then you lost your trainer and figured what the hell. A bird in the hand... '

She did laugh now, a big boomy laugh that filled up the airspace between them and made her hair jiggle in little scythes around her chin.

'Er... exactly,' she said.

In the ninety or so seconds that followed, Jack found himself in the unusual and rather enjoyable position of being with someone who was plainly hoping the ground would swallow them up. She was only joking, really she was. Though if she was being scrupulously honest she never much listened to Radio Wales, so no, she didn't actually know who he was before she met him, but someone called Simon, who was apparently in the accounts department where she worked, did listen to his show and said it was very good. And that it wasn't true that she'd tried lots of people and they'd all turned her down, because they'd not actually got to that stage in the planning yet. (She was blushing by now.) But that she had to concede that had they got to that stage in the planning then, no, she wouldn't have thought of him because how could she when she'd never heard of him? And, truth be known, she'd already composed a sort of list in her head and she'd thought she might approach the woman who did the weather on HTV – you know, what was her name, Emma... Emma Hepplewhite, that was it. Not because she really knew who she was either, but because her mother went to flower club with her mother and thought she might be able to swing it for her, but then she had lost her trainer and he'd found it and picked it up and Madeleine – who was the boss there, apparently – had come up with the idea that it being a trainer and their fun run being, well, a fun run, the two things went rather well together and this would be a perfect opportunity to get someone big-league on side, and perhaps some sustained radio coverage in the build up, and therefore more in the way of sponsorship perhaps than they would otherwise, and... and...

'And... well,' she said at last, grinding to a halt and still slightly pink around the cheekbones. 'That's me. Dig me a hole and I'll fall in it for you.' She laughed again, this time in a less voluble and rather pleasingly embarrassed way. And Jack knew at that moment that he had the upper hand. He hadn't articulated to himself how or when having the upper hand in this encounter was going to benefit him specifically, just that not being on the back foot in a conversation with a member of the opposite sex – and one in black suede boots, moreover – was an exceedingly pleasant position to find himself in.

'So,' he said, clasping his hands together on the table and smiling benignly at her. 'What do you want me to do, exactly?'

Jack had, in the last two years, opened a village fête, an out-of-town designer outlet mall, a school science block (though that didn't really count, as it was Ollie's school), a dog training outfit and a garden centre. Oh, and he'd given a speech at the Cougar's prize-giving evening, but that didn't count either, as it was Ollie's football team. Hardly an illustrious list, particularly given that five years and a morning slot earlier, he had been receiving requests to do such things almost weekly. Still, a fun run was a first.

She was consulting the handwritten list on the table in front of her. There were a row of little squiggled asterisks acting as bullet points down the side of the page.

'We were rather hoping,' she said, 'that we could get you on board. We're going to be producing the publicity material soon – you know, the flyers and sponsorship forms and so on?' Jack nodded to indicate that he did. 'And we'd love it if we could put a picture of you on the front, with a quote, perhaps – you know, that sort of thing. Valentine. Hearts. And… well. Hmm. Anyway. Obviously I don't know where the BBC would stand on things financially, but, I mean, we really are the bottom of the heap as far as charities go – heart disease just isn't sexy, I'm afraid – and they do do Children in Need, don't they, so they wouldn't have any objection to supporting the event through your show, would they?' Jack said he didn't think they would. 'And there's the event itself, of course. We're pencilled in for an early evening start, but that's still negotiable. I mean, we'd be anxious to fit in with whatever suits you best. Assuming you'd be… well. That's about the size of it.' She smiled hopefully at him.

'I'll have to think about it. Check my schedule and so on,' he said. 'But that all sounds do-able on the face of it.'

'Does it?' She looked pleased. 'And we'd like you to present the prizes and so on.'

He nodded.

She'd got to the end of her list by now and was just folding it up when the waiter brought their starters. The polo-necked top had turned out to be a dress. A soft, short thing – there were several inches of leg between the hem and the boots – which was unadorned bar a thin gold chain necklace with a chunky ring hanging from it.

She wasn't twenty-seven, she wasn't blonde, she wasn't leggy. On the other hand, Jack found himself musing as he studied her, she *was* rather pretty. And she was rather sweet too. 'So,' he said, this time with absolute conviction. 'How long have you been divorced?'

'Oh God oh God oh God' said Hope, pulling off a boot. 'What a prat.'

'Was he? I always thought –'

'Not Jack Valentine!' she said with feeling. 'Me! He must have thought I was the doziest, most irritating person on the planet.'

Her cheeks still burned at the memory of her faux pas. How had her composure deserted her so utterly? Why did she feel so jangly all of a sudden? She had, after all, just been doing her job.

Kayleigh was at the reisograph, reisographing something. She peered into the hole where the paper was supposed to come out.

'I'm sure he didn't,' she said. 'Bloody thing. Do you know what it means when the zig-zag light comes on?'

'It means the paper's jammed. You need to –'

But Kayleigh was already sorting it. Hope wrestled with her other boot. And sighed. She had, she realised, become all too used to the schizophrenic nature of her present situation. No – she had created it. The brave face, the stoicism, the affectation of feeling OK. At first as a shield against well-meaning sympathy, but then, as the months passed, it had come to feel normal. The best way to manage the demons within. Thus there was the work her: confident, outgoing, ambitious, ever smiling, and then the *real* her: the duck legs underneath the swan, paddling fretfully and anxiously, out of sight. Yet somehow, today, the distinction had blurred. She had, she realised, felt her real self laid bare. It had been only the one and a half glasses of wine, but the afternoon now stretched unprepossessingly ahead of her, fuggy and distracting and full of paperwork and phone calls, when what she really wanted to do was put her feet up on her desk and consider the unbearable lightness of being. She didn't know what that meant exactly, only that it seemed to suit her mood. And the consideration of such things was suddenly an altogether more enticing prospect than the pile of work that beckoned her now. Secretly, because it embarrassed her hugely, she was in a state of high, if somewhat worrying, excitement. She knew this was in some part due to the wine, but even so, a germ of daydream had lodged itself in her mind. A germ of a daydream about *him*. Him and her. Them, in fact. Silly, but it wouldn't go away.

Work, she told herself. This was work. Nothing to be frightened of. Jack Valentine had been absolutely right, of course, and the evidence was now sitting on her desk. She picked it up. Yet another letter from yet another agent, explaining that yet another big-shot celebrity would, regrettably, not be available to support their worthy cause. That he got requests all the time and that sadly it was impossible to support all of them. But at least this one had a cheque in it. For fifty pounds. And now she had someone anyway, even if she hadn't known who he was.

She put the letter down and kicked her boots under her chair. Her head might feel like the middle of a pavlova, but her feet felt like balls of angry wasps.

'Ah!' said Madeleine, coming in and parking her bottom on the corner of Hope's desk. 'The wanderer returns! So. Tell all. What's he like? Is he nice? Is he on side?'

'He's going to speak to someone,' she told her. 'He said he's very happy to give us a quote and do a photo – and do the race itself, if it fits in with his schedule – and he's going to speak to someone at work about the rest. He's going to ring me next week.'

'Excellent,' said Madeleine. 'Pity he isn't in television, but there you go. I expect he's well-connected. And, besides, the trainer connection is eminently exploitable too. I was talking to George from the sports shop this morning and he thinks we might be able to wheedle some freebies out of Reebok, so, all in all, it's looking like we might have some serious progress on our hands.' She clapped Hope on the back. 'Well done, sweetie. Great work.'

'I enjoyed it. He's nice.'

'As in "nice" or as in *nice*?'

Hope coloured. 'As in nice. As in helpful. As in pleasant. As in –'

'Rubbish! Come on. Come clean. As in *nice*.'

So, Maddie could tell. And this, therefore, was a conversation that would have gone the way of all such conversations with her (and therefore straight to Hope's soul without stopping at the services) were it not for the fact that the phone on her desk was now ringing.

Madeleine plucked it up, and listened for a moment.

'Ah,' she said, grinning at Hope, 'no, it isn't. But she's right here beside me, so if you'll just hold the line –'

She pulled the receiver from her ear, and then cupped her hand over it.

'Cinderella, guess what? It looks like you've pulled.' She winked again, and held the phone out to Hope. 'For you. It's that nice Mr Charming.'

That was the tricky thing about getting some sex, Jack decided. You had to find someone to have sex with. Up till now, this had proved an intractable problem. There had been Allegra, of course. (When had there not been Allegra?) He could have had sex with Allegra aeons ago. Before the divorce even, if he'd instigated it. But he hadn't. Still hadn't. Though having sex with Allegra was in no way an undesirable thing to contemplate on a rainy night when there was no football on the telly, Jack didn't think it would be too clever. This was the woman charged with making him a television celebrity. This was the woman in whose hands his new career rested. No. It wouldn't be too clever to make a move in that direction. The complications were altogether too obvious.

But then – hello? – there was the rest of the world. All the other available women who must be out there. But where did you find them? Jack had never been much of a one for lads' nights out, except those that his five-a-side team sporadically semi-organised, and as these mainly consisted of a lot of drinking followed by a lot of dancing, followed by a lot of swearing, followed by a lot of pretending to be something other than a bunch of ageing married blokes with night-passes, followed by chips and curry sauce eaten at a cab rank (with a wooden fork) there was little prospect that such evenings were likely to prove productive on the sex front.

But he had made an effort. He had been to two dinner parties – reluctantly, and rightly so. They had both proved the point that friends – and almost all his were still married – only invited single men to dinner parties if they had newly flayed and disembowelled female friends to take care of, because that way they got a break. Got to shriek and guffaw in their kitchens while you – OK, *he* – had to sit at the table while said disembowelled females spent hour upon hour telling you how much they felt raped by the experience and what draconian maintenance agreements they had. He'd been to town, too. Twice. Where else *did* you go, frankly? Once with Danny, and once with a sometime journalist friend from the *Echo*, and both times had been pretty grim. Unexpectedly so. Where had he been all his life? Had it always been this way? He'd had no idea that so many married women went out in the evenings, *en masse*, wearing sparkly tops, swigging fluorescent drinks out of bottles, and pretending they wanted to have sex with you. And if this had been a revelation (and it had), then even more so had been the realisation that he didn't actually want to have sex with the sort of women who prowled dance floors in town, in push-up bras (yes, he knew about those – the type that stood up by themselves in the washing pile) and too much make-up, whether they were married or not. He wanted to have sex with girls who didn't need to do that. But where on earth did you go to find them?

Most depressing of all was that he didn't actually seem to fancy *anyone* any more. Well, he did, but not anyone to whom he wasn't invisible. He cherished the fanciful, if unrealistic notion that one day someone would just walk up and want to have sex with him who wasn't in a sparkly top thing and didn't feel the need to leap up and whoop when anything by Shania Twain came on. Perhaps an evening class in Bikram Yoga, which Patti had suggested, wasn't so way off-beam after all. At least there'd be the benefit of spiritual replenishment while he ogled the flesh on display.

But now it had happened. He had met someone with whom it was not wholly unrealistic to suppose he might be able to have sex. She might not be exactly the siren of his dreams, but when he recalled the way her breasts sat so unassumingly in her dress-thing, he decided that he hadn't the least reservation about inventing a new category specifically for her. And he still had her trainer, so he had a reason to phone her.

'Did you get back all right?' he asked her now.

'I seem to have done,' she said jauntily. 'Didn't lose any footwear, at least.'

'But I still have your trainer.'

'Indeed you do,' she answered. 'And a bottle of champagne, for that matter. I meant to mention it over lunch, but I completely forgot.'

'So I should get them to you, perhaps.'

'The trainer would certainly be helpful. I don't know why I didn't think to ask for it when I came on your radio show. Just – poof! – went straight out of my head.'

'I know what you mean. It can be nerve-racking, the first time.' Why had he said that? In that way? He cleared his throat. 'Anyway.'

'Anyway.'

'Anyway, I was thinking.'

'And what were you thinking?'

'I was thinking that I owe you a meal.'

This was entirely true. There had been a bit of a tussle over the lunch bill. She had upped and paid it while he'd been in the men's room, leaving him with little choice but to tick her off politely and accept defeat. Now he waited.

'No, really,' she said. 'Please don't worry about that.'

She wasn't supposed to say that. 'Sorry,' he said. 'No. What I mean is, that I'd like to take you out to dinner. I've bent a few ears here, and we've lots to discuss. About your fun run.'

'We do? That's marvellous! It's looking hopeful, then, is it?'

Yes, Jack decided. It's looking very hopeful. Looking very hopeful indeed.

When he got home from work Ollie was already there, installed in front of his computer and playing something that seemed to involve the random slaughter of a lot of multi-horned beasts. He looked like he'd been there some time. He looked, moreover, like he'd be there some time. An open carton of orange juice was stationed beside him, with a half-empty pint glass parked alongside. Jack peered over his fourteen year old son's newly

39

shorn head and tried to make sense of the row of icons at the top of the screen. He ruffled Ollie's scalp. It was warm and hedgehoggy. He always used to be the one who took Ollie for haircuts. But no more. He wished he still did.

'Hello,' he said cheerfully, because despite that small caveat, he felt very cheerful. 'How was school? Did you have a good day?'

Ollie killed something, and glanced up only very briefly, as if busy piloting a jumbo jet through a storm.

'Mmm,' he said.

'Any homework?'

'Dunno.'

Jack picked up the juice carton and closed the flap at the top. 'I thought we might go out for supper this evening.'

'Hmm?'

'You know. For a pizza or something. Or the Hard Rock, maybe. What do you think?'

'Hmm?'

'About supper. We could get a take-away in, but I thought perhaps it would be nice if –' The speaker interrupted with a violent squawk. 'Ollie?'

Ollie's head snapped round. '*What?*'

'Supper. I thought we might–'

'Look, Dad. Could you, like, you know, hang on a minute?' He gestured to the screen. Skeletons and Viking-things were loping around a cluster of huts in a clearing.

'Oh.'

'Because I'm, like, in the middle of something?'

'Oh.'

'And it's, like, a pretty crucial bit?'

'Oh.' Jack pointed at one of the skeletons. It had an oscillating red halo thing round it. And cross hairs. And a long bow.

'This one's you, then, is it?'

Ollie's expression was one of derision. '*No.*'

'Oh.' He pointed again. 'That one over there, then?'

'NO.' Ollie stopped stabbing at the keyboard and turned to face Jack. 'Look, Dad, can we, like, just leave this? Like, you know, leave me alone?'

For a second or two Jack considered bringing to bear the absolute and unquestioning authority he'd enjoyed over Oliver this time last year, but which seemed, by some process that had occurred entirely without him realising, to have evaporated quicker than the bone-men Ollie was now so busy vaporising. At about the time when their time together became finite. Too precious to be spent in acrimony and sulks. So he didn't.

'Oh, OK. When you've finished, then,' he said.

It was a cloud, this thing with Ollie. This fact that some mindless technological blood-fest was so much more alluring than talking to him. He'd come to the flat, he'd grunt, he'd go to bed, he'd get up, he'd grunt a bit more, he'd go off to school. But not a heavy cloud today. Just a mere wisp of cirrus. In what was, for the first time since he'd taken to noticing again, a decidedly sunny blue sky.

Chapter 6

'Well, I think it's absolutely lovely,' said Hope's mother, as she blanket-bombed the kitchen table with germ-busting spray.

Hope sidestepped the mist, frowning. 'I do wish you'd shut up, Mum. It's just work. That's all.'

Her mother paused to scrutinise her, which made her feel self-conscious and therefore cross with herself. She really had no business with all this make-up and frock lark. She was not seventeen. And tonight was not a date.

'Nonsense. He's taking you out to dinner, which means it's a date.'

'No, it doesn't. People do have meetings over dinner, you know. And breakfast, come to that.' Which was entirely the wrong thing to say. Why had she said that? She was thirty-nine. Was it really necessary to justify herself to her mother? Or anyone else for that matter? No. Yet this was what she did all the time these days: let people dispense wisdom and advice like prescriptions, as if anxious to fill the gaping hole in guidance that had opened now Iain wasn't around to provide it. As if she had an L plate affixed to her bosom. Or 'PDP' plate perhaps. Post-Divorce-Person. In need of help. Dozy. Still a great deal to learn.

Yet she had got a great deal to learn. Like not daydreaming. Therein lay demons. But she had been daydreaming. Endlessly. Compulsively. Madly. And as her daydreams gained clarity and substance, so did the anxiety, the ever-present, unbidden, unsettling anxiety, like a sprouting of strong weeds around a newly planted shrub.

'Everyone feels like that starting out again,' Madeleine had told her. Hope had believed her. Of course they did. But everyone feeling like that – like this – lent no practical support, and offered no comfort. She just wished she didn't. It wasn't her.

'Pssh! You read the wrong sorts of magazines,' her mother said now. But didn't qualify as to which wrong sort she meant. *Essentials*? *Marie Claire*? *The Cefn Melin Newsletter*? 'Anyway, it doesn't matter what you choose to call it,' her mother added,

42

returning to her labours, circling the table with an aggressively wielded J-cloth. 'Work or date. It's high time you got yourself out and about a bit more. Where is he taking you? Somewhere nice, I don't doubt.'

'I don't know. A restaurant I haven't heard of. I'm meeting him outside the Hilton again.'

Her mother sniffed. 'He could have picked you up.'

'I told you, it's not a date. Do you think Tony Blair offers to pick Gordon Brown up when they get together to discuss the Trade Deficit?'

He had offered to pick her up, in fact, but she had declined. Way too date-like. Her mother tutted now. 'That's different. They live next door to each other. Anyway, there's no point you taking your car, now, is there?' There was a gleam of salacious excitement in her eyes. 'I can drop you.'

Hope grimaced. 'There's really no need, Mum. Anyway, you'll be here, won't you?'

'Nonsense. I'll drop you off and there's an end to it. I'm quite sure Tom and Chloe can cope for twenty minutes. Goodness me, I used to leave you in your cot every day when I went to collect your brother from school. Or Chloe can come with us, can't she?' She finished wiping the table and went to wring the cloth out. 'There,' she said. 'So.' She plucked fluff from Hope's shoulder. 'What time do you want to leave for this non-date of yours?'

There was no point arguing with her, so Hope didn't bother. But it wasn't a date, even so. She wouldn't let it be.

There was a thin drizzle falling when they pulled up outside the Hilton, and this time Jack Valentine was nowhere to be seen.

'I'll get out here, Mum,' Hope said, with some relief. At least she would be spared the embarrassment of her mother leaping from the car and making screechy small talk at him. She pulled over to the side of the road.

'Don't be daft,' her mother responded quickly. 'It's raining. And what if he's late?'

'Mother, I am quite capable of being out in the rain on my own.' Hope slid from the driver's seat, leaving the engine running. 'Go on. You get off home.'

'Best I stay a bit. There's no rush, is there?'

'Yes, there is, Gran,' reminded Chloe from the back seat. 'Casualty's on in ten minutes. Mum, can I stay up and watch Emergency Nine One One tonight?'

Hope had by now jogged around the car and opened her mother's door to let her out.

'Certainly not, Chloe. You've got school in the morning.'

'Mu-um...'

'Well now. Here we are again!'

It wasn't a date, but, even so, Hope felt herself go a very mild shade of tingle upon hearing Jack's voice behind her. So much so that when she finally managed to extricate him from her mother's conversational clutches – Jack had been so sweet with her, Hope didn't like to seem short – she determined to reign in her febrile imaginings and concentrate wholly on the job in hand.

Though he, clearly, had other ideas. They set off down the street under the ample cover of his golf umbrella which, being blue, made it feel vaguely subterranean inside. 'Elbow?' he said, once the car had puttered off. And there was his, suddenly, stuck out at right angles beside her. 'Two people,' he added. 'One umbrella. It's easier.'

Out-manoeuvred, she slipped her arm self-consciously into the crook of it, and he tucked it back in with a grin.

'There,' he said happily. 'That's much better, isn't it?'

Was it? Hope swallowed. She wasn't so sure. She must, at all costs, keep her eye on the ball.

'Right,' said Jack, whose confidence and merriment and general air of jollity seemingly knew no bounds. 'I imagine the lady'll probably be wanting a wallpaper of lightly poached paperclip goujons set on a bed of mixed watering cans and drizzled with an emulsion of lampshades, please.'

Hope, like the waiter, who was writing it all down, took a moment or two to digest this. She laughed. Jack laughed. The waiter laughed too. Though in his case the laugh was obviously a cover, because he looked for all the world like he was chewing on a cockroach.

'Not really,' said Jack, who didn't seem to notice. Or maybe didn't care. He was in the media, after all. He gestured, and asked

Hope what she actually wanted. Once she'd told him, he raised his menu and pointed to an item. Hope was still laughing behind hers.

'And I'll have that.' He grinned at her.

'That?' asked the waiter.

'Yes, that.' Jack closed the menu and handed it back.

'What's "that"?' asked Hope.

'The mushroom thing.' He leaned across the table and whispered. 'Only I can't say it.'

'Say what?'

'*Mille Feuille.*'

'You just did.'

'Yes, but appallingly. And not to him.'

'You said it just fine.'

'I said it like a dork. Doesn't matter how hard I try to say "me foo-ee" in a restaurant situation it always comes out all wrong. I'm no better with *rognon*. You'd think a writer would have a better handle on pronunciation, wouldn't you? But there you go.'

Hope handed her menu back to the waiter, and wondered why he'd brought her somewhere so cold and pretentious. To impress her? If so it was a shame, because it didn't.

Though his words did. 'Wow. I didn't know you were a writer as well.'

He widened his eyes. 'Didn't you? I can see I've made a spectacular impression on you all round. You don't follow the sports pages in the *Echo,* then?'

'I don't, I'm sorry. Is that what you do then? Write for the *Echo*?'

'Among other things. I do all sorts of freelance. Though in this case, more for love than money, it has to be said. I cover the junior leagues.'

'Football?'

He put his palms up and pulled a face. 'Oh, dear. Guilty as charged. Yes. I'm afraid so.'

'Don't be daft,' said Hope, meaning it. 'I like football.'

'You do?'

'Well, OK, only up to a point.' He looked disappointed. 'But my son plays.'

He looked pleased again. 'Who for?'

'Well, it used to be the Cefn Melin Greens, but they've split into three teams this season, or something. It's hard to keep track. You know, I'm not actually sure what they're called any more.'

'Well, if it is the Greens, then you should read the *Echo*. I gave them an excellent write-up last week. I run the Cougars.'

'Really?' she said politely. She hadn't heard of them. Football was Iain's thing, not hers. But it could be… Oh, God. Job in hand. Job in hand.

'Absolutely. And we're going to win the league. Remember, Hope, you heard it here first.'

He leaned back as the waiter reappeared to splash a dribble of wine into Jack's glass. 'Oh, go on,' he said, flapping his hand. 'You look like an honest enough kind of guy.' The waiter looked mortified, but did as he was told. Even so, Hope decided she really didn't like him. Or this kind of restaurant. Too full of itself. Too altogether snooty. She looked around and wished she'd worn something else. Was someone else. The someone else she'd been way back before she'd met Iain, who'd never worried about such rubbish. Where was she now she was needed so badly?

Jack raised his glass, so Hope did likewise.

'Well,' he said. 'Here's to us.'

'And the fun run,' she added.

'Oh, go on then, if we must,' he answered. 'To the fun run. Though I was thinking more along the lines of a toast to our divorces.' His eyes twinkled fetchingly. Must be the light, Hope decided. Or the wine. Or… well, something.

'Seems a funny thing to be toasting.'

'You had a party, didn't you?'

'Yes, but that was then. This is, well, now.'

'Now it's sunk in, you mean? But you're wrong. We should toast,' he said, clinking glasses with her again. 'You're here, aren't you?'

Oh, dear, thought Hope. How did she respond to that?

'We're both here,' he said quickly, as if reading her reticence. 'Weary fellow travellers along life's rocky road. So tell me,' he asked her. 'How was it for you?'

Hope had never expected to find herself talking about her divorce in those terms, least of all with a man she knew so little about. Though she did know, because he'd told her, that his wife had left him, and not the other way round. Perhaps that was it. Here was someone who knew how it felt. Hope knew no one, she realised, who knew how it felt.

'I don't know,' she said now. 'It's difficult to say without a yardstick. Same as it is for everyone, I suppose. Grim.'

'Was it messy?'

She shook her head. 'Remarkably uncomplicated, actually. Straightforward infidelity. He had previous. Lots of it.'

'Well, that's something. I mean not that he had previous, of course. But that it wasn't too messy.'

'No. It wasn't.' She frowned. 'Lots of other awful things but not messy. You?'

He considered for a moment. 'Um. Let's see. Let me grope for a word here. Sort of expected. Which is three, I know. But not messy. Let me think. Sad. Sad, mainly. Yes, sad about does it.'

'It *is* sad, isn't it?'

He frowned. 'Very. They don't tell you, do they?'

'They don't. But, well, I guess we live and we learn.'

He looked serious suddenly. 'And tell me, what have you learned?'

Hope shrugged. 'Nothing good, really.' She thought for a moment. 'Oh, dear. Not to trust, I suppose. I wish I hadn't. Had to learn that, I mean. It makes you feel so vulnerable. So, well, fragile. You know?'

He nodded sympathetically, and she felt suddenly self-conscious. And as if she'd been hoodwinked into saying too much. Why had she said that? It had sounded so pathetic. It was true, but it was so not how she wanted to come across. The victim. The cuckold. The one who got dumped. The one who was sitting in a restaurant at this moment, palpitating in such a juvenile fashion about being out socially with a man, for God's sake. She'd no idea it would be such a terrifying business. That she'd feel so overwhelmed with apprehension.

'Yes,' he said. 'I do. But you can unlearn it, you know.'

Hope picked up her glass. Yes, she thought. She should. She just didn't feel equal to the task yet. 'What about you?' she said. 'What have you learned, then?'

'Ah,' he said. 'Thought you'd be coming to that. Um. Let me see. That I married too young, that I married the wrong person...

47

that I was the wrong person… ' He grinned. 'But mainly that I'm forty, I'm free, and I have one hell of a lot of lost time to make up for.'

'I wish I felt like that.'

'You should try it on for size.'

God, she envied him his confidence. Why didn't he feel as she did? It didn't seem fair. 'Your ex-wife – sorry. I don't mean to pry. But what –'

'Oh, pry away. Same as you. Infidelity was the one we plumped for in the end. But that was just detail. Just for the sake of speed, really. If there'd been a "sorry, Jack, just got fed up with you" option, I think it might well have been her first choice. She's dumped him already, of course.'

He said this without a trace of self-pity. A grin, even. Hope, who had laboured under a similar cloud for so long, shook her head firmly. 'I can't imagine anyone getting fed up with you,' she said, meaning it but immediately kicking herself furiously for actually having said it. He poured them both more wine and considered her as he did so.

'Know what, Hope Shepherd? I rather like you,' he said.

Oh dear, thought Hope. Damn. So much for plans. Hers seemed to have been sidelined now. Utterly. Somewhere between the main course and the dessert she realised that despite her absolute conviction that she wasn't going to get involved with any man at any time in the foreseeable future (or indeed the unforeseeable one, just for good measure), she was beginning to find herself more than a little taken with Jack Valentine. There was the way he looked. He was so achingly good-looking. With his dense ochre hair and his big turquoise eyes. Then there was the way he looked at her. He was looking at her now, as he threaded his way through the tables to rejoin her after visiting the men's room. It was a speculative kind of looking, an appreciative kind of looking. Not lascivious exactly, but definitely the kind of look that made her feel she wouldn't mind in the least if it was. And there was the feeling. It had been so long since Hope had felt that simmering excitement in the pit of her stomach that it quite took her breath away.

48

She didn't know what to say to him when he sat back down again. She felt suddenly, unaccountably, debilitatingly self-conscious again. She should talk. About him. 'Come on,' she said. 'Tell me about your football team.'

'Absolutely not,' he said, smiling in a perfectly relaxed and happy way. 'I'd kind of like to have you awake for the evening. How about you tell me all about you instead?'

Oh, God. 'Me?'

'Yes, you. I was just thinking. I might write a feature about you.'

'Me?'

He stirred in his seat. 'Oh, and Heartbeat, of course. Nice human interest story. They like those at the *Echo*. And very good publicity for you, of course.'

This was better. Back on track. 'Oh. Yes. Yes, I suppose it would be, wouldn't it?'

'Indisputably.' He laced his fingers together and propped his chin on them. 'So, go on then. Shoot.'

'Oh dear. That's the only trouble. I'm not sure there's much to tell.'

He shook his head. 'There's always lots to tell. How d'you come to be there for instance? Doing what you do?'

'That's easy enough. I used to help out in the shop. We have a nearly-new shop, and I used to work there a couple of days a week when the children were smaller. But then, well, you know, with the divorce and everything, I had to get a proper job again and Madeleine asked me if I'd like to work for them full-time. Her husband had died and she'd taken on the running of the whole charity, and she needed someone to take on her old role.'

'The fundraising.'

'Exactly. And, well, I said yes.' She shrugged. 'Not much of a story there.'

'Nonsense,' he said. 'I think that's a nice story. But what about you?'

'What about me?'

'Hopes? Dreams? What d'you do when you're not busy extorting money out of people?'

'Oh, dear. Now there really isn't anything to tell. Not right now, at any rate. I don't know. I guess I have the same dreams as everyone else. To get through all the bad bits and move on to the good bits. God. I don't know. What do I do? I go to work. There never seems to be much time for anything else. I run. I read books. I watch TV... er... I make cushions.' She winced. 'Jesus, but that sounds grim, doesn't it? I wish I could tell you something else, but I can't. I don't do anything creative, like you do. I go to work, I come home from work, I do stuff with my kids. I go out running. I make cushions. There.'

She sat back in her chair while the waiter brought her dessert. Jack studied her. 'Cushions? '

'Oh, I live life on the edge, me. Yes. Cushions. It's not quite as dreary as it sounds. I make them out of leather, suede, that sort of thing. I have a bit of a fetish for skin, you see. God, that sounds worse! But, you know, out of all the old jackets and coats and stuff we get in at the shop. We get heaps of them. Even the odd fur. I don't use the fur, of course.' She leaned forward again. 'Well, not officially. I do. But just for me. Don't tell anyone that, will you? I have a big heap on my bed. *So* not PC. I don't – I mean, I don't approve, or anything. But we get these old furs, and they're only going to be binned, and they're so... well, anyway. Yes, I make cushions. I just got the idea, and made a couple to sell in the shop – I've got my mum's old industrial sewing machine – and, well, they went like a bomb. And then I made some for the office, because Maddie liked them, and nowadays I can hardly keep up with the orders. They must be in vogue or something, because everyone seems to want them.'

'There we are then. A one-woman cottage industry. That's pretty creative.'

'You think?' said Hope, who had never really thought about it. 'Well, I suppose. If you say so. Actually, Maddie thinks I should tout them round Liberty's or somewhere. See if I can't get some big deal going. But I haven't gotten around to it. It's just therapy, really. Something to do.' She pushed her teaspoon into the top of her crème brûlée, and it broke with a snap. 'God, does that make me sound sad, or what?'

'Not at all.' A smile played at the corner of his mouth. She lowered her eyes because his were becoming too distracting.

'I'm prattling now. Ask me about Heartbeat. Much more interesting.'

But he didn't.

He just sat there and smiled and watched her while she ate a mouthful of pudding. And another. And another. Still he looked at her, twiddling his glass stem and smiling. She lowered the teaspoon again. 'What?'

His eyes were trained on hers. 'Can I try some?'

'Some of this?'

He nodded. 'You seem to be enjoying it. Is it good?'

'Yes. Yes, it is. Here… ' She proffered the dish and the spoon.

He shook his head. 'No,' he said. 'You do it for me.'

So she loaded the spoon with a glistening mouthful and slid it gently between his waiting lips. She licked the spoon herself then, though she hadn't meant to.

'Thank you,' he mouthed. He still hadn't taken his eyes off her.

Holding his gaze, Hope knew something else had happened. That the man she was looking at had broached her defences. Somewhere along the line, by some glorious oversight, she had taken her eye off the ball.

Chapter 7

The taxi was somewhere between the castle and the University entrance when Jack made his mind up. Decided that what he would most like to do in all the world was to lunge at Hope Shepherd across the back seat and snog her until her teeth rattled. The thought, together with its profound inappropriateness at that moment, began to fuddle his cognitive processes. Hope was still talking thirteen to the dozen. This time about whether he thought it a good or a bad thing that the Welsh Assembly had decided to make museums free, which had followed on from what she'd been talking about while they'd been waiting for the taxi, which was how difficult it was to get any sort of government funding for little charities like hers, which followed on from what she'd been talking about while they waited for the waiter to bring his credit card back, which was, he only dimly remembered, something about how they hadn't managed to get a lottery grant. Or something. He'd lost track. For someone so shy – and her diffidence at the start of the evening had surprised him – she had an opinion about *everything*. An informed opinion, to boot. That hypothetical feature article (such a devilishly clever idea) would have to become actual now. She'd half written the bloody thing for him already. He smiled to himself. He was sitting slightly angled towards her, and could see the full length of her left leg, right down to the couple of inches of black leather boot at the bottom. It made him feel horny as hell. He imagined her left leg without its trouser. He imagined her left arm (which was lying inert in her lap, while her right one batted the air in time with the points she was making), peeled free of its jumper and lying encouragingly across his own thigh. He imagined (well, what the hell) what she would look like if she were sitting in the taxi with nothing on whatsoever, how the contours of her tummy – a smallish swell beneath her breasts – would rise and fall every time she drew breath. How her dark – no, black hair...

'Don't you?'

52

Jack rounded himself up and fixed his eyes on her face. She lifted her left arm and coiled a liquorice lace of loose hair behind her ear.

Didn't he what? Shit. He'd have to wing it. 'I'm not sure.'

She turned a little herself now, the better, he assumed, to engage him in the crux of her argument. The hand came down again and sat on the seating between them, the polished nails mere centimetres from his thigh. He pondered on the possibility of moving his leg. 'That's exactly it, isn't it?' she was saying. 'I mean, on the *one* hand –'

'Which part of Cefn Melin was it you wanted, lovely?' The cab driver jutted his head to fix his eyes into the rectangle of rear-view mirror. Hope leaned forward a little to meet them. Jack could smell her perfume every time she moved.

'It's the top end. Up by the park. If you head up through Roath and then on to Llanishen I'll tell you the way after that. You really didn't have to do this,' she added, training her dark eyes on Jack once again. 'Going all this way out of your way. I could easily have got a separate cab.' Then she smiled at him coyly, as if she was pleased nevertheless.

'It's not that far,' he said. 'Only a couple of miles.' How much could he read into that smile? Was he reading her right, period? She'd certainly revved up in the last hour or so. Did she fancy him, too? Her lips were glossy in the gloom. She must have put something on them when she went to the Ladies. Would a kiss be appropriate currency with which to end the evening? A peck of some kind? A brush of his lips against her cheek? Something nearer her mouth? On her mouth? The buzzing of every part of him south of his waistband was matched only in its intensity by the furious campaign instructions his neurones were firing at him. Would there ever be a time again when situations like this just happened? It seemed to Jack that sex (if and when he ever got some) was just one big round of manoeuvrings these days. It didn't used to be like that, did it? You just got the hots for a girl and went for it, didn't you? But his fond recollections of his teenage libido had been unpicked, every last one of them, since his divorce. His easy flirtatiousness with the opposite sex while he'd been married had evaporated as surely as a puddle in the sun. It was all decisions now. Imports. Consequences. Angles. He would so like to kiss her.

Would so like to kiss her while taking a well-aimed palm and smoothing it over the woolly mound in her jumper that he knew outlined her right breast. And then move on to the left... Was there any way he could wangle it so that he could send the taxi away?

But her mother would be there, he remembered belatedly. Her mother was babysitting, that's what she'd said. Though didn't she say her mother had driven her down? In which case, wouldn't she be driving home at some point? Why hadn't he brought his car? He'd drunk comparatively little. If he'd brought his car there would have been so many possibilities. *Carpe Diem*. But now he was stuck with the bloody cab. He tried to imagine himself standing outside Hope's house and kissing her while the taxi driver sat and waited for him. He couldn't. But he clearly couldn't kiss her in the taxi. It would seem tacky. It would be tacky. God, but he wanted to take her to bed.

Llanishen came and went. More directions were exchanged.

'Oh, I am so excited,' said Hope suddenly, lifting her arm up again and relocating it halfway along his forearm. A different part of his anatomy rose momentarily in agreement. But then he felt the mild pressure of her squeezing his arm through his jacket. Squeezing forearms was not, to Jack's mind, a ticket to ride. 'I just can't tell you. This means so much to me... what with, well, you know, everything... and I just know we're going to raise loads of cash. And it's so kind of everyone–' She stopped speaking for a moment to squeeze his arm again, before patting it. As if he were an amiable terrier. 'It's so kind of *you,* Jack. God, to think I almost didn't ring in about my trainer! Serendipity, don't you think?'

True serendipity, thought Jack, would be the happy coincidence of her deciding she'd like to take him to bed too. Among her secret fur cushions – now, there was a picture. Her boudoir. And preferably tonight. With her mother and children spirited away somewhere. 'It's a pleasure,' he said, holding her gaze long enough so that she wouldn't fail to register quite how much of a pleasure. An anticipatory one, admittedly. But then he always travelled hopefully.

She kept looking at him, her hand still on his forearm, then whipped it away suddenly and lowered her eyes. This was good. This was progress. Perhaps he had read things right. She looked thoughtful. Shy even. Maybe he should consolidate and make some sort of move.

'It was a lovely dinner,' she said hurriedly, beating him to it. 'And you must please, please let me give you something towards the taxi.' She starting fiddling with the clasp on the little bag in her lap. Aha! An opportunity. He reached out and placed his hand over hers. Her skin was warm, almost hot. And very, very soft. Following her lead, he now squeezed her hand gently, wondering, as her other hand hovered between them, if she might plonk it on top of his own now, in some sort of famous-five-pact ritual thing. Which would be fine. Just fine. He had another hand available. Pre-pubescent foreplay was OK by him. But she didn't. She just sat.

'I will not,' he said sternly, to consolidate. 'And no arguments.'

'But –'

He shook his head. 'No buts.'

'But –'

'Where here, love?'

Hope stopped butting and gave the driver more directions. Was it the light, or had she coloured a little? They were in her road now, it seemed, and approaching her house. 'But nothing,' said Jack smoothly. 'Like I said, it's been a pleasure.' He looked intently at her, smiling. It would be a pleasure. Decided, Jack let go of her hand as the taxi pulled up, and leapt out while she re-fastened her bag. She looked bemused to find him standing to attention by the door as she climbed out.

Flustered, in fact. 'There was really no need –'

Should he go for it? *Should* he?

'So,' he said instead. 'Here we are, then.'

'Here we are indeed.' She pushed a bit of hair around again. 'Thank you so much for this evening. I'd ask you in but I suppose you'll want to be getting back.' She gestured towards the taxi. The driver inside was fiddling with a knob on his radio set.

'I guess I will,' he said. And in one fluid movement he clasped her shoulder with one hand, shut the car door with the other, leaned forward, pursed his lips, changed his mind, opened them, and made satisfying contact with her mouth. She'd proffered her cheek, of course, but he was wise to that one. Their lips met

55

and parted in an untidy muddle, which was more than she'd expected and the best he could hope for. She looked mildly shocked.

'It's been lovely, Hope,' he said, drawing back and reluctantly letting go of her. She was blinking at him now. He smiled in what he hoped was a reassuring manner. He didn't want her thinking he was some sort of letch. She grinned coyly at him, so he smiled the smile wider. 'I hope we can do it again soon.'

As Jack got back into the taxi he'd already mentally ditched the word 'again' from this statement. A sporting analogy seemed rather fitting. God, just do it. To just do it at all would be nice.

She waved as they drove off. Damn, he felt horny. Damn, but he wished he'd brought the car.

Chapter 8

'Well, well!' Madeleine's chuckle rang loudly down the phone line. 'So you and Prince Charming have struck up a bit of a rapport, then?'

Oh God. She should have stopped and thought before yammering on so much. Madeleine was on the case, big time. Hope's lack of a love-life was Maddie's favourite project. Had been since the day Iain had left. Why hadn't she kept her mouth shut? More to the point, if the prospect of a love-life filled her with such a palpable fear, which it manifestly did, why was she letting it dominate her thoughts? Why not call a moratorium on love and be done with it? She really didn't need all this angst.

'He's very nice,' she said carefully.

'You told me that already. We still on *nice* nice?'

'Just nice, Maddie. Stop it.'

'Babe, I haven't even started. Besides, what's the big deal?'

'It isn't a big deal.'

'Yeah, and I'm a kipper.'

'It isn't. He's just nice, OK? No more than that.'

'Come on. Own up. You fancy him rotten.'

'OK, then. I fancy him. Satisfied now?'

Saying it felt strange and unreal on her tongue. And filled her with trepidation. Maddie was right. There was a whole world of difference between a little light rapport and the something that was happening to her now. She had, she realised, been snatching up the phone every time it rang since she'd arrived at the office. 'Anyway,' said Maddie, 'you can spill the beans later. I was really ringing to let you know I was going to be a little later than I'd planned. I'm at the chiropractors.'

'Chiropractors?' asked Hope, pleased to change the subject. 'I didn't know you had problems with your back.'

'I don't, stoo-pid. But, hey, I'm wearing my lucky thong, so perhaps I'll get lucky today.'

'What, get back ache?'

Madeleine guffawed.

'Darling, get real!' Her voice grew a little quieter. 'A recommendation. A friend of mine said I really should go see him. He's a bit of a sweetie, apparently. So I thought I'd come and check him out. Prophylactically, so to speak. Anyway, you can cope OK, can't you? Just be sure to remind Kayleigh about the mailshot. I left it on her desk.'

'No problem.'

'Right. I'll see you about twelve. You can fill me in then.'

'On what?'

'D'oh! Prince Charming, of course!'

Hope had been addressing the envelope when Madeleine called. The envelope for the card she'd sent Jack, to thank him for the dinner. And to reiterate, again, how thrilled they all were that he'd so kindly agreed to lend his support to the fun run. She'd signed the card Hope, with an X underneath it. Which she wasn't sure she wasn't now regretting. It felt so adolescent. And it wasn't very businesslike. But it was already done. The kiss would have to stay.

As had the memory of his. Something big and important had happened to Hope, and she wasn't sure quite what to do about it. She had, she realised, become possessed by a feeling she could not remember having felt for the last twenty years. It wasn't quite lust and it wasn't quite love; it wasn't quite anything she could readily pin down, just a preoccupation and a chemical reaction every time she brought Jack to mind. It was, she decided, the single most distracting and disabling feeling she'd experienced in the whole of her life.

She had been floating when he'd left her. She'd floated across the pavement, up the path, through the door, and into the hall. Once inside (and while floating across the carpet) she'd become conscious of both a faint tang of popcorn and a sensation of ringing in her ears. Her mother had been dozing on the sofa in the living room, the television transmitting pictures but no sound. She'd glanced at herself then, in the hall mirror, on her way into the kitchen. Her face – *a* woman's face, at any rate; it felt strangely unfamiliar – had a patina of sparkle. An end-of-evening glow, a not unattractive slight dishevelment. She'd run her tongue across her lips, then, to recapture the taste of him. God, that's what it was, she'd thought. The ringing was the sound of her heart beating faster. Not a lot. Just a little.

She'd smiled as she'd passed by, rather charmed at the thought. And having woken her mother and fielded all her questions, she'd waved her off hurriedly and floated on up to bed.

She was glad that her mother had been there. Had she not been, and Hope's feelings were somewhat mixed on this point, there was little doubt (there was the wine to consider, after all) that she would have invited him in. Little doubt she'd have encouraged him to kiss her some more. And then?

A wholly novel state of affairs. It was interesting, and not a little disquieting, to find that a pulse of sexual desire still actually beat in her. That it was possible that, buried beneath the layers of mistrust and denial, she wanted to be made love to again. That the sensation of arousal could be so profoundly physical. That this thing, this phenomenon, was actually happening to *her*. He liked her too. That much was evident. She closed the card and slipped it back into the envelope. He liked her. And as Madeleine was ever fond of commenting, a little light frisson never failed to help the cause.

She ran her tongue along the paper edge. But that was last night. However good it felt to have been courted by him, however delicious it was to feel sexy again, with morning had come the return of common sense. And with that, a reminder, as evidenced by her telephone frenzy, of the terrible nature of infatuations. He was dangerous territory. Not as cheesy, perhaps, as she'd originally decided. No. Not cheesy at all, in fact. Charming, just like Maddie had said. Too charming? Probably. Certainly a man used to female attention, and, no doubt, given his ex-marital status, used to capitalising on it without a second thought. Someone, as he'd been at pains to point out, who had a lot of lost time to make up.

'Someone's birthday?' asked Simon, who had appeared at her desk, in the stealthy way he had that always made her feel slightly fretful. He was pointing at the lilac envelope. He was unsettlingly observant.

She sealed it, feeling scrutinised. 'What? Oh... no, no. Just a card for the DJ man.'

'Ah, the fun run.'

'The fun run.'

He thrust his hands into the pockets of his trousers. 'We really ought to get in training.'

'Hmm?'

'Training. You know. For the race. I mean we'll want to run ourselves, won't we? I was thinking, actually. We ought to form a little running group. You know. Get some sort of regimen organised. It's only a few months off.'

'It's only five K.'

He nodded violently at her. 'Absolutely. Chicken feed.' He opened his mouth and emitted a sound that might well have been an attempt at a cluck. 'But, you know. I was just thinking about working on our times and all that. Might be fun. Tell you what. How about I send a memo round? See if we can get a gang of us together. Be quite apposite to lead the pack, so to speak.'

Apposite (if he must) but unlikely. Hope had only that morning received confirmation from the North East Cardiff Harriers that yes, they'd love to be part of the publicity, and yes, they'd be there for the run. She was about to remind Simon that they had at least three county champions among their number, when he shifted his sheaf of papers from one arm to the other and said, 'How about later this week? Are you free Thursday evening, say? Weather permitting, of course.'

Hope considered. He seemed awfully keen. 'Um… yes, maybe. I normally don't run on Thursdays. But the children will be at their dad's, so I suppose I could.'

There would be no harm in running with Simon. It would be company. As long as she kept him at arm's length.

'That would be brilliant,' he said, with worrisome sincerity. 'Brilliant. I'll get on to it now. Oh, by the way –'

'What?'

'Did Kayleigh give you the message about the press release?'

Hope scanned her desk. 'What press release?'

'They need a press release so they can write something to go with the photo. They called back half an hour ago. Kayleigh told them you'd do one for them.'

'What photo?'

'The photo for the paper.'

'You've lost me, Simon.'

'Oh, of course. You wouldn't know. They're all coming at three.'

'Who are coming at three?'

'The people from the *Echo*. To do a piece on the fun run. And take a photo.'

'Of who?'

'Of all of us. With Jack Valentine.'

The sensation was electric. 'Jack's coming *here*?'

Simon nodded.

'What, *today*?'

'Apparently so.' He was, she noticed, looking rather irritated by this. 'He said he's going to pop along after his show.'

'He is?' She tried hard not to appear too excited. But Simon's expression made her realise she'd failed.

It changed. Now he was smiling at her sweetly. 'Yes, he is. Apparently. Only I just remembered. You're not going to be in then, of course.'

Damn, damn, *damn*. She wasn't. And there was no earthly way she could get out of her engagementt. Mr Babbage was expecting her at half past two and fulfilling Mr Babbage's expectations was a non-negotiable commitment. Not only was he one of their most enduring patrons, he was also principal sponsor of the fun run. Damn.

She returned to the office having missed Jack Valentine by a scant ten minutes. She might have passed him on the road. She could have passed him on the pavement. She could, she was sure, still smell his aftershave in the air. Surely not. Now, that was just mad.

'I'm impressed,' said Madeleine. She was clearly energised by her brush with back manipulation because she was sitting cross-legged in the middle of her office floor, eating from a bowl of grapes, a beatific – or satisfied? – smile on her face. 'That's the wonderful thing about life. Doors open more doors. At this rate we'll fetch up on the six o'clock news. How was Mr Babbage?'

Short, fat and balding. As opposed to tall, slim and gorgeous. Hope shrugged. 'Oh, much the same as ever,' she said. 'He's already sent a mailshot to all his clients to sponsor him to run it himself.'

Maddie paused, grape in hand. 'Run it? Mr Babbage? You must dissuade him at all costs, Hope. It'll kill him, for sure. And that's just the sort of publicity we need right now, I don't think.'

Hope nodded. Maddie knew all about exercise-induced cardiac problems. 'I will. Er… it went well, then, did it? The thing with the *Echo*?'

'Excellent. It's a shame you weren't here, though,' mused Madeleine. 'You would have lent a little class to the photo.' She looked gleeful suddenly. 'And your absence was noted. You were *missed.*'

Hope didn't care if she was in the photo or not. Just that she'd missed him. But she didn't dare probe. Maddie had the antennae of an Elephant Hawk Moth. And the nose of a tapir.

And a lucky thong. Perhaps Hope should go out and get one. 'I'm in the photo,' said Kayleigh, who had come in with a tray of tea and Garibaldis. She side-stepped Madeleine and put the tray on the desk. 'Mum'll be well made up.'

Hope took her tea and a compensatory three biscuits.

'He's ever so nice, isn't he? I've never met a famous person before. Do you know, he's actually met Tom Jones? I mean, how cool is that?'

Kayleigh reclaimed the biscuit packet and ambled out with the tray.

'Oh, yeah, Hope,' she said, as she negotiated the doorway. 'I nearly forgot. He really liked your cushions, by the way. He told me to make sure I told you.'

'A thank you card? Hmm. She's keen, then.' Danny peeled off his vest and stooped to disentangle his football shorts from his feet. 'God, what a bastard of a fall. Look at that!' He lifted his knee, the better to show Jack the oozing burgundy smear that was crusting on top of it. 'Anyway, what's she like?'

Jack threw his towel over his shoulder and headed off towards the showers.

'Nice,' he called back. 'She's, you know, well, nice.' He knew that "nice" wasn't the right word, but that was the word that, rather frustratingly, kept coming, unbidden, to mind. He wished it didn't. It really bugged him that it did. He so wanted to stick with the fur.

Danny was padding along behind him.

'Bit of a babe, then?'

'Well, I doubt you'd think so. But, yes. *I* think so. Very attractive. But, oh, I don't know –'

He stopped, and Danny caught him up. 'But what? Go shag her, mate.'

Jack turned around. 'I don't know. I mean, yes, she's certainly shaggable, but, I don't know… '

'Don't know what?'

'You know. Whether I want to get involved with someone like her right now. I mean she's thirty-nine, she's divorced, she's got kids, she's got –' He shrugged. 'Look, don't get me wrong. I'm not saying I'm only in the market for vestal virgins.'

'Just as well, mate. You'd have no chance.'

' – or girls who only want a good time.'

'You sad man, you. But that still leaves pretty much everything else in between. So what's the problem?'

'Well, it's just that, well… she's got – well, she's got –'

Danny rolled his eyes. 'Don't tell me, mate. Baggage.'

'Whatever you want to call it. Yes, I suppose. Yes. At any rate, all the kind of stuff you'd expect her to have. Like an ex-husband who's been a bastard to her. And a big downer on men.'

'Hmm. See your point. But not all men. Not you.'

Jack shook his head. No, he had already decided. Not from the way she'd reacted when he'd kissed her. She'd certainly been startled, but she hadn't seemed to mind. He thought again what a fool he'd been not taking his car that night. If he had, the question might have been academic by now. There wouldn't have been time to start pondering how nice she was. He'd have been too busy finding out how hot she was instead. He'd missed the moment and now he'd started thinking. Never a good thing to be doing.

'No. Not me, I don't think,' he agreed, with some regret.

Danny spread his hands. 'So. What's the problem?'

'She's too nice.'

'You what? How can she be too nice?'

Jack pulled his towel from his shoulder and hung it on a hook. 'Because I don't mean "nice", Dan, I mean "*nice*". A nice person. A caring, intelligent, principled person. Someone with whom you wouldn't generally associate the word "shag".'

Danny rolled his eyes again. 'You do talk some crap, mate.'

63

Yes. He knew that. He did. Truth be known, he didn't know quite what it was he *did* think about Hope Shepherd. Only that much as he liked the idea of *shagging* her, he wasn't sure he was so keen on the idea of shagging *her*. And who was to say he'd get that lucky anyway? With her background, it didn't seem likely that she'd jump into bed with the first guy who asked her. And he wasn't up to fragile, or vulnerable, or untrusting, frankly. Too big a remit. He was in no shape for that kind of responsibility right now.

Not ready. He stepped into a shower cubicle and trained the shower head over his face. She was nice, no question. If he was honest with himself, she was probably exactly the sort of person he could see himself ending up with. No. He didn't mean that. Exactly the sort of person that he'd be happy ending up with. Just, well... just not yet. He wasn't stupid. There was no way in the world he was going to become some wizened Lothario. It was just the "ending up" thing that bothered him. The notion that if he started getting involved with the sort of woman he might end up with, what happened to the bit in between? All the dreams, all the plans, all the shagging scenarios (however preposterous) that had sustained him through the doldrums thus far? The *Jack* bit of his life. The him bit. The *me* bit. He was just, only just, getting the hang of being single, and he didn't want to slam shut all the doors that had just opened for him as a result of that state. He wasn't ready yet.

He knew exactly what it was that he did want. That was the problem. He wanted the same thing he'd been wanting for the last umpteen months. Some uncomplicated congress with the opposite sex. Some sex, in fact, period. Not commitment, or a life plan, or to have to spend months and months manoeuvring-in-hope. Just some sex. Some fun. Like the rest of the world. Everything would feel different once he'd crossed that particular hurdle. So why wasn't he getting any? Everyone else seemed to manage to do it. Why not him?

He wished he could see himself the way everyone else seemed to see him. Wished he could morph into the rabid, testosterone-fuelled automaton of Danny's imagination. Perhaps then he'd actually have some hope of getting his shagging campaign off the ground. But he fretted too much. That was the trouble. When he first got divorced it had all seemed so simple. He'd get out there,

God help him, and he'd have a good time. Trouble was, it hadn't turned out to be easy being rabid and rampant, not when he spent so much of his time seeing himself as the person Lydia had always seen him as, which was understandable given that they'd been married so long. It wasn't easy to have to start all over with your self-image. To pick over the clutch of adjectives that were generally associated with him (unambitious, a little introspective, no great shakes in any department) and remodel them into less damning ones – like free-spirited, creative, a catch.

Perhaps he was a little fragile himself. But why should he be? Deep down he knew he probably was the same person he'd always been. It was just his perception of the value of that person that had changed. Lydia, on the other hand, had changed a great deal. In that oh-so-well documented way that women, or so he'd been told, always did. Thus their paths had diverged. That was it. Yes. He should keep reminding himself of that. A simple case of divergence. It had been the OU course that had started it.

'I feel unfulfilled,' she'd announced one day, apropos of nothing. 'Like my life is slipping past me and that I haven't achieved anything.'

Fine, he'd said. Great, he'd said.

'I need to go back to college and learn something new.'

Fine, he'd said. Great, he'd said. Whatever you want to do.

Except that they couldn't afford for her to go back to college. Not with Ollie's school fees and the mortgage and everything else – the carpets, conservatories, industrial expresso makers – that Lydia deemed necessary for bearable living. It was out of the question for her to give up work. Which was Jack's fault, of course.

He couldn't blame her. They had both, he knew, approached life with a number of expectations, and it was to both their discredit that they hadn't bothered consulting each other about what exactly those were.

So she'd started studying part-time with the OU, and re-acquainted herself with the self she'd once been. And acquainted herself with someone else too.

He had about eight letters after his name, a chair in epitheliology or some such, a Caterham Seven and a *pied-a-terre* in Bordeaux.

Jack had a radio show, two columns and not-quite-half-a-book about football. No contest, really. So she took him (and all his bloody letters) to bed.

He rinsed the shower gel from his hair and let cold water stream over his body for a few moments. 'Still,' Danny was shouting at him now, from the other cubicle. 'She's worth a shot, don't you think?'

As Jack had failed to hear what had been said prior to this, it made little sense to him.

'What? Hope?' he shouted back.

'No, you dick. Forget *her*. Allegra Staunton! Didn't I tell you?'

Oh God. 'What about Allegra?'

'She collared me in the corridor yesterday. God only knows what she was doing there.'

'And?'

'And what?'

'And what about it?'

'She told me to send you her love.' Danny's shower curtain zipped back with a tinny rattle. He pulled Jack's open too and stood there naked and dripping before him. Then winked. 'She's gagging for it, mate. *Gagging* for it. No baggage with that one. Like I said, def worth a shot.'

It was only after Jack had got home and sorted his kit out that it occurred to him what Danny had meant. Well, as long as Danny didn't know about the TV thing, that was OK. Let him enjoy his vicarious pleasures. He pulled Hope's card from the inside pocket of his jacket and frowned. Danny was right. Best not to go there. Not now. He propped it on his bedside table with a sigh.

The only other object on Jack's bedside table was a photograph of his parents. Looking at this photo now filled him with woe. Made him yearn to scuttle back to the bolt hole of his youth. To all the safe summer holidays and Christmasses of his childhood. Try as he might, in almost all of his memories, it seemed it was one or the other. Or his birthday. Egg sandwiches, paper streamers, butterfly cakes. And lollies made with Kia-Ora orange squash.

And woe. How'd it go? That was it. *Monday's child is full of grace, Tuesday's child is fair of face, Wednesday's child is full of woe, Thursday's child has far to go...* That was him. Wednesday's child. He hadn't known what the word 'woe' actually meant, then. He could remember asking his mother as if it were yesterday. Right down to the smell of custard tart cooking in the kitchen. Right down to her warm floury hand on his cheek. 'It's when you're feeling a bit forlorn,' she'd said. He hadn't known what 'forlorn' meant either. 'You know,' she'd said. 'When you've got that little serious face on of yours.' His serious face. He had it on now. He could feel the weight of its creases on his forehead. Well, he sure knew what woe meant now.

He picked the photograph up. It had been taken when his father must have been almost exactly the age he was now. Black and white. A little faded and creased at the corners – until Jack had dug it out, it had resided in his dad's photo box for many years. He smoothed his finger across the dust that had settled there. His mum and dad, hand-in-hand on a beach in West Wales. He couldn't recall where now. Only that it was a picture that he himself had taken. He didn't remember doing so, but his father had told him he had. Also in the photo, was his precious tin bucket. The one with the farmyard frieze around the side, abandoned upside down in the sand, by his spade. There they'd all been, a happy family. A happy couple. So where was *he* right now? At this same point in *his* life? He put the picture back down and looked ruefully around him. At the stained anaglypta, the listless, sprigged curtains, the clumsy marquetry on the junk-shop chest of drawers. How did they get to there and he get to here?

This really wouldn't do. He checked his watch. It wasn't late. After he'd called Ollie to sort out tomorrow, perhaps he'd ring the nursing home and say hello to his dad.

Chapter 9

OK, then. Since when was it decreed that there were just the two categories of women – those that did and those that didn't, and that those that did were strictly for the doing of it with, and those that didn't were strictly for, well, the not doing of it with, and that never the twain should be confused? Jack, who had awoken to find himself dragged reluctantly from a happy hypothetical re-visit to the contours of Hope Shepherd's body, was trying very hard to talk himself out of mindless chivalry. He had lived his life following all sorts of daft rules like that and precisely where had it got him? In under-stairs cupboards with girls who looked as if they might actually be up for most things if encouraged, but then in a church vestry with a woman for whom sex was, and always would be, like root-canal work. Uncomfortable, unfortunate, but one of those things. And then divorced. Oh yes. And that.

Well, perhaps that should tell him something. That changes were long overdue. In that department of his life, at any rate. Other departments, Jack knew, must stay reassuring constants. Life rafts to cling to. There were his columns, the one he did for the *Mail*, which paid his half of the mortgage – and the one, though less well paid, less high profile, less *everything* – that he wrote for the *Echo* on the junior league. He'd been doing the column since Ollie started at the Cougars, his arrival on the scene having happily coincided with the coaching retirement of the already-retired headmaster who'd been writing it (pretty listlessly) for the last fifteen years. He had a whole page to himself, so seriously was the junior league taken, which he'd fill with noteworthy snippets about the various league matches, and the sort of photographs – taken by himself, wherever possible – that he knew would be cherished long after the subjects had grown and the ink had all but faded to grey. They would be put in fancy frames, or stored lovingly in albums, to be brought out, decades later, for grandfatherly chit-chats about days and excitements and triumphs long gone. Being part of the making of these small, unremarkable but precious pieces of history gave Jack more pleasure than almost anything he did.

There were other constants, of course – there was his book, for one. Jack had embarked, several years back, on an ambitious project. To write a definitive sporting and social history of his father's beloved Portsmouth Football Club. It was a daft project, the sort of project you didn't discuss with people at parties. And moreover, there were at least two such books to his knowledge already in print. Why on earth did the world need another? But the enormity of what he'd already done (300-odd pages and rising) coupled with the enormity of what he still had to do (at least that again) compounded with the reality that, having done it, he would have to find someone to publish it, made him feel so anxious that he tried not to think about it when he wasn't actually doing it, in case he became so frightened that he never picked it up again. He remembered Lydia's scathing eye-rolling whenever he ventured to mention it. Now the manuscript sat on the chest of drawers in Ollie's room, and, except on those days when Ollie inhabited it, it was there, siren-calling him every time he passed. But finish it he must. Because it was his dad he was writing it for.

The other constant Jack loved in his life was coaching the Cougars. He'd been a helper there since the day Ollie started, believing, then as now, that the opportunity of watching your child play football on a Saturday morning to be one of the greatest privileges parenting could bestow.

Though right now, he decided, there might well be others. This particular Saturday was not shaping up well.

They were playing the Roath Rovers, and their manager, a man he'd had few dealings with except on presentation days, was not in the jolliest of moods. Earlier there'd been dissent about which pitch they should use – many of them being more mud-bath than playing field – and Jack, refereeing, and therefore nominally in charge, had had to stand firm on his choice.

No surprise then, that not long into the first half the boys were already chopsy and scrapping. While he was helping up a lad who'd slipped in the mud just in front of him, almost tripping him up, there'd been a corker of a cross towards the open goal. So conscious was he now of the two lads on a collision course to receive it, that he was only belatedly aware of the linesman – the Rover's manager – blowing his whistle, and of some sort of ruck that was already underway.

Jogging across to break up the tussle, Jack chided himself that he'd missed the tackle. He was sure it was no big deal, but he was ever conscious that he needed to be impartial where his own son was concerned, and Ollie, it seemed, was a part of this spat.

'Come on, lads,' he yelled equably as he approached. 'Break it up!'

Ollie was holding his hand to his face. Jack shoved the gaggle to one side. They were still sniping at each other.

'Bollocks!' Ollie was saying, 'You bloody elbowed me on purpose!'

'Hey, hey, hey –' Jack began.

The other boy scowled, his face hot with rage. They were all breathing heavily. The ground was like treacle and the air prickly in his nostrils. Breath clouded in front of him.

'I did not!' said the boy vehemently, stabbing a finger in Ollie's general direction. 'It was an accident! Anyway, you fucking chopped me!'

'I didn't!'

'You bloody did!' He turned to Jack. 'He bloody did!'

A couple of the boys from the Rovers nodded mutely. He turned to Ollie.

'Well?' he demanded.

'Look, OK – it was a late-ish tackle, but you bloody elbowed me on purpose!'

'I didn't!'

Jack took a closer look at Ollie's reddened cheek. 'OK, OK, calm down both of you. Ollie, you can come off till half-time and we'll put something on that swelling.' He looked towards the Rovers coach who was doing the right thing and not interfering. He could speak to him afterwards. Best thing, experience told him, was that they just calm down and get on with the game. 'And… you… er, what's your name, son?'

'Tom,' said the boy.

'Why do I have to come off?' demanded Oliver. 'I don't want to come off. He was the one who elbowed me. He –'

'I fucking *didn't*!' said Tom.

'Boys, boys, *boys*!' began Jack, who managed such hormonal outbursts at least once every Saturday and knew there was no point trying to tease any more facts out of either party right now. 'Will you both cut this out, *now*, so we can get on with the game!'

'*Thomas!*' came a voice. A strident, shrill, and indisputably female one. 'Thomas Shepherd! If I hear so much as one more expletive come out of your mouth, you are grounded till next Christmas! Do you hear me?'

Jack turned towards the sideline, where the small gathering of parents had parted to allow a woman in a grey duffel-coat-thing to march through. He blinked. A woman he recognised.

A woman, he realised as he watched her approach, that other bits of him recognised too. And why not? If they did, then so be it. She wasn't the Vicar of Dibley, for God's sake.

'Hello!' he called out to her. But even as he did so, he felt a bump against his shoulder, as the Roath boy, Tom, pushed angrily past him and stalked off towards the edge of the pitch.

Hope Shepherd drew level. 'Oh dear,' she said, her voice now substantially lower and her expression one of mortification. She glanced behind her. 'I am *so* sorry.'

'Please,' said Jack, spreading his palms. 'There's no need to be.'

She was shaking her head. 'Yes, there is. I am so sorry. I'll go and… well, er, look, I think I'd better go after him, hadn't I?' She frowned. 'I'm *really* sorry.'

She turned on her heel and stomped angrily after him, leaving Jack with the lingering and not unpleasant image of the two carmine spots that had flamed on her cheeks.

'I have never – *never* – been so embarrassed in my life. Do you hear me? How dare you behave like that! Is this what professional footballers do? *Is* it? Do you consider that to be sportsman-like behaviour? Well?'

Tom sat, sullen and damp and still perspiring in the passenger seat while Hope drove furiously home. 'Well?'

'But he chopped me, Mum! He knew exactly what he was doing. He chopped me!'

She took a hand from the steering wheel and flapped it angrily in front of him. 'He chopped you, he chopped you… So what if he did? Does that make it right to stick your elbow in his face?'

'I didn't mean to. I –'

'I'm sorry, but I simply don't believe you, Thomas. Do you think Alan Shearer would have behaved like that?'

'Yes,' he said, sulkily. 'He –'

'I don't think so, young man. I don't think so. I have never been so embarrassed in all my life. And your language!' She changed gear and the clutch screeched an expletive of its own. 'It's not the point, anyway. Whether you meant to or not is irrelevant. You should have apologised! You don't go around barging into people and shoving them out of the way with your elbows and then expect everyone to believe it was just –'

'Mum, *God!* It's football, OK?!'

'Don't you "God" me! And don't you "it's football" me either, young man! It won't wash, I'm afraid. And don't give me any more excuses. I'm not interested whether he chopped you or not, quite frankly. It's –'

'But he should have blown for it!'

'Well, he didn't. So deal with it. Because that's life, my boy, and you –'

'But it's not fair. And it's not life either, it's just because he's his son!'

Hope's head snapped round.

'What? Whose son?'

'The ref's son!'

'*What?* That boy? That Oliver boy?'

Tom spread his hands in his lap. 'Yes! *Exactly,* Mum!'

Oh, brilliant. *Brilliant*, thought Hope.

It wasn't, she told herself, that she'd engineered it. Not really. It was just that she had found the fixture list and happened to notice that Tom's team were playing the Cougars, and it didn't take a great deal to persuade Iain that as she was going to be in the area anyway, it made sense for her to take Tom. That was all. Just one of those things you do on the spur of the moment. OK, on the spur of Friday evening, which *was* the spur of the moment in Iain's organisational terms.

Who was she kidding? In all her adult life, Hope had never, not once, found herself so utterly preoccupied with a man. With Iain, well, in the early days there'd been moments, of course, but that felt different to this. This was more complex. Less comfortable. This unmanageable mania was consuming almost all her waking thoughts. So, no. Not spur of the moment at all. Spur of a moment two weeks and five days back when a man called Jack Valentine had pressed his mouth against hers. It hadn't even been a proper kiss, not really. Even so, the mere thought of it, along with the pictures that, as a result, kept suggesting themselves to her, made her light-headed with lust. She felt drenched in it, trapped in its velvety tentacles, and so intoxicating, so compelling, so heady was the feeling, that it actually made her very frightened.

Yet on she'd trolled. On with her scheming and dreaming, as if someone else altogether was now running her life. Chloe, conveniently, was at a friend's for a sleepover, and off she'd gone, head over her bloody Cinderella heels.

She'd known he would be there, of course. The first rule in the management of a crush, Hope had reluctantly conceded, was that all reason must be abandoned on the altar of desire. So yes, of course he'd be there, inconceivable that he'd not be – bounding about the place, all tracksuited and trainered, all smiling enthusiasm and skill. And he had been. Though she'd not seen him at first. The pitches were a good way from the car park, so she'd dropped Tom off and gone back to park the car, and they were already playing by the time she'd trudged back. She'd huddled at the back of the knot of chilly parents, content to enjoy the experience of just seeing him and looking forward to saying hello at half time.

But now this. This shame. Let down by her own son. She could just about cope with the fact of his outburst, but this subsidiary bombshell that Oliver wasn't just any old Oliver, but Oliver *Valentine*... well... it was too much. Horror upon horror. What would he think of her?

'Right,' she said, decided, once Tom had showered and calmed down and thought he'd slunk off and got away with it. 'Two apologies are in order. One, I apologise for coming on the pitch and shouting at you. It was wrong of me and embarrassing for you and I won't do it again, OK? And two, I want you to go up to your room and write a letter of apology to Mr Valentine, and you can come with me to deliver it later on, when I go to pick up my suit from the dry cleaners.'

Tom looked horrified. '*What*?'

'You heard. You will write a letter of apology and you will come with me to deliver it.'

'What, to *him*? What, personally?'

'Yes, young man,' she said sternly, in her don't-mess-with-me voice. 'Personally, Thomas. To him.'

So he did. They picked up a box of Roses from the supermarket, and then drove on to Jack's house. She knew where it was because she had all his details in her handbag. He'd scribbled his home address and phone number on the back of his card when he'd taken her out to dinner. Just in case, he'd said. Just in case you need to get hold of me for anything.

And now, as she stood in his porch, ringing the doorbell, the 'anything' felt particularly ill-judged and stupid, and her feet felt spectacularly, cringe-makingly cold.

It was important that Tom do the right thing. Of course it was. But right now? In the form of this impulsive madness? Coming round here and turning up on his doorstep? When she could have sent it, or given it to him when she next saw him, or had Tom go round on his bike or something and drop it through the letterbox... she didn't want to examine her motives, for she knew they were agents of a whole other preoccupation.

Some time passed. She hadn't heard the bell ring inside, and there was no indication of life beyond the frosted glass panel in the door.

'They're probably out,' observed Tom, looking hopeful.

Hope cupped her hand around her eye and peered through the glass. A dark shape was growing inside now, coming down the stairs.

'Ah,' said Hope.

'Oh,' said Tom.

Jack Valentine then appeared at the door. He was barefoot, wearing very little clothing. A pair of shorts – boxer shorts, even – she didn't like to look too closely – and a T-Shirt that said 'Real Men Don't Ask For Directions' on the front. He looked slightly crumpled. Like he'd recently been asleep.

'Goodness!' he said, looking shocked. 'Well, hello!'

Hope smiled cheerily at him, wishing she could simply disappear or explode.

'We're sorry to bother you,' she said. 'But Tom wanted to – well –' She nudged Tom and he proffered the envelope. 'We came – *Tom* came – to apologise.'

'Oh,' said Jack Valentine again, smiling at Hope as he took the letter. 'Oh, right. But you really didn't have to do that.' He smiled at Tom now. 'I know it was an accident. These things happen. Heat of the moment and all that.'

Lots of things happened in the heat of the moment. Not all of them necessarily good. Hope swallowed. 'That's very gracious of you. How's Oliver's eye?'

'It's fine. A little bruised, but no permanent damage.' He opened the door wider. 'Why don't you come up and say hello?'

'You're not in the middle of anything, are you? I should have called, I know, but I thought, well… as we were passing anyway… and, well, Tom –'

Hope fell silent, feeling more than ever like this had been a very bad idea. 'No, no,' he said. 'Not long home from work, actually. Watching TV. Nothing special.' He glanced at the chocolates clasped in Tom's other hand. 'Well? Are you going to come in?' He stood aside and waved an arm towards the stairs.

Hope stayed on the doorstep. Tom, beside her, continued to look down at his feet.

'I don't want to intrude or anything.'

'You're not. Not at all. Come on in.' He held the door open wider still, while Hope and Tom filed past him. 'Up the stairs,' he said, shutting the front door.

It was an old house, the hall wallpapered in violent floral swirls. Down the hallway, two further doors were both closed. A copy of the local newsletter lay unopened on a spindly hall table, next to a spider plant sitting in a tide-marked saucer. Hope headed up the stairs, Tom's footfalls heavy behind her.

At the top, eighteen inches of brick-red carpet led to another door, which was ajar. Clearly the door to Jack's flat. It had a Yale lock on it.

'Go on. Go on in,' he called up from behind them. The landing continued, only now it was more correctly another hall. There was a phone on the floor and a phone book beside it. And there were two black and white photos of football teams on the wall. Teenagers. But not his. These were a generation or two older. She hovered while Jack shut the door behind them.

'My dad,' he said proudly, pointing to the first one. 'He played for the Portsmouth under twenty-ones.' He pointed out a slight boy with the same grin Jack had.

'And this one?'

'Ah. That's me. I'm afraid I wasn't quite so talented as a player. That's just the local team. But I'm kind of hoping these things skip a generation – you know, like twins do? And that Ollie'll be doing it for me instead. I'm working on him.' He grinned. 'Anyway, come on in.'

Through the far door, Hope could see a teenage boy hunched over a computer at a small gate-leg table. He glanced up as they entered.

'Ollie, look who's here. And bearing chocolates, no less! D'you want to go on in, Tom?'

Tom looked like he'd rather have a six-inch nail drilled through his toe without anaesthetic and Hope wondered again quite what it was that had possessed her to frogmarch him round here. But he stepped forward anyway. There was little else for him to do.

'Peace offering,' quipped Jack, clearly also a bit lost for words. 'Hey! There's a thought! Are you genned up with this Legend of Mir game, Tom?' He followed Tom into the living room and ushered him across to the computer, where sounds of distant carnage intermittently cawed from the screen. Oliver looked embarrassed. Hope could see Tom nod.

'Ollie's obsessed with it, aren't you, mate?' He turned back to Hope. 'What's new, eh?' he added knowingly. Hope didn't know. She didn't have a computer right now. A source of much scowling resentment at home. Jack turned around and grabbed another chair from the other side of the table. 'Here, Tom. Have a seat. Ollie'll be glad of some intelligent discussion about it, I'm sure.'

'Er… right,' said Tom, sitting down, and placing the box of Roses at the side of the desk.

Ollie turned to face him, reaching for the chocolates as he did so. 'You on this?'

'At my dad's.'

'What level you on?'

'Twenty-three.'

76

Oliver offered Tom a chocolate. ' Twenty-*three*?' He looked awed.

So that was all right, then.

'Well,' said Jack, once the boys were installed in front of the monitor. 'Whatever they say about the anti-social nature of computer games, I think we pulled off a social coup there, don't you? Cup of tea? Coffee or something? Drink?' He was standing close enough to her that she could smell him. A woody smell. Pungent. Aftershave or shower gel, she supposed. The hair on his neck looked slightly damp.

She shook her head. 'No, no,' she replied quickly. 'I really don't want to impose. I just – Tom just – well, we wanted to apologise, that was all. I couldn't leave it. His behaviour was unforgivable this morning, and –'

'No problem,' said Jack graciously. 'Happens all the time, believe me.' He nodded towards the boys. 'Thanks for the chocolates,' he said, smiling at her. 'My favourites.'

'I'm sure they're not.'

Jack Valentine placed a hand on each hip and studied her. He seemed entirely unconcerned at his state of undress. 'Go on. At least have a cup of tea or something, now you're here.'

He led her through to a little kitchen. It was only slightly wider than the hallway, with a couple of take-away containers on the worktop and two plates sitting in the sink. Like the rest of the flat it was painted white over the wallpaper, only in here the paper was woodchip, and the units were all beige with a leather-look finish. The floor was chipped cork tiles. It was, Hope thought, grim.

Jack bent down and fished two mugs out of a cupboard. Hope couldn't help noticing there was little else in there. And the handle was coming off. She hovered by the worktop self-consciously.

Jack glanced across at her. 'Here,' he said, pulling a stool from under the end of it. 'Sit down.'

She felt uncomfortable seeing him here, in this place. Profoundly uncomfortable. As if she had strayed into a part of his life that she had no business to. It was so not what she had expected. She was embarrassed by the sight of his smeary washing-up-liquid bottle, by the little memo board on the fridge saying 'coffee' and ' beans', by the pair of grey socks that were lying on the floor in the corner, by the crocheted tea cosy, the Indian take-away calendar on the wall. The peeling paintwork. The cheap, aged furniture. She was embarrassed for *him*. It hadn't been like this for Iain. How was it like this for Jack? She was desperate to know. But couldn't bring herself to ask.

'Quite the bachelor pad,' she found herself saying instead. Saying very jovially, barely even as she'd thought it, as if her subconscious mind simply had to acknowledge it. He turned around, a chrome caddy of tea bags in his hand.

'As shit-holes go, it's pretty top notch,' he said, his expression mock-serious. 'I had to beat off hordes to get it, you know.' He plopped tea bags into the mugs and reached for a large chrome kettle. 'You know what they say. Location, location, location.' He grinned. 'It's near the pub.' He seemed entirely unconcerned.

Hope smiled too, her disquiet now stilled. 'Where did you live before?'

'Oh, not far. Roath.'

'Well, I never! I used to live there. Well, near there.' How had she never seen him before? 'You rent this place, do you?' He couldn't have bought it. Surely. He nodded.

'I had a place lined up to buy before Christmas, but it fell through at the last minute.' He picked up a tea towel from the work top and folded it over the handle on the oven door. 'So it was either rent somewhere quick or unpack and stay in the spare room a bit longer.' He grinned at her wryly. 'I chose the shit-hole. Wouldn't you?'

Hope nodded, remembering. 'I guess I would. We – my ex-husband and I – decided to sell our house. We had to live together while we waited for it all to go through. He wouldn't go. It was horrible.'

'You could have made him.'

'So everybody told me at the time. But it's never that simple, is it? It was –' she shrugged. 'Sensible. Rather than him have to move twice.'

The kettle boiled, and Jack poured water into the mugs.

'Lucky him, then!' he said cheerfully.

Yes, thought Hope, looking through to the airless little living room, with its threadbare sofa, its hideous chintzy cushions, its tired brown carpet. Lucky him.

'Your wife kept the house, then?'

Jack nodded. 'She didn't want to move. And she's got a pretty well-paid job, so she was quite happy to take on half the mortgage.'

'But what about you? I mean, if you're still paying for it, don't you get a share in it?'

'Oh, I will eventually.' He stirred the tea bags around in the mugs. 'I'll start looking for a place in the spring, I guess. I'm in the middle of a lot of stuff at the moment. No rush.'

Hope nodded. 'Seems a bit unfair, though. I mean, you having to live here, while –'

'Believe me, I'm not complaining. You could put me in a cardboard box and I'd be happy. I'm just glad that it's over. That I'm out of it. Free.'

Hope watched while he fished out the tea bags, and then stirred in milk. His profile, she saw, as if noticing for the first time, was angular, Roman. The sort you might describe as heroic. He'd have to be, she thought, living here.

She accepted the mug he passed her. 'And in your bachelor pad,' she said.

'You said it! No, I'm quite happy to let the dust settle. See how things pan out. I don't want to commit myself to too much else right now, but I've got some irons in the fire workwise… so we'll see.'

'That sounds exciting. What sort of irons? On the radio?'

He shook his head. 'TV. But it's early days. Like I say, we'll see.'

She sipped the tea. It was Earl Grey, which surprised her. 'Wow. Quite the Renaissance man.'

'Do what?'

'You. Your life sounds so exciting compared to mine.'

He blew steam from his mug.

'You know what?' he said, meeting her gaze and holding it. 'It certainly has its moments.'

They stayed for over an hour.

Poor Jack Valentine, she thought, as she and Tom pulled out into the road and drove away while he waved. He'd made the flat cosy enough, but it was still pretty dismal. It seemed so unfair. He was, thought Hope, as they drove off down the street, such a very nice man. So much not what she'd originally thought. She wondered what kind of woman he'd been married to. It was hard to reconcile the person she had just been with, with the idea of a wife playing fast and loose. What was wrong with him, she wondered? What was the hidden character defect that would make a sane woman want to leave someone like him? But thinking that made her realise that perhaps, even at this very moment, he might be wondering that very thing about her. Divorce. Such an ugly word. Full of uncomfortable implications. That was the greatest tragedy of divorce, she decided. The nagging unease that there had to be something not quite right about a person to make another person want to leave them. Try as she might, she couldn't get past the feeling that there must have been something very wrong with her for Iain to have had all the affairs that he did.

She pushed the thought away angrily. There was nothing wrong with her. Nothing whatsoever. She'd just had the misfortune to have married a man for whom fidelity in marriage was an optional extra. And then the even greater misfortune of not having realised this until she'd produced two children and was effectively pinioned to her position in the triad. Leaving Iain then had simply not been an option, however much society might have had it that it was. She had no job, no money, no financial security, no pension, no nothing. And two children to consider. No. All she'd had in any real quantity was a feeling of stultifying fear. So she'd practised forgiveness. She'd been great at forgiveness. And Iain, who didn't want to leave her in any case, had been good at reassuring her that he wouldn't do it again. He loved her. It didn't mean anything. It really didn't mean anything. He just couldn't help himself sometimes. He loved her. Yes, yes, he knew he'd done it before. But he wouldn't do it again. He promised.

The change, when it came, had been a revelation to Hope. When it dawned on her that she didn't need to feel scared any more. The children were older, she was working part-time, and Madeleine, dear Madeleine, had given her the belief that she *could* have a different future. It was easy after that. Painful, but still easy.

As with childbirth, the light at the end of the tunnel went a long way towards dulling the pain.

Well, she was free now, and could count her blessings on all ten fingers, while Iain could get on and count his regrets. Not, she was sure, that he had very many. But that was fine, too. She'd got past all that now. She could allow him some happiness. This, to her mind, and to her quiet relief, had turned out to be the greatest freedom of all.

Chapter 10

But the trouble with freedom, Hope decided, was that there were only so many varieties of it that were actually life-enhancing. The freedom to eat crisps in bed was good. The freedom to watch 'EastEnders' without a disparaging commentary was even better. The freedom to do what she wanted when she wanted and with whom she wanted was not all it was cracked up to be.

Most freedoms, she decided, were not the holy grail they had seemed. They were simply manifestations of the fact that she had too many choices. The scary potentiality of her current state. The most fundamental of these was the freedom that was inherent in not being part of a couple, and while she was becoming perfectly used to, and even appreciative of, the many benefits of this particular state of affairs, it did not come without its downside. There was the sex, for a start. The freedom to moon about like some ditzy fifteen-year-old over a guy she hardly known was becoming an unmanageable side-effect of that one. She picked up the half-finished cushion cover that had fallen on the floor beside the bed and wondered, not for the first time, if she was losing her senses. What was she doing? And had she really been up sewing so late? She couldn't remember falling asleep. She shoved the cushion in with the others at the bottom of her wardrobe, and sighed. There was the love downside too. Hope didn't want to head off down any love downsides right now, for sure – way too frightening – but on the other hand she had to dip her toe in the water sometime. Just as she couldn't imagine celibacy as a lifestyle, she also couldn't really see herself growing old without someone to grow old with. And now, as if to remind her, it was her first Valentine's day as an officially single woman, and she was entirely without a Valentine.

Hopeful or actual. Paper or flesh.

But no. She was wrong. She'd got mail.

'Oh God.'
'Oh what?'

Hope's mother had come early, to take Chloe to school, because Hope had to go to the printers before work to check the proofs for the race registration forms. She closed the card again quickly, wishing it would dematerialise in her hand.

'Aha!' said her mother, plucking the card from her fingers. 'Would that be a Valentine card?'

Hope nodded. 'I'm afraid so.'

'How wonderful! A secret admirer!' She opened the card again. 'Oh, ho! Not so secret!'

'Exactly,' said Hope, dragging the brush through her hair and scowling at her reflection in the hall mirror. She should have expected it, shouldn't she?

'So who's this Simon, then?' asked her mother, putting the card on the hall table while she shrugged off her coat.

'Simon Armitage. He works with me. He's the accountant at Heartbeat.' How could she face work today? Thank God she wasn't going straight there. Her mother plopped her coat over the newel post and picked the card up again.

'And?'

'And what?'

'What's he like?'

'Late thirties. Brown hair. A bit overweight. Wears sleeveless sweaters. Jolly. Unassuming –'

'And is he nice?'

'No! I mean, yes, he's nice. He's perfectly nice, Mother. But he's not *nice*. Oh, God. What a pain.'

'A pain? How can it be a pain?'

'Because it is, believe me.'

'Well, I think it's sweet. Never look a gift horse in the mouth, my girl.' Her mother narrowed her eyes, the better to train them on her soul. 'Nothing from your Mr Valentine, then?'

Thinking about looking in Simon's mouth made Hope feel quite queasy. Thinking about Jack Valentine made her feel altogether different. And nice though that was, she was beginning to wish that it didn't, because it made her feel so anxious as well. But she couldn't seem to help it. He kept invading her brain. She wished he'd phone her. When she'd seen him it seemed so, well, as if he might do. And yet he hadn't. She frowned. 'Mum, he is not *my* Mr Valentine.'

Her mother clucked dismissively. 'You'd think with a name like that he'd send lots, wouldn't you? I'll bet he gets a fair few.'

'I'm getting five, Gran.' This was Chloe, who was still in her pyjamas and stumbling blearily down the stairs. Oh, to be nine again, thought Hope. To be nine and untroubled by the vicissitudes of love.

'I don't doubt that, young lady,' said Hope's mother, smiling. Hope glanced at her daughter and smiled too.

'And just what makes you so sure about that?'

'We did an arrangement,' she said. 'I couldn't decide who I was going to send one to, so I told them all if they sent me one I'd send them one back.'

'So you're sending five Valentines?' said Hope's mother. 'You little minx, you!'

Chloe arrived at the foot of the stairs and accepted the kiss Hope planted on her forehead.

'Oh, no,' she said airily. 'I just made that up.'

Hope wondered if there was enough time to change her top, belatedly recalling that Simon had commented on how much it suited her the last time she wore it. God. Signals. Signals. She mustn't send him signals. Did she have anything shroud-like upstairs?

'Like mother like daughter,' said her mother, chuckling to herself as she followed Hope out to wave her off. 'You were always a right one with the boys. Bees round a honey pot.'

'Huh. Whereas now all I get are the drones.' Which was unfair. There was nothing wrong with Simon. She just wanted to kill him, that was all.

'There's no need to be so testy, love. You got a Valentine's card. You should think yourself lucky. I've not had one for twenty-two years.'

Hope went down to the car and got in, her day already altogether spoiled. She wasn't feeling testy. Relieved, not testy.

She had so nearly sent Jack one. So very nearly. Well, thank God she hadn't.

'You have heaps, you bastard,' Patti announced equably when Jack arrived at the studios. '*Heaps.*' She scratched her stomach. Today's ring was green. Nestling in her flesh like the eye of a witch's cat. 'I

84

only got seven,' she went on. 'And three of them are from that mad bloke in Neath. I thought the signal didn't reach Neath, Hil.'

Jack sat down at his desk. Big bloody deal. He surveyed the pile of envelopes in front of him. Getting Valentine cards simply came with the territory. He opened the top one without interest.

"To Jack," he read out. *"The knave of my heart."*

'Do you think he's a stalker?' Patti interrupted him. 'I mean, listen to this. *"Dearest Patti, will you come and pat me? Come sit on my lap and straddle my knees?"* – yuk! That's a bit near the mark isn't it? And look, the postmark's Cardiff.'

Jack threw the card back on the pile. 'You should be so lucky.'

Later, once the show was over and they'd written most of the links for the next day, Jack sat and went through his pile of cards more carefully. A pleasing thought had wormed its way into his mind. There might be. You never knew. He fished out the latest letter she'd sent him about the fun run and studied her signature. For all he knew, any one of these cards could be from Hope Shepherd. Since seeing her again, he'd been thinking about her, often, despite his determination not to. Had even been into Smith's and looked at cards himself. But he hadn't bought one. For one thing, he'd felt a prize prat – the place had been teeming with women – and, for another, he wouldn't know what to put in it. Valentines cards were just a commercial cash-cow, strictly for adolescents and girls. He scanned the remaining envelopes for matches, but none looked hopeful and he put the letter back in his drawer, feeling stupid. If he wanted to let Hope Shepherd know he fancied her he had only to call her up and tell her, didn't he? How many times had he asked himself that question and found himself groping for a sensible answer? There was the niceness thing, of course, but Jack was reluctantly beginning to visit the notion that perhaps that wasn't all there was to it. Perhaps his reluctance was more about *him*. Perhaps his hypothetical shag 'em and leave 'em mentality was not, in reality, about seeing what was out there, but about avoiding any scrutiny of what was within.

Christ. How did he get to be someone who did all this prevaricating? He blamed Lydia, he decided. Utterly. You couldn't go to bed with someone like Lydia for fifteen years without some residual damage to your sexual self-esteem. He wondered if perhaps she'd been dipped in liquid nitrogen at birth. He flicked through more envelopes. He was halfway down the pile when he noticed one with distinctive spiky handwriting. Allegra Staunton's, in fact. She'd used an italic pen and chocolate-brown ink. Like she always did. Where did you buy chocolate-brown ink, for God's sake? He opened it with some trepidation.

The card slid out easily – a stylish affair, hand-painted and assembled, by the looks of it. So very Allegra. There were no words on the front, just a collage thing – two hessian chillies, if he wasn't mistaken.

Inside the card, it said very little. Just *'Jack – phwoarrrrrrr – Allegra'.*

She was, Jack reflected, slipping it safely away again, a very singular species of woman.

It had been a busy afternoon, and an even busier evening. Jack still had a couple of pre-records to get done, and the last of these had become a protracted affair, the production assistant, who had fixed the thing up for three, having failed to point out that the subject of his interview (a crumpled academic they generally consulted on all matters sociological) was not in Caerphilly, as she usually was, but on an 'Emotional Intelligence at Work' seminar in North Dakota. And therefore, when they'd first called her, asleep.

It was almost nine when he finally downed tools and made it home. There was another small pile of post for him on the hall table downstairs and, having got himself a beer, he went into the living room to go through it.

He was no longer thinking Valentine card at this point, and had no prior expectations when he opened the typewritten white envelope. He was surprised, therefore, to find a card inside. No hearts on this one, just a bunch of pink flowers.

Hope sprang eternal. Perhaps she was making a move after all. He opened the card and his heart sank immediately.

'Dear Jack,
Just to let you know I'm thinking of you today.
Thanks for the happy times,
Lydia xx'

His first reaction was to laugh. The woman needed therapy. Or an Emotional Intelligence seminar. North Dakota would do the bitch nicely. His second was to feel really, physically, wall-punchingly angry. So much so that he was half out of his chair and heading for the phone before he stopped himself. Instead, he ripped the card neatly in two. And then four. And then eight. How dare she? How *dare* she! Patronising cow. He downed the rest of his beer in one swallow and stomped off to get another from the fridge.

Chapter 11

Jack had just finished emailing his youth team round-up to the *Echo* when the phone rang. It was Saturday evening. Ergo 'Stars in Their Eyes' and another exciting night in. He used to enjoy 'Stars in Their Eyes', in a slumming-it, detached, wind-up-Lydia sort of way. Now he just watched it. How sad was that? He padded out to the hall and stooped to pick up the receiver.

'Hello,' said a voice. 'It's Hope Shepherd. Are you in?'

Jack wiggled his bare toes. This was a surprise. 'I certainly seem to be,' he said.

'Only I'm around and about and wondered if I could pop by.' She paused. 'Er… I've got something for you.'

A pleasant surprise. A *very* pleasant surprise. This was telling him something, and he really ought to listen. He nearly said 'that sounds like an offer I can't refuse' but stopped himself. Too lewd. Too suggestive. She sounded a bit nervous.

'Well, that sounds most intriguing,' he said instead. 'What sort of something?'

'Ah. You'll have to wait and see.' He could hear a smile in her voice now. 'About half an hour or so? Would that be OK?'

She was calling from a mobile. He could hear white noise around her. 'That,' he replied. 'Would be very OK.'

By the time Hope's car pulled up in the road Jack had done the two things most important in an unscheduled-female-visitor situation. Removed his boxer shorts from the bathroom floor and cleaned his teeth. He'd been in two minds about re-freezing the chicken tikka biriani he'd been defrosting for his supper, but in the end plumped for relocating it to the fridge. There was always room in the day for curry. Breakfast tomorrow, if need be.

He opened the door even before she was through the front gate, a manoeuvre she was executing with a fair degree of difficulty, as she seemed to be more dustbin liner than person from his vantage point. He walked down the path to help her, wincing as his feet made contact with the cold ground. She had the grey coat-thing on again. And – hurrah! – the boots.

'Dismembered corpse? Hippo?' he asked her as he heaved the bag from her. She scooped some hair from her face with a gloved hand.

'Thanks. It's not heavy. Just a bit bulky. There.' She carefully shut the gate, as per Leonard's laminated instruction, and followed him up the path. He could hear her heels click-clicking behind him.

The smell in the hallway was an unfortunate blend of cauliflower and damp carpet, and Jack was pleased he'd sprayed a bit of Ollie's Ben Sherman anti-perspirant around before coming down. He must get some air freshener. He never seemed to think of things like that when he was shopping. But at least it had faded a little once they got up the stairs.

He wanted to usher her into the flat but the bin bag made the action potentially dangerous, so rather than sending her flailing off back down the staircase he went on in. He heard her shut the door behind them.

'So,' he said, dumping the bag down on the sofa. 'This'll be the something, then, will it?' She nodded, beaming at him. 'So what is it?'

She slipped her handbag from her shoulder and deposited her car keys in it.

'See for yourself,' she said, her expression a little bashful as she pulled off her gloves. 'And you must tell me if you don't like them. I won't be offended. We can flog them off in the shop, no problem. So, you know. After I came round… well, I just wanted to do something. I just thought perhaps you'd appreciate something to… well… anyhow… I hope you don't mind.'

She was saying all this while he was fiddling with the knot that held the bin bag together. Unsuccessfully, because it needed pygmy fingers. Or girl's ones. So in the end he just ripped it open, man-style. A jumble of large cushions burst out. Six of them. Three leather patchwork, three suede. In various shades of brown and distress. Like the ones he'd seen back at the charity office.

And admired. Of course. 'These all for me?' he said, picking one up now and smoothing his hand across it. It was beautifully made. She nodded again and put her own hands in her pockets.

'I just thought, with the flat and everything… well. Do you like them? I remembered the sofa was beige.'

He was lost for words. No-one had ever done anything like this for him before. Been kind like this. 'Like them? They're great, Hope. And that's really –' Not 'nice', for God's sake. 'Really thoughtful of you. But you must let me give you something for them. They must have –'

'Don't be daft.' She took her hands out of the pockets and did the double hair-behind-the-ears thing. 'I told you. I get all the jackets from the shop. It's only a few cushion pads. And a bit of time. And as Kayleigh told me you'd said you –'

Jack ditched the rest of her sentence by stepping forward and planting a wholesome, closed lips, what-a-pal smacker on her mouth. Then hugged her.

'You are *so* sweet, you know that?'

He let her go. She was scarlet. 'I'm so glad you like them. They'll work well in here.' She reached across and picked up the empty bin bag, crumpling it in her hand.

Jack thought the only thing that would work well in his living room was a hefty JCB with a pile-driver on the front. But who cared. They would work perfectly well on their own. They were classy. That's what they were. 'They'll look just – well – perfect,' said Jack, groping for some interior design vocabulary and failing. 'A darn sight better than these manky things, that's for sure.' He strode around the room, plucking the old ones up. Cushions. Fancy that. Fancy her making him cushions.

She was following his circuit now, placing the new ones where the old ones had been. Then she stood, hovering, while he shovelled the flowery ones into the back of one of the cupboards. Jack turned.

'You taking your coat off, or what?'

'Oh, right. I –'

'Unless you're in a rush or something.' Jack suddenly wondered if she'd left her children in the car. But it was all right. She couldn't have done. She was beginning to untoggle the toggles.

'I'm not doing anything,' he went on, to consolidate. 'Just chilling. Heavy night last night. Stay for a while, why don't you?'

The coat was undone now and she slipped it from her shoulders. She was wearing the wool dress she'd had on when they'd first gone out to lunch. Well, now. Saturday night. Nothing doing. Frozen Indian. Crap telly. And now cushions. And Hope. Here, in the flesh, in her boots and her dress. And tomorrow, and the day after, and the day after, and the day after... well, they could go hang. She was here. This was now. 'Well, if you don't have to dash off anywhere, let me get you a drink or something, yes?'

'That'll be great, thanks.'

'Beer, beer or beer?' He paused a moment in the kitchen doorway, taking in the legs as she sat down on the sofa. 'Only joking. I have meths too.'

She looked at him sideways. 'A glass of wine would be good if you've got one. Just a small one. I'm driving.' She sprang up again, and followed him into the kitchen.

'Kids?' he said, opening the fridge door as little as possible so she wouldn't see how sad the contents were.

She shook her head. 'At their father's this weekend. Back tomorrow night.' She'd moved across the kitchen now and pulled back the net curtain that hung across the door down to the garden.

'It's big, isn't it?' she was saying. 'You'd never guess these houses had such long back gardens, would you? What does it back on to? Is it the railway?'

Jack started peeling the foil from the bottle of wine that had sat in the fridge since the last high school quiz night and raffle. It could be crap, easily. And the raffle ticket was still on it. He pulled it off. 'Not quite. There's allotments before that, just beyond the trees there.'

'Nice in the summer.'

'I wouldn't know. I don't intend – I sincerely hope – finding out. Anyway, I don't use it. It's not for the flat. I have that rope thing to hang out washing – as if!' He uncorked the bottle and poured her a glass of wine, then picked up a Becks and opened it. 'The garden's Leonard's. The landlord. That's just a fire escape, really.'

She peered into the blackness outside. 'But you have this little balcony.'

'I have that little balcony. And if I'm still stuck here in the summer no doubt I'll pop a few tubs of pansies on it. You know. Brighten the place up.'

She turned round to smile at him. 'Yeah, right,' she laughed. 'Of course you will. But what's that down the end? That big shed thing?' She turned back to look outside.

'At the end of the garden? Oh, that's Leonard's menagerie. He keeps all sorts down there. He's got finches and canaries and chipmunks –'

She raised her eyebrows. 'Chipmunks?'

Jack nodded and took a swig of the beer. It wasn't quite cold enough. He must turn the fridge up a bit more. He had no evidence, but he wasn't altogether sure that Leonard didn't let himself in when he was out and turn it down.

'Chipmunks. He's very fond of his animals, Leonard.'

'Oh, chipmunks are so *sweet*. I had no idea you could keep them as pets.'

'Oh, they're not really pets. He doesn't handle them. Just likes looking at them.'

Like he was liking looking at Hope now. Her face was reflected in the glass in the door, and she caught his expression before he had time to remove it. She smiled shyly at him. Then turned round.

'Well,' she said. 'So what are your plans for the rest of the weekend?'

Was she being conversational or up front? She moved back across the kitchen and began studying the list of football fixtures on the fridge door. 'I found it really strange at first after Iain went. When he had the children. Disenfranchised, you know? I'm sort of getting used to it, but I still feel not quite relaxed. Like I'm skiving off or something. I'm never sure quite what I should be doing.' She sipped her wine. And didn't grimace. 'It must be *really* strange for you.'

Making conversation, then. But, hey, the night was young.

He gestured that they go back in the living room. He would put on some music. Yes, that would be good.

'Like you say, you get used to it. But you're right. It feels like a whole lot of time to fill sometimes. I only see Ollie Thursdays and every other weekend – this isn't one of them, as you probably

92

figured – so it's a big life change, yes.' He pulled out the CD rack and started flicking through it. Nirvana? Was she a Nirvana kind of person? Or would she be more Lighthouse Family? In which case he was well scuppered. 'And no. No plans. I'll spend some time writing tomorrow, probably. Meet up with Dan for a drink at some point, no doubt.'

She was crossing the room, looking over his shoulder as he flicked.

'Dan?'

'Danny. You met him at the studio, didn't you?'

She shook her head. 'I'm not sure.'

'Well, anyway, he's got three kids. One of them a baby. He needs to get out more.' They both laughed a been-there-and-done-that-one laugh.

'Oh!' she said, arresting his flicking with her hand. 'You have the Chili Peppers! I love the Chili Peppers.' She pulled the CD out and handed it to him.

'Put that on. Track twelve.'

'Yes, miss,' said Jack. It was one of Ollie's. It had his little sticker in the corner. Jack put his thumb over it. 'Right away.'

By the time he'd put the CD on and an arresting electronic twanging had started up, Hope was back on the sofa and unzipping her boots. She glanced up.

'I hope you don't mind,' she said. 'But my feet are killing me. I've been in these all afternoon.'

'Around and about?' he said, sitting in the armchair the better to view her.

She yanked them both off and tucked her legs up under her.

'Shopping mainly. As you do. Plus, I had to go down to the Heartbeat shop to sort out the race application forms with Bet. Which reminds me. Are you going to be able to make the meeting OK next Tuesday? We've got both our main sponsors coming. I called your secretary but she wasn't sure what your movements would be.'

Secretary? Fat chance. But Jack had already put it in his diary. Along with the meeting with Allegra in the afternoon. He was pinning so many hopes on his meeting with Allegra that he didn't even want to think about it. Getting out of this hole, for one.

'I'm sure it will be fine,' he said. 'Another drink?' Her glass was still a third full but his beer was finished.

She looked at her watch then shook her head. 'I'd better not.'

'There's no rush to go, you know.' He stood up.

'Go on then. Just half a glass.'

'Great.' He headed off to the kitchen. 'What about food?' he said, though he wasn't quite sure why. He had no food apart from the Indian for one. But he could always have a take-away delivered. That would work. 'You eaten?'

'Oh, don't worry,' she called to him. 'I don't want to impose on your evening. I'll probably have some soup or something when I get home.'

'No rush,' he said again, bringing the wine bottle back in with him. 'My evening is more than happy to be imposed upon. And if it's soup you're after, I can easily oblige. As long as you like tomato.' This time he sat on the sofa beside her and put another two inches into what was left in her glass.

'I do, as it happens,' she said, nodding to indicate there was enough in the glass now. She sipped at it and settled herself back against one of his stylish new cushions. 'Well,' she said. 'Isn't this nice?'

There were so many routes to a successful seduction, but, for the life of him, Jack couldn't get his head around what they were. All he knew – all that he could think right now – was that Hope (female, warm, fragrant, soft, smiley, yielding and ultimately, gloriously, alien) was sitting on his sofa, in his flat, and that they were all alone. And she was looking gorgeous. What the hell had he been thinking? There was absolutely no possibility that he was going to let the next hour or two pass without making an attempt at seducing her. He had absorbed all this information at lightning speed around the time, if not before, she had taken her boots off. He was a man and she was a woman and whatever reservations he might have had about the wisdom of getting involved with anyone like her right now, chances were that she had not, he figured, had sex for perhaps even longer than he had. That fact, together with the boots and the dress, was sufficient to make him determined that baggage could bugger off, that biology would out, that two people of the opposite sex in circumstances such as theirs would be committing a grievous crime if they didn't allow their proximity to reach its evolutionary conclusion. But Hope was a woman. And women didn't necessarily see things like that.

'The first boy,' she was saying, 'that I really fell in love with – well, in that way you do when you're thirteen – he had two chinchillas.' She sipped the wine again, glancing at Jack as she said this as if it were the most natural conversational direction imaginable. Now that was a woman thing. That ability to hang on to a train of thought while you were busy talking about something altogether different and plop it back into the conversation seemingly at random. Lydia used to do that. They'd be talking about the cladding on the pipes and she'd suddenly say, 'did you?' Did he what? 'Did you speak to Kevin about the life assurance?' As if they'd had the conversation not yesterday but five seconds ago. But he didn't want to think about Lydia while sharing airspace with Hope. Didn't want to think about Lydia, period. Which, happily, he didn't much. Except as a dusty archaeological artefact capable of throwing light on the present. Like a severed head, or particularly unattractive old urn.

'I had a stag beetle,' he replied now.

'Ugh.' She curled a strand of hair behind her ear. 'I'm glad he didn't. D'you know? One day when I went round to his house we got talking about a previous chinchilla he'd had that had died. And he dug up the skeleton to show me. Isn't that bizarre?'

'Very bizarre. Perhaps it was a ritual. Don't some Amazonian tribesmen give their women the bones of rival tribesmen to ornament their hair?'

She shrugged. 'I don't know. But I definitely remember the jawbone. Chipmunks. *Bless*. How sweet. We have two hamsters, you know. Ant and Dec. '

Seduce her he must. If that was the right word for it, which Jack doubted. Seducing someone involved an element of corruption, didn't it? It wasn't as if he was trying to deflower a virgin. He just wanted to have sex with her, and he needed a game plan. The trouble with women, it seemed to him, was that where sex was concerned, so much of the communication had to be non-verbal. Life would be so much simpler if women were more like men. If he could just ask her if she'd like to make love with him and be done with it. It was all the guesswork that vexed him. All the

95

reading of body language. The fretful business of having to work on assumptions all the time. Was she looking at him like that now because she *did* want to have sex with him, or just because she thought he was nice? He wished he had more yardsticks. More conquests under his belt.

They'd moved away from mammals and on to teenagers by now, occasioned by more rootling in his CD collection, and her comment that his tastes (which were more than half Ollie's) were a lot more eclectic than most. She seemed not at all as if she were thinking of going. Indeed, her legs, which were now stretched out in front of her, crossed at the ankle, seemed like they were thinking of staying, if anything. If such a thing could be read into the wiggling of female toes.

'Right. I really should be getting back,' she said. Jack ripped the last page from his mental instruction manual. Clearly not, then. But then again, women worked this way sometimes. This might just be code for 'tell me you want me to stay'. He stood up and held out his hand for her glass.

'Why?' he said. 'What's the hurry? Anyway, I thought you were going to have some soup with me.' He gestured with the glass. She looked undecided.

'No, I really mustn't. I have to drive home.'

'Get a cab.'

'Listen to you!'

'Go on. My treat.'

'I don't need treating.'

'Yes, you do. I insist.'

She seemed to like that. She pulled the sleeve of her dress up and consulted her watch. Chewed on her lip.

'I don't know –'

'I insist.'

She pushed the sleeve back down. 'Oh, go on then. What the hell. I guess I could always cycle over and pick the car up in the morning, couldn't I?' She chewed her lip again. She seemed to be waiting to hear something from him. He wished he knew what. This was a very big deal. He wished she'd just tell him what she was thinking.

'Or you could run,' he offered. 'It's probably about three miles, isn't it?'

'Less than that, even. Yes. Yes, that's a brilliant idea. I'd be going for a run tomorrow anyway. *Yes.*' She uncrossed her ankles and stood up. 'Yes. What the hell. I'll have another glass of wine then, thank you very much.'

Back in the kitchen, Jack was conscious that a highly significant milestone had been reached. Had she not followed him in there he would have mimed a yes! yes! yes! worthy of Beckham scoring against Argentina, perhaps have even knelt down and put his T-shirt over his face. But as she was behind him he had to make do with doing it in his head.

She drank a full two inches from her wine in five seconds, as if some stellar gateway had sucked her in and spat her out again in a different time continuum. As if some internal switch had been flicked. He remembered a bag of Doritos he had in the cupboard, so he got them out and put some into a cereal bowl. Hope took one and munched on it. She was back looking out into the garden again.

'Where do they come from?'

He topped up her wine glass and got himself another beer.

'Where do who come from?'

'Not who. What. Chipmunks. America, isn't it?'

Jack nodded. 'The Appalachians or somewhere, I guess. Though I imagine they're indigenous to pretty much the whole continent, don't you think?'

She took another slurp of her wine. 'Only I was wondering if they felt the cold out there. Wouldn't they normally hibernate in the winter? You know, in the forest?'

Jack didn't have the first idea what chipmunks got up to in the forest, or, indeed, anywhere else. Mating and eating and sleeping, no doubt. And looking cutesy for the tourists.

'D'you know? I don't actually know,' he said, trying hard to sound like it was something he might have.

'It probably doesn't get cold enough,' she decided. 'But even so, bless. It can still get pretty chilly. Does he have a heater for them or anything?'

He really didn't have a clue. Chipmunks. They weren't in any sex manual, but Jack was all for trusting to instinct, and his instinct told him right now that if he could oblige Hope's evident affection for small rodents by taking her down and actually showing her the chipmunks, something useful would be achieved. She was clearly into stuff like that. And the flat below had been dark when he'd last looked. Perhaps Leonard was down the pub.

'Do you want to go down and see the chipmunks?'

'Oh, I'd love to see the chipmunks,' she said, putting her glass down. 'I'll go fetch my boots, shall I?'

'Don't bother. They'll only get caught in the fire escape grating. It's not that cold. Besides, we'll have to be quiet. Just in case.'

'Oh, if it's a problem –'

He shook his head. 'Absolutely no problem. Leonard won't mind.' He would. But what the hell. This was business. Jack unlocked the back door.

'Come on then,' he said. 'Let's go down and see the chipmunks.'

Hope grinned at him. 'Barefoot? In the dark? What fun!'

That was the thing about Hope, really. She was up for it. It wasn't a quality he'd ever given much thought to, but he suddenly realised that was what he most liked about her. She had a natural *joie de vivre*. A way of interacting with life that made you feel it could be something other than basically shite, if only you knew how to approach it. She was giggling now.

Jack held the back door open for her. She was shorter in her stockinged feet – getting on for a foot shorter than him, in fact. It made him feel very masculine. Very protective. Hell, very horny. He clicked up the latch and pulled the door shut behind him, then padded after her down the fire escape stairs.

'It's a nice garden,' she whispered when she got to the bottom. Jack, who had always seen gardens as merely another domestic drain on his football-watching time, thought he'd probably have to shoot himself should it ever seem a good idea to have a garden as a hobby. This kind of garden, at any rate. He had no problem with the mad stuff that Irish guy on the telly did. It was only March, but already Leonard had been out and shaved the lawn, as well as tying the daffodil foliage down in little bundles so they seemed to pepper the flowerbeds like eruptions of cysts. Jack generally tried to avoid opening the back door in daylight, as Leonard could talk about hard-pruning his forsythia with a fact-packed obsession that bordered on mania. Like a serial killer in an interview room when the game's up and he might just as well revel in his work.

But it was neat and tidy and had big wavy borders. A woman probably would like it, he supposed.

They made their way down the little stepping-stone path, each concrete circle of which was etched with a bird, or a frog, or a hedgehog. Hope's perfume was scenting the air in her wake, and the breeze, which was more of a wind now, lifted skeins of her hair from her neck. It was cold because it was a clear night, an almost full moon and a smattering of stars lighting their way to the sheds at the end. The birds were quiet, of course, but as they approached they could already hear the chipmunks as they streaked back and forth, up and down, round and round, a blur of striped backs and button eyes.

'Round here,' he said, placing his arm around Hope's shoulder to steer her along to the side of the shed. Which felt very nice.

'Did he make all this himself?' she asked.

Jack didn't know. 'I suppose so,' he said. The chipmunks were housed in what was more giant cage than shed. Though the lowest two feet were panelled in wood, the rest of the structure was simply long struts between reinforced chicken wire, and there were also various wooden assemblages in the cage, nesting boxes and sloped runways, up and down which the chipmunks – he thought there were about six of them – moved at great speed, doing whatever it was that chipmunks did.

'Oh, look, there's one!' said Hope. 'Oh bless. It's so sweet!' She had the fingers of one hand laced through the wire.

'And they bite,' said Jack. She took the fingers out.

'But they're *so* sweet,' she said again. 'They're so tiny, aren't they?'

'Tiny,' agreed Jack. Women always seemed to like tiny things.

'And there's another one! Look!'

They looked. Looked for some minutes, in fact. He didn't think he'd felt so happy in a long time. The chipmunks were being obliging, Leonard's flat was still in darkness, it was Saturday night and there was a soft womanly body not five inches from his. He still had his arm around her shoulder, moreover, and she wasn't making any gestures that suggested she minded. But then he felt a small shiver run through her.

'You're cold,' he observed.

'I'm freezing, as it happens.'

'Shall we get back inside, then?'

She nodded and leaned forward a little. One of the chipmunks was poised on a branch, still as stone, bar small twitching undulations of its tail. 'Bye bye, little chipmunk' she crooned at it, waving her fingers. Women, eh. So other. So exquisitely other. He squeezed his hand against her shoulder. This was shaping up well.

But Jack knew from long experience that when things started shaping up well there was always scope for a downturn. And now one happened.

He'd led the way back up the fire escape stairs light of heart, tall of bearing, decidedly joyous of spirit. But then the back door wouldn't open.

'Shit,' he said, pushing against it.

'What's the matter?' Hope was standing behind him, one step down.

'The door's stuck.'

'Oh dear.'

He pushed it again.

'Shall I help?'

'Oh, bugger.' He shook his head. 'You can't. It's not stuck. It's bloody locked.' In his haste to implement Operation Chipmunk he must have failed to engage the little lug on the latch properly. Which meant – oh, *damn* – that he had locked them both out.

'Oh dear,' she said, smiling up at him. 'Can we get in another way?'

He peered down through the grating. Leonard's flat was still dark.

'Er, probably not.'

Hope joined him on the balcony itself.

'What about round the front? Or is there a window?' She leaned around him. 'That window up there, maybe. Look. Isn't that one open? That's your bathroom, isn't it?'

Jack was still shouldering the door, albeit pointlessly. Bloody hell. Why did they put a bloody Yale lock on a back door, anyway?'

Hope moved around him. 'Funny having a Yale lock on a back door,' she said.

'Security,' he answered grimly. Oh, ho bloody ho.

She'd moved along the balcony now, and was looking up at the bathroom window. 'There,' she said, pointing to it. 'It *is* open. Crisis sorted.'

She looked elfin, almost, with her nose tilted upwards like that. Crisis sorted. Spit spot. She was so sweet.

But sweet or not, it was a very small window. And head height. A good six feet up. Though Jack's flat was a flat, it was in the kind of house that pleased itself in the matter of floor levels. The bathroom, just off his bedroom, was reached via three extra stairs. And the window, in addition, was set high in the wall.

'I'll never get through there,' he said.

She looked him over. 'Hmm. You might not,' she said finally. 'But I definitely will.'

'You can't possibly –'

'Don't be daft. I can get through there easily.' She grinned at him fetchingly.

'If you give me a leg up.'

Though Jack could imagine all sorts of scenarios that would give him a legitimate opportunity to get his face five inches from Hope's stockinged thighs, this would not have been one of them. But here it was anyway. On a plate. 'Are you sure?' he said.

'Well, unless you'd rather stand out here in the dark all night with nothing on your feet,' she said. 'Or call the police. Come on.' She gestured to him then turned to face the wall, her back to him. 'Come on. Let me get my foot up.'

So he cupped his hands obligingly while she lifted her leg, then took the weight of her right foot as she hoisted herself upwards, rising, as if a small fragrant wraith from a lake, before swivelling to open the window to its widest and pulling her body over on to the sill. 'You see?' she called down to him, grinning. 'Piece of piss.'

He was still marvelling at her unexpected turn of phrase when the pressure eased in his hands and she was manoeuvring through the window, slithering her body over and down into the room. She was grunting a little. He tried not to look up her dress.

'You see,' she called again, as her legs disappeared inside. 'There we are – *oof*!'

'Hope? Hope? Are you all right?' He reached up and grabbed the sill himself now, mildly impressed at the sudden surge of power in his biceps. He really must get back down to the gym. He could still hear her wincing. And now he could see her. She was sprawled on the bathroom floor, clutching her leg.

'Oh, God,' he said, balanced over the fulcrum of the sill now. His feet skittered ineffectually against the brickwork. There was no way, NO way he was going to get through this window. She scrabbled to a sitting position on the bath mat and blinked up at him.

'Don't be daft, Jack. Get down. I'll come round and let you in.'

But he was half in already. He heaved his arms against the windowsill.

'No problem,' he grunted. 'I'm in already.' And with an extra heave he scraped his hips in along with him, landing, with a thud, by the toilet. She was sitting, one knee up, with her back against the bath, scrutinising her leg.

'Damn,' she said.

'What?'

'I've laddered my tights.'

He gathered himself up, hitting his head against the towel rail. He rubbed it.

'Oh, dear. Sorry about that. But, oh well –' Sod his head. He was feeling rather jolly. He peered at the ladder. 'They're disposable, aren't they?'

Her head snapped up. '*Disposable*? What planet are you on?'

Oh dear. Had he blown it? Weren't tights disposable? Lydia's always seemed to be. So much he didn't know about. He sat back on his heels and smiled sheepishly at her.

'Then I'll buy you some new ones.'

And then, without any evident reason or warning, she threw back her head and laughed. The biggest laugh he'd ever heard in his life. From a woman, for sure. If you didn't count Hil. Which he didn't. Inexplicable. And though he knew his bathroom wasn't really the place for it, he knew it was also high time to move in.

His opening parry, a rather clumsy two-handed approach on his knees, was greeted with more enthusiasm than he'd dared hope for, and in moments he was going at the kissing with gusto, her arms around his back and his hands in her hair. But he had been on the receiving end of enough bangs and scrapes and bruises to know that however urgent and beguiling the idea seemed right now, there would be little satisfaction in having sex with Hope on his bathroom floor. Quite apart from its decidedly bijou nature, it sported all sorts of paraphernalia that were not conducive to libidinous abandon. The dental floss on the side of the sink. The duck-in-flight terracotta plaque on the wall. The faint whiff of Sainsbury's summer breeze toilet cleaner. The proximity of the loo brush to his left knee. All this he registered while he was still kissing her. As well as something else. That she was kissing him back. Boy, was she kissing him back. It was this, more than anything, that had him decided. *Carpe diem*. Sod it! *Carpe* Hope Shepherd! There was a perfectly serviceable bed not five yards from the patch of lino, and it was there, not here, that they needed to be. But it was getting from the one place to the other that was going to be the problem. Hope (being female) that was going to be the problem. Give a man anything vaguely erotic to look at and he was instantly, wholeheartedly, unstoppably aroused. A woman, on the other hand, was wired altogether differently. In Jack's experience, women were all too prone to getting sidetracked. Give a woman a moment for sober reflection and her neurones could so easily be diverted from their course. From 'yes, do it now' to 'what the hell am I doing?', or even worse, to 'oh, God – what knickers am I wearing?' Or, in Lydia's case, to 'Sorry, I'm just not in the mood.' Hope *was* in the mood. No question about that one. The sticky bit, the trick, as with tuning a telly, was to get a fix on the signal and keep things that way. He moved exploratory hands over various soft bits of her. He kissed her more. He moaned into her hair. He had to get her to the bed now, but without giving her sufficient time to take stock and engage thought. Eye contact. That was it. Keep her focussed. On task.

Her hands were round his neck and she was kissing his whole face now.

Then she stopped. 'Jack, you do have a bed, I presume?'

Bloody hell. Bloody hell, this was going like a bomb now. There was clearly less danger of her going off the boil than there was of him reaching it way too soon. Within seconds of her question, which he had answered with some feeling, she was up on her feet and almost dragging him there.

He'd made the bed, which was good, but left his pile of dirty washing on it, which wasn't. But he figured that given another five minutes, she wouldn't even care. Didn't care *now*, by the look of it – his right arm, effecting clearance, only narrowly avoiding being pinioned by her bottom as she threw herself prostrate and panting on the bed. This was becoming surreal. Did women actually *do* this? He'd anticipated a little more vertical fumbling, a little *soupçon* of shyness, a little light undressing, a little his 'n hers probing-among-underwear stuff.

But there was no time for that. She was feral. Like a wild cat. An exquisite mass of glossy (if laddered) legs and black baby-soft wool. He peeled his T-shirt from his torso, all the better to feel it. Then joined her on the bed and disengaged his neocortex, very slightly shot through with performance anxiety, and not quite believing his luck.

Chapter 12

'I don't believe we did that,' said Hope, some half an hour later. She was lying flat on her back on the bed beside him, her naked body, disappointingly, now covered with the duvet. There were some unexpected benefits to long-term abstinence. It had been barely ten minutes since they'd collapsed, panting, against the pillows, yet already Jack could feel the troops massing for more. It was a quarter to ten. The night was still young.

He turned to face Hope, but she was staring at the ceiling.

'Well, we did,' he said. They had, he thought. He had. *Finally.* He couldn't keep the smile off his face. But her own expression was grim.

'No, actually I don't mean that.' She continued to look up at the ceiling. 'I mean I can't believe *I* did that. Which is different. I mean, well, I don't mean that to sound... well, you know, I mean you're a man, obviously, so... I mean, it was great –' She turned her head and looked at him. Her eyes were slightly smudgy. Mascara, he supposed. He could see now that her irises weren't as opaque as he'd thought. There were a few amber flecks among the brown. 'Great,' she said again. 'And, I mean, you... you're so... well, it's been... well, you know. It's just that... ' She stopped again here to emit a heavy sigh. Women. So unfathomable. So very other. All this post-coital analysis. All this gobbledegook. All this squinnying, as his mother would have said. Jesus! How did his mother crop up? Perhaps he'd better put his hand back somewhere pertinent.

He did. 'It's just what?'

Her lips twitched at the contact. She twisted her body towards him a little. Which was encouraging. 'It's just, oh, Jack, I don't know. I feel a bit like... well, like – God, what got into me?'

'Er, me?' he offered. But she didn't smile. Instead, she drew her brows together. 'It's all right,' he said. 'Go on. Tell me I'm utterly incorrigible. I can take it.'

'I wasn't going to say that,' she said, as if chiding him. 'I was just thinking how I came here tonight expecting, well, kind of hoping, I suppose, that you might – well... ' She looked uncomfortable. 'You *know*.' He didn't. 'Which was fine. And... but –'

And what? But *what?* She had her chin resting on the palm of her hand, and she was looking across him. To the bedside table. Jack knew, without even having to turn his head, that her eyes had come to rest not on the photo, but on the packet of twelve that was lying open beside it. The packet of twelve that Patti had ceremoniously bought him and that had sat in the drawer for all those months. And that she was thinking. He knew it. Not good. ' But you didn't for a moment imagine you were going to ravish me at any point in the evening,' he said quickly. 'Well that makes two of us. I'm still gobsmacked, believe me.'

She sat up violently now, casting his hand off her breast like a badly lobbed tennis ball. And put her face in her hands. Her back was very smooth.

'God, that's it. I'm just stupefied. I can't believe I just did that. Really I can't.'

So not the right thing to say, then. Jack sat up too, and put one arm around her shoulder. Which still left one available, which he deployed again pretty smartish.

'Hey, tell you what,' he said. 'How about I ravish *you* now? Even things up a bit. We'll be quits then, won't we? Then we can go have that soup.'

She stared into his eyes for such a long time that he began to feel he was playing the lead in a black-and-white foreign language film. Then she looked down at her hands. They were folded in her lap on the duvet. And then at his hand, which was still moving in circles over her right breast. A tiny smile twitched at the edge of her mouth. He tweaked her nipple encouragingly.

'Hmm?' he said.

She looked at him again, but by this time there was something rather different in her expression. A little-girl-in-a-sweet-shop coquettishness, maybe. She moved one of her hands back under the duvet and slid it along the inside of his thigh. 'It's just that, well. It's been such a long time. Such a long time, Jack.'

'For me too.'

'Honestly? Really?'

He nodded vigorously. 'Oh, yes. Really.'

Her hand stopped moving.

'So it's all right?' She was doing the staring thing again. 'I mean, it *is* all right, isn't it?'

Jesus, she was gorgeous. And he didn't have a clue what the hell she was on about.

'Of course it's all right, Hope,' he said.

Chapter 13

Hope pulled into her drive to find Suze walking down it towards her.

It was ten past nine, and if someone had handed her a survey containing the question 'who would you least like to see at this point in your life?' this vision of fun-fur and novelty cats 'n dogs umbrella would have been her immediate response. God, what was her sister-in-law doing here?

Waving at her, at this point. If only Hope had spotted her sooner, she could have driven on down the street. She glanced in the mirror to see her brother sitting in their car, which was parked across the road. Reluctantly, she lowered the window.

Suze had placed her spare fist on her hip by now. 'There you are,' she said, smiling the special smile she had perfected for letting people know she was-not-at-all-impressed. 'We'd almost given you up. You're out and about very early this morning.' She stooped now to peer in at Hope. The car filled instantly with the sort of cloying scent that Hope guessed cost Paul heaps of cash from various in-flight duty-free wagons.

'Um –'

'Where've you been? We kept calling.' Hope wondered if perhaps she'd lost a few days. It had been an awful lot of sex, after all. And why were her brother and sister-in-law here anyway? 'We called last night,' Suze went on. 'Several times. And then we called again first thing this morning –'

How first was first thing? Suze was looking at her more intently now.

Hope switched off the ignition and the wipers stopped mid-arc on the windscreen. Iain had always ticked her off about that. Wipers first. Ignition after. Why? What was going to happen to them, for God's sake? 'Why?' she said now, suddenly irritable herself. 'Is there a problem?'

'Well, no. Not a problem. It's just that when you didn't call back… anyway, no matter. We're off to Ikea.'

'At this time? They don't open till eleven on a Sunday, do they?'

'We're stopping for breakfast. And we want to get parked. So are you coming or not?'

'What – to Ikea?'

'Yes, of course to Ikea. I thought you said you wanted to come with us.'

She had? When was that?

'Um, well actually… I mean, thanks for asking me and everything, but I've got –' God, *what*? 'Football. Tom. You know –'

'How come? It's Sunday. Anyway, I thought the children were with their father this weekend.'

God, she was sharp. 'They are. Only there's a –'

'I thought you wanted to get that table.' Recollection kicked in as Suze pointed towards her husband. 'Paul's put the seats down and everything.'

'God, Suze. Sorry. I had completely forgotten.'

Why was she apologising? They had made no plans to go to Ikea. Ever. They'd just had a conversation a couple of weeks back about the fact that *if* they were going there sometime in the near future that she might – *might* – like to go with them. No. That wasn't how it had been at all. Suze had suggested that she might like to go with them. Hope had thought she rather wouldn't. Still wouldn't. And had never said she would. Only nodded at the 'might' to be polite, for God's sake. That was all. No dates. No plans. So why was she acting as if she'd done something wrong?

Suze sniffed and looked at her watch. Then reached across and opened the car door. 'Well, no matter. Plenty of time still. Did you have a nice evening?'

Hope swung her legs out, grateful that the ladder in her tights was hidden under her boot. 'Evening?'

'Last night. You were out.'

'Yes, I… er… had to deliver some cushions. To a friend.'

'Oh.'

Hope clamped her lips together while Suze stood to one side to let her out. She looked at her watch again. 'Well, come on, then,' she said. 'Let's get a move on.'

For a moment, Hope felt Iain's absence in her life. And felt it keenly, unwelcome though the realisation was. Had Iain been here, Suze wouldn't be bullying her like this. God, why did she have to say everything twice?

'It's very kind of you to think of me, but I really can't, Suze. I've got too much to do.'

Suze exhaled. 'Well, it's a pity you didn't let little old me know that before we trolled all the way here, isn't it?' She said this with a smile, but her eyes blazed fury. She blinked. 'Eh? So shall *we*, then?'

'What?'

She looked exasperated. 'Pick up the table for you!'

'No. No, really.' Jesus! She didn't want the bloody table! 'I've got to measure up and everything. And I'm not sure it's the one I want anyway. I need to… Look, thanks, but no. Don't worry. No rush for the table. You go.'

Hope stayed standing by her car while they drove off, her brother giving two long toots on the horn to signify their departure to the rest of the neighbourhood, and Suze, with a face like a driven-over biscuit, staring very pointedly ahead. She felt for all the world like a teenage girl who'd just been caught smoking by the bike sheds.

Except it was so much worse than that.

He'd been asleep when she'd woken, edged into consciousness by the unfamiliar ticking of a clock somewhere. Fast asleep. She'd slipped quietly from the bed, so as not to wake him, and pulled on a T-shirt that was crumpled in a pile of clothes on the floor. Then she'd taken their soup bowls out into the little kitchen, washed them both up and stacked them on the draining board. She'd pulled back the net curtain but there was a man down in the garden – Leonard, she supposed – so she'd lowered the net again quickly and made a pot of tea. There was only just enough milk for two mugs.

She hadn't known quite what to do or think. Only that she shouldn't be there. She'd taken the tea in and put his beside him on the bedside table, only inches from his nose. His features, in sleep, looked smooth and untroubled. She could fall in love with this man, she knew she could, and the thought, so powerful and so utterly unwelcome, was almost enough to make her run from the room. She didn't want to feel like that. Not now. Not about him. But she couldn't seem to help it. She was awed by his body, bemused by his maleness. The way the hair under his flung-out arm was so pale and wispy, yet the rest of it was so dense and wiry, running in a cross over his chest and almost from neck to groin. She had been glad the duvet covered that bit. She didn't want to see such an intimate part of him in the cold light of day. It would feel too personal. Too intimate, in fact. Altogether more so than the sex.

She let herself into the house and dropped her bag on the floor by the hall table. The answer-phone light was winking frantically at her, recording, no doubt, the chain of events that had placed her sister-in-law on her drive. She wondered if Jack's voice would be on there too, but she didn't press the button. She didn't think she could bear that it might not be. She went up to shower instead.

It was the knickers, really. The stepping back into the pair of knickers that she had worn last night. They never seemed to mention things like that in books or movies. The dirty-laundry implications of unscheduled sex away from home. Of staying the night. Of hanging around. Of still being there in the morning. Oh, God. Stupid. *Stupid*. Thank heavens she was home now and could get it all off.

She hadn't been able to shower at the flat – there wasn't one – so, not wanting to breach any house rules by filling the bath, instead had washed herself all over at the sink. The bathroom window, she'd noticed, was still wide open. She gazed out of it while she cleaned her teeth with his toothbrush, watching the blobs of rain streak down the window frame, pooling at the bottom before re-falling below.

And then she'd had to go back into the bedroom and re-dress in the clothes she'd scattered to the four winds last night. Unswizzle her knickers, unravel her laddered tights, pull the now shapeless wool dress back over her head. All this while he'd slept. She didn't want to wake him. She knew if she did he'd be on her in an instant, which, given that she knew she'd be unable to resist him, would only compound the angst now crowding her mind. Or worse. Or *worse*, he might be indifferent. Vaguely hostile. Be unable to hide the fact that he didn't want her there. Why did she feel this way? Would he really be like that? Yes. Yes, he would. If not immediately, then soon after. She stepped into the shower to wash it all away. She'd never in her life felt so ashamed.

The house was as she'd left it. There was no reason why it wouldn't be, but as she had never spent a night away from it since moving in, it felt strangely unfamiliar – cold. As if she'd just returned from two weeks in the Med. She rubbed herself dry and padded back naked to the bedroom, where the sight of her torso in the dressing table mirror brought new waves of horror to wash over her again. What had got into her? What had possessed her to let him have sex with her like that? What would he think of her?

God, but why did she think so little of herself? She was an adult, wasn't she? A single adult. There was no reason on earth why she shouldn't have sex with anyone she saw fit to have sex with, at any time she saw fit, and without reference to any of the cock-eyed rules of morality that had informed her teenage years. She was an adult. She needed to have sex. Sex was something fundamental to life, wasn't it? And hadn't she enjoyed it? Yes. *Yes*. But she still shouldn't have done it. She pulled on fresh underwear and scowled at her reflection. She shouldn't have let him. She shouldn't have done it. What would he think of her now?

She needed to talk to Madeleine. Madeleine would make her feel better. Less the victim of a stupid adolescent crush, and more an independent woman who had just happened to have sex with a man. Madeleine, now in her late fifties, had sex whenever and with whoever she felt like, and it never seemed to bother her in the slightest. Hope wondered if it wasn't something to do with having been bereaved as opposed to divorced. Madeleine's sex life with her husband had been legendary. If it wasn't actually in the middle of a shag that he'd keeled over, even Madeleine herself wasn't fazed by the notion that their energetic couplings might have been a factor in his untimely death. A short life but a happy one. She'd said that more than once.

Maddie hadn't been rejected. That was the thing. She didn't have that switch, so it couldn't be turned on.

She called Madeleine, while still in her bra and pants.

'I've done it.'

'Done what?'

112

'Been to bed with someone.' It sounded, surprisingly, all right, saying that to Madeleine. Sort of rugged. Uncompromising. Cosmopolitan-esque.

'Sweetness! That's marvellous! Do I know him? Was it good?'

'Yes, you know him.' She took a breath. 'Maddie, it was Jack Valentine.'

There. She'd said it. And she felt a little better for it, which surprised her. Madeleine whooped. 'Finally! You harlot, you! Mind you, I knew it was only a matter of time.' Of course she'd known. But more to the point, had Hope known that too? Yes, of course she had. It was just the amount of time that she'd miscalculated. But it was all right. She could be a sexual animal when she was talking to Madeleine. It felt like it had been – exciting. Spontaneous. It didn't feel shabby. She could pretend it didn't matter if he didn't call her now.

But he hadn't called her yet. And where, oh where, was her optimism now?

'You won't tell anyone, will you?' she added anxiously.

'Not if it's a secret. Though why it would be I have no idea. You're both available, aren't you? Wow*ee*,' she added. 'So how did all this come about? I mean, I knew you had a bit of a thing for him, but, my word, you're a shifty mare.'

Hope told her about the cushions. It had seemed such a nice, uncomplicated idea at the time, untarnished, she'd told herself, by ulterior motives. Just a gesture. A gesture of friendship. Of empathy... She sighed. That wasn't true, and she knew it. '... and then, *God*, I don't know. It just sort of happened.'

'And I can hear the glow in your voice, darling.'

'It's not a glow. It's a tremor. I feel awful.'

'Awful? Why on earth do you feel awful?'

'Because I just threw myself at him, Maddie. Went round there and threw myself at him. God, I can hardly bear to think about it. How could I do that? How could I be so forward?'

How indeed? Madeleine made a tut tut sound down the phone. 'Sweetness, get real. Which century do you imagine you're living in?

'I know. I *know*. But it still feels wrong to me.'

'But why?'

113

'Because he must think I'm so, well, easy.'

'Dear me, Hope – you sound like *Jackie* magazine circa nineteen-seventy. The world doesn't work like that any more. It's only sex, darling. That's all. Who cares about the logistics of who made the first move?'

It was actually not so much the logistics. She knew that. It was her crushing insecurity. Would there ever be a time when she didn't have to lump it around with her? When she loved herself enough again not to care who else did?

The telephone rang finally, at a quarter past six, and she eyed it for a moment, almost too frightened to pick it up.

It was Simon.

'Only me,' he said. He always said 'only me.' As if he didn't much matter. As if it being only him would never be anything other than a disappointment to anyone. To her, at least. Which, right now, it was. There was a brief pause. 'Well,' he said then. 'Are we on?'

They were supposed to be running at seven. She had not forgotten. Merely put her head in the sand. Hoped that if she did nothing and he did nothing it simply wouldn't happen. Which was stupid. She had answered the phone and now she would have to go running with Simon. How could she not?

'We're on,' she said, trying to sound like she meant it. Perhaps a run would do her good. Clear her head. If not her conscience. 'Anyone else coming?'

'Just you and little old me,' he said happily. Oh dear.

'I can't make it a long one,' she said quickly. 'I have to be back for the kids.'

It would do her good. The evening was dry and crisp and threatening a frost, and her breath was cotton wool in front of her as she jogged up to meet him. She liked running best when there was a chill in the air.

They met at the park. Two circuits of the pavement that ran around the perimeter of the park, Simon told her, came to exactly three point two miles, as long as you included the war memorial. Just a spit over five kilometres, which was perfect. He knew this, he said, because he'd driven it earlier, to check. He had a chunky watch on, one of those watches that could tell you the time in Buenos Aires while simultaneously monitoring your mean gradient and reminding you how far off sea level you were. He spent some moments fiddling with it before they set off.

'Right,' he said finally. 'Let's kick some gravel.'

Hope kicked, pushing on hard, in order that she would be breathless, and wouldn't have to talk back to him too much. He didn't seem to care. He matched her stride easily, keeping up a commentary on the fun run as they ran. Hope wasn't really listening. He was banging on about one of the sponsors, and how he'd offered to have his team all dress up as comedy hearts.

'I think he's mad,' he was saying. 'But it might help with the TV coverage.'

'Hmm.'

'Oh, and talking of TV, that reminds me. I spotted our man, as it happens.'

Hope slowed a little as they approached a junction, knowing, precisely, which man he meant, because there was only one man on her mind.

'Saw who?'

He was becoming breathless himself now, his early pace obviously catching up with him. 'Jack Valentine,' he panted, jogging on the spot while a train of cars streamed past from the lights. He placed a hand against her back now and began to herd her across the road. She wished he wouldn't. She lengthened her stride again. He caught up. 'In that free magazine. The one you get at the doctors. You know –'

She was listening now. 'No.'

'That one they give away. *Ladies Only*, or something? I meant to bring it in for Madeleine.'

'Oh, right.'

'Well, she's so keen to get someone from the television involved. Only he was with that woman. I thought Madeleine might be interested. I mean if his girlfriend's a big shot at HTV, it might be useful, mightn't it? You never know, do you?'

Hope didn't know. More to the point, Hope didn't much want to know. 'What woman was this?' She kicked her legs harder. *What* woman?

'That woman from the telly,' he panted. 'You know her. Used to present that news programme. Hey – we on a mission here or something?' He was gasping audibly by now. 'Allegra something. Allegra S something… Staunton, that's it. Hey, he gets about, our boy, doesn't he?'

Hope didn't watch a lot of television, but the name rang a definite bell. 'In a magazine? How come?'

'The CancerCope ball. One of those society features. They always do them. The great and the good. The "*glitterati*".' He said this with what Hope took to be a wry flourish. We are not worthy.

Hope couldn't imagine why someone like Simon would be a reader of society pages. But then there was lots about Simon she didn't know. And she was perfectly happy for that state of affairs to continue. Though not perfectly happy right now. How could he have a girlfriend? How could he have a girlfriend and sleep with *her*?

Their cars were coming into view, and Simon began to slow. Hope ran faster, sprinting now. She was breathing in gasps as Simon drew level with her.

'Well,' he said, beads of perspiration crowding his forehead and nose. 'Twenty-seven thirty-two. You certainly know how to make a man build up a sweat!'

Hope wiped the back of her wrist across her forehead. She felt nauseated. And dizzy. She'd had nothing to eat since midday and her body was yowling its protest. She walked a few paces up the road to cool down, while Simon stood, bent-backed, his pale hands on his paler knees. Yes, she did know who Allegra Staunton was. She could picture her. A telly blonde. That was the accepted vernacular, wasn't it? Just the kind of woman Jack Valentine *would* have on his arm. Simon was sniffing now. Loudly. Then swallowing. Horrible. But better, she supposed, than spitting. Iain always used to spit when he ran. She fished her car key from the little pocket in her shorts. She needed to get away from Simon now, before any other nuggets of innuendo occurred to him. She started back. Simon had fished out his own key.

'You know, it's daft us bringing both cars down here,' he was saying. 'I'll pick you up next time. Make much more sense.' He seemed to be hovering.

It would make no sense at all. It would place him outside her house when they finished their run and leave openings for him to hover even more.

'I'm happy enough to drive myself,' she said, conscious as she said it that she must also avoid intimating that her picking him up would be workable. Simon was getting too close for comfort. She unlocked the car and opened the door. 'I've got to stop off at the Spar, anyway.'

'Oh, right.' He began walking towards her. 'Wednesday? Thursday? Er… Hope, I –'

'We'll sort it out at work,' she said hurriedly, sliding into her seat. 'Better dash or the kids'll get there before me.'

Hope drove through the darkening Sunday evening streets and tried to still the new waves of regret that washed over her. The woman wasn't necessarily his girlfriend. Even if she had been when the picture was taken, that meant nothing. The CancerCope ball had been three months back – January? Before Christmas, even. She recalled Madeleine mentioning it. Commenting that a fundraising ball was something they might attempt at some point. God, she wished she could get hold of a copy of that magazine. But what would be the point? What possible purpose would it serve except to confirm her suspicion that Jack Valentine was someone who went out with glamorous women? Why wouldn't he? By his own admission he had a lot of lost time to make up. He'd made no bones about it. God, why had she slept with him? It wasn't even as if they were seeing each other. A slick of ruby shame burned on her cheeks. When had he ever sought her out? When had he ever *asked* her out? They'd had dinner, yes, but that had been work. Must have been, in hindsight, because nothing had come of it. Since then – God, it was too awful to contemplate. Her first real connection with someone of the opposite sex and she'd run completely away with herself. She'd chased him, that's what she'd done. She'd sought him out. *She* had. With her stupid cushions. Trotting round there, all smiles and eyelashes. What had she been thinking? She'd simply handed her body to him on a plate. She pulled her keys from the ignition and hated herself.

Why would he call her? He'd already dined.

Chapter 14

By three on Sunday afternoon, Jack had decided he would stop hanging around at the flat in case Hope phoned him, and went off to visit his father instead.

He'd woken at ten, feeling refreshed and relaxed in an entirely unfamiliar way. It was a full half minute before he realised why, but only twenty seconds more before he realised she'd gone – all evidence of her being there having vanished, bar a single black hair that was coiled on his pillow and the mug of cold tea that sat inches from his nose. He'd padded around the flat, naked, grinning, and fisting the air, as the rewind of the previous night spooled through his mind. Result! Re*sult*! A fine night. A night to remember. A watershed night, in fact. He'd broken his duck and he felt like a lion. No. He just felt like a man again. Sated. Which was plenty to be going on with. Though it was a little strange she'd shot off like that. No note or anything.

Still, he'd thought, peering hopefully into the fridge for more milk, perhaps she had to get somewhere early, and had decided not to wake him. That was probably it. His discovery that he didn't have her number was a bit of a blow. Quite apart from the fact that he'd quite like to talk to her, being sated was something with a limited life span. What he'd most like to do would be to drag her right back and have sex with her again. And this, in itself, was an interesting thing to contemplate. His memory of similar encounters pre-Lydia was that his principal, number one, morning-after feeling was one of wanting one of them – himself, her, whichever – to be gone. To be somewhere else. And yet, here she was, gone, and he wished that she wasn't. Curious. But no matter. He went to fetch the mug of tea, and brought it back out to the kitchen to microwave. She'd call him, no doubt, when she could.

But by the time he was ready to leave for the nursing home she still hadn't called him, and his entire journey there – a one-way trip of about thirty-five minutes – was punctuated by bouts of post-coital insights small and large. Many of these were of an unashamedly carnal and ebullient nature, but nestling among them now was the nagging thought that perhaps it was not such a bad thing that he didn't have her number, because it was never a good thing to seem too keen where women were concerned. He'd been there already and where precisely had it got him? No matter how much his loins were telling him he wanted to see her again, there was another more insistent voice telling him not to start getting too over-enthusiastic about a woman he hardly knew. Not to regard his morning-after euphoria as anything more meaningful than it actually was. Not to confuse the message with the messenger, in fact. It had been an awfully long time. And not just that. He'd done what he'd set out to, hadn't he? Why go inventing problems that might not even be there? The words 'commitment' and 'relationship' ebbed and flowed along the shore of his consciousness, and despite knowing full well that these were simply two staples of the old-bag lexicon that had informed most of Lydia's bitchings about men (bloody rich, as it had turned out), he was fairly certain they were endemic in much of womanhood. Along with walking in front of the TV during replays and leaving things halfway up stairs. No. He shouldn't fret about not being able to call her. No rush. He could get her number in work in the morning. Whatever. Bloody hell, but he'd shagged someone at last!

His father, Jack knew, was going to die. Some days he could deal with this knowledge better than others. Some days he would arrive at the nursing home and stride up the long drive, with its rose-stumps and leaf mounds and air of quiet stoicism, and feel strong and accepting and able to cope. Other days, like today, perhaps to bring him back to earth, it made him feel vulnerable in a way he rarely felt elsewhere in his life. It was an inevitability he didn't feel remotely equipped to have to live through. It scared him. His father would be gone and there'd just be him and Ollie. Just him and his only son. Alone in the world. But thinking of Ollie always made him feel better, albeit in a frightened kind of way. That was the way it worked, having children. You had them and then you moved up to the next notch. He'd soon be the one at the top of the pile. No longer receiving but dispensing advice. Strange how a scant few years could shift the dynamic so profoundly. He and Lydia and Ollie had been a family. As had his mum and dad. But

Lydia's parents – her git of a brother, even – they had been a part of his family too. His extended family. The whole web of relationships – the tussles over Christmas, the remembering of birthdays, the inevitable rows – and now, today, it was almost all gone. He no longer had an extended family. Sooner or later his father would die, and that would be it. His family would consist of just him and Ollie. That was all. Finite. That was *it*.

He had already stopped at the Esso garage and picked up some wine gums. Jack's father had always had a great fondness for wine gums, and as the food at the nursing home was bland, at best, and he had so little appetite now, he was always grateful for this little treat. It wasn't much, but then his father didn't want much. He was glad that at a time in his father's life when there was so little he could give him, he could proffer *something*, at least. He paused, as he habitually did, to look back across Cardiff before going in. The nursing home was set high to the south west of the city. From one side the lawns sloped gently away with views over the Bristol Channel, and to the other, the city itself was miniatured before him, the white prongs of the Millennium Stadium winking sunlight in the distance. The last time he had been a regular here – when his mother died – the Millennium Stadium had not even been built. All that construction, all that life going on. All the things and events she'd never lived to see.

There was one nurse in the nursing home that Jack would have fancied, were it not for the fact that the whole notion of fancying someone at this time, in this place, was vaguely distasteful. Something he registered without really connecting to. Her name was Shelley, and she greeted him now.

'How is he?' he said. He always said this, even though the answer could only be 'the same', or 'a little worse', or 'a lot worse', or 'dead'. He wasn't ready for dead yet. Not ready at all. So there was always a welling of mild panic as he entered the stuffy entrance hall, that his father might actually pass away without him – a ridiculous anxiety, he knew. His dad could die at any time on any day. He could die while Jack was on air. He could die while he was away reporting on a match. He could die while he sat in the cinema with Ollie, with his phone switched off. But Jack didn't think so. He thought – thought with some conviction, in fact – that in any of these scenarios there would be time to alert him.

That there'd be a call in sufficient time that he'd be able to make it to be with him. But, irrational though it was, he had a fixation that what would actually happen was that he'd set off to visit entirely as per usual, and that his father would die while he was en route. Jack knew this was simply a manifestation of his anxiety; even so, his outbreath when Shelley said 'comfortable' was heavy with relief. That it wasn't today. That it wasn't yet.

'Nice that the rain's cleared up,' she said next. 'You could take him outside, perhaps.'

'Yes, nice,' agreed Jack, nodding. 'I might.'

Jack's father was awake and reading the *Daily Mail* when he got to his room, sitting in the chair by the window with a blanket over his knees. Jack visited often – at least once a week, but always felt unprepared for the deterioration he saw. As if time moved more quickly here. Like cat years or dog years. As if the man beneath the face was slipping rapidly away from him, growing ever more difficult to recognise, incarcerated and fading beneath a veil of sallow skin. He held up the wine gums.

'Splendid, son,' his father said, nodding. 'Just the jobby.'

He always said the same thing. Splendid, son. Just the jobby. Jack, smiling, put them on the bedside table and sat down on the bed.

'So,' he said. 'How've you been feeling this week?'

'Not great,' he said, throwing the paper on the bed. 'You saw it I suppose? Typical. Just threw it away.'

Jack nodded. He was talking about football, of course. Football was in his father's blood every bit as much as all the red cells and white cells, so it was no surprise that the performance of his teams (Portsmouth and Manchester United) acted as a barometer on any given week, indicating the state of his mood. It had ever been thus. It was the same with Jack, too. And Ollie? Yes, definitely. Jack liked the sense of continuity that gave him.

'What about you?' His father examined him. 'You're looking very chipper. More than you've a business to.' He inspected Jack more carefully. 'Come on, out with it, son. What's her name?'

*   *   *

121

Hope. Where was she? What was she doing? He'd checked the answer-phone as soon as he got home, but still there was nothing. And when she hadn't called by the time it had grown dark, Jack decided he either needed a very cold shower or a breath of fresh air. Not having a shower, there was just the one option. So he telephoned Danny to see if he fancied a pint. It was handy, he decided, him moving into the Cefn Melin flat, because both Danny and the local were only a walk away. Predictably, Danny had been up for it.

Though this was beginning to look as if it wasn't necessarily a good thing. Jack had told his father all about Hope. At some length. Not just because he was feeling so ridiculously pleased with himself, but also because he knew it was what his father wanted to hear. That he was seeing someone. Well, that wasn't strictly true. But at least there was a chance that he wouldn't die and leave his son all alone. Jack's father worried more about Jack than anything else. He worried that he needed a proper home. That he needed a family. He worried whether he'd be all right once he was no longer there. So Jack had told him. Not about the sex, of course. But much of the rest. The chipmunks. The lock-out. The cushions. He'd liked that.

'She made you cushions?' Danny said, after they'd downed their first pint and Jack had told *him* about Hope's unexpected visit. Why did he do that? Why couldn't he just keep his mouth shut? 'Blimey,' Danny went on. 'You want to watch that, mate. Sounds a little cosy to me.'

Jack knew that. He also knew that to tell Danny about the cushions had been a spectacularly grave error of judgement. Not because there was anything intrinsically wrong about Hope having made him cushions, but because telling Danny about it immediately flagged up every one of the vague discomforts that he was beginning to have about it and lobbed them back, irrefutable and set in stone, in his face. Why hadn't he thought that before he told him? He was glad he'd decided not to tell Danny they'd had sex.

'It'll be a hearthrug next.'

He knew.

'Or she'll start making you casseroles. Before you know it, she'll be wanting you to get a door key cut for her.'

He *knew*.

'Don't be daft,' he said, depressed by Danny's relentless ribbing. Perhaps coming out for a drink with Danny had been an error of judgement, full stop. He was a great friend, but sometimes, particularly after he'd been with his dad, it felt all wrong. He needed to be on his own. He couldn't talk to Danny about his dad. Not really. There were whole areas of Jack's life that Danny simply didn't penetrate, and that was just fine. But thinking this seemed disloyal. He was a good, supportive friend. Just wearing at times. Not least because it sometimes felt Danny had taken ownership of him since his divorce. Like he was some counselling guru who always knew what was best for him. He didn't like the inequality it had caused in their friendship. He just wanted things to get back to normal. To talk to Danny about football. Just football and sex. Though not this sex. Because that felt wrong, too.

But Danny had been there for him when he'd needed him. That was what really mattered. Jack sipped his pint. 'I think you're barking up the wrong tree there, mate. It was just a gesture. A nice gesture. She's a nice person.'

Danny blew out his cheeks and tapped a beer mat on the table. 'Nice. Exactly my point, mate. Make no mistake. She's getting her claws into you. And once a woman starts getting her claws into you with cushions, it's only a matter of time before you're back down the slippery slope and dragged back up an aisle. Beware the power of the penis, mate. It'll get you into trouble.'

Danny said it with feeling. 'Hardly,' Jack replied. 'She hasn't phoned me, after all.'

'Ah,' said Danny. 'That'll be because you haven't called her –'

'But I *can't*!'

'– and now she's sulking.' Danny stared mournfully at his pint for a few moments. 'They're good at that, women.'

'Don't be daft, mate,' Jack said again.

When Jack got home from the pub Hope still hadn't called, and once he'd abandoned the idea of driving to her house – where *was* it? He didn't know the street name even – he remembered that he did have Hil's number, and that Hil being Hil, she'd probably have Hope's number in her Palm Pilot. She was efficient like that. She'd have taken her details when she came on the show. He leafed

123

through his address book. He ought to ring Hope. Sod being circumspect and cool. He wanted to ring Hope. It was only ten. Not too late. Perhaps they could meet up in the week. Perhaps he could take her out for a meal. Go on a date. That would be novel. But if he rang Hil he'd have to submit himself to an interrogation. An in-depth interrogation. Why was it that since he had found himself single his love life was so much the *plat du jour*? Why did people feel they had the right to scrutinise his every move? Why was his sex life (or lack of) suddenly a matter of public record? He didn't ask Hil, or Patti or Dave, for that matter, to keep him posted on theirs, did he? Sex. That was what it was really all about. Yes, they were anxious to see him happy again – and he did appreciate that – but there was also (and this was true of Danny as well) an element of straightforward voyeurism about it. And Hil would tell Dave and Dave would tell Patti, and Patti – bloody Patti probably wouldn't be adverse to telling South Wales on air. She'd been bad enough over that ridiculous Cinderella nonsense.

But it *was* sex. He wanted to have sex with Hope again. That was what it was really all about. The pull of his loins. Which didn't feel particularly laudable, and reminded him of Danny's words not half an hour earlier. He picked up the cushion on the chair beside him. Why should wanting to have sex with Hope Shepherd make him feel so anxious all of a sudden? He liked her. She liked him (oh, yes – no doubt about that), so what, precisely, was the problem? He grimaced. Probably the one he'd already had pointed out to him. That she was too nice. Certainly too nice to be messed around with. And how could he guarantee that he wouldn't mess her around? He was a man, for God's sake. A single man. A newly single man with newly single designs on the opposite sex. *Lots* of them. Unless – he picked up the receiver and cradled it in his hand – unless, hell – why was he presuming so much? Why wouldn't she be up for it? It wasn't as if she had told him otherwise, was it? She'd certainly been up for it last night. Where was the harm? He punched out the digits and waited.

Hil's number rang and rang, but Hil herself clearly wasn't home. Bollocks. He put the phone down again and flipped the cover shut on his address book. He was kidding himself anyway. It was simply wishful thinking. If he'd worked out one thing about Hope, it was that she was emphatically not the sort of person who'd be interested in recreational sex. She'd be interested in sex as a part of a monogamous relationship. She was fragile. Vulnerable. She'd made a point of saying so. In fact, she was probably waiting for him to phone her right now. Quite possibly she was sulking because he hadn't done so, which was all the more reason not to, perhaps. He couldn't in any case, could he?

Women. He pushed the address book back into the drawer. He'd ring her from work in the morning.

Chapter 15

It was about ten minutes before Hope stopped crying, and she felt much better for it.

When she'd got in from her run, the answer-phone light had been flashing, and, deciding to save the message till she was out of her kit, she'd run upstairs for her shower feeling suddenly invigorated and light of heart. It would be him. She just knew it. What did it matter who he'd gone out with before he'd met her? In any case, she wasn't sure Simon didn't have his own agenda where Jack was concerned. The way he called him 'our man' when he really meant 'your man', almost as if by professing joint ownership he was challenging her to tell him he was wrong.

But then she'd come down and pressed the play button, and it had only been Iain, to let her know he'd be half an hour late with the children.

They'd come in then, and she'd spent another half an hour in her fortnightly Purgatory, listening to how lovely their weekend had been. How much fun it had been compared to boring life at home, how they'd been (oh, how wicked!) to TGI Friday's, how (oh, the sweetheart!) he'd taken them ice skating, how (oh, go on, then) he had let Tom borrow his *Saving Private Ryan* DVD, despite all the gore at the start. And also how they'd gone to have lunch with Daddy's new girlfriend, who was called Rhiannon, and who (oh, how *lovely!*) had a really lush Mini and bright red, *mega*-lush hair.

It might have been partly listening to that, she reasoned. Not because she cared; she was through all that – he could do what he liked now. But because it was an uncomfortable reminder of how cruelly compartmentalised all their lives had become. There were parts of her children's lives that weren't part of hers now. They were peopled by Rhiannons and Emmas and Ffions and whoever else he hung on his treacherous arm.

But maybe not. The phone had started up again while she was tucking Tom in and this time it was Suze, with her interminable wittering – this time about how she'd batch-cooked some chilli which Hope could pop in to collect the next day. Not 'might like to pop in'. Oh, no. 'Could pop in'. Which meant *would* pop in. Or expect retribution, you ungrateful cow. Suze hadn't been any more irritating than usual, but nevertheless, as Hope had put down the receiver, the tears started and they just wouldn't stop.

Having stopped crying now, Hope could see her tears for exactly what they were. The fall-out from an infatuation. Yes. All that pent-up sexual tension. That and feeling so shameful. Only to be expected, really. There was the sex itself – there must be some hormonal component to that, mustn't there? But it wasn't like her heart was broken or anything. Just that it was so painful to recall how stupidly she'd behaved. That and the fact that Jack Valentine had been the first man who had shown the least interest in her since she had left Iain. (If you didn't count Simon, and she definitely didn't.) The first person she'd allowed herself to imagine she could have a romantic relationship with. What a fool. What an idiot. She was thirty-nine, for God's sake. What business did she have becoming infatuated with the first man who paid her the compliment of fancying her? What the hell was she doing crying?

She went into the kitchen on heavy legs and ripped a piece of kitchen roll from the holder on the wall. God, why didn't she just phone him and be done with it? It had to be better than all this juvenile snivelling. At least it would put an end to all this wretched speculation. But she couldn't. She mustn't. She absolutely knew it was the one thing she must not do. She'd had quite enough humiliation for one weekend, and ringing him now would only make things worse. Suppose he wasn't alone? Suppose he was alone but sounded like he wasn't pleased to hear from her? And even supposing he did sound pleased to hear from her – it would still feel all wrong. It would *be* all wrong. Would she actually believe it when he hadn't already phoned *her*? Surely, *surely*, if he liked her, phoning her would have been the very first thing he'd have done this morning. And he hadn't. So there was no point in phoning at all. The only way forward was to wait. Wait and see. God, but the world was a cruel place to be in. Why did men wield so much power over women?

She blew her nose aggressively on the piece of kitchen roll. No. She wouldn't phone him. She'd slept with him and she couldn't undo that. All she could do now was limit the damage.

That and learn from her mistake. Good luck to him. Let him go screw every woman in Cardiff if he liked. She'd walked away from the situation. That was what mattered.

Bastard. *Bastard.*

'That's fabulous, darling. Absolutely perfect. Don't you think so, gentlemen? What a star our Hope is.'

Oh, God. She wished Maddie would shut up. What was she on?

In honour of the fact that Jack and the sponsors and the President of the North East Cardiff Harriers were going to be present at the meeting today, Madeleine had borrowed the conference room that belonged to the solicitors in the offices downstairs. Thus they had the use of a large oval table, chairs that matched each other, and a tray bearing a cut-glass water jug and tumblers, which Hope had only five minutes ago filled. And he was here. So very much here. She lay the rough of the poster on the table in front of her, heavy of heart, and with hands that just wouldn't stay still.

They were here to discuss the ongoing publicity and to finalise details and dates. Their two main sponsors were both in place in their chairs, smiling benefactors' smiles, finishing their coffee and custard creams, and wholly unaware of the one act (oh, God, *post*-act) melodrama that was being played out in their midst. As, indeed, was Madeleine. Hope had seen little of Madeleine on Monday, a state of affairs not without future ramifications. Maddie clearly thought she was sitting in the midst of something altogether different from what she actually was.

'Absolutely! Hear, hear!' said Mr Babbage.

'Hear, hear,' agreed Jack heartily. 'Yes, indeed she is.'

He was seated across the table and two seats along from Hope. They hadn't spoken except to say good morning. But he kept glancing at her and grinning. She wished he wouldn't. The act of seeing him again had been a dreadful shock. Having spent much of Sunday night and a good deal of Monday reminding herself that she needed a man in her life like she needed a cold sore, she had assumed that when she did see him the event would be manageable. But here he was and her stomach was fluttering ridiculously. Here he was and she couldn't stop stealing looks at him. Here he was and she was so distracted by him. She had so comprehensively forgotten the unbearable intensity of it all. She hadn't felt this way in decades. And she wasn't, she realised with sudden conviction, ready yet to feel this way again.

Madeleine, seated next to Hope, kicked her under the table. 'So. Mouse mats,' she was saying. Saying to *her*. Hope riffled through her notes and pulled out the sample, conscious that everyone's eyes were now on her. Which meant Jack's were, of course.

'Er… oh, right. Yes.' She held up the sample. 'They've agreed to do us five hundred.'

'And they're lovely too. Though I'm not sure five hundred will be enough, will it? But you can do the business on him, can't you? You're good at that.' She nudged Hope. 'She's good at that,' she added to the men. Jack specifically. Horror upon horror. How could she? How *could* she?

'Oh, yes, indeed,' said Mr Babbage. Jack smiled. Or did he smirk? Madeleine consulted the list in front of her again.

'Sun block.'

Sun block? What? Oh God. Yes. For the runners. Get your head together. Sun block.

'Sun?' said Mr Babbage, nodding towards the window. 'Fat chance of that. Rust remover might be a more useful option.'

'The sun always shines on the righteous,' said Mr Pinkerton.

'Not in Wales it doesn't,' said Mr Babbage brightly. 'Either that, or we've all been very naughty!' He guffawed. He really thought he was funny.

Jack was looking at her still. She could feel it, sense it. He could see right through her dress and straight through into her soul. She tightened her grip on her agenda. She decided that if she had to look at him much more, she might just dissolve into tears.

'Anyway, you're on to that as well, aren't you, sweetie? Hope? Hel-lo?' Maddie kicked her again. 'Are you still with us, darling, or what?'

Oh, God, she hoped he'd gone. That was all she hoped and she hoped it with more sincerity than she'd ever hoped anything in her life. Except perhaps the time she'd first hoped she'd been wrong about Iain (which had been the mother and father of all hopes).

But he hadn't. He was talking to Kayleigh and Mr Pinkerton from the Harriers. She hovered by reception while Mr Pinkerton pulled a bungee from his pocket and strode off outside to unlock his bike. Which left Jack, who was showing not the least sign of doing likewise, so there was no choice but to go up and either deck him or speak to him. The phone rang in the office. Kayleigh went off to answer it. Speak to him, then. It was all she could do.

'So,' he said, rounding on her as soon as the door had closed behind her. His expression was warm. 'How are *you*?'

She stood stiffly to attention. What was the '*you*' bit all about? It sounded so suggestive. It made her feel like a trollop. 'I'm fine,' she replied crisply. 'You?'

He nodded. 'I'm fine. Just fine.' Then he threw his hands out in supplication. 'I'm sorry I never managed to get hold of you.'

She nodded back. 'Right.'

'Only I didn't have your number at home so I couldn't ring you Sunday, and what with one thing and another yesterday –'

'That's OK,' she said levelly. 'I didn't ring you either, did I?'

He waggled a finger towards her chest and grinned. 'No, you didn't. I thought you might have. You should have.'

He looked all eager and anxious to please, like a puppy.

Or a penitent. Didn't have her number. That was lame. She'd given it to him the first time they'd met. But even if he hadn't had it, her phone him? As if.

She shrugged. 'Well, you know… ' She left the words hanging. Did he? Did he have the first idea what she'd been through since Saturday? Obviously not. She was suddenly pleased beyond measure that she hadn't succumbed and picked up that phone. She'd been so very close. Thank God – thank every deity in the universe – that she hadn't actually done it.

'Well,' he said, 'I've got it now.' He patted his breast pocket and looked like he'd appreciate a sticky star for his efforts. In that instant, Hope knew that it didn't matter. They could chew over logistics all they liked, but it wasn't relevant. This was nothing whatsoever to do with day-to-call ratios, and everything, oh but everything, to do with her. Just her.

She didn't need this. Didn't want it. Didn't have to put herself through it. She nodded at him. 'Fine.'

She said nothing more, and he looked at her without speaking for a long moment. She looked back. She couldn't not.

'So,' he said eventually, flicking his eyes down and then back again. He cleared his throat and pushed his hands into his trouser pockets. 'Have you got any plans for the weekend? If you're free I thought we might –'

'Sorry,' she said, decided. It was easy. 'I'm pretty busy. Chloe's got her interim dance examinations and my mum's looking after my brother's kids for a few days, so I'm all out of babysitters, and in any case, I've got a lot of paperwork to catch up on so I really need to stay in and... er... catch up.'

He had smiled politely throughout this but now he stopped smiling and nodded briskly instead. 'Right,' he said, cheerfully. 'I'll guess I'll have to take that as a no, then.'

But he didn't look cheerful. He looked hurt, and also shocked. Which made her hesitate. Did it really matter so much about him calling? So she'd gone and got herself in a state. Understandable, really. It didn't mean... God, but it was Tuesday. Two whole days had passed. She thought of a future dominated and punctuated by such anxieties. Of waiting for phone calls. Of fretting all the time. No. She didn't need this. Not now, she didn't. She folded her arms across her chest. 'I'm sorry, Jack, it's just that... well, when I didn't hear from you... well, I've already made other plans. You know how it is.'

'No, I don't,' he said, looking like he meant it. His mouth twitched at the corners. 'I wish I did.'

'I'm sorry. It's just... ' Someone, surely, would come out into reception soon and rescue her from this torture. He was still so *there*. Filling the small space. His eyes boring into hers. She could almost hear the cogs in his brain whirring. She could almost hear the steady drip of her own resolve melting. ' ...I'm –'

'Am I in the doghouse?' he said. There was still a trace of a smile on his face, but the edge in his voice now belied it.

'No.' She tried to make it sound light, but as soon as she uttered it, she knew it had come out all wrong. All spiky and pointed. More like a yes, in fact. He looked even more upset.

'Are you sure? You've gone very frosty on me all of a sudden.'

'I haven't gone frosty.'

131

'Yes, you have. One minute you're all over me –' Hope winced '– and the next you're treating me as if I've got a notifiable disease. Why?' He spread his hands now. 'Is it really because I didn't phone on Sunday?' He slapped them back against his sides again, looking incredulous that this could possibly be true. 'Or did you just go off me?'

Hope had so not been expecting this. Her mouth dropped open.

'No! No... well... *No*.' She should, she realised, just tell him the truth. Or a version of it, at any rate. With the flutterings in her stomach edited out. 'Look,' she said. 'I'm just feeling a little shellshocked, OK? I shouldn't have let myself get so carried away on Saturday, and I just... ' She glanced behind her to check that Kayleigh hadn't returned. 'Jack, I just feel a bit uncomfortable about it. I don't want to get too involved, that's all.'

He rolled his eyes. 'What's all this "involved" stuff? Either you want to see me again or you don't. I'm not asking you to marry me.'

She didn't know what to say to that. He raised his eyebrows a little. He was smiling at her again. 'Hmm?'

'I just... well, I just don't want to put myself in a position where... '

'Where what? Look, if you don't want to see me again you only have to say so, you know. I'd just rather you told me. That's all.'

'It's not that. I do. It's just that I don't want to put myself in a situation where – well, I just don't want those sort of complications in my life right now. I'm not ready for it. I haven't the energy for it.'

This seemed to strike a chord with him. He nodded immediately. 'Neither do I,' he agreed. 'Believe me, the last thing I need right now is to get into a heavy relationship. I've done that to death just lately, thanks.'

'So have I.'

'So where's the problem? We go out. We have fun. We see what happens. I'm not talking drawing up contracts here.'

'Exactly!'

'What do you mean "exactly"?'

132

'I mean that's exactly why I don't feel comfortable about seeing you again. Not yet. Because it's just all too complicated.' Because it *wouldn't* be fun.

'But how is it complicated? You just agreed you didn't want to get heavy – and I'm not getting heavy. God knows, I'm not. See this?' He stuck his fist out, startling her. 'See?' he said again, tapping his jacket. 'Sleeve. See what's on it?'

'Um.'

'Red squashy thing. Pumps blood. A little worse for wear, you'll note.'

She couldn't help smiling, in spite of his exasperation. 'Oh, I've got one of those. But I try to keep mine somewhere a little safer.'

Belatedly. Why hadn't she thought about that before?

'Evidently,' he said slowly. He put his arm down again and took a step towards her. God, he wasn't about to try and kiss her in reception, was he?

'Look,' he said, his expression softer. 'All I'm saying is that I can't be doing with you playing hard to get. Here I am. Take me or leave me.'

That was rich. Coming from someone who'd made love to her three times and then not phoned her for two days. '*I'm* not the one playing hard to get, here. I hardly qualify any more, do I? I'm just not playing easy to get, that's all. In fact, what I'm playing is keep your head, don't let your heart have unprotected sex with strangers, retain your dignity and don't get hurt.'

'Just the simple life, then.'

'Exactly.'

He fell silent. She could tell he was thinking. She wondered what.

'You reckon I'll do that, then, do you? Hurt you?'

'You might.'

'Why exactly?'

'Because you've been hurt yourself. Because –'

'So I'm going to get my own back on womankind by hurting you? Well, that's really nice of you.'

'No!' God. This was coming out all wrong. She spread her hands. 'Because you've already told me you're not ready to have a serious relationship yet.'

He looked affronted. 'When?'

'When I came over with Tom that time.'

He paused to digest this. She could see him thinking again. His face was so open. So easy to read. 'Hang on,' he said eventually, pointing his finger at her again. 'So did you!'

'Yes, but it's different for you. You're a man.'

'So?'

'Well, you've got a lot of lost time to make up. You told me. And there's lots of other women out there.'

He stabbed a finger towards the door. 'So? There's lots of men out there too, and *you're* the one who said –'

She put her hand up to silence him. 'Yes, but I'm not interested, am I? I'm not a man.' Or someone like Madeleine, however much she wished she was. And, boy, she did right now. If *only* he had phoned her on Sunday. But then again, perhaps it was much better that he hadn't. She could get out of this before she was sucked further in.

His expression hardened again. Had he been thinking her thoughts? 'I'm well aware of that. It's probably why I don't have a clue what you're on about.'

'It's quite simple. I'm not a man, so I'm really not interested in casual sex, flings, one-night stands, whatever you want to call it. There's only one type of relationship I'm ever going to be interested in having, and it's not the kind I think you and I are able to have right now. That's all.'

He rolled his eyes again. 'Oh, and I am, of course. You see? You *are* being frosty.'

'I'm not,' she said firmly. 'I'm just trying to be straight with you, Jack.'

'No,' he said. 'Believe me, Hope. You're being frosty.'

She opened her mouth to correct him, but closed it again immediately. Because of the way he had spoken her name. Because of the way the smile had left his face all of a sudden. As if a penny – no, an anvil – had dropped on his head. Whoosh. Just like that. So wholly and comprehensively it felt as if she'd been slapped. 'Well,' he said shortly. 'When – no, *if* – you thaw out a bit, you know where to find me, don't you?'

He turned around and stalked out of the building, the words hanging like icicles in his wake.

Chapter 16

There was a new Saturday afternoon football show in development at HTV, and Jack Valentine was going to present it. That was all there was to it. Nothing was going to come between him and getting this job. No more languishing in the dusty reaches of daytime local radio. This was prime time. This was television. This was the start of the rest of his professional life.

He had, he realised, a lot to thank Allegra for. Admittedly, principal among these tributes was the fact that she had the hots for him (and there was no knowing what sort of shelf life that circumstance had, which was something that perhaps he ought to address) but right now she was rooting for him and he was very, very grateful.

The meeting had been scheduled for four-fifteen, which had left Jack precious little time to get out to the TV studios, but he had made it, and could now enjoy a few minutes in the car while he went through his notes once again.

Not that he needed to. He knew everything a man could conceivably know about football. This wasn't a conceit. It was a fact.

He knew less than nothing, however, about women.

Hope, damn her. What was all that about? All that just because he hadn't phoned her? God, he'd tried, hadn't he? It was incomprehensible.

More to the point, having failed to get hold of her, why had he not even had enough intelligence to see what was coming? He had gone to the Heartbeat offices that morning looking forward to seeing her, and had come away feeling angrier than he could remember feeling in a very long time. And not just angry. What had he done to deserve such a comprehensive character assassination? He felt manipulated. Self-righteous. Rejected.

Danny had been in the office when Jack returned to the studios, doing something to one of the printers. Jack's anger had dissipated a little, though not much – at least twice on the journey from Roath over to Llandaff he had almost stopped the car and phoned her for a rant. But something had stopped him. Mainly the nagging feeling that what she'd been driving at added up to a great deal more than what she'd actually said. In that way women's mad logic generally did. But mad logic wasn't logic. Bloody women. Bloody *that* woman.

'God,' he said, throwing himself at the nearest swivel chair and flopping into it. 'Why do women have to analyse so much all the time?'

Danny looked up from the machine and scratched his nose with a screwdriver. Then he nodded.

'It's evolution,' he decided. 'They can't help it. They don't have penises to direct operations.' He put the screwdriver down and smiled. 'You got a problem?'

'Hope Shepherd.'

Danny's smile grew wider.

Jack shook his head. 'She's barking. That's the only word for it. You know, I show up and everything, all friendly and – well, I sort of thought I might ask her if she fancied an evening down the Bay or something – you know – and I all but get my face slapped!'

Danny smirked. 'Perhaps you need to look at your chat-up technique, mate.'

'Pah! I didn't get that far! Listen. Sunday to Tuesday. Is that such a long time? Really? I mean, I tried, didn't I? God, she could have called *me*, couldn't she? I explained about not having her number at home, but it was like I'd driven over her cat or something –'

'She has a cat? It figures. Never trust a woman with an over-attachment to a cat, Jack. Trust me on this. She's –'

'No! God, I don't know. All I know is that I was subjected to a load of bloody bollocks about how she'd decided she didn't want to see me again anyway because though she *did* want to see me again she'd decided that it probably wouldn't be a good *idea* to see me again because I've only just got divorced, so I probably want to shag lots of other women before getting hooked up with someone like her –'

'Which is true.'

'Pah! And because – get this – I'm a *man*. Jesus! Am I up to here with that line! Oh, and how she really shouldn't have gone to bed with me in the first place and that –'

'Hang on! You've shagged her?' Danny's eyes widened. 'Way to go, mate,' he said heartily. He clapped Jack across the back.

Jack scowled. 'Yes. I went to bed with her, OK? Big deal.' What was he saying? It was a very big deal. Bigger than he'd ever imagined it would be.

'Excellent,' said Danny.

'No, not excellent. Because she doesn't do sleeping around, as she calls it, and is apparently far happier doing no sex at all until such time that she meets someone who's already done all that stuff and isn't interested in doing it any more and then she can go out with them instead. Or me. But not now. Just in case. I mean, what the hell's all that about? Does that make any kind of sense to you? Can you believe anyone would get so much in their heads just because someone didn't ring them for two days?'

Danny picked his screwdriver up again and sucked the end of it thoughtfully.

'You've got to remember. Women sulk. And, hey, sounds like she's got you sussed, mate.' He scratched his head. 'Anyway, like I said, if she's got that much baggage – if she's that needy, you're well out of it. On to the next one, I say!'

Jack sprang up from the swivel chair and went to glare out of the window, not at all happy to realise that his original instincts had been proved so comprehensively right. Why hadn't he trusted them in the first place? Like *before* he'd got bloody embroiled with her? Like before, it, hell, it *mattered*. He swung around. 'But who goes around saying all that stuff? Even thinking that stuff? Did she read it in some tit-faced woman's magazine? 'Oh, yes, first principles, ladies. All men are utter bastards and divorced ones are even more dangerous than most. Cavort with them at your peril!'

'She's got a point.'

'Well, thanks a lot, Dan. Cheers.' He slumped against the wall heater. 'I mean why can't I just take her out and see what happens, for Christ's sake? What's with all the Nostradamus bullshit? I can't see into the future, can I? How should I know how I'm going to feel six months down the line? I don't know how I'm going to feel five minutes down the line! Christ! Why can't life just happen?'

Danny chuckled. 'Can't live with 'em, can't live without'em. It's the wonderful world of birds, mate. Listen, the bottom line is that she's right, isn't she? Look, I know you like her –'

'I *liked* her.' He shook his head. ' *Yes*. OK. I *like* her.'

'Yeah, but do you like her enough? Do you like her in a "right that's it, I'm sorted on the sex front till death us do part so no, no, hold me back from any gorgeous young women" kind of way?'

'How should I know? I've only known her a couple of months! I've only been out with her a couple of times! Why should I even have to *think* about stuff like that?'

'You don't. You keep your options open. You hang loose. You hang out. You play the field. Face it. She's not young enough, blonde enough or leggy enough for you, and she knows it. Like I said, you're well out of there.'

Now, sitting in the car outside the TV studios, Jack wished he wasn't divorced. He wished it as wholeheartedly and earnestly as he had ever wished for anything. It was the biggest failure of his life. He didn't want to be married to Lydia any more – which was just as well – but he wished it had all never happened. That he could unravel time and do the whole thing again. Be more careful. More circumspect. More sure of what he wanted. Marry the right person in the first place. For the right reasons. Do whatever it was you needed to do to stay married instead of just blithely assuming it would happen by default. It didn't really matter that it was Lydia who left him. The marriage broke down. It didn't work. So he was as much to blame as she was. He thought about his father and his mother. Married so long and so happily. None of this to deal with. He almost wished they hadn't been. Not really, of course, but if they hadn't – if it hadn't always seemed so effortless – perhaps he wouldn't have taken it so much for granted.

It was almost four. He'd better get on and get in there. He pulled his case from the passenger seat and opened the car door. Danny had been right in the first place. He really wasn't ready to do those sort of relationships again. Hope was right too. She was no different from him, really. Only difference was that she'd already thought about this stuff. Which made her much cleverer than him.

Too clever by half, damn her. And way too demanding. The last thing he needed in his life was another bloody woman flagging up his deficiencies and making him feel he wasn't up to scratch. Too much of that and he'd begin to start believing it again. Wasn't sure he didn't believe it again already. He wasn't having that. Danny talked sense. He *was* well out of it.

He straightened his tie and pushed thoughts of her away. So many women, so little time. He watched idly as a young girl, couldn't be more than late teens or early twenties, half walked, half ran towards a waiting car. Her hair, long and corn-coloured, streamed out behind her in ribbons, and her legs, in brown boots, moved in sinewy rhythm. The automatic twitch from his loins reassured him. Nine out of ten. Now he'd go get that job.

'Hey! The boy done good!'

Allegra had caught up with him on his way back across the car park, all dusky cheeks and lipstick and set-square-aligned teeth. She was dressed in a charcoal suit and a pair of outrageously pointed scarlet stilettos. Not foot shaped at all. Why did women wear shoes like that? Their click-clack across the car park was what had made him turn around. It put him in mind of the crocodile in Peter Pan.

Or, no, perhaps fangs. 'I'm not counting any chickens,' he said.

'No, *really*,' she purred, plucking a speck of something from the lapel of his jacket. 'You made quite an impression. How d'you know all that stuff? I've never seen the Führer quite so animated. Did you know about his Portsmouth fetish or something?'

She hitched her handbag strap higher on her shoulder, and a flash of lilac coloured bra peeped out from the little gap that had appeared between the buttons of her blouse.

'A happy coincidence,' he said, trying not to look at it. 'But like I say, let's wait and see, shall we?'

Allegra turned and slipped her arm through the crook in his. 'It's in the bag,' she said. 'I just know it. Anyway.' She smelled of coconut. 'What are you up to now? Off to pen some sparkling copy for the *Echo*?'

'I'm going home to get out of this suit,' he said, as they reached the first line of cars. He checked his watch. 'And catch the end of the 'Simpsons'.'

'Whoah! You're making me giddy. You sure know how to party, don't you? Look, d'you fancy a drink first, maybe? I've got a few ideas I wanted to run by you. I mean, I'd hate to come between you and Marge, but... '

'I don't know –' he began.

She pouted at him. 'Spoilsport.'

'Oh, go on,' he decided. 'What the hell. Why not.'

They went to the bar in a hotel nearby, Allegra travelling in his car to save them taking both. Jack had known Allegra for some time. They'd worked together back in pre-history, when the world was still flat and he still had a six-pack. And the breakfast slot on Red Dragon, while she was just a lowly researcher on 'South Wales Today'. But she hadn't been around long. She went off to pursue her acting ambitions (was there anyone there who didn't have 'acting ambitions'?) and managed to get a part in some soap or other. Then came back to Wales (all acted out, presumably) three years later, and somehow – Jack didn't know quite how – here she was producing the very programme he wanted in on. Funny how tables got turned.

Back then he'd been married, of course, not that that would have stopped her. She was married too. But that was then, in the days when he thought fidelity was something married people did. Back before Lydia had re-written the rules. After a lengthy affair with the deputy controller of religious programming, Allegra had divorced her husband and hooked up with someone else. A string of someone elses. It hadn't harmed her career one bit. Though Jack didn't believe *all* the rumours about her prodigious talent for making men in powerful places curl up and pant for her, he wasn't impervious to the potency of her charms. It was just that she'd always scared him. She was the kind of woman you wouldn't want to find yourself in a broken lift with. Not if she decided she wanted to seduce you. Not if you wanted to come out alive.

He'd been divorced, what, five months now? – in his flat for longer – and he knew she was chipping away at his defences. An image of Hope's face swam before him as he thought it. He blinked it away. Allegra, like Hope, was a demanding woman. But there were demanding women, and demanding women. Allegra's brand of demanding didn't involve commitment, or fidelity, or love. It just involved sex, pure and simple. On demand.

She insisted on buying the drinks, which addled him. He'd tried to stand his ground, but she was having none of it. That was the thing with women these days – come on too heavy about paying for things and they lobbed the equality card into the arena. Like you were the spokesman for a whole millennium's worth of chauvinist bastards. Perhaps they had a point. He was feeling chopsy. He would very much have liked to have said 'I'm buying the fucking drinks, OK?' but instead he backed down and it made him feel emasculated. Crazy. *Crazy.* He stood beside her, breathing in her tropical-paradise aura while she extracted a stiff twenty pound note from her wallet. He didn't for one moment believe she had any 'ideas' to run by him, unless you counted the one he could see simmering in her eyes now, as she passed him his gin and tonic.

'*Sante,*' she said silkily. 'Here's to us, eh? Here's to you. May the good Lord grant us Des Lynam's viewing figures, and may Portsmouth prevail in all things.'

He clinked glasses with her and smelled the sharp acid tang as he swallowed the top inch of his drink. He wasn't sure why he'd asked for it. But he hadn't felt like sinking a pint right now. And there was no way he'd ever ask for a half.

'Shall we sit down?' he asked, once she'd stashed the wallet away. 'There's a couple of tables free over there.'

'Sitting works for me,' she agreed, leading the way across the bar and giving him an unrestricted view of her tautly-clad bottom as he followed. 'If I have to walk much further in these I might just keel over.' She sat down, slipping the bag from her shoulder and slipping one foot from her shoe. She had big breasts. Jack trained his gaze at his glass. 'So,' she said, crossing her legs and leaning down to massage her stockinged foot. 'How's things with you, then? You've been keeping a very low profile lately.'

'I've been keeping busy,' he corrected her. 'I've got the two columns now, plus that series I'm doing for the *Mail*, plus there's the show, of course.'

'I do listen, you know,' she said, straightening and tutting at him. She slid the other shoe off. 'Often. I like hearing the sound of your voice when I'm working. And how is the lovely Patti?' She re-crossed her long legs at the knee. Jack couldn't help his eyes straying down her shin. A ski-run of smooth honey flesh.

'Patti?' he said. 'She's fine. Er. Lovely.'

'And you?' She inspected his face. 'No developments there, then, I take it?'

Jack almost choked on his drink. The idea that he and Patti might get together romantically was about as ridiculous a notion as the idea that he and Hil might indulge in the odd quickie over her desk.

'Er, no. No developments there,' he assured her. Though there was really no need. She hadn't thought so for an instant.

She was casing the joint, that was all.

By the time they were back at the car, Jack could sense that the input from his loins was fast gaining ground on the input from his brain. And what of it, he thought, as he clicked up the lock and opened the door for her. The only reason he'd been reticent about getting involved with Allegra was that he didn't want to get *involved* with Allegra. The sort of cock-eyed, romanticised, faux-moral thinking that could have earned him a pedigree in lost opportunities with girls. With Hope Shepherd, for certain. Damn her. He hadn't wanted to get involved with *her* either. Well, perhaps now was the time to stop worrying and start living. Danny was right. He did have a penis. Why the hell shouldn't it direct operations for a while? A simplifying system all round. So many women. So little time.

They climbed into the car and he pushed the key into the ignition.

'Allegra,' he said, swivelling in his seat now to face her. 'Are you doing anything Friday evening?'

She leaned across and planted a kiss on his cheek. 'Jack,' she breathed at him, just to the left of his earlobe. 'I really, really thought you'd never ask.'

Chapter 17

Almost the last thing Hope would have wanted to see sitting on her desk when she arrived at work on Thursday morning was an A4 black-and-white picture of Jack Valentine's face. The absolute last (since she was trawling her *bete noires*) would have been Simon wearing nothing but his pants and a come-hither expression, so she did suppose it could be worse, but, even as the lesser of two evils, what she was looking at now did not please her one bit.

'What's this?' she asked Kayleigh, who was standing on a chair across the office, poking a watering can into the dessicated fronds of the spider plant on top of the stationery cupboard. Kayleigh paused in her pouring.

'Hmm?'

'This.' Hope picked it up by its corner, almost reluctant to touch it. 'This thing on my desk.'

Kayleigh climbed down from the chair.

'That's Jack Valentine,' she said.

'Yes, I know that,' Hope said patiently. 'But what's it doing on my desk?'

Kayleigh shrugged. 'I dunno. It's a printout of the jpeg, isn't it?'

'What jpeg?'

'The jpeg he sent through for the posters.'

'What jpeg he sent through for the posters?'

'The one he sent us. For us to put on the posters for the fun run.' She climbed back on to the chair again and shrugged. 'I dunno.'

'Yes, but what's it doing on my desk?'

Kayleigh's expression became agitated. 'I dunno.'

'Well, who put it there?'

'I dunno.'

Hope plonked her handbag on her desk. 'Is Madeleine in yet?'

'I dunno. I'll – '

'No. Don't worry. I'll go check myself.'

*　　　　*　　　　*

Wednesday. Where had Wednesday gone? Oh, yes. She'd spent
the morning helping Kayleigh collate the paperwork for the fun run
registration packs and the afternoon stuffing the envelopes. Other
than that it had been a blur. Thinking mournful and regretful
thoughts about making such a fool of herself over Jack Valentine
was occupying such a substantial part of her waking hours that she
felt she was traversing life as if trapped beneath the surface of an
iced-over pond. She had spent insane amounts of time on Tuesday
evening dithering over whether to call him and apologise, except
that she could think of little to apologise for except for having
become almost debilitatingly obsessed by him.

Yesterday had been a little better. She would come out the
other side of all this nonsense a stronger and better and altogether
less screwed-up person.

Madeleine was sitting in her office eating a banana and flicking
through *Elle Decoration*.

'What's this?' asked Hope, yanking aside the chair that was
holding the door open, and letting it sigh shut behind her.

Madeleine swallowed gracefully.

'What?'

'This picture.' She thrust it in Madeleine's face. 'It was on my
desk.'

Madeleine grinned at her.

'Oh, that. I just thought it would bring a little ray of sunshine
to your morning's endeavours. I've been working on ideas for the
poster. It's rather nice, isn't it? These publicity photos can be so
cheesy. He's very photogenic, isn't he? His face is, anyway. I'll
have to take your word for it about the rest.' She laughed.

Hope cringed. 'Yes, but where did you get it?'

'He emailed it to me.'

'When?'

Madeleine closed the magazine and shrugged. 'I don't know.
Monday? Tuesday? No. It couldn't have been Tuesday. He was
here for the meeting on Tuesday, wasn't he? Monday then. Yes, it
was Monday I spoke to him. Why? Is it important?'

144

'Monday?' It came out as a squeak. 'You spoke to him on *Monday*? Are you sure?'

'Yes.' She grinned at Hope again. Then folded her arms and winked. 'God, of course. Is that it? Well, don't you worry your little head about it, sweetie. I didn't say anything to him. Though why you insist on all this cloak and dagger palaver, I –'

'You definitely spoke to him on Monday?'

She nodded.

'On the phone?'

She nodded again.

'Did you phone *him*?'

'Nope. He –'

'So he phoned *you*?'

'Yes!' Madeleine eased the last knobble of banana from its skin and popped it into her mouth. She chewed on it as she spoke. 'Well, no, of course he didn't. It was you he wanted to speak to, naturally. But you weren't here, so I dealt with it.'

'Dealt with what?'

Madeleine flipped the banana skin back into shape and lobbed it into the bin. 'With the jpeg, of course! He didn't have our email address. What's the –'

'Oh, God. Did he leave a message for me?'

'No.'

'Are you sure?'

'Well, only to let you know he'd called, of course.'

Hope sat down before her legs had a chance to give way beneath her. 'But you *didn't* let me know! God, Maddie, you didn't let me know!'

'Hope!' Madeleine said. 'Remove your hands from your face and stop groaning like you're giving birth to a wardrobe.'

Hope removed her hands from her face and stopped groaning. What was the point? What was the bloody point?

'That's better,' said Madeleine. 'Now. What the hell is the matter?'

'The matter is that I have just made a very serious error of judgement and I think it might be sensible for me to hand in my notice at this point as I have to go and kill myself. Now.'

'What?'

'Or Kayleigh.'

'You can't kill Kayleigh. She's on a government youth training initiative and it wouldn't go down well with the trustees. You can't kill yourself, either. I'm way too busy to have my number two drop dead on me. Now, pull yourself together. Here. Have a banana. And tell me what in heaven's name the problem is.'

Ten past seven and Hope's problem was simple. What to do with three containers full of gunk (bolognaise, chicken Marengo and goulash, according to the stickers) before heading off to Suze and Paul's.

She wrenched irritably at the first till it gave up its contents and they fell, with a guilt-making but nevertheless satisfying plop, into the bin. But how much more satisfying, she thought, as she picked up the next one, if she'd not agreed to go there at all. She could no more stomach Suze right now than her interminable culinary creations.

Hope had never really got on with Suze. Though it was a truism that you didn't get to choose your relatives, Hope had always assumed that her brother, who was nice, would marry someone else who was nice. Why she'd blithely assumed this, she thought now, was a mystery. Iain was a low life. And she'd married *him*.

She extricated the contents from the other containers, then threw them all into the sink and trained the hot tap on them. She didn't not like Suze – she considered it a failing to decide not to like people *per se*. You should try to like everyone, shouldn't you? But in Suze's case, it was taxing. This was partly because Suze was everything Hope was not (tidy, well organised, possessed heaps of bloody Tupperware) but mainly because she was also one of those women who seemed to want to make it their life's work to organise those women who were not like them. There was almost nothing Hope did that Suze did not appear to know how to do better, or, if not better, at least more efficiently, from wallpapering an alcove to making guacamole, to getting toddlers to consume Brussels sprouts. It was only in the losing-of-husbands stakes that Hope had the upper hand and this, of course, made Suze doubly irritating; since Iain had left she'd adopted – or, more accurately, grown into – a whole new set of facial expressions, ones which

146

made it clear that had Hope been just that little bit more like Suze in the first place Iain's infidelities would never have happened.

But families being families and Hope being Hope she had nevertheless agreed to go and have dinner with Paul and Suze, on account of lacking plausible excuses not to, or indeed, sufficient nerve to just say no. Or, indeed, to tell Suze that her perfectly prepared delicacies were now gently defrosting in Hope's bin. She added washing-up-liquid to the containers in the sink. Not a good day.

Earlier, she had explained all to Madeleine, tearfully, and in some detail. Including the bit about telling Jack how she wasn't going to let her heart have unprotected sex with strangers, which made her howl uncontrollably until Madeleine – who was by now laughing like a drain and going 'Priceless! Priceless!' – grabbed her by the wrists and threatened to shake her. She had then made a resolution to ring Jack and apologise. That being the only sensible way forward, as Madeleine saw it. But as the day wore on it felt less and less like an option. What on earth would it achieve? He would just think she was even madder than he must do already. And not only mad, but a stalker. Were she him she was quite sure she'd never want to speak to her again. She didn't want to speak to her again, for God's sake. The bottom line was that she could hardly unsay all the dreadful things she'd said to him, could she? And even if she could, she wasn't entirely sure she didn't, deep down, believe most of them. OK, so he *had* called her on Monday, but what difference did it make? Had she taken the call would she have felt different? Any happier with her actions? Any less insecure? The water bubbled and frothed and she attacked it with her washing-up brush. Did she want to run such a gauntlet? No. When you totted things up, she had made every single move in his direction, and the thought of it still made her blood run cold. Forward was not a directional option. Of that she was almost certain.

If only she could stop replaying and re-writing the script all the time. In her ideal scenario he would have had her home number, and he would have rung her on Sunday, and they would have arranged to meet up again – hell, even *on* Sunday – why not? – and he would have reassured her that no, there was absolutely nothing wrong with her leaping on top of him in such a bestial fashion on their first proper date – which wasn't a date anyway, because he hadn't even asked her to come round – she just *had* – which was… no, no, no! NO!

No. He would have reassured her, would have told her he was just itching to be leapt on in a bestial way, and she would have fallen into his arms and then they would have made love again and everything would have been all right and she wouldn't be feeling as if she'd done something wrong, because she'd be too busy feeling like her life was about to turn around just a little and that there was now A Vestige of Hope.

Or not. Wouldn't she still be writing the script of their ending, even before their relationship had begun?

She finished washing the Tupperware, then rinsed and dried it. But what about *him*? The actual scenario was that he probably turned up on Tuesday worried that she'd snubbed him – what with her not leaving a note or anything on Sunday, and then not returning his call on Monday, and then – oh, God, it was all so obvious now – all that smiling at her and seeming so unsure of himself and bashful and asking her if she was doing anything on Saturday and looking so crestfallen when she'd – oh, it was just so awful it made her want to staple her tongue to the top of the kitchen table – and God, she'd been so, so, so, well – damn, it, frosty. She shovelled the boxes into a Sainsbury's carrier. Late already. She'd have to get her skates on.

Yes. Frosty. He was right. It was the only word for it. She *had* been frosty. And she'd been so hell-bent on letting him know how little she thought of men – of him – Christ, what made her think all those things? – and all he'd done wrong was to fail to have her home telephone number, and the misfortune to have called the office while she was down in bloody Queen Street with Mr sodding bloody Guttridge from the wretched bloody printers.

She snatched up the carrier. It was all just a mess.

Half an hour later, and she still felt no better. She parked, messily, outside Suze and Paul's tidy front garden and stomped up the drive, drenched in gloom.

Chapter 18

Allegra lived in a tree-lined street in Pontcanna, in a tall skinny house with a big beech hedge outside that looked like it could have been in Chelsea. It was the sort of house Jack had himself once fancied occupying, before marriage to Lydia and the absolute necessity for a decent state school and a double garage had had her drag him out to suburbia.

He had bought flowers – a small cellophane-wrapped bunch that he'd found in the supermarket, which he'd chosen because they were all the same colour – mindful of something Lydia had once said about style being all about understatement. They smelled nice, at any rate. Allegra, who had expressed fulsome delight, had then given him a glass of white wine and ushered him into a sparsely furnished living room, the most arresting feature of which was the complete absence of anything that hadn't been put there as decoration. There were bookcases but no books, a sound system but no CDs, coffee tables but no coffee. The only evidence that organic life existed in the place was the flower arrangement thing on the low table in the centre. But even here – it consisted of three stems of some outrageously enormous lily-type plant – the life that had created such magnificent blooms had been all but strangled out, for they were tied up with lengths of artfully twizzled copper wire and set rigid among a kilo of black pebbles. Jack wondered, not for the first time in his life, why on earth anyone would think that was nice. But thinking this, as usual, made him feel out of step with the world, and he now contemplated his own floral offering with dismay. He felt decidedly scruffy in his suede jacket and chinos. He was glad he'd worn a shirt, at least.

'Great! Come to mine first,' she'd said, when he'd suggested a restaurant, and Jack had immediately wished he'd thought of somewhere else. The *Pot au Feu* was currently *the* restaurant to be seen in in Cardiff. Not because the food was anything particularly special, but because it was the result of a much-hyped collaboration between an ex rugby international with a side-line in falling out of pub doorways and the 'cockney charmer' (so it was said) Jimmy Bath, the television embodiment of The New Estuary Cuisine. Jack had only been there once, on the night it had opened – some twot clearly thinking it would make sound business sense to send a freebie to a journo who wrote only about sport – and, like the hack he really was, he hadn't been that impressed.

He swilled wine around his mouth. He'd regretted his choice even before that, in fact, because he actually couldn't afford it right now. And as she went there so often she'd hardly be impressed. But no, she was enthusiasm personified. 'Perfect, perfect!' she'd cooed at him. So here he was.

He'd spent the preceding days in quiet and anxious conversation with himself about what exactly he had hoped to achieve by inviting Allegra out to dinner. It would boost his limp self-esteem to bed her, for certain, but beyond that he really didn't know. Assuming they did have sex (come on, who was he kidding?) would she then expect to be serviced on a regular basis? Would she want to 'go out' with him? And if she did, would he want to 'go out' with her? He'd not quite thought that through. (No. Surely not. Allegra didn't 'go out' with people, did she? She had lovers. Affaires. A different thing altogether, he thought.)

There was a large gilt-framed mirror hanging above the fireplace. He looked at himself and saw the face of a man for whom indecision had long been the lifestyle of choice. It was the face of a worried man, the forehead etched with the rift valleys and tributaries of stress. As if every one of the pounds he'd shed since his divorce had been scooped out specifically with crenelation in mind. Was right now the start of his mid-life crisis?

Another face came to join his. Allegra, who'd answered the door to him in a blink-making firework explosion of a kimono and a large helping of feminine fluster (she was not-yet-ready on purpose, he judged), had returned, primped and painted and ready for action. It may have been an illusion, but she seemed to have even less on now. It was only late March but she had nothing bar a length of green crepe stuff between her and the elements. It could have been a dress, or a top and skirt, or some altogether different variety of womenswear. He wasn't sure. But, whatever it was, it shimmered and plunged and generally moved around her body as if busy making love to her itself.

She popped her chin on his shoulder.

'You look nice,' he said. Meaning it. She generally did.

'So do you,' she said. 'And I love that tie. Is it Hermes?'

'No, it's St Michael's,' he said. Which made her laugh. It was funny. Making Allegra laugh was something that came easily to him. He didn't have to do anything funny. Didn't have to think about it. Didn't they say women got turned on by men that made them laugh? There had to be something in it, when you looked at Woody Allen. Jack didn't think he was particularly funny, but perhaps that was why Allegra wanted to shag him so much. Right now, quite possibly. Because he could feel her hip bone pressed up right against his left buttock.

'And you smell so delicious, too,' she said, giving him his shoulder back and drawing alongside him in front of the mirror to roll her lips around a bit and poke at her hair. He resisted the urge to check if there was now a beige blob on his jacket. Her face did have an awful lot of powder on it. You didn't see it from a distance, but up close she was seriously dusty.

And she seemed shorter tonight than she usually did. She couldn't have been, of course, and she was still in the spindly footwear she tended to favour. And he hadn't grown, so perhaps it was just that she was stooping a bit, in an attempt to appear less scary. Whatever. It was cheering. And very much in her favour. She was scary enough at five foot seven, or whatever height she was.

He drained his wine and she led him out into the hallway, where she put on a long black leather coat. She then spent some moments hoicking the sleeves up her forearms. It made her look as though she intended a veterinary diversion, to shove her arms up a cow's bottom or something. Then she swirled a stripy woollen scarf around her long neck, and announced herself ready to go.

It wasn't a good choice, as it turned out. Almost as soon as they entered the restaurant people started waving and cooing at them – OK, mainly at her – and by the time their drinks arrived (together with a small white dish containing what looked like the droppings of a large, sick rodent, but were apparently date-and-cambozola *hors d'oevres*) it was beginning to feel as if they were not sitting in a restaurant at all, but behind a post office counter on benefit day.

'Chester!' she panted. 'Adelia!' she breathed. 'Oh, Timmy, you old devil! I thought you were in Penang!' It was pretty tedious. Even the arrival of an elderly lady in a poncho saying, 'Goodness – Jack! How lovely to see you! I still listen in, you know,' was insufficient to quell his increasing irritation. He didn't like to tell Allegra that it was only Hil's grandmother, who'd been a presenter there herself in about 1803. Jack didn't like this sort of thing. No. He hated this sort of thing. He had forgotten quite how much.

But Allegra was as astute as she was sociable, and when the oily waiter came up to take their order, she leaned across the table and beckoned him to do likewise.

'Jesus, this is dire, don't you think? Shall we just order main courses and head up to the Stones for a drink after?'

He didn't think she thought it was dire for one minute. You didn't get to know almost the entire clientele of a restaurant unless you frequented it a very great deal. But that didn't matter. He would much rather be in a saloon bar with a pint in his hand. Plus she'd seem less scary in the pub.

Except that when they were finally in the pub, lubricated by two small buckets of wine, she became voluble and not a little amorous. She kept stroking his jacket, which made him feel like a Pekingese dog.

'You,' she said, prodding him in the chest with a fingernail, 'have been a very very naughty boy, you know.'

Jack slurped the head off his pint. 'I have?'

Allegra slipped her hand along his thigh and pinched his flesh. 'For keeping me waiting so long.'

They didn't stay long. Half an hour after they got there a loud and drunken hen party fetched up. The women, who were mainly corpulent and plain, were all wearing big T-shirts with stupid slogans daubed on the back and, to a man, black stockings. The bride-to-be sported a range of flashing accessories and a novelty condom-based hat.

'Home, I think,' announced Allegra, after she'd been barged from behind for the third time. Jack nodded. There was no point in staying anyway. The DJ – who up until then had been tinkering listlessly with chart staples at low volume – clearly felt invigorated at the arrival of so many women in suspenders (the lighting was dim), and had cranked up the music to a level where the only form of communication possible was semaphore or signing. Worse than that, he'd dug out a microphone from somewhere and four of the hen-ees, or whatever they were called, had mounted his rostrum, huddled sweatily around it, and were now massacring 'Angels' so loudly and comprehensively that Jack wouldn't have been surprised if Gabriel himself had flown in from on high to tell them to shut the hell up.

'Home,' he repeated, though unsure which home she meant. But not for long. She had her hand under his jacket and was stroking his bottom.

Allegra's kitchen was like the flight deck of a cartoon spaceship. Everything was either white or silver, bar the contents of the chrome bowl that sat on the work surface. These were lemons and limes and oranges and grapefruit, all so artfully arranged and so unrealistically gleamy that he wasn't sure they weren't plastic. But, no, she plucked out a lime now and lobbed it playfully at him.

'Deal with that, will you, big boy, while I go get the gin?'

So he found a knife and cut two thin slices from the lime, while Allegra poured slugs of gin. Then she splashed in some tonic, said, 'Upstairs, I think, don't you?' and led the way up her long hill of stairs.

She kissed him a bit then, all citrus saliva, then slipped off her stilettos and went around lighting candles, before disappearing, purring at him, into the en suite.

Marooned in the vast bedroom, Jack began to feel more than ever as if he was on the set of a stylish television drama, or strolling through the pages of a glossy magazine. The bed itself, low and wide, was heaped with jewel-coloured cushions and backed with some sort of padded hanging that was strung along an iron pole. It wasn't a bed you could imagine eating toast in.

Allegra returned from the en suite still dressed. He had been concerned on this point. She'd become so pointedly, aggressively sexual by now that he had half expected her to return completely naked, thus depriving him of the initiative and a chance to draw level on the lust front. She had, though, he noticed, removed her tights. Or stockings. He didn't know which. Her slender legs were the colour of French mustard, and her long toes were painted a mother-of-pearl colour, as if they'd been trailed in meringue. She sat on the end of the bed and patted the space beside her.

He sat down and for want of appropriate conversation, began kissing her, still feeling self-conscious perched beside her, but grateful for the presence of an (albeit scant) item of clothing or two that he could concentrate on, twiddle with and generally explore. He duly explored. He slid his hand under the hemline, then back up under the shoulder strap, he pulled it down, he pushed it up, he slipped his fingers under the bit that gave access via her armpit to her breast, and, as her tongue began ferreting around the tops of his molars, he was rewarded with a reassuring flood of intense animal arousal. He kissed her harder still and began to relax. They lay back. It would be all right, after all.

Anxious to take the initiative now, he moved his hand down her arm and brought it inwards to cup her breast in his hand. It was a nice, approachable, un-scary breast, full but not too full – not the sort of breast that would burst out once released, all creamy and challenging, and make him think of his mother. There was no bra under the fabric and he could feel the nipple as a hard, pea-sized nugget under his fingers.

She sat up, suddenly, and then rose to her feet, crossing her arms and gathering up the fabric of the dress before peeling the whole thing up over her head. Now she *was* fully naked and he was still fully dressed. Not good. But she clearly intended to address that disparity, for she straddled his legs immediately and lowered herself into his lap. The breasts, now at face height, with their petits pois nipples, wobbled in front of him while she busied herself removing his tie from his neck. Then she started on the buttons of his shirt – bish bash bosh – and slipped his trouser button from its button hole with a deft flick of her thumb. And then, suddenly, she had her hand on the front of his trousers, clamped around his scrotum like a cricket ball she'd just caught. Jack had always thought – always – that bedroom nirvana would be a woman such as Allegra – God, was she growling? – taking him so masterfully in hand. It was the stuff of dreams, wasn't it? But here it was, happening, and it wasn't. It wasn't at *all*. He remained passive, trying to keep focussed, kissing her still while she tugged down his fly. Her hand began ferreting, fishing around for the waistband of his boxers, then slipping down, warm and deliberate and questing, inching ever closer to her quarry.

'Hello,' she said, grinning at him. 'What have we here? I think our little fella's gone to sleep!'

He had pleaded a need for a wee.

The en suite was dimly lit, tiled in intricate mosaic tiling, and the floor was icy beneath his bare feet. He stood in front of the washbasin, legs slightly apart, hands on hips, and tried very very hard to think deeply sexy thoughts. This had never happened to him, ever, in his life and he didn't know what the hell to do about it.

Never happened to him before in his *life*… He straightened his back. OK. Allegra on the bed… legs spread… What was happening to him? No. Allegra on the bed, legs spread, beckoning him to come and… Completely floppy. Like a jelly baby! Like a… OK. Try Natalie Imbruglia. Or Britney Spears… How could it do that to him? Just straight down. *Down*. Down and out. Not interested. How did this happen? Why couldn't he… OK. Relax. Britney Spears. In one of those little tops, with her airborne breasts jutting, and her stomach, her belly button. Oh, shit. Patti. No. No. This was no good. Limp! As flaccid as a piece of liver. Noooo. No liver. Liver bad. OK. Not Britney Spears, then. The girl who read the weather bulletins on HTV. Her. OK. On screen – suit jacket, prim expression, meteorological expertise. Occluded fronts. Isobars. Scattered showers… whereas *below* screen. That was the one. That one always worked. Nothing on below the south coast of the Isle of Wight…. Come on. Isle of Wight… but not this time, obviously. Non-functional. Come on. Come *on*… He could do this. Surely he could. He looked at his expression in the mirror. It was a frightened expression. It was a terrified expression… It was…

'Jack? Jack, what are you doing in there?' The doorknob squeaked. Shit. He hadn't thought to lock it.

Allegra appeared behind him, ruddy in the gloom. He pressed himself up against the basin. Cold porcelain. Absolutely the worst thing. She was right behind him now. He could feel various soft protuberances making warm contact with his flesh. No. Hang on. This actually felt better. This felt *hopeful*. She snaked an arm around his torso and traced circles across his chest with her fingernail. He could see his own face growing more cheerful. This *was* better. The bed had been a vast and forbidding gladiatorial arena. This was better. This was warm, cosy, arousing. This was – or he could at least think of it as – spontaneous sex in an unusual setting. Yes! The sort of sex Lydia would never have with him. Ever. Yes. This was progress. There was even a mirror! He smiled at it. Smiled at Allegra. Who smiled right on back. Who started inching her fingers back down over his stomach, and – yes! Progress! There might even just be something for her to take in hand when it got there! And then – suddenly – there was a buzzing noise in there with them. And Allegra was purring. He tried to place it. An odd noise. An electric-toothbrush kind of noise.

'What's that?' he said, concentrating to keep the momentum. Her other hand appeared from behind his back in the mirror.

'Why, this!' came the silky reply.

It was supposed to be windy in March, but someone somewhere had tinkered with the settings.

Jack locked the car and ran through the now teeming rain with a copy of the *Western Mail* over his head. Leonard's flat was still in darkness – it was just before midnight, so probably a lock-in at the pub – but the lamplight burned yellow through the net curtains in his own window, lighting the front path just enough for him to see.

He clicked the latch on the gate and walked dejectedly up it, his burning sense of shame now replaced by regret. He should never have done it. He should never have gone there. However much he tried to convince himself otherwise, the simple fact was that he didn't fancy Allegra, and this knowledge – so cruelly and irrefutably now proven – had depressed him far more than he could possibly imagine. She was beautiful by any yardstick, so what was his problem? What kind of man was he that when a desirable woman started taking all her clothes off his principal response was terror?

It had been such an ignominious retreat. She'd been fine. She'd been solicitous and sweet, even. Nice. But there'd really been nothing more to say. He had needed to get home and be alone.

Approaching the front door, he rootled in his jacket pocket for his door key. Bed. Oblivion. That was what he needed. And perhaps a large glass of that brandy that he'd been given at Christmas by the girls in the office. He was just thinking how thinking about Christmas was depressing him further, when he became aware of a noise coming from the porch. The house, being old, and presumably grand in a former life, boasted a brick porch with an arched frontage and red flagstone tiles. There were recesses on either side of the front door, one of which contained the downstairs loo window, and one which contained a small wall-mounted carriage lamp that didn't (and, knowing Leonard, wouldn't ever) contain a bulb.

Hence the blackness. He stopped on the path and listened harder. The pathetic puddle of light in the front garden only made the porch blacker. The noise had stopped. Was he about to be ambushed now? Mugged for his mobile at his own front door?

He took another step forward. This was silly. It was probably just a cat.

'Er… anyone there?' he said.

The noise started again, its components becoming louder and in doing so identifying themselves more readily. The squeak of footwear on flagstone, the rustle of clothing, the grunt of a male voicebox, the exhalation of breath. A tramp? A dopehead?

'Who's that?' Jack said, more sharply. There was no response. 'Leonard?' Of course it wasn't Leonard. He *knew* it wasn't Leonard. Leonard wouldn't lurk in his own porch.

All of a sudden a form emerged. Jack tensed, his fists clenching as the figure approached.

'Thank fuck. About time!' Danny drawled.

Chapter 19

Had Danny been in any way physically compromised – a limb hanging off, say, or a severed artery spurting blood all over Leonard's mahonia, Jack might have felt more sympathetic. But Danny looked every inch fully functional and was, though soaking wet, also grinning rather sheepishly, so Jack's response, now his fear had abated, was to be simply nonplussed. And peeved. He had wanted to get in and brood.

'Are you drunk?' he asked, needlessly. Had Jack spent another moment hovering on his front path it would have been the fumes rather than the movement that would have alerted him to Danny's presence.

'Of course I'm drunk,' he said, now back in the recess of the porch and picking up a large holdall. 'You'd be drunk, believe me.'

Realising that there was a chance that Leonard might fetch up from the pub at this point, Jack hurried to get the front door open and Danny inside. He pushed the door open and waited for Danny to stumble through.

'Though not that drunk,' he was saying, as he stamped the rain from his shoes. 'I was drunker. Some things have remarkable sobering properties.'

Yes, thought Jack bitterly, they do. Not that he was drunk. Perhaps if he had been drunk – a little merry, at any rate – the evening would have turned out differently. No, being drunk was the thing he needed to address. He needed to GET drunk right now.

He followed Danny up the stairs to the flat, and reached past him to turn the key in the lock.

Danny dumped the bag in the hallway and Jack had to step over it to get past.

'So,' he said. 'What's going on?'

Danny smiled mirthlessly. 'Julie's chucked me out.'

Jack digested this statement with a sense of resignation. Every day, it seemed, had an endless capacity for getting worse than it already was.

'Why, exactly?' he said.

'Well... ' Danny scratched his head. 'Look, you got a beer or something?' He strode off in the direction of the kitchen. Jack followed.

'An "or something",' he said. 'Unless you want a warm one.' He peered into the food cupboard (a loose-ish description) and reached inside for a bottle of red. He'd run into Sainsbury's earlier that evening – for the flowers – but hadn't yet unpacked the rest of his few purchases. He hadn't, he thought, wretchedly, been anticipating being home quite so early, or, indeed, so in need of a beer.

Danny was ferreting in the carriers on the worktop. 'I'll shove these in now then, shall I?' indicating the two four packs he now held in his hand. Jack began opening the red.

'Well?'

Danny opened the fridge door, which made his normal pallor look even more ghoulish. Like he was something that had been yanked up from the ocean floor by David Attenborough. He put the beers in.

'I have been rumbled,' he said, in tones of great gravity.

'Rumbled?' God – had Danny been unfaithful to Julie? '*Rumbled?*' he said again.

Danny nodded. 'She has, rather unfortunately, found my little stash.'

Jack eased the cork from the wine bottle.

'Stash? What stash?'

'Well, I say stash, but I'm not being strictly accurate. Given that it's all on the hard drive.'

The penny dropped. 'Porn, then.'

'Yes, porn. Come on, get that wine poured, will you?'

It had, apparently, only ever been a matter of time, and, boy, was he was kicking himself about it. Since Julie had become secretary of the Cefn Melin Little Sprouts mother and toddler group, she'd developed a taste for home publishing. She produced a monthly newsletter, created posters for events and generally fiddled about in that way women did. It had been while in the process of trying to access the photos from the Easter Hunt 'n Cookout (which she had taken with Danny's digital camera and now wanted to cut and paste into her 'Sprout and About' wall display) that she had inadvertently stumbled upon a number of other photographic files – ones that didn't include nappies or potties or bottles, although plenty of bottoms and breasts. It being Friday, and Danny at work, she'd had several uninterrupted hours in which to explore a great deal of the canon – her horror growing more acute with every click of the mouse. The first Danny had known of her discovery was when he'd arrived home from work to be welcomed with the greeting 'I hate you, you disgusting pig'.

She'd said nothing more then. But the minute their eldest was tucked up in bed, she'd let rip.

Danny glugged down the last of his wine and held the glass out for a refill.

'And then some. But I mean, for Christ's sake! It's only bloody pictures!'

Jack pulled out the stool and sat on it.

'Yeah, but what sort of pictures?'

Danny looked affronted. 'God, mate, what do you take me for? Nothing illegal or anything. Just women. Nothing heavy. Nothing grim. But the way she went on, you'd think I'd been out and shagged every woman in Cardiff!' He shook his head sadly. 'I wish!'

'Oh dear,' said Jack, not really knowing what else he could say. His own forays up to the top shelf had been few. He'd read his fair share of *Playboy* and *Razzle* as a teenager, but marriage and a pathological terror of actually making such purchases had all but expunged such urges from his life. There'd been one video – *Mandy goes to Hollywood*, that was it – that some guy on his MA course had lent him. He'd taken it home for Lydia and him to watch together, but there'd been so much eye-popping debauchery in it (the scene with the garden hose remained wincingly vivid) that Lydia had pronounced herself queasy and retired to bed with a headache and an improving book.

He had no particular problems with it. Not really. He'd even been to a lap-dancing club with some of the boys at work. Though the proximity of so much female flesh on display made him so anxious about getting an unstoppable hard-on that he had a Pavlovian droop for the best part of a week, he had quite enjoyed it. But it had always seemed to him (perhaps not always, but certainly since the breakdown of his own marriage, and most definitely in its aftermath) that there was something terribly sad about the idea of a grown man sitting hunched over a computer screen looking at other people having sex. Grim or not, it felt grim. Like the worst kind of substitute for real life. For real lovemaking. So however non-existent his own sex life had become, he'd never felt comfortable about doing it himself. Perhaps that was his problem. Perhaps he was too idealistic. Perhaps he *was* out of step with the rest of the world.

Danny stomped off into the living room and plonked himself on the sofa. Jack followed.

'Oh dear,' he said again.

Danny stared moodily into his half-empty glass. ' It's my own stupid fault,' he said. 'Downloading stuff.'

'Yes, why d'you *do* that? Why couldn't you just, well, look at it and be done with it?'

Danny shrugged. 'What planet is she on, eh? I mean, what does she think I do? What does she think blokes do, period? I'm lucky if she lets me near her most of the time. What does she expect me to do, for God's sake? I'm not a bloody monk! I mean, what would she rather?' He jabbed a finger in the air. 'That's what I told her. What *exactly* would she rather? Would she rather I went down Caroline Street and picked up a prostitute? Or went off and had an affair?'

'You said that to her? I bet that didn't go down too well.'

'Too bloody right it didn't.' He nodded towards the open doorway, where his holdall still sat, bulging ominously, on the floor. 'That's what she's told me to go and do.' He stood up again. 'Shall I go and check on those beers? I can't drink any more of this stuff.'

'If you like,' said Jack. 'They won't be cold yet, though.' He didn't feel like a beer now. Didn't feel like drinking any more. Perhaps he'd make himself a coffee. He followed Danny into the kitchen.

'She'll calm down,' he said. 'Once she's thought it through.'

Danny turned around to face him. 'That's just it,' he said. 'She has thought it through. She's had all day to think it through and she's decided I'm a disgusting pig. It's –' He sighed, heavily. 'It's just, you know, so bloody depressing. It's like we live in totally different places in our heads. I always thought Jules was – look, I'm not stupid. I know she's never been particularly adventurous about sex and I know it's never been such a big deal for her. But I can't help thinking there must be something fundamentally wrong about a relationship where we can't talk sensibly about such a basic life function. Can't talk about it at all, in fact. We don't, you know. Not ever. When we were younger, and I'd look at a girl, or make a comment about her legs or something – as you do – I always thought it was rather nice when Jules got all huffy about it. It made me feel good. It made me feel wanted. It was what it was all about. Being with someone. So I learned to keep my mouth shut, so I wouldn't upset her. But, I don't know, the more I think about it, the more I can't help feeling it's all wrong. I feel as if she doesn't accept me as a person. That there's a whole part of me she finds distasteful but just puts up with. I tried to explain it to her, you know? Tried to make her understand that just because I can look at an attractive woman and fantasise about what it would be like to have sex with her, it doesn't mean I love *her* any less. It doesn't mean I actually want to. Doesn't mean I would. It's just normal. Isn't it?' Jack nodded. 'But she can't see it.' He shook his head. 'She really can't see it. It isn't about feeling possessive. I used to think it was about feeling possessive. But it's not. She really does believe it's all a bit unsavoury. That thinking about sex is a bit unsavoury. That *I'm* a bit unsavoury. That I'm bad.'

'A disgusting pig.'

'A disgusting pig.' He pulled out the can again and tested it against his cheek. 'I mean, how would you feel if someone described *you* like that?'

Jack thought that half the population had been describing the other half of the population pretty much like that since time began. Slugs and snails. That was it. Slugs and snails and puppy dogs' tails. Danny was right. It was depressing.

'I'm sure she doesn't mean it. I mean, I'm sure she did at the time, but it's just words. That's all. Said in the heat of the moment. And, well, she's not long had a baby, has she? Women go off sex when they have babies. It's their hormones. They can't help it.' So Lydia had told him, at any rate. Some pretty potent hormones, in her case. They'd lasted the best part of a year.

162

He wished he knew Julie better. They'd never socialised much as couples. Since it became clear there were to be no further little Valentines, Lydia didn't like being around women with more babies than she had. All he really knew of Julie was that she seemed a quiet, fairly unremarkable woman, who got on, rather stoically, with the business of bringing up her family. But you never did know with most people.

'So,' he said. 'What are you going to do?'

Danny opened the can and foam surged over the top. 'Kip here. If that's all right. Till she's calmed down a bit.'

Jack thought of something. 'Hang on. What about next Saturday?' Their youngest, Fergus, was about to be baptised. And Jack was to be godfather. Which scared him a little, moved though he was to have been asked.

'What about next Saturday?'

'Isn't it the christening next Saturday?'

Danny scowled. 'Next Saturday week. In theory.' He slurped noisily at the overspill and stared at the carpet.

'It *will* be OK, mate,' Jack told him. 'You'll see. These things blow over. You'll sort it.'

The words were empty platitudes. He didn't know any such thing to be true. But he hoped it, hoped it more sincerely than Danny knew. He gave him a reassuring squeeze on his forearm.

'You'll sort it,' he said again. 'And in the meantime you can have Ollie's bed. She knows where you are, and –'

'No she doesn't.'

'Haven't you rung her?'

'No, I fucking haven't.'

'Shouldn't you?'

'No.'

'Don't you think –'

'*No*. She can ring me on my mobile if she wants me.' He upended the can to his lips and walked back into the living room, shoulders drooped. 'Where were you, anyway? I've been trying to get you all evening.'

Jack followed him. 'I was out having dinner.'

'Really? With who?'

Jack hesitated a second. 'Allegra.'

Danny turned around, looking suddenly animated. 'What – Staunton?' Jack nodded. Danny rolled his eyes. 'Tsk! You lucky bugger. Now there's someone I wouldn't kick out of bed. There's someone –' he waggled the can towards Jack, 'who definitely wouldn't call a man a disgusting pig. Why can't all women be like that? Any joy?'

Jack, all the while that Danny had been talking, had been readying himself for this question. He could, of course, not have mentioned Allegra at all. He hadn't at work. He could easily have made something up. But what was the point? Half the BBC had been at the bloody restaurant. It would be all over the office by Monday.

'Joy?' he asked, to give himself a moment.

Danny gave him what his mother would have described as an old-fashioned look. Though it might have been a leer. 'Matey-boy, you don't take Allegra Staunton out to dinner without having at least a small hope of there being a shag on the menu somewhere.'

'I guess not.' He felt very tired, all of a sudden. It was all too much stress. Too much stress and manoeuvring.

Danny raised his eyebrows. 'So?'

'So, no,' he replied. 'No joy.'

It had mainly – no, wholly – been the fault of Allegra's vibrator. The anxiety had already been present, to be sure, but up until she'd bought that wretched thing out, he'd thought! or at least hoped, he could ride it. But not then. After that it had become almost blackly comic. She'd do whatever he fancied with it, she'd told him. Whatever he liked. And then she'd started twerbling on about prostates or something, and how nice he might find it if she... He'd had to go then. Had to dress and just go.

Funny he should be sitting here talking to Danny about sex and pornography. He'd always thought he'd rather enjoy watching a woman doing things to herself. But did he? As for her other idea... God. There was so much sexual stuff that he'd taken for granted while it was all safely hypothetical – that he'd be up for a threesome, that if Liz Hurley walked into the studio and offered him her body he'd have her up against a wall in a flash, that wife-swapping between interested parties was something he wouldn't *absolutely* rule out – but now it all seemed risible. Ridiculous and stupid and risible. He didn't really want any of those things – it was just years of conditioning and blokey banter and pub lore. All he actually wanted right now was someone to love him and cherish him. Someone to help him make dinner, choose a new rug with him, stroll in the woods with him. Someone to love. Which meant his penis – that most cruelly treacherous part of his anatomy – was not actually capable of directing him anywhere he really wanted to go.

Which was why it had failed him this evening.

'Bloody women, eh?' said Danny now. He added a tut, and Jack realised he was saying it off the back of an erroneous assumption. That Danny thought it must have been Allegra and not him who had bought the evening to an unconsummated close. This struck him as sad. Even sadder than Julie finding his porn stash. It had obviously not occurred to Danny that it might be Jack. Never occurred to him that Jack wouldn't have been able to perform. Or if it had crossed Danny's mind, it would not be acknowledged and therefore would not be discussed. Which, when you thought about it, Jack decided with painful clarity, was the really sad thing about men.

'Bloody women,' he agreed, grateful to collude in this falsehood nevertheless. 'I'll go sort the bed out for you, mate.'

Lying sleepless in his own bed at three-thirty in the morning, Jack felt as wretched as he thought it was possible to feel. More wretched, he realised, than he had at any point during or after the divorce. At that time, though it was often pretty grisly, there had at least begun to blossom in him a keen sense of relief. They would not need to keep up the pretence any more. They could communicate at last in a currency other than one of denial and simmering resentment. And as for afterwards – well, after the divorce, there had been the future to look forward to, hadn't there? Thoughts of a different and better life. Women. Attraction. Affection. He'd felt liberated. Liberated from Lydia's expectations of him. Free to pursue his real goals – goals that had all but been quashed with her. His coaching, his writing. The real things he loved. Sure he'd be poorer, but as he had always wanted and needed money far less than Lydia had, it didn't worry him unduly. Another relief. Their financial personalities were perhaps even less well matched than their sexual ones, and his lack of financial ambition had irritated her, he knew. Funny, then, that this TV opportunity should come along now. Funny that after years of steady-state salary and the quiet brown-envelope anxiety of the freelancer, he would perhaps be better off now than at any point in his life. He could tell by her expression the last time he had seen her – and told her – that she thought he had actually planned things this way.

What he hadn't expected, all this time down the line, was that something so commonplace, so unremarkable, so ordinary as not being able to hang on to an erection, should affect him so profoundly. What exactly had happened there? He imagined himself as a participant in a quietly earnest documentary, where men with shadowed faces talked candidly (though anonymously, naturally) about the shame and indignity of their potency problems, intercut with cameos from patient, understanding wives. Was this him now? Was this the next step? This shift from the animal to the essentially cerebral? There was no doubt that it had been his brain which had damned him. 'Overruled, OK, penis? Overruled, I say!' And his penis, the wimp, had obeyed.

But that was the thing about sex. He'd spent most of his life working so damn bloody hard to try and get some. As a teenager (and a reasonably good-looking one – if only he'd realised it then) he had had no shortage of girls to go out with. Trouble was, the ones he *wanted* to go out with were generally of the 'kiss on the first date, bra on the third or fourth, knickers after four months (if you were lucky), and sorry, but that's your lot' variety. And they'd only touch him on the outside of his trousers, which always struck him as wildly unfair.

University had been better – he was a classic late-developer – but after losing his virginity while too drunk to notice (ironically, no erection difficulties in those days – it would never go *down*) and having no more than three unremarkable encounters with girls he felt bad about screwing, he'd met Lydia, who was at that time doing anthropology and whose passionate debating style and breadth of knowledge about indigenous populations and global politics and apartheid had somehow led him to reach the mistaken conclusion that this fiery, committed and intelligent girl just had to be the one for him. (Two years after her degree she had swapped

166

the dungarees and spiky rhetoric for a job as a marketing assistant at a cruise line, the fire in her belly all gone. But where?)

In any event, sex after that had been on a steadily downward trajectory. Twice a day for six months, twice a week for six months, and then they'd somehow slipped into the routine of him wanting sex and cajoling her to have it, with varying degrees of participation and success. Jack wondered if Lydia was experiencing a sexual renaissance with the man who should have been on the divorce papers.

Was that his problem? Was he so conditioned to sex being something he had to work hard at getting that when offered to him freely by a woman with her own sexual agenda, his brain couldn't cope? But how could that be? Hope Shepherd (damn her) had been all over him, hadn't she? And his reproductive equipment had been truly joyous to behold – unstoppable, rampant, efficient, enduring – moreover, he recalled with some regret (*damn* her, damn *him* – how had he screwed that one up so completely?) – it had barely stopped twitching at the memory all week.

Well, it had certainly stopped twitching now. That had been all about *her*. So wild and passionate, but so feminine with it. So self-conscious. So tender. So sweet. Not that he wanted to dominate anyone, but her incredulity that he should awaken such behaviour in her had been the greatest aphrodisiac of all. Because it made him feel strong. Made him feel like a man.

Jack sat up and rubbed at his eyes with his palms. That was it, wasn't it? Yes, Allegra was beautiful. Yes, she was sexy. Yes, she was all those things that inhabit male fantasies, and more. But she had made him feel emasculated. With her slick, film star home, that made him feel poor and her seem so powerful; with her self-assurance, her ease, her practised hands on his body; 'I know what *you* need… ' It made him cringe to recall it. He knew what *she* needed too, but he couldn't supply it. Not for all her sex toys, her candles, her velvet-smooth, almost hairless body. Everything about her was so perfectly, artfully, libidinously arranged. There was nothing he could give her but his raw masculinity. And that one thing, that unremarkable constant, his maleness, had shrunk back, inadequate. Recoiled.

He drank some water then lay back against the pillows, tucking his laced hands behind his head. He had always taken his male state for granted. That he would pursue a woman (oh ho, hypothesise, why don't you, Jack?) and if she responded – as, well… well, Hope Shepherd had – *that* was the thing that governed the process. Gave it momentum. With Allegra he had felt like a rabbit caught in headlamps. Scrutinised. Assessed. Not masculine at all. Biology had more hold on humanity, he decided, than sophisticated people sometimes gave it credit for.

Basic biology. He thought about the second time he had made love to Hope Shepherd. A little on the bed and a great deal on the floor. He remembered how he'd tugged a pillow from the bed and tucked it behind her head so she wouldn't bang it against the bedside table leg. He recalled the exact contours of her face as she'd smiled up at him and mouthed the words 'thank you'. Thinking this caused his own biology to respond now, gloriously, and quite without direction. He considered the phenomenon, the autonomy of the process, even as he lay there and surrendered himself to its images and sensations, at four a.m., in the dark, with the rain lashing down outside. Here was her face now. And here was her body. Basic biology. *QED*.

Damn her. *Damn* her, he thought.

Chapter 20

Damn Jack Valentine, thought Hope. *Damn* him. It really was high time she stopped mooning over him and started taking charge of her life. It was getting on for six and she hadn't even showered yet, and she really did not want to go to Paul and Suze's pot luck party. Tom did not want to go to Paul and Suze's pot luck party. Chloe did not want to go to Paul and Suze's pot luck party. Truth be known, Paul and Suze probably didn't even want them to go to Paul and Suze's pot luck party. Yet what was she doing right now? Cancelling? No, she was standing in her kitchen, still damp and sweaty from her run with Simon, cutting small resistant vegetable items into amusing shapes with a sharp knife. And that, she thought irritably, should have been another New Year's resolution. Never say 'anything I can do to help?' to a person who keeps an itinerary in her knickers.

Her mother, naturally, was very much looking forward to Paul and Suze's pot luck party, and had been saying so at roughly five-minute intervals, in order, Hope suspected, to 'jolly her along'. Which was because, when she had arrived mid-afternoon, she had been bearing news.

'Hmm,' she'd said, in that way she had that seemed to indicate she'd already started the conversation some minutes before she'd actually arrived. 'You've had words then?'

Hope, who hadn't had the slightest idea who or what she was talking about, had raised her eyebrows in enquiry.

'You and Suze,' her mother had elaborated. 'She sounded terribly upset.'

Hope was entirely mystified by this, but also suddenly alert. The conjunction of the words 'Suze' and 'upset' in one sentence was too daunting a prospect to ignore.

'First I've heard of it,' she'd said. 'What about?'

'About the casseroles, of course. You know, you really could give her a little more credit, Hope. She's always been very kind to you. It's very hurtful. I had her on the phone in tears.'

A sliver of recall wormed its way into Hope's mind. 'Hang *on*. Hang on just one minute, Mother. Words? What 'words' do you refer to, precisely?'

Her mother had fastened her eye on Hope then, the better to gauge her reaction. 'Now don't let's go getting all uppity, dear. I only thought I'd mention it.'

Right. Things were beginning to make sense. 'Oh, I'm *with* you,' she said with elaborate emphasis. 'Casseroles, eh? Well, if we're talking about the casseroles I think we're talking about, the only words *I* exchanged were entirely non-combative. Something – let me see – along the lines of her saying "I've made another couple of casseroles for you", and me saying "thanks ever so, Suze, but you know, I'd feel awful taking them from you, because Tom and Chloe don't actually like puy lentils or borlotti beans – or whatever pulse it was she'd put in them – and it seems such a shame for them to go to waste". And then –' she could feel the colour rising in her cheeks, 'yes, *I* remember. *Her* saying – no, *sniffing* – something along the lines of, "well if you'd *told* me that, I could have made them something else, couldn't I?" And me saying – let me get this right – yes, that was it. That as I hadn't *known* she'd been busy making more casseroles for us, I was hardly in a position to do that, was I? And that, grateful as I was for her thoughtfulness, perhaps it was high time I started making my own casseroles, instead of putting her to so much bother. I think she answered that by saying – no, sniffing again – "well, if that's how you feel… " in that conversation-stopping way she's so good at. So yes. OK. Words. But *hers*. Not mine.' She glared at her mother. 'OK?'

'But –'

'And as far as I'm concerned I should have done it months ago. I've spent way too much of the last couple of years meekly letting her tell me how to run my life. Oh, yes! I missed a bit! Yes. She also pointed out that she'd only put the pulses in because she wanted to make sure they were getting a balanced diet. Bloody cheek! Frankly, Mother, with the day I'd had, she's lucky I didn't punch her.'

There was a brief, and clearly digestatory, silence. 'Oh.'

Hope planted a hand on each hip. 'Quite. Well now, aren't we going to have a lovely time this evening? In fact, tell you what? How about I just don't go?'

Hope's mother looked horrified.

'You can't do that! Then she'd know I told you! She specifically asked me not to say anything!'

'But you did.'

Hope's mother looked stricken. 'Please, Hope. You know how sensitive she is. She would hate to think she'd upset you.'

'Yeah, right, Mum.'

'No really.' She'd stood in the hall all the while, still in her coat. But she took it off now, with an air of maternal resignation.' Look, I know she can get on your nerves at times. I know she can seem a bit, well, overbearing and bossy. But she doesn't mean anything by it. It's just her way. She's not like that underneath. She means well, really she does. Don't be too hard on her, love. Come on.'

'Hard on her?' Hope spluttered. 'Me? Hard on *her*? Mother, are we talking about the same person?'

Her mother tutted. 'I just think you could be a little more charitable towards her, that's all.'

'Oh, you do, do you? Well thanks for the character reference.'

Her mother looked defiant. 'Now you're just being silly.'

'I am not being silly! God, you sound like her now!' Hope grimaced. 'You really have no idea, do you? There's hardly a week goes by when she's not bustling in, telling me what to do, pointing out my failings as a mother – not to mention as a wife – chipping away all the time at my self-esteem. Have you any idea how that feels? Have you? We're not all as perfect as she is, OK? We know. We don't need reminding. Perhaps she'd like to spend some time thinking about *that*.'

'I only said –'

'Well don't, OK?'

'You're a very good mother.'

'Don't start.'

'You *are*. How can you even think such nonsense? You're –'

'Mother, I said don't start.'

'All right.'

'All right.'

'Shall I put the kettle on, dear?'

That had been that, and Hope had been for her run, and she had calmed down a little, and yes, OK, they would all go to the party. What was the point of not going? She was too tired, too bored to have a family scene. Order restored, her mother had since been flitting around the kitchen, in that flitty way that set Hope's teeth on edge at the best of times, but which she would try, strenuously, to ignore today.

Hope's mother flitted particularly irritatingly whenever a social engagement with Paul and Suze loomed, even without revelations like today's. And later she'd become manic, to boot, laughing too loudly at things that weren't funny and washing up like a woman with a wet-crockery fetish. Hope really didn't mind that her mother was her brother and sister-in-law's doormat – that was entirely her business. But she was sick and tired, frankly, of being expected to be likewise. To worship at the temple of Suze. This had been a small victory. Yes, she'd caved in and would go to the party, but at least she wouldn't be taking a bloody casserole home.

Hope's mother, who had at last stopped flitting and come to help Hope with the food, executed an impressive radish rose and lobbed it into the bowl in the sink.

'He seems like a nice man,' she observed in her sly way. 'Very chatty. Not at all like you described.'

Though she had been adamant that it would not happen, Hope had been forced to relent in the matter of Simon driving over to take her to the park for their runs. This was the second time now, and the complicating factor of her mother being in the house (and like a whippet whenever the doorbell rang) meant that he'd now stepped over the threshold. She should have stuck to her guns, she knew she should have. But Simon had a crafty way of creeping up on her absolutes. It was madness, he'd said, for him not to collect her. He'd be driving almost past her house on his way there, and was really more than happy to drop her back as well. There were only so many times you could politely say 'it's too much bother for you' and no occasion whatsoever when you could less politely change tack and say 'I just don't want you to – *OK?*' in its place.

'He *is* a nice man, Mum, and I never described him differently.'

Her mother sniffed. 'Yes you did, dear. You made him sound very dull. Oh, yes. And talking about men friends –'

'We were?'

'We were. I remember what it was I was going to tell you now.' She reached across Hope and picked up a cherry tomato. Why was it ever necessary to do *anything* with a cherry tomato? 'You'll never guess who Biddie saw in the *Pot au* whatsit the other day.'

Hope glanced across at her mother.

'Biddie?'

'You know – Biddie Hepplewhite from the flower club. She goes there with her daughter.'

'Lucky her,' observed Hope, trowelling away at a mushroom and scowling.

'Oh, I don't know about that. She says the food is a Shakespearean tragedy. Anyway, the point is, she saw your Jack Valentine in there.'

Hope put the distressed mushroom in the dish with the others and picked up another. Then thought better of it, put the mushroom down and picked up her glass of wine. Hell, her mother was driving, wasn't she? She swallowed a mouthful. 'Mum, he is not *my* Jack Valentine.'

'No, I know, dear. More's the pity.' She shook her head. Hope had told her nothing beyond the black eye at the football match. 'But you know what I mean,' her mother chided. 'Anyway, he was there with that woman who used to be in Emmerdale. What *was* her name? Biddie did tell me. You know. The one who played the veterinary receptionist and ran off with the communicable diseases inspector they sent in to sort out the pigs.'

Hope swallowed another mouthful of wine. A bigger one. 'Allegra Staunton.'

'That's it! Well done! Allegra Staunton. Yes, her.'

It didn't mean anything. They could have been having a meeting. Quite easily, in fact. These broadcasting types kept funny hours, didn't they?

And, bloody hell, what was it to her, anyway? OK, she had still been toying with the idea of calling him. But that was all.

173

Every reservation in the entire book of reservations had so far stayed her hand on the receiver, and, well, this unexpected piece of intelligence was truly a gift. Her unspoken questions had been answered now, hadn't they? Just as she'd predicted. Just as she'd feared. Forget the self-pity. The satisfaction of having been proved right so conclusively almost made her feel jaunty. Paul and Suze's pot luck party notwithstanding.

'Isn't that lovely!' trilled Suze when, some ninety minutes later, they arrived at the house.

Hope pushed the tray of crudités towards her and reminded Tom and Chloe crisply about removing their footwear, even as they were doing so. Why did she do that? Why the need for automatic pre-emptive strikes? She must stop doing it.

There were already enough trainers outside the front door to stock a small shoe shop, into which heap Chloe cheerfully lobbed hers, while Tom, scowling pointedly, because his were new and very precious, stepped inside in his socks and placed his own ones at the foot of the stairs.

'And how are you two?' enquired Suze now, flicking her pony tail and turning to march off down the hallway. It was expected, and invariably achieved, that they'd follow. A curious ritual. It always put Hope in mind of mother goose.

'We lost one of our stick insects today,' said Chloe, who had not yet told Hope this. 'I've had to leave privet leaves all round the house.'

'My Lord, how grisly!' came back the laughing response. 'Now you two, let's see – they had now reached the kitchen – a quick glass of Ribena before you go and join the fray?'

Tom, third in the crocodile, glanced back at Hope with his eyebrows aloft. She shook her head minutely, knowing what was coming. He raised his eyebrows further. He was now six inches taller than both of them, and eyed the Ikea plastic cups that stood in a rainbow row on the table with enough pained derision to fell a rhino.

'Actually, Auntie Suze, I don't like Ribena. Er… any chance I could have a beer?'

Had Paul not stepped into the kitchen at this point, Hope would doubtless have inserted a reedy 'certainly not!' into the conversation – Suze's face was already gearing itself up to express rigorous disapproval, and she was anxious to forestall it – but he had, and now clapped his nephew on the back.

'Course you can, mate,' he said, ignoring his wife's look of horror. 'Howdy, sis,' he added, clapping Hope on the back as well. 'How's your love life?'

Paul had asked this question with tedious regularity from the day after her divorce had come through. She wondered quite how he'd respond if she told him. In detail. In millilitres of body fluids exchanged, if he bloody liked. He went across to the fridge and pulled out a bottle of something European and duty-free and held it out to Tom.

'Marvellous,' she answered, smiling sweetly at Suze. 'I'll have one of those too, if I may. How's yours?'

Chapter 21

'Marvellous,' Jack said. 'That's really good news, mate.'

It had been touch and go, and a trifle overcrowded in the bathroom, but good sense had prevailed and the lovely Julie had relented by the Thursday. Not, she'd been at pains to point out, because she'd completely forgiven Danny his misdemeanours, but simply because christening slots were hard to come by and it wouldn't sit well with the vicar if she had to cancel at such short notice.

Danny had been uncharacteristically quiet and thoughtful about it.

'You think?' he answered, while packing his few things into his holdall. 'I'm not so sure, mate. I can still see me here.'

Jack, just home from work and swigging on a Becks, and still in thoughtful mode about his excuse for a life, scanned the shabby room and raised his eyebrows.

'You can?'

'I was thinking about something you said to me once. Way back. When Lydia first said she wanted to divorce you. You said something about feeling you'd lived half your life feeling not quite up to scratch. Like something she'd just had to tolerate, like eczema. It's a bit of word, isn't it?'

'What, eczema?'

'No. Tolerate.'

Jack shrugged. 'I guess.'

'I mean, that's what it's really all about, isn't it? With men and women. That women just 'tolerate' men these days. Don't much need them. Don't particularly want them. Just tolerate them because they have to.'

'But that's it. They don't have to any more. Not if they don't want to. Lydia didn't, did she?'

He looked searchingly at Jack. 'Yes, but doesn't that bother you?'

Jack shrugged. He was way past analysing all the reasons why his marriage had ended. And wearier still of attributing so much of it to his deficiencies as a husband. He'd had more than enough of that before it had ended, despite Lydia prefacing every lecture she gave him with the words 'Jack this isn't about *you*, you know. It's about *me*. You must understand that.' Blah blah blah. She had a special face for that one and it wasn't dissimilar to the one a priest might adopt for speaking to a condemned felon. Besides, the football would be coming on soon.

And at least Danny had a wife to go home to. She was probably whipping up a moussaka even now. 'No,' he said. 'Not unduly. It's not all women. It's just some women.'

'Yeah, like Jules. I mean, you know what she said? That she could just about tolerate my 'wandering eye', but that she really couldn't tolerate any more of that computer stuff. Well, I'm not sure I want to be tolerated. I feel like I'm on bloody probation. Is that right? Is it?'

Jack passed him a pair of balled socks that had rolled away across the carpet.

'She loves you, mate. You know she does. She's just, I don't know, a bit twitchy about sex. She'll come round. What time's she expecting you?'

On the Friday, a whole week since the Allegra debacle, Jack still felt he hadn't moved on. What he needed, he decided, was to get himself out of the rut he was slipping into. He needed to find a new place in the world. More pressingly, he needed to find himself a new place in which to live. To which end he'd popped into an estate agent's on his way home from work. The girl in there, a pleasant twenty-something with a dip-dyed scarlet ponytail, had been friendly, effusive even, when he'd told her his name. She'd printed off several colour copies of property details for him and told him her mother listened to his show every day and thought he was really, really lovely.

Jack, for whom this particular endorsement was beginning to feel more than ever like a hail of Sanatogen bottles raining on his unprotected head, was reminded (via trying hard to remind himself that he was not old and worn out but young and fit and virile) of Allegra. She hadn't called him, and he wasn't sure whether this was a good thing, a bad thing, or something to which he should ascribe no particular importance. (There was no reason to hear about the TV show yet – they'd already written to tell him they'd be getting in touch again next week.) And he wasn't sure whether to call her. If he did he'd feel obliged to have a big grown-up talk with her, either attempting a further assignation, which was pointless, or explaining that while he found her immensely attractive, that he wasn't ready for – well, *that* – right now. While this option had the benefit of being honest and less scary, it might not augur well for his TV career. A woman scorned and all that. What to do?

And now it was Saturday and he was about to become a godfather. Almost eleven. He'd better get a move on. Better think himself into the role.

Jack had been to only one christening in his life – Ollie's – and wasn't sure what to expect. He'd spent some time in town the preceding week, trying, and largely failing, to decide what sort of gift would be appropriate for him to give this new charge. His gut instinct was for a seriously good football – Danny would appreciate that – but logic told him this would not go down half so well with Julie, so, in the end, with the help of a kindly lady in the jewellers, he'd plumped for a little silver musical money box, which tinkled *Finlandia* when you wound it up, and had an assortment of silver forest animals gathered around a tree stump on the top. No chipmunks. He so wished he could stop thinking about Hope. It was doing him no good at all.

The local church – less than a mile from his flat – was a Norman affair, with towering cedars in a rank around the graveyard and a daffodil-filled garden at the side. A big banner affixed to the low wall outside exhorted him to come and find out what life was really all about, but as this involved telephoning someone called Peggy for a friendly chat and/or joining their informal group for tea and discussion on a Tuesday (or so the permanent marker squiggles written below told him) he felt he probably wouldn't find useful answers there.

He wasn't sure he wanted to know, anyway. He had been doing too much thinking lately as it was. Jack wasn't given to bouts of despondency and depression. But, right now, in this little cache of existence in which he had found himself, he felt he could, should he allow himself to try one on for size, very easily find himself doing so.

There was a small knot of people in suits and pastel clothing gathered at the entrance. Dan and Julie's relatives, he supposed. He knew none of them, which made him feel like an impostor, turning up here all on his own. A shady character who had shuffled up in the hopes of a free cup of tea and a little light redemption.

'Jack!' said one of them now – a woman about his own age. She waved and approached him. He smiled automatically, even though he didn't have a clue who she was.

'Caryl Phelps,' she told him obligingly. 'Julie's sister? We met at their Christmas party a couple of years back. How are you? I'm so sorry to hear your news. It's always a shock when these things happen.'

Shock for who, precisely? It certainly hadn't been a shock for him. Indisputably hadn't been one for Lydia – she'd written the script. For Caryl then. For everyone who hadn't broached the veneer of their marriage. Jack tried, and failed, to place her. The only thing he could recall about Dan and Julie's Christmas party a couple of years back was that, in keeping with just about every social event in the last two or three years of their marriage, Lydia had spent most of the evening sitting on other men's laps and/or shimmying around the kitchen clutching wine bottles with her shoes off and an expression of studied abandon on her face. And that he had been far from sober and rather sad.

'Yes.' He shrugged. 'Well, that's life.'

'Yes.' She shrugged too. 'Well. These things are usually for the best, aren't they? Nice to see you again, anyway.' She smiled at him sympathetically, having presumably run out of polite conversation and/or interest in attempting more. 'Well,' she said. 'I'd better go and round up my brood, I suppose. Looks like rain.'

Yes, thought Jack. Heavy storms expected. Lydia was approaching from behind.

She was wearing a particularly unattractive outfit. A stiff turquoise skirt suit that he didn't recognise. It pleased him. For several months after the separation he had found himself gripped with a frustrating sense of bitterness nearly every time he saw her. She looked so damn thrilled to be no longer with him. So groomed. So confident. So altogether like a woman who had blossomed. Jack

179

tried hard not to read anything relating to the subject of divorce, but even he knew – it was so generally well documented – that post-divorce women so often found happiness, while post-divorce men often lost their way, like old limb-challenged lions in the veldt. And killed themselves sometimes.

He knew he was only feeling sorry for himself, but he couldn't help it. She'd put on a little weight which, he had to concede, suited her. And emanated self-assurance. Like a diamond might emanate sparkle, perhaps. Or an overfilled burger bun might emanate ketchup, this metaphor pleased him more.

Lydia also looked at him sympathetically. Which was what she always did these days. Always had done, perhaps. As if he'd been an orphan puppy she'd taken in once but in whose future she no longer had any faith.

'You're looking well,' she said. Which, likewise, was what she always said. 'How's Dad?'

He wished she wouldn't call him Dad. She shouldn't be allowed to. Not any more. There should be legislation, thought Jack, to stop it. He knew he was being childish, but, right now, a child was what he very much wished he could be.

'Ollie and I popped in to see him last week. Did he tell you?' she was saying. 'He's not looking too good, is he?'

Jack shook his head. 'He's much the same.'

'The nurse was saying they didn't think it would be too long before they'd have to see about getting him a hospice place. It's terrible, isn't it? Seems like only yesterday that he was fit as a flea and chasing Ollie round the garden. Such a shame. Poor Dad.'

Jack stood and studied his newly polished shoes. He really, really, didn't want to talk to Lydia about his father. He felt her hand on his arm before seeing its approach.

'If there's anything... if you want to... well, you know you only have to ask, don't you?'

Or have her pat him either. She was looking sympathetic again. What the hell did she think she could do for him? Effect a cure? Invent immortality? Mop his fucking brow when it all got too much? He looked at her pointedly and she took her arm back.

He really, really, wished she wouldn't call him Dad.

*　　　　　*　　　　　*

Jack hadn't known quite what to expect, but one thing he definitely hadn't expected was that he would have to sit through an entire church service before the christening proper began. He had assumed, clearly wrongly, that, as it was a Saturday, it would be a quick in-and-out affair.

There was also talk of some sort of lunch party to follow, at Dan and Julie's. Which wouldn't ordinarily have been of any consequence, except that it was almost lunchtime and he was supposed to be getting in the junior league scores. He'd missed his own match, of course, but he'd still promised to have his copy in for early evening. So he'd persuaded Ollie to stay home to deal with the calls, and that, he'd thought, would be that.

Except it hadn't been. The sun, appropriately, was breaking through a wash of violet clouds as they emerged once again into the light with the newly blessed child, inspiring many a happy whoop and coo. But Lydia, who was bearing down on him now, had left her sympathetic voice back in the vestry with the cherubs and the cassocks and the communion wine.

'Honestly,' she barked at him. 'What the hell did you think you were doing taking telephone calls? This is a christening, for God's sake!'

Jack wondered quite how God would feel about the question of his sake being discussed in a church vestibule, and thought he might find it amusing. Less amusing was that Lydia had taken it upon herself to seek him out and chastise him, as if she were in some way still responsible for him. As if he had made *her* look bad.

It had only been the one call. Half way through 'All Things Bright and Beautiful'. And with the church full of caterwauling women his few mumbled words were almost entirely drowned out. When the second came in he had checked the number, ignored it, and switched the phone to vibrate instead. Which it had. Several times. Like a bluebottle in his trouserleg. More scores. So Oliver must have gone out. Or, it occurred to him, was sitting at the computer, entirely oblivious of the phone.

He nodded. 'I'm well aware of that,' he said levelly. 'It was work.'

She rolled her eyes. 'Oh, and of course that's so much more important than good manners, isn't it? Why didn't you just switch the thing off?'

He met her eye, annoyed but all at once also rather pleased. 'I never switch my phone off. You know that,' he answered.

'Well, you should,' she said haughtily. 'Your precious football scores, I take it? Hardly life and death. The world won't end if you miss a couple, you know. '

Jack smiled a mirthless smile.

'Probably not,' he said smoothly. 'But I never switch my phone off. My father's dying, or did you forget?'

It was ten to four. And no more than half a mile from where Jack, frowning, was climbing into his car, Simon, smiling, was climbing out of his.

Hope, who had been watching for his arrival from the living room window, moved quickly into the hall and out of the front door. It was silly, she kept telling herself, but the whole thing with Simon was beginning to addle her. She felt that the minute she let him into the house again, a very tangible threshold would have been crossed, and their running, right now just an exercise in mutual training, would take on the cadence and timbre of an assignation. That she would, having invited him in, have to offer him a glass of water. Or a cup of tea, even biscuits, and heaven knew what would happen then. She knew she wouldn't *really* have to, but if she let him into her house and didn't do any of those perfectly normal-in-any-other-circumstance, perfectly polite and sociable things, it would be tantamount to accepting that there was another agenda where Simon was concerned. Which there was. And though she knew there was little she could do about it bar grow a great deal of facial hair or not wash for a week, she also knew that tea and biscuit gestures could so easily be construed as invitations. She was half way down the front path when he got to her.

She lifted up her secret key-hiding stone and popped her door key underneath it.

'D'you want to put your car key under here?' she asked him.

He glanced beyond her, towards the house. 'Oh,' he said, looking confused. 'Oh. Righty ho.' He bent down to do so, and as he did she could see three inches of pallid stomach bulging between his stringy running vest and the top of his shorts.

She tugged her own T-shirt down extra hard.

But Simon, it turned out, was the least of her problems.

'How odd,' she panted.

'What's odd?'

'That.'

They'd been on the move for a little over ten minutes, and were both, by now, out of breath. Hope's running had come on in leaps and bounds now she was motivated not to make conversation.

Running to the park, as opposed to around it, took them through a number of footpaths that criss-crossed the area, which in turn took them through the close Paul and Suze lived in. And, naturally, past Paul and Suze's house. As they did so Hope had noticed a large transit van parked outside. Which would have been of no consequence (except to Suze, who had standards) except that it had the words 'Pest Arrest' written down the side. There were various illustrative decals, too. Of wasps. And cockroaches. And rats.

'What about it?' puffed Simon, as they ran on past. Hope explained that it was her brother's house. 'I presume they've got pests,' he shrugged, re-entering the footpath. 'My mother had an infestation last year. Silverfish, I think it was.'

Hope smiled to herself. Well, hey nonny no. The squeaky-clean Suze with her very own infestation. She wondered what she'd say about that.

When she got home, and had seen Simon swiftly off, Hope picked up the phone to ask. Despite her earlier indignance, she did feel a little bad about Suze and her casseroles. Not least, cross with herself, for doing what she always did, letting things get out of hand in the first place.

'Suze?'

'What?'

No hello. Just a bark. Which should have told her something. Her sister-in-law never answered the telephone with a bark. Always the number. And the area code.

'I've just been past, on my run,' she explained. 'I saw the Pest Arrest van outside. Is everything OK? Have you got a wasp's nest or something?'

There was a silence. Then a sigh. Then another silence. Then a sigh again.

'Suze?'

'No,' she snapped. 'We have *not* got a wasps' nest.'

Hope waited but Suze obviously wasn't going to elaborate. 'Well,' she said at last. 'That's a relief. Something else, then?'

'Yes,' came the toneless reply. 'Something else.'

'Well, what something?'

The line went silent again, then Suze exhaled loudly. 'Moles, if you must know.'

'Moles? In the garden?'

'Of course in the garden!'

'Oh, dear. But, oh, bless!' said Hope. 'Oh, moles are so sweet! Have you seen one?'

Another silence.

'Suze? Are you still there?'

The silence continued. And then, suddenly, it was broken.

'That's right!' Suze hissed. 'You laugh, why don't you? Well, you can just sod off and laugh somewhere else!'

'Um… '

'You heard me! Just leave me alone! This isn't bloody funny, *OK*?'

Chapter 22

Hope was woken abruptly the next morning. By Chloe, who was standing at her bedside, in pyjamas, and pummelling her shoulder with both hands.

'Mum, wake up. Auntie Suze is on the phone!'

Suze? Hope groaned and swung her legs from under the duvet. She'd thought about calling Suze back. Several times, in fact. But she hadn't. If Suze wanted to slam down phones and immerse herself in histrionics – make a mountain out of her wretched mole hills – then she could bloody well get on with it. Hope was done with pussy-footing around her. She glanced blearily at the bedside clock. It wasn't even seven. She sent Chloe back to bed and padded irritably down the stairs.

'I mush apologise,' said Suze as soon as she picked the phone up.

At least Hope thought that's what she said. She was still half asleep.

'Pardon?'

'I *mush*. Apologise to you.'

She hadn't imagined it. Suze's voice sounded strange. Really strange. If she'd got little sense out of her last night – and she hadn't – then this was something else again. 'Er... what for?' she said at last.

'For last night. For swearing.'

'Oh, forget it. You don't have to apologise –'

'And for everything!' Suze's voice rose ten decibels. 'I do. I see it now.'

Really strange. 'See what?'

'That's why they've come for me.'

No. Not strange. Hope was fully awake now. Drunk. Suze sounded *drunk*. But that was impossible. Suze didn't drink. She rubbed her spare fist against her eyes. 'See what?' she asked again. 'Who've come for you?'

Suze's voice dropped so far now that it was barely a whisper.

'The moles, of course!' she hissed.

185

A moment passed before Hope could gather her thoughts into any response to this statement.

'What, the moles in your garden?'

'Of course the moles in our garden!' The voice was still a barely audible hiss. Hope was dumbfounded. Was this some sort of joke?

'You're not making any sense, Suze.'

'I am. You know there's new ones now, don't you?'

'New what?'

'New mounds! Right at the edge of the lawn. Right by the patio!'

'Suze, I –'

'D'you think they'll get under? D'you think –' She stopped speaking then, and emitted a loud sob.

'Suze? *Suze*?'

Hope heard the phone knock against something. Then Suze's breathing. It sounded laboured.

'It's all right,' Suze whispered. 'It's all right. I've got a plan.'

This was becoming more alarming by the minute. 'Suze, where's Paul?'

'Not here, Paul. No.'

'Where is he?'

'Away, of course. Always away. So *I'm* going to deal with them.'

She was becoming indistinct now. The words becoming soupy. Merging into one another. Then the silence returned.

'Suze? *Suze!*'

'You won't tell him, will you?' She sounded suddenly alarmed. 'You won't, Hope, will you? You promise?'

'*Yes!*' But the line had already gone dead.

Hope called straight back but the line was now engaged. What on earth was going on? She'd never heard her sister-in-law sound so peculiar. It didn't make any sense. And what on earth was all that stuff about the moles coming to get her?

Chloe was heading down the stairs.

'I'm awake now,' she announced. 'Can I go and watch telly?'

Hope was busy rummaging in the hall table drawer for her address book. Paul's mobile number was in there. 'Yes, you can go and watch telly,' she said.

Chloe started off down the hall and then turned.

'Did she sing to you, as well?'

'I beg your pardon?'

'Auntie Suze. Did she sing to you?'

'No. Did she sing to you, then?'

Chloe nodded.

'What?'

She shrugged. 'Some mad song about holes.'

Paul's mobile wasn't responding, and after several more fruitless attempts with the home number, Hope was becoming increasingly anxious. She'd have to go round there. It was almost seven-thirty now and Tom was up, too. The two children, by now dressed, were already installed in the kitchen, spooning cereal into their mouths on automatic pilot, while they gaped at some rubbish on TV. Another quarter of an hour and her mother would be here, and she could get over to Paul's and find out what was going on. She ran upstairs and showered as quickly as she could, and was fully dressed and ready when her mother arrived.

Hope let her in and kept her in the hall while she explained about the phone call. And the one the night before. And the moles.

'You know,' said her mother, looking worried. 'She called me last night, too. I thought she sounded a bit odd then. What did she sound like to you?'

'Drunk.'

Her mother frowned.

'And I can't get Paul on his mobile.' Hope pulled on a jacket and picked up her car keys.

'I'd better come with you.'

'No, no. We can't both go, can we? You stay here and look after the kids.'

'I really think –'

'Mum, I'll deal with this, OK? I'll call you as soon as I know what's going on.'

It only took ten minutes to drive over to Paul and Suze's house, but when Hope got there there was no sign of life. Suze's car wasn't on the drive, and for a minute she worried that she'd upped and driven off somewhere, but, no, if Paul was away somewhere on business, he might well have taken it. He generally did if he was parking at the airport. He left Suze with his.

She swung into their drive and peered up through the windscreen. There were a couple of upstairs lights burning. Another thought struck her. Where on earth were the children?

She climbed out of the car and strode up to the front door. The sound of the bell reverberated round the hallway, but no-one came to answer it. She peered through the letterbox. She could see the telephone receiver dangling from its wire. She tried the bell again, unsure what to do next, then took herself off round to the side of the house. But the side gate was locked, and she couldn't see through it. She frowned as she looked around her. She couldn't climb over it. It was made out of vertical planks of wood. Where the hell was Paul?

She fished in her bag. Perhaps his mobile was on now. If not, she would just have to call the police. But the phone started ringing as she got her hand around it. It was her mother, anxious for news.

'I can't even get in!' she said. 'She's not answering the doorbell. And the gate's locked. And what about the children? Where could they be?' She felt the first stirrings of panic welling inside her. 'I think I'm going to have to call 999.'

'Ah!' said her mother. 'You *can* get in! They've got an emergency key.' She told Hope where to find it, and having instructed her mother to keep trying Paul, Hope went off to track the thing down.

Gaining entry to the house did nothing to quell Hope's unease. Not because it looked like any sort of chaos had been wrought there, but because, as she jogged from room to room, all the little details were wrong. The phone, of course, which she had placed back on its base, Suze and Paul's unmade bed, the children's neatly-made ones, the empty glass on its side on the floor on the landing, the general sense of mild disarray, that would have been normal in most people's homes, but not Suze's. But there was no sign of either her or the children. Perhaps she'd been wrong. Perhaps Suze *had* gone off somewhere. But her handbag, its contents disgorged on the kitchen table, was still there, as were her car keys. All this Hope absorbed in the thirty or so seconds it took to do one circuit of the house, calling out Suze's name as she ran. The next thing she took in, and took in with dismay, was a big Bacardi bottle, almost empty, in the living room. Her heart sank. She'd been right, then. Suze *had* been drunk.

She picked up the bottle and ran back out to the kitchen. *Was* drunk. Was very drunk. And was nowhere to be found. She placed the bottle on the draining board and gazed out across the garden. There were indeed a great number of molehills, punctuating the lawn like an outbreak of acne.

And then she spotted her. Or something like her, at any rate. A wraithlike form, emerging from behind a hedge at the far end of the garden, and bounding at some speed across the grass. Hope made for the back door, turned the key and yanked it open. She could see Suze now, an indistinct figure in the drizzle. She was on her knees, in a nightie, soaked to the skin, and stabbing violently at the ground with a very large fork .

It took Hope mere seconds to cross the sodden lawn. By this time, Suze, who had jerked up, startled, when Hope called her name, was up on her feet, her soaked nightie clinging to her small frame like wet paper, and her hair, which was usually so neatly tied back, hanging in slimy brown ropes around her face. She looked, if such things were actually possible, as if the real Suze, the one Hope knew, wasn't at home. Seventeen years. A whole seventeen years. She'd never, *ever* seen her like this.

Hope eyed the fork, unsure what to make of it. It was a big kitchen one. The kind you used when carving roasts. A foot long, twin pronged, and no doubt very sharp. She swallowed. But at least it wasn't a knife.

'Suze, what are you doing?' she asked, in what she hoped was a calming voice.

Suze swung the fork in an arc, sending globs of glistening mud winging through the air.

'Killing them, of course. Whaddya think?'

Hope took a step towards her, noticing with alarm that there was a rip in the nightie and a ruddy reddish stain around it, over Suze's left knee.

'OK,' she said softly. 'OK, Suze. I see… ' God, she really didn't have the first clue what to do. Suze was still brandishing the fork and now glancing around. 'OK,' Hope said again. 'Now, how about you and I going inside in the warm, and we'll get you out of those wet things, and… '

She proffered a hand. Suze lowered her arm and seemed to consider it for a moment.

'No! I haven't finished!' she barked suddenly. She sank to her knees again and started stabbing at another mound.

'Suze –'

'I haven't finished!'

Hope moved towards her. Got a hand on her arm.

'Come on… ' she coaxed. But Suze shook her hand off. Then suddenly she leapt up, swung round, and was off down the garden, moving like a terrier in a novelty dog coat, hair streaming out behind her like jellyfish tails.

Paul and Suze had a very large garden. Just how large, however, was only now becoming clear. Suze was running at great speed across it, with Hope, blinking raindrops, in pursuit. It wasn't just a very large garden, it was a very complicated garden as well. As with most things, Suze didn't do her gardening by halves. There was a pond, and a pergola, and an assortment of shrubberies, and, at its end, like most of the gardens around here, it had an area that, while it couldn't really be called woodland, was tree-filled and dark and unkempt. The houses here all backed on to a strip of real woodland that circled the reservoir beyond. Quite a selling point, Hope remembered, as, panting, she approached it. So lovely for the little ones, their very own fairy glen. Hope jogged towards it. Like others nearby, Paul and Suze had installed a Wendy house in here, and it was behind this, having zig-zagged her way round all the bracken and wild garlic, that Suze's nightie-clad form had now plunged.

There was no choice but to follow her, and as soon as Hope did she realised with relief that Suze was effectively cornered; the fence that separated the garden from the woodland was tall and topped off with a robust stretch of barbed wire. Added to which, the little area she was in now was hemmed in by two substantial and aggressive-looking shrubs. Suze saw this too and looked petulant and cross.

'Leave me alone!' she called out. 'I haven't *finished*.'

Hope could see that a firmer approach was required.

'Yes you *have*,' she shouted back, in equally firm tones. 'So just put that fork down right now, or I'm coming in there to get it off you.'

Suze glared out from beneath her frondy fringe.

'Go away!'

'I will *not*! Now put down that fork!'

To Hope's utter surprise, she did so. But just as she was taking a step closer to her, Suze wheeled around and started off again, tracking along the line of the fence, her nightie catching on the branches as she went.

There was nothing else for it. If Hope wanted her she'd have to go right on in and get her. She pushed up her sleeves and strode in.

But Suze was determined otherwise. She seemed oblivious to the thorns and was inching further away from Hope with every step.

'Go away!'

'Come back here!'

'Go *away*! Go AWAY!'

Hope pulled in frustration at a thorn caught in her jacket. Suze must be covered in scratches though she obviously wasn't feeling them. Hope could hear the snap and thwack of the branches, as the thorns alternately gripped and then relinquished the fabric of the nightdress. She stopped a moment, a pungent onion smell sour in her nostrils. It was pointless trying to follow. Suze was going nowhere. She should go back to the house and call someone for help. But even as she decided this, Suze began whimpering, and Hope could see she was now stuck and in pain. She was pulling ineffectually at a fretwork of branches that criss-crossed her torso and had pinioned her there.

Releasing her was easier than she expected. The silence now punctuated by Suze's increasingly hysterical cries, Hope cast around and found a fallen tree branch, and, thus armed, was able to make much more efficient progress through the undergrowth. Once close enough, she managed to free the tangle of branches, while keeping a firm grip on Suze's left arm, in case she tried to escape. But she didn't. All the fight seemed to suddenly go out of her, and Hope was able to pull her out of the woodland with a great deal less effort than she'd expended getting in.

They emerged onto the lawn to find Hope's mother jogging across it towards them.

'Gracious me!' she called out, almost gaily. Hope blinked at her. Almost jolly, in fact. 'What a palaver!' she declared as she reached them 'What a to do! Come on. Come on, chicken. Let's get you inside.'

Suze, who had by now become floppy and inert, allowed herself to be supported by Hope's mum's arm as well, and between them they half dragged, half carried her back into the house.

'I dropped off the children,' Hope's mum told her, almost conversationally, as they walked. 'And I got hold of Paul. He's only in Bristol, so he won't be long. Paul's on his way, chicken,' she added, to Suze.

'Oh dear,' Suze cried suddenly. 'Oh dear. Oh dear.'

'Shhh, sweetheart. Shhh. And I've called an ambulance.' By now they were shovelling Suze through the back door. Her sobs were growing more voluble with every step.

'Oh dear,' she cried again.

'Now don't fuss,' said Hope's mother, sternly, as if talking to a whining child. 'Come on and let's get you sorted.'

Between them, they manoeuvred Suze through the kitchen and into the living room and Hope helped her mother lay her down on the sofa.

'Oh dear,' she kept saying. 'Oh dear, oh dear, oh dear.'

Hope's mother pulled Suze's nightie up and inspected the cut on her leg. She tutted.

'We'll have to get some Savlon spray on this. Dear me. And on all these grazes. Oh, and that's a thought. Hope, go upstairs and grab her a few things, will you, lovely? Clean nightie. A wash bag. Some undies and that.'

'But what about the children, mum? Where are they?'

Hope's mother nodded. 'Oh dear. Of course. I should have told you. Dear me, I'm getting old. I should have remembered. They're at their other Gran's, of course. They've gone to stay for a few days.'

Suze's mother lived in England, on the coast somewhere in the south east. And Suze's children, of course, were at private school. So they'd already broken up for Easter.

Hope ran upstairs and gathered all the things she thought were needed, her mind in overdrive and teeming with questions. About her mother, for one thing. Unlike Hope, who was still reeling, she seemed to be busily taking charge of a situation that was no surprise to her at all.

Suze was flat out on the sofa under a blanket when Hope came back downstairs, and her mother was bustling about tidying the place up.

'Mum, do you know something?' Hope asked her pointedly. 'About this?'

Her mother paused, half-plumped chenille cushion in hand.

'Yes,' she answered, sighing. 'Yes, dear. I'm afraid I do.'

Simple psychosis. That was what the doctor said. Hope didn't know what a complicated psychosis was, so was none the wiser until Paul, who had by this time travelled back and joined them at the hospital, explained.

'It's the sleeping pills that caused the psychotic episode,' he said. 'She takes the pills and then they react with the alcohol. And then – well, you saw. I'm sorry, sis. Must have been a bit of a morning for you.' He was drinking coffee from the vending machine. Hope felt more like a proper drink. Could it really still be only eleven-thirty? 'God, I shouldn't have gone. I should have seen it coming. It's been building up for a while.' He glanced at his mother and she patted his wrist. 'I certainly shouldn't have left her on her own. But it was only the one night. I thought it would be OK.'

'Well, it doesn't matter now, dear,' Hope's mother reassured him. 'She'll sleep it off and that'll be that. I doubt she'll remember a thing about it.'

Paul looked tired. And tangibly different. Or perhaps it was just that Hope was seeing him differently. He drained his cup.

'We'll have to do something about those wretched bloody moles, though. Perhaps I'd better see if the guy can come over later. Don't want to start her off again.'

Hope's mother nodded. 'Good idea.'

Hope felt she was watching a movie, and that she'd come in too late and didn't know the plot. She drained her own cup and crumpled it in her hand.

'This has happened before, then?' she asked them both.

Her mother and brother exchanged glances. Paul nodded. 'Not this exactly. But yes, this. That's the trouble with all these bloody drugs she's on.'

Hope threw her cup at the bin. 'I had no idea, Paul.'

He looked uncomfortable. 'No. Well, you wouldn't. It's not… well, you know. It's not something we tend to talk about.'

'But what drugs?' She spread her hands. '*Why*?'

'Ah,' he said thoughtfully. 'If only we had the answer to that one. It's just, oh, I don't know. She's just anxious. There's always been… well, she's always had a tendency to anxiety. Panic attacks. She's not depressed. It's not like that. She just has trouble dealing with stuff. She's OK. I mean it's not like it's anything progressive. But she's been popping pills for years.' He smiled wanly. 'One of the merry band, eh? But you know, from time to time something just, I don't know, tips her over the edge. And then she can't sleep, and then she's on the sleeping pills, and then she gets it into her head that she wants a drink… and then… well, you saw.' He looked miserably back towards the ward.

'And you're telling me all this has all come about just because you've got moles in the garden?'

'Oh, it's not really about that. That was probably just the trigger.' He smiled a mirthless smile. 'Mountains out of mole hills, eh?'

Hope nodded ruefully. 'I already thought that.'

And had done nothing. *Nothing*.

'You got it,' said Paul. The smile left his lips and he pushed his hand through his hair. 'God knows what it's really about this time. It's never clear cut. Mid-life crisis. Her dad dying last year. The kids getting older. It could be any number of things. Shit. I shouldn't have gone on that trip.' He crumpled his own plastic cup in his hand now, his expression so full of guilt and woe that Hope wanted to take him in her arms and cuddle him. So much she didn't know. So much she'd never even suspected.

'So is drink the main problem, then?'

Paul shook his head. 'God, no. Not at all. She hardly touches the stuff. Because she knows she shouldn't. Not with the drugs she takes. But every now and then… '

'Tell you what,' said Hope's mother. 'I'll come and stay for a few days. How about that? I doubt they'll keep her in more than a day or two, and you need to go to work. You're the one who keeps it all together, you know, darling. Come on. It's not your fault. Don't feel bad.'

Paul smiled wanly. 'Thanks, Mum. I'd really appreciate that.'

'That's what mums are for,' she said, almost jauntily. 'That's what we're best at.' She turned to Hope. 'And what about you, sweetheart? You've got work to get to haven't you? Will you able to drop me back for my car on the way?'

She stood up. Yes. She did have work to get to. The BBC, at least, for another Heartbeat interview. It was too late to go into work first, so she'd have to call them from Paul's. 'No problem. We'd better get going, I guess.'

Paul stood up too.

'Thanks, sis,' he said, putting his arms around her and hugging her. 'You're a trooper. What would I do without you?' He held her out at arms' length.

'I just wish I'd known, Paul. I wish... ' What *did* she wish? That she could unthink all the uncharitable thoughts she'd always had about Suze? What good would that do? What help would it be? But she wished it even so. 'I mean I know it's none of my business, but –'

Paul shushed her with his hand.

'No,' he said slowly. 'It's not like that. Please don't think that. It's just not your problem, sis. There's a difference.' He looked carefully at her. 'And I think you've had quite enough problems of your own to deal with.' He smiled. 'OK? You get me?' He hugged her again, and she felt her eyes fill with tears for him. Yes, she said, kissing him. She did.

Was that what it was about? The unbearable lightness of being? Hope still wasn't sure. Only knew that she felt suddenly unanchored. As if the landscape of her life had shifted and deformed. Knew that she'd been cast loose, and was flailing to get purchase again.

The events of the morning felt like a dream by the time she arrived at the BBC. Something other and unreal that had happened in a parallel universe.

'I'm so sorry I'm late,' she said breathlessly. Automatically. 'You got my message OK, did you?' She tugged her arms from the sleeves of her jacket as the producer lady – who she remembered was called Hilary – held the door to the stairway open for her. She felt as though she'd been dragged through a hedge. But then she *had* been through a hedge. Been the one doing the dragging. She shook out her jacket. She was cold. She was wet. Her nerves were still jangling.

'Yes, yes,' Hilary reassured her, taking it from her. 'No problem at all. We just re-jigged the schedule a bit. Swapped you with the chicken carcass story. You've got time for a cup of tea, even. Everything OK at home now?'

Hope nodded and they made their way up to the first floor. She'd dropped her mother back at Paul and Suze's – he was staying on at the hospital for a while – and telephoned work to say she wouldn't be coming in, and then the BBC to let them know she'd be late. They'd told her the schedule was reasonably fluid and just to get there whenever she could. 'Everything's fine,' she said, managing a nonchalant smile. 'Just a minor domestic panic. All sorted.'

She was still breathless when Hilary ushered her into the little cubicle. It had been a very long run up from the car park. There'd been no sign of Jack anywhere, but she'd half expected this. His own show had finished now, so he'd either be in an office somewhere preparing the next one, or off home to write one of his columns, perhaps. Or whatever else he did in the afternoons. What did he do in the afternoons? She swallowed her disappointment. Now she was here, even though she hadn't really admitted it to herself, she realised how much she wanted to see him. To talk to him. She realised how much she longed to put things right. Especially today. Paul's words had stayed with her. She did have enough problems of her own. Most of them, just lately, she knew, of her own making. Like making an ass of herself over someone. Like making judgements. Like leaping to conclusions. Like not giving people – giving Jack – a chance. But he'd be probably long gone by now, even though Patti was still in evidence. She'd passed them on the stairwell and called a breezy hello.

*   *   *

196

The interview itself, which was really just an update on the fun run for one of the afternoon programmes, took mere minutes, and it occurred to Hope that it would have been altogether easier if they'd just done it over the phone. Except that that thought would never have occurred to her, not when there was a chance she'd get to see Jack. God, she'd got it bad.

'Right,' said Hilary brightly as she ushered Hope back into the cubicle afterwards. 'Better let you out of the madhouse, then.'

Hope managed a smile at this. If only she knew. She slipped her arms into the sleeves of her jacket. Someone had evidently put it on a radiator, for it was now dry and warm.

'Right,' she said back. 'Thanks for that.'

'No problem at all,' said Hilary. 'Always happy to oblige for a good cause. I think we've even got a bit of a team coming ourselves, as it happens. Did Jack tell you?'

The mention of his name caused Hope's stomach to turn over. The reflex was automatic now. She was powerless to control it. She shook her head.

'Actually,' she said, because there was always *some* chance he'd still be there. 'He's not about, is he? I've got a couple of things I wanted to check with him.'

Hilary glanced at the clock on the cubicle wall.

'He might be. D'you want me to see?'

Hope said she did, and Hilary rang through to an office somewhere, and then the canteen, but without success.

They set off down the corridor, Hilary still chatting. He quite often stayed and had lunch there, apparently. But evidently not today.

'Oh, but there's a thought –' she said suddenly.

She stopped in the corridor and pushed an adjacent door open, putting her head around it as she did so. Hope couldn't see anyone, but there was obviously someone in there, behind the door.

'Ah, Danny,' said Hilary. 'Just the person. You don't know if Jack's still around anywhere, do you?'

Hope could hear a male voice answer. The name Danny rang a bell.

'Jack? No. He's long gone,' it said.

'Is he?' said Hilary. 'Where to?'

197

'Hey, of course,' said the voice now. 'You don't know, do you?'

'Know what?' said Hilary, leaning further round the doorway. Hope rather got the impression he must be beckoning her. His voice dropped a little.

'Allegra,' he said quietly. 'Came to pick him up. Word has it she was taking him out for lunch.'

Hilary's eyebrows shot up. 'Was she, now, indeed?' She stuck a thumb in the air. 'That's excellent news!'

Hope remained in the corridor, smiling politely at the carpet.

'Anyway,' said Hilary, who was beaming now. 'No matter. But if you do see him later, could you let him know Hope Shepherd from Heartbeat wanted to have a word?'

'Hope Shepherd?' said the man's voice, suddenly changed in its timbre. Hope's ears pricked up. There was a silence. Then a laugh. 'Oh, did she?' he said then. 'Well, well!' She could see Hilary's expression doing sudden gymnastics, but they were obviously lost on him. Or, if not, way too late. 'Well,' he was busy saying, and she could tell he was smirking. 'You'd better go and tell *Ms* Hope Shepherd from Heartbeat that she'll just have to join the queue.'

Hilary, embarrassed, bundled her off down the corridor then, and though Hope's mind was teeming with questions she would have killed for answers to, she meekly accepted Hilary's goodbyes and good lucks, and her promise that she'd leave Jack a note to call Heartbeat. Almost before she knew it, she was back in the car park. And now, all things considered (and she couldn't help but consider them), pretty comprehensively sad.

Chapter 23

The estate agent Jack had arranged to meet had a slim, boyish figure and a twinkle in her eye. Jack wasn't altogether sure what he was doing here, but here he was anyway, just like he'd said.

In truth, he felt no pressing need to be looking at property right now. There was his big new TV career, of course – a penthouse in the bay would sit very well with that, even if it felt so not *him* – but the impulse was more because he knew he had to make some sort of effort for his father. And *now*. His father had been so agitated about it when they'd last spoken, and he wanted to have something to show him.

Jack wasn't about to inherit any great fortune, but his dad had insisted he put his own house on the market, and was anxious to know Jack was moving things forward.

'Charlie Jones,' said the woman, extending a hand and pumping Jack's enthusiastically as they drew level outside the building. 'Building site' might have been a better description, for there were girders everywhere, cranes clawing at the skyline and the whole area, once just a back basin of the docks, was speckled with a mid-makeover patina of dust.

'Did you manage to get a parking space all right?' she asked as they walked. 'Dreadful day for it, isn't it? Though I have to say, I always think it's better to see a place when the rain's hammering down and it's blowing a gale, don't you? So easy to be seduced by the sunshine.' She smiled at him, revealing a row of perfect white teeth. Her hair was as ebullient as her manner, milk-chocolate brown, wild and very curly. In a different universe, one in which he wasn't pining for someone else so wholeheartedly, he would have fancied her, for sure. Yet she wasn't young, she wasn't blonde and her legs weren't even long. Hell, truth be known, did he really even go for young, long-legged blondes anyway? No, thought Jack. He went for petite elfin types with long liquorice hair. It was a very reassuring revelation. As if a weight had been lifted from his loins.

'I parked in the multi-storey and walked over,' he told her, increasing his pace as they approached the entrance so he could open the door for her.

'You'll have your own garage underneath, of course. And they've already started the second phase of the development,' she told him. 'There's covered visitor parking there, too. Have you looked at much already?'

She was right. There was no sunshine to be seduced by. Just a choppy, leaden sea under an irritable sky. But it did have a kind of moody beauty about it. Perhaps that was why it worked. Perhaps that was why he could sort of see himself here. The door drew open with an expensive sigh and his feet hit yielding blue carpet.

'There's twenty-four-hour security, of course, and a gym – planning permission for a swimming pool, too. But I'm not officially allowed to say so yet. That won't be finalised till phase three.' Her smile was warm, uncomplicated. A smile of contentment. She wanted a sale, but everything in her manner told him she liked her life very much anyhow, thank you, so if he didn't go for it, well, *c'est la vie*.

By the time Jack got back into his car he was feeling quite positive. He liked the notion of 'phases'. The idea that the way he felt now was just one of them. That a new, better one, was in the offing, rising phoenix-like from the ashes of the past. He watched Charlie Jones stride across the car park and get into her car, then headed off to get into his. It was getting late, and he still had today's script to finalise, not to mention an article for the *Express* to get finished, and all his football kit to get washed, too.

He'd just reached the car when his mobile started up. It was Allegra. Oh ho. At last.

'Lunch', she commanded, in her oh-so-forward style. Not a sniff of a mention of their date. Just 'lunch', then 'today' then 'well? How you fixed?', then, 'Come on. Just an hour. I'll pick you up.'

Was it Jack's imagination or was she sounding a little sharp? Her manner when they'd parted had suggested this was not the way she'd be. Quite the opposite, in fact. Or was this yet another woman with a date-to-phone-call egg timer? Had he got on the wrong foot even with her?

'Hi there!' he said cheerily, refusing to join in. This was a business relationship as well, after all. 'Look, hey, I'm sorry I haven't been in touch –'

'Jack. Look. I'm sorry too.' She sighed. 'Look, I may as well tell you now. It isn't going to happen for us, OK?'

Jack felt a surge of relief. So he'd been let off the hook.

'Allegra, I'm so glad you feel like that, because, well, you're right. I've got a –'

'*Jesus, Jack!*' Her explosion of exasperation was so loud he had to hold the phone away from his ear. 'I'm not talking about us, you dope! I'm talking about the bloody show!'

C'est la vie. It hadn't taken too long, the complete dismantling of everything he had been building his future career happiness on. Just the hour, which he'd spared her – she'd indeed come to work and collected him – and a brief resumé of why it had been axed. Nothing to do with him, as it turned out. Just that someone else, another thrusting producer, had come up with a different format and a bigger big name, and the powers that be, being powerful powers, had decided in the end to go with that. This was the way it worked in television. Nothing was set in stone until it happened. As with the highs, the hard knocks were very hard.

Strangely, he felt kind of OK. Not OK in a leaping-joyfully-up-and-down sense, but OK in the sense that now that the almost worst had happened he'd only the actual worst left to deal with. He had his job on the radio, he would continue to have his job on the radio. It was *OK*. Actually, a stress off his plate. It was something he didn't have to think about any more. As with Allegra, it seemed – and it did seem – all the excitement had been in the anticipation.

It was Allegra he felt sorriest for. Though she was at great pains to sympathise with *him* – she had other irons in the fire, of course, other projects to get green-lighted – it soon became clear to Jack that all was not as cut and dried as he'd thought. She'd squeezed his arm as she dropped him back at the BBC car park. Asked him to phone her. Pouted even. Looked shy. Asked why he hadn't phoned her. Strange how his one ignoble brush with a sexual appliance should have injected this marked shift in the dynamics of their non-relationship. It could have been pity, he thought, compassion, even, but everything in her demeanour told

201

him otherwise. Something had changed. Her hold over him, maybe? His reason to cultivate her affection, for example, which, though it had left a slightly unpleasant taste in his mouth in the long nights following their unfortunate encounter, seemed to have been some sort of unspoken contract between them. And now he was no longer being cultivated by her, he held the cards, suddenly. The ball was in his court.

Which made it doubly important he made his position clear.

'Look, Allegra,' he said as he climbed out of her car, 'What I said before about us –'

But she was having none of it. She obviously valued her dignity too much. 'Us? You big pussy! We're pals, you and me, right? Let's keep it that way, OK?'

He'd gone back to his own car, then, and sat in it for a moment or two. The rain had stopped and the sun had emerged from behind the remaining wisps of high cloud. He was happy enough to sit a minute and let it warm his face. He hadn't even realised he'd fallen asleep until a ringing sound jolted him back into consciousness.

It was the matron at the nursing home.

'We've got your father a place at the hospice, Jack.'

C'est la vie. It was now. The actual worst was on its way.

The doctor was in residence when Jack arrived at the nursing home. She was a tall, commanding woman, with aggressively sharp tailoring but the sort of face that made you want to ask her to hug you. She emanated care and empathy and goodness and warmth and she wasted no time telling Jack anything positive, just that it was important that they get his father installed in the hospice as soon as possible and that they do their level best to get to grips with his pain.

Again, a sense of events moving up a gear washed over him. The fact of his father's imminent death was no longer something he'd have to dwell on, alone, in the car. It was out of the closet. Official. Jack's father was going to a hospice, therefore he was going to die sooner rather than later. And with that came an almost welcome realisation that no one would tell him to try not to worry any more.

There was lots of other talk as they moved him from bed to wheelchair to corridor to ambulance. What a wag Jack's father was. How he'd always charmed all the nurses. The way he liked to go to sleep with his earphones jammed in. Book at Bedtime, or Radio Three, or even Red Dragon, sometimes. How they'd all miss him so much. It was strange, thought Jack, how these people had taken ownership of his father. How they'd become his new family. His final family. How he, himself, had been relegated to visitor status. He still felt a degree of guilt about this. When his father's health had begun failing, Jack and Lydia were at the start of the slope they were about to tumble down maritally, but they both, nevertheless, had entreated Jack's father to come live with them. They would manage, they assured him. They would look after him. They wanted to look after him. But Jack's father, the painfully diminished form semi-conscious in the chair beneath his hands now, had been bigger then. Stronger. And would not be swayed.

Jack had tried again, afterwards. More than once. But his father, if anything, was even firmer in his refusals. He did not, he'd said sternly, want to go to his grave knowing his only son wasted his formative years mopping up after a doddery old man.

His father's head nodded up as they entered the lift.

'Teeth,' he said.

'Yes, Dad?'

'Teeth,' he said again.

Jack squeezed around the side of the chair to face him. The lift, though capacious, held Jack, his father, Shelley, another nurse, and a porter. If there was little room to swing a cat there was so much less for dignity.

'Teeth?' he asked him again. His father looked fairly lucid.

'They're in his toilet bag,' said Shelley.

'It's all right, Dad. They're in your toilet bag,' Jack said.

His father blinked at him and nodded.

'You told Liddie?' Jack's father had always called her Liddie. 'She came last week.'

'I know.'

'She worries about you.'

'I know.'

'*I* worry about you.'

'You don't have to.'

203

'How's that girl of yours?'

'What girl?'

His father rolled his eyes. 'What girl! Listen to him! The girl you were telling me about!'

Out of the corner of his eye, Jack saw the two nurses exchange covert grins.

When they came out of the lift, Jack was gripped by a powerful vision of an elderly man, in a chair much like this one. Only the elderly man was himself, and the son pushing the chair was Ollie. In that instant Jack decided that it mattered very much that he live to be very, very old, and that he die very quietly in his sleep.

The entourage finally made it out to the forecourt. The ambulance, its jaws open, stood ready to receive his father, while the nurses made minor adjustments to his drips. The doctor patted Jack's shoulder and said she'd see him at the hospice. Jack wanted to ask her how long his father had, but he couldn't. It felt a little bit too much like he wanted to organise his diary.

He was just about to get into his car when another nurse, a young girl he didn't recognise, emerged from the front porch and started calling out to him.

He left the car and walked across the drive towards her.

'Mr Valentine? Oh, I'm glad I caught you. I'm ever so sorry,' she said, drawing level with him. She must be new. He didn't know her. 'But I forgot all about these.' She had a large cardboard box in her arms, which she now raised towards him. It said 'Venflon' on the side. 'They've been sitting in the office since we cleared your Dad's things out. Matron had thought you might be happy for us to send them on down to the local primary school. They've got their Spring Fayre coming up and she thought they could maybe sell them. Seeing as how they've not been opened or anything. But they can't. You know, health and safety. Sell by dates and all that. Anyway... ' She proffered the box.

Jack took it from her, confused.

'These?' he asked.

'The wine gums.' She nodded at the box. 'There's packets and packets of them. You know what elderly people are like for hoarding things.' She paused, whether from uncertainty about the possible impropriety of what she'd just said or simply because she had nothing else to say, Jack didn't know. He flipped the box top open. Inside there were, indeed, packets and packets of wine gums.

'Bless him,' said the nurse. It was getting increasingly blowy and the little tails on her nurse's cap were dancing in the breeze. 'Anyway,' she said briskly. Nursily, in fact. 'I'm sure you'll find a use for them. Get through them in no time if you're anything like me!'

Jack looked up from the box at her young, untroubled face. Wine gums. Splendid, son. Just the jobby.

He cleared his throat, which felt tight. 'Would *you* like them?'

'Me?'

'I mean, would the staff like them?'

She grinned at him.

'Is the Pope catholic?' she said.

Jack watched her go back inside, returning her wave as she entered the building, his other hand gripping the open car door, the strengthening wind lifting his jacket lapels. He felt so small all of a sudden, so young and vulnerable, so unprepared, so not ready to relinquish his father. So not ready to face the rest of his life without him. So ill-equipped to become him now. But it was about to happen. The ambulance was already moving off down the hill. He got back in the car and poked the key into the ignition, swallowing hard at the pain in his throat. He had never felt so much like curling up into a ball and crying.

Chapter 24

Go away, Hope thought. Perhaps that's what she should do. Once the run was done, maybe she would take the children off somewhere. To a caravan, or a cottage, perhaps, just the three of them. If she could just remove herself from her normal life for a few days perhaps she might shake off the gloom. If she could just *find* her own life, amid the muddle of everyone else's, perhaps she might find a path that would make her feel hopeful again.

But right now she had to keep her happy face on. Because it was Kayleigh's eighteenth birthday and they were having a bit of a do.

Any excuse for a party, Madeleine had said, and that was what this was turning out to be. An excuse for a party. An excuse *of* a party. A dozen of them, gathered in the main office on a Wednesday, drinking champagne and eating take-away pizza, and everybody getting drunk. Not that Hope was. The pizza had looked like something that had been disgorged by a bilious buzzard after a heavy night's carnage, so she'd stuck to the champagne. Only a prudent one and a half glasses, but it was nevertheless fizzing and buzzing in her brain.

Kayleigh, by now, was certainly drunk, and clearly also of the opinion that it was her duty to provide the entertainment. She had fished out a Kylie Minogue CD from her back-pack, and someone had found a CD player, and now she was dancing with a box file.

It was only just gone seven, but already Hope was trying to formulate an excuse of her own. One that would sound plausible enough to get her out of the place. She wasn't quite sure what she'd like to do instead, only that she was tired and crotchety and not feeling very sociable. And Simon was beginning to cloy.

'They've done a good job,' he was saying to her now – shouting to her, in fact, even though his mouth was but inches from her ear. 'With the radio build-up. Don't you think?'

She nodded. Simon had been trailing around after her since five. Trailing pointedly, persistently.

Betty, who'd come over from the shop, nodded vigorously. 'You can say what you like about these celebrities, but I must say your Mr Valentine's come up trumps for us, hasn't he? We've been listening to him on the radio. He's been ever so good.'

Hope nodded.

'You going to do the run yourself, dear?' she asked Hope.

Hope nodded again, about to speak, but Betty's attention had been diverted by Simon, who was nodding pretty frantically himself. 'We both are, Betty,' he interrupted happily. 'We're becoming a bit of a double act, actually. We've been in training together.'

'That's nice,' said Betty.

'Haven't we?'

He smiled at Hope. She nodded again.

'I was even wondering if we shouldn't have a couple of T-shirts printed. You know. "Two Hearts Become Run" or – get this – "Beauty and the Beast". You know, "beauty dot dot dot... " on yours and "... dot dot dot and the beast" on mine.'

Hope felt appalled. But she nodded again. 'Ri-ght.'

Betty looked at Simon, then at Hope, and then at Simon again. Simon glugged down champagne and beamed.

'That's nice,' said Betty.

Simon beamed some more. 'This year the fun run – next year the London marathon, eh?'

'I don't really see myself running a marathon,' said Hope. 'Five K is plenty for me.'

'Nonsense!' said Simon, reaching for the nearest bottle and filling his glass to the brim for at least the fourth time. 'It's only a question of commitment. Only a question of us getting in training for it, Hope. You're very fit. She's very fit,' he added, to Betty. 'Always keeps me on my toes, I can tell you.' He did a little running mime then patted his stomach. Which was certainly a little smaller. The 'us' however, loomed fearfully large. He patted his stomach again. 'I'll probably have lost a stone by the time she's finished with me!'

'You're looking well now, Simon,' Betty said. 'I was only saying to Iris the other day how well you're looking these days. You always used to look so peaky. Nice to see. So, the transformation's all down to you, then, is it, Hope?'

'Hardly –'

'Absolutely!' said Simon.

'That's nice,' said Betty. 'You make a nice pair, you two.' She smiled. 'Nice to see.'

Simon beamed.

She'd kept away from him after that. But she was still conscious of his eyes, which seemed permanently angled towards her, as if connected by invisible string. She had never ignored Simon so pointedly, and she could tell he was aware that she was doing it now. Which was why she should have really seen it coming. But when an hour later she became aware of his sudden absence, she simply assumed (no, hoped) he'd gone home.

'No, he hasn't,' corrected Madeleine, who was getting the birthday cake out of its box. 'His coat's still on the coat stand. He's probably gone off to the office or something. Perhaps he had to make a call. Perhaps he's beavering away on some anomaly in the purchase ledger. You know what he's like. Go and fetch him, will you, sweetie?'

Yes, of course she should have seen it coming. That was the trouble with champagne on an empty stomach. It smoothed away the edges of your mental vision. She should have seen it coming and taken evasive action. Sent Kayleigh or Kevin for him instead. Stayed well away. As it was, she found herself alone in the unlit office with him, its forms and shapes murky against the darkening sky. She heard the door sigh shut, the click of the latch, the indistinct sounds of the rest of the staff partying so near yet so far away beyond it. He had a pencil in his hand, which he was using, but no calculator. No serried ranks of figures jumping through hoops before him. Just doodles. Endless doodles.

'Are you all right?' she said.

'I'm OK,' he replied, glancing up at her and nodding slowly. 'Just needed to sit down.' He had taken off his brown pullover. There were dark smudges beneath his eyes. 'I thought I'd grab five minutes.' He put the pencil down and pushed his hands slowly through his hair.

'Only Madeleine was wondering where you'd got to. She's about to do the cake.'

Simon stood up and started straightening his tie. It was an instinctive action, one so familiar you hardly noticed it. Like the way he always said tickety boo when his figures balanced, or the way he stirred sugar in his coffee so fast. *Ding ding ding ding ding ding ding ding ding!* There was an almost full glass of champagne on the desk in front of him. He picked this up now and downed the contents in one gulp. She watched his Adam's apple bob. She started to turn back towards the door. But even as she did so, she knew he'd try to stop her. Knew this was the moment she'd have to let him down. Poor Simon. She should have done it sooner, she knew. But how could you tell someone you didn't want to go out with them before they actually asked you if you would?

'Dutch courage,' he said now, lowering the glass and considering her over it.

She smiled. Feigned lightness. 'I beg your pardon?'

'That's what they say, don't they?' He put the empty glass down and moved out from behind the desk. He was looking pointedly at her now, like a predator assessing his chances. A mild anxiety washed over her. How much had he drunk? 'Why Dutch?' he went on. 'Why do you think they call it *Dutch* courage particularly? Are the Dutch a particularly uncourageous people, do you think? I've always wondered about that.'

He couldn't pronounce the word 'particularly' properly. Hope took a step back, making a gesture as if she were headed to her own desk, to get something.

'I don't know,' she said. 'I don't know any Dutch people. Isn't it something to do with soldiers?' He was advancing on her now, straightening his tie again as he walked. 'Isn't it a war thing? Something to do with the army? I don't know. I –'

He was in front of her now. She could smell the fabric conditioner on his shirt. See the shadows beneath his arms, the sheen of sweat on his face, the grooves in his forehead as he frowned at her.

'Oh, Hope,' he said slowly, enunciating carefully. 'Look at you.'

She blinked at him. 'What?'

He opened his arms wide, startling her. '*Look* at you!' he said again. The arms began moving up and down, for emphasis, his palms open, his gaze bobbing over her with them. 'Look at you! Oh, Hope, have you any idea what you do to me?'

'*What?*'

He slapped them back against his sides. 'Oh, Hope.' He swept the arms out once more and this time he left them there. '*This!*'

She stared at him, stunned. She was completely unprepared for this kind of drama. A mumbled invitation to dinner perhaps. A shy declaration. But not this. 'Simon,' she lied, 'I really don't know what you're talking about.'

His brows converged as he advanced closer. 'Don't say that. Please don't say that, Hope. You know very well. The way you look, the way you act, the way you –' He grabbed her hand. Held it tightly between his own. They were big hands. Big powerful hands. Warm and moist. 'The way you look at me, Hope. *Me*. Don't try to tell me you don't know. Please don't.' He squeezed it now, his gaze locked on to hers. 'Don't try to tell me you haven't been aware – that you really don't know. That you're not a part of this. That you haven't been waiting for me to – look, I know it's been a difficult year for you. I don't want to push things, really I don't. I know you feel a bit shy. I don't want to... ' He moved his thumb tenderly in small arcs over the back of her hand. 'I don't want to pressure you or anything. But sometimes, *sometimes*, when you're sitting there across the office, and I look over at you, and you catch my eye and smile back at me – the way you smile back at me, Hope. I can't help but believe that –'

She pulled her hand away and stepped backwards, horrified. Her bottom was now against the edge of her desk.

'Simon, you're stressing me. I don't –'

'*Stressing* you?' He pushed his hand through his hair again. 'Why on earth would I be stressing you?' He looked genuinely appalled. He took another step towards her. 'Why on earth would you be stressed? There's nothing to be stressed about. I'm just talking about *us*, Hope,' he said quietly. 'You and me.'

His arms were around her before she could properly digest this. And his face – God, his lips – were heading for her own – collision-course heading, like surface-to-air missiles. She wriggled away from him.

'Simon, come on. Stop this, please. You've had a little too much to drink, and you'll –'

'Hope, come on. Don't do this to me.' He was crowding her again, a half-smile twitching on his lips. 'Don't play games with me. Just relax. Just let me hold you. There. That's all I want. See?

Just to –' His arms encircled her again, and this time she could feel the steady pressure of them against her sides. 'Just to kiss you, that's all. I've been waiting so long, I can't let you –'

She pressed her palms against his chest and pushed him gently but firmly away. 'Simon, stop it,' she said. 'Stop it. You'll regret this in the morning. Come on. Don't be silly.'

His arms were still around her and his face was still angled to kiss her, but his lips, slightly open still, reined themselves in. He was looking at her now with unmistakeable determination, his eyes glittering with lust only inches from hers. Though his ears, evidently, weren't working.

He licked his lips. 'Oh, Hope… '

There was an unsteady thickness in his voice now. God, but he was dogged. She'd never seen him like this, and it filled her with foreboding. 'Come *on*,' she urged again, more firmly this time. 'Don't be silly, Simon. It's just the champagne. You'll be kicking yourself in the morning –'

But it was fruitless trying to reason with him. The pressure against her shoulders grew, if anything, stronger. She could feel the warm bulk of his thigh against her own. And he was grinning at her. *Grinning* at her.

'Come on,' he whispered. 'Look, we both know you want to really.' He licked his lips again. 'I do understand your reticence, you know. I do know how it's been for you… '

He was edging her back against the desk, albeit gently. Albeit only in his quietly persistent way. He was a persistent man and he was persisting right now. Also, as was becoming increasingly apparent, stupid and ignorant and immune to reality and persistently trying to get his tongue in her mouth and to press his fat knee between hers. There was no room for discussion. No point in cajoling. She shoved her hands against his chest hard enough to make him stagger backwards and collide with his own swivel chair.

'The *hell* you do!' she roared at him. He looked incredulous. Poleaxed. 'The hell you bloody do! Do you hear?'

There was a moment of absolute silence. And then, either as a result of the push, or her expression, or the alcohol level in his bloodstream having dropped just half a millilitre below that required for the continuing application of Dutch courage – Hope really didn't know – his expression changed from one of stupefaction to one of mild horror. And then, even as her own was busy forming one of forgiveness and compassion, it moved on to one of barely restrained anger. She grew frightened. She hadn't expected anger either. Not at all.

'The hell you do!' she said again, his narrowed eyes and curled lip acting as fuel to her own fury. 'You know nothing about me, Simon! Nothing!'

He was flexing and unflexing his fingers at his side now. Staring at her with as much hate as there'd been love moments earlier. She didn't doubt it. Oh no. Not now. Where once she'd simply seen a gentle person with a puppy-dog devotion, she could now see the reality of his feelings for her. The raw intensity of the ardour of the man underneath. To think she'd caused this. To think she'd fanned such a fire. To think her innocent gestures of friendship and camaraderie had been so wrongly interpreted, so mistakenly read. Even as he stood there hating her for it, she couldn't help but feel wretched that she'd let it come to this. How on earth would she deal with him now?

He was still staring at her, breathing heavily and raggedly. In – out. In – out. Flex – unflex. In – out.

'I'm sorry,' he said, his voice low and cold, his eyes shining. 'I'm sorry I ever laid eyes on you, Hope.' Then he turned his face away from her, lifted his arm, and punched his fist, like a piston, at the wall.

'*There* you are!'

Madeleine's voice, mere seconds later, entered the office along with a bright stripe of light, as she'd swung open the door, blinding Hope. It had grown quite dark. She hadn't realised. Madeleine flicked on the light switch.

Hope was on her knees beside Simon, who was crying. Great gulping sobs as he rocked on his haunches. Her hands were shaking, she realised.

'Hope?' Madeleine said, peering across the office at them. 'What's happened? Is Simon all right?'

Hope could hear him trying to still his sobs.

'He's fine,' she said over her shoulder. 'Just fine. No panic. Just tripped on one of the computer leads trying to pick up his pen. You're all right, aren't you, Simon?' He made some sort of noise.

Madeleine was crossing the office now, and Hope, still with her back to the door, swivelled her head to catch Madeleine's eye.

'Too much champagne, eh?' she said, ostensibly to Simon, but inclining her head and signalling with her eyes to let Madeleine know not to press. She would have to tell her, of course. She couldn't not. But not now. Not with everyone around. 'I think we're all a bit worse for wear,' she went on. 'Maybe you could call him a taxi or something? Wouldn't do to have the other staff see you like this, eh, Simon?' She felt his shoulders heave beneath her hands.

Madeleine, though clearly perplexed, was also blessed with a quick brain and a keen nose for trouble. She nodded. Stuck a thumb up. Winked knowingly.

'Absolutely,' she said now, while rolling her eyes at Hope and grinning. 'No problem. On its way. Hey, Si? I'll make sure they save you some cake.'

And she was gone. Hope rose to her feet, heaving Simon up too and hooking his chair with her ankle. He sat down on it listlessly, silent and acquiescent. He was, she realised, far more drunk than she'd thought. The sour tang of alcohol eddied around him as he breathed. His knuckles looked livid. Two angry cuts oozed bright red blood. She found a packet of tissues in her desk drawer and wrapped several around his hand, which was already swelling, then spat on another and rubbed away the smear of blood on the wall. He watched all this through glazed eyes.

'Right,' she said finally, not knowing quite what to do or say to him, and retreating to the safer ground of getting organised instead. 'That'll have to do. I'll go and get your coat for you and fetch you once the cab arrives, OK?'

He lifted his head and looked up at her. 'Thank you,' he said dully.

'Do you want some water or anything? A coffee?' He shook his head. 'Right then. I'll be back soon.'

*   *   *

'I need a proper drink,' declared Madeleine some forty-five minutes later, once everyone else had left and the offices were dark and silent again. 'And so do you, by the looks of it. You in a hurry to get home?'

Hope looked at her watch. It wasn't yet nine. And no, she wasn't in a hurry to get home. She felt too strung out. Too tearful. All out of energy for dealing with people. Besides, with her mother out of commission at the moment, she'd had to ring round and get the girl down the road to babysit. She'd come with her boyfriend. No. She'd be in no rush. Hope shook her head. 'Now I'm out, I may as well get my money's worth, eh?' So they walked the few streets to the local wine bar, and perched themselves gratefully on stools at the bar.

'Ah, a cigarette at last,' Madeleine said, pulling a packet from her handbag. 'You can't imagine what a trial it is having to pretend I don't smoke all the time. Makes me feel like a naughty school girl.'

'What *I* need,' said Hope, resting her elbows on the bar top and sipping tentatively at her expresso, 'is a large mug of cocoa, some slippers and a hot water bottle, and to go to bed – under a candlewick bedspread, ideally – and stay there for the rest of my life. Look! See? My hands are still shaking. Can you believe that? Do you think he broke anything?'

Madeleine lit a cigarette and inhaled deeply. 'God. That's better.' She shook her head. 'Broke anything? I doubt it.' She winked. 'Bar his heart.'

'You didn't see it. He really punched it hard, Maddie. God, it was horrible. What got into him?'

Madeleine smiled broadly as she drank a mouthful of red wine. 'Well, half a bucket of Sainsbury's finest, for one thing. But mainly you, of course, sweetie. What else? It would be rather romantic if it wasn't so pathetic. Just goes to show. You never know with people, do you?'

Hope felt this statement to be profoundly true. She felt she didn't know anything about anyone any more. 'But Simon? Simon, of all people! If I'd had the first idea –'

'Come on, darling. He's been mooning over you since the day you started. No. Tell a lie. Before that, even. He used to come back

214

to the office with a dozy expression on his face when you were still helping out at the shop. It was only ever a matter of time.'

'Yes, but the way he lunged at me! I mean I know he's been keen on me, but if I'd thought for one minute he'd behave like that – he really didn't have a clue. He really thought I was up for it. I was gobsmacked! I wouldn't mind, but I've never given him even the tiniest indication that I was interested in him. Never!'

Madeleine placed a hand on Hope's forearm. 'Darling, you are so touchingly naïve. You didn't need to. Some men are highly accomplished self-deluders. And you are just the sort of woman that men like that have no difficulty fixing their fantasies upon.'

'Me? How d'you work that out?'

'Because you're just so damn sweet and pretty, honey.'

'Come on!'

'Believe me, you are. Hope, if I was gay, even *I'd* fancy you, sweetheart.' She laughed. 'You just have those looks that bring out the beast in a man.'

'Thanks, but I think I already knew that. Iain was perfectly civilised when I met him.' She pushed her coffee away. Perhaps she needed a real drink too. 'Oh, stop depressing me, will you? I don't want a beast. What do I have to do? Become one?'

'God, Hope, no. Stay as sweet as you are. It's just something you have to factor into your dealings with men, that's all. Mind you, you are way too nice. If he'd tried it on with me like that, you wouldn't have caught me patting him and offering to call him a taxi. I'd be too busy stamping on his other hand.'

'I know, I know. But I just felt so guilty. I mean, what is it with him? Months and months of looking like he's – Christ – and then this!'

Maddie flicked her ash into the ashtray. 'He has a little difficulty expressing himself, our Simon. Bit of baggage, that's all.'

'Baggage? What sort of baggage?'

'Oh, I don't know the ins and outs, but I believe he was jilted. There was certainly an engagement, or so Betty told me. Five or six years ago. I think she pulled out pretty close to the wedding. Like I say, I don't know the details. And I certainly haven't asked. He keeps himself pretty much to himself, but to the best of my knowledge, there hasn't been anyone since. You want a text book on low self-esteem? Well he wrote it.'

'I should have read it. God, what a mess. This has been brewing up for months, and I've just shut my eyes and let it. I've been running with him so often –'

'Well, there's that for starters. Frankly, sweetie, with a body like yours, it doesn't do to don Lycra with a man you've no carnal designs on. He's probably been trotting round ogling that little bottom of yours, thinking his excitable little thoughts, planning his little campaign, imagining his –'

'Oh, don't, Maddie!' Hope put her face in her hands. 'I *know*. God, I can't imagine how he must be feeling right now. How's he going to face me tomorrow?'

'That's his problem, darling. Not yours.'

'Maybe, but how am I going to face him?'

'Look. Do you want me to speak to him?'

'Oh, I don't know. Is there any point?'

'Probably not. Unless you want to slap a harassment action on his head, I'm happy enough to let it go. Look, it's done now. At least it's brought it to a head. And let's face it – it *was* an office party. Everyone does appalling things at office parties. Even the Simons of this world, apparently. So – hey - there's hope for him yet! Er… ' She raised her glass. 'No pun intended, of course.'

Hope wished she was still married. Wished it vehemently and profoundly. She didn't wish she was still married to Iain, of course, she just wished she could return, by some miracle, to the safely married state. She wished she didn't have to inhabit the real world any longer. Or could inhabit it differently. In a nun's habit and iron knickers, or with an obsessive compulsion to play bowls. Sex, it felt, had never loomed larger in her life. It was all around her, latent yet suffocating. It was all too exhausting, this business. Too time-consuming and racked with anxiety and insecurity. Too much a world of playing games. Of small rushes of hope and great storm clouds of disappointment. She thought she'd done that bit. She *had* done that bit. But now she was back, full circle, doing it all again, only this time with the handicap of hard knocks and experience, and the awful knowledge that the field on which she was now playing was no longer in the premier league. That most of the players on the other team were either the subs that didn't get a game last time, or the ones that got injured, or the ones that got sent off.

Which made her at once think of football and Oliver Valentine, which took her instantly, wretchedly, straight back to Jack Valentine, which made her feel hopeless and sad. There were so few nice, normal men on the planet, and, depressingly, so very many Simons.

Chapter 25

Stick with it, thought Jack. That was the thing. A routine was comfortable and familiar. Routine didn't invoke much in the anxiety department. Didn't change, didn't tax, and didn't make demands.

When he'd got back from the hospice he had sat straight down in the middle of the lounge floor and tipped out all his files for the book. In fact, THE book, because it said so in bold marker pen on the side of the box. He didn't remember having written the words. An act of confidence, he supposed, from more optimistic times. Whatever. It was a joke, any idea he might have had about getting it finished soon. That simply wasn't going to happen, and he just had to accept it.

But finish it he would, if not this year than next. It wasn't much of an ambition. Wasn't an ambition at all, really. Not now. Now it was more of a need. That he'd finish it, get it published, do whatever it took. Just so he could put those precious words on the flyleaf: *for my father, with all my love*.

The file had all still been there when he set off for the studios the following morning. Sorted and organised, looking like business. Looking like he might yet make something of it. Filling him with hope that he actually could.

'You're wanted,' Hil announced as soon as she saw him. She nodded. 'Upstairs. By the boss. One-fifteen.'

While Jack was busy getting his show out, he didn't think a great deal about this summons. Which was for the best, he decided afterwards, or he might just have got straight back in his car and gone home.

'I'm not going to waste your time with small talk,' Graham said. Which told Jack he wasn't going to like what he was going to hear next. He was getting used to this.

'My contract,' he said.

Graham nodded, looking sad. Jack wondered how many years of this sort of meeting had sculpted the sincerity he could see writ upon his face. But he liked Graham. He wouldn't want his job.

'As you know, we're making some pretty big changes.'

Jack nodded too.

'One of which is with the daytime schedules.'

'And my show's axed.'

Graham sighed now. 'You got it, mate. I'm sorry.'

Jack shifted in his chair and crossed his legs. He thought Graham probably genuinely was sorry. They went back a long way, he and Graham. Back to the day when he'd sat in this very office, probably only days after someone else had sat in it, hearing the same news he was hearing now.

He shrugged. 'That's life,' he said simply. Because it was.

But Graham was still grimacing. 'We're giving the slot to Patti,' he added quickly, as if anxious to have his worst news hitch a ride with the first news, the better to minimise the pain. 'Quotas, you know. That sort of thing. A change of emphasis. The Target Listener and all that.'

Jack shrugged. He did know. This was how things worked. He wasn't even surprised, once he thought about it. Why wouldn't they give the show to Patti? She was a vibrant and talented broadcaster. In her twenties, leggy, and, intermittently at least, blonde. He made a big show of smiling in a nonchalant manner.

'Hey, I can take it,' he said. 'In fact, the timing's about perfect. I was thinking it was perhaps time for a new challenge. Easy to get stale.'

Graham looked relieved. 'I'm glad you said that,' he answered. 'Because actually, potentially, there is some rather good news, too. Sport Scene.' This was a show Jack had at one time presented on Saturdays. Till he'd got Valentine's Day. Did he really want to take that up again? It felt like demotion. Stupid, but it did.

'What about it?' he said. 'Is Connor moving on then?' Connor, who was thirty and on a roll and ambitious. A little like he'd been. Full circle. *C'est la vie.*

Graham grinned. 'Of course not! No, I mean how do you feel about taking over as producer? They've not quite crossed the I's, so don't broadcast this one yet, but Brian's moving over to ITV Wales.'

Brian had come to them from television in the first place, following a move down from London five years back. They'd been lucky to get him, and they'd known they wouldn't keep him.

'Really?' Jack's brain began whirring in an altogether unsavoury way. Was that why Allegra's show hadn't been commissioned? Because Brian's had? What a bloody irony that would be. He wondered which big name he'd managed to poach for it. Then stopped wondering, abruptly. He realised he didn't care.

Graham was nodding. 'You'd make a good fist of it, mate. You know you would. But take some time to think it over. No hurry.'

No, thought Jack, no hurry at all. He rather wished time would just stop.

'Coo, get you!' said Patti when he returned downstairs. She was flicking through the brochure for the Cardiff Bay development that Charlie Jones had given him, and it occurred to him that either she didn't know what had just happened or she was making a fine job of pretending she didn't. The former, he judged. The former, he *hoped*.

He scowled at it now. 'You can bin that,' he told her.

'How so?'

'Because.'

'Because what?'

He hadn't the energy. Not today. 'Because nothing.'

She laughed at him. 'You're not getting enough, Jack.'

'Enough what?'

'Enough sex.'

'Is that right?'

'That's right. I can see it in your eyes. Tell you what. You wanna come clubbing with me later?'

'I don't think so.'

'You should.'

'I don't think so,' he said again.

Patti poked him. 'You old saddo.'

He nodded. 'You got it.'

He wasn't *that* old, but he was sure as hell sad.

'I want to apologise.'

It was almost five-thirty, and Hope had not seen anything of Simon since the night of Kayleigh's party. Madeleine, having spoken to him, had decided to have him work at home for a couple of weeks. It was year-end, so this was perfectly reasonable. There'd been emails, of a '*Hope. VAT receipt for this? Can you clarify?*' variety, but no phone calls, no contact, no nothing. It was a relief having him gone from the office. She supposed he was licking his wounds.

But this afternoon he had arrived for some meeting with Madeleine and now everyone else had gone and they were alone in the office. He sat down heavily on the chair on the other side of her desk.

'You don't need to, Simon,' she said levelly. 'It's forgotten. I've forgotten it. OK?'

He seemed to wince. Straight away, she realised this was the wrong thing to say. Or the right thing, perhaps. She must stop being kind to him.

'I haven't,' he said.

'Well, you should,' she persisted. 'If we're going to carry on working together, you must.'

He managed a smile. A tight and halting affair, which made his face, already pasty under the striplight, look like a wax mask.

'Just like that, eh?' he said. There was no sarcasm in his voice, only sadness.

Hope put her pen down.

'No, Simon. Not just like that. Look, I'm sorry too. I feel awful about it. What else can I say to you?'

He didn't answer. His face was a picture of perfect misery, and there wasn't a thing she could do about it. He remained sitting, as if uncertain whether there was anything further he needed to add. Then he stood up.

'And I wanted to let you know I'm looking around,' he said finally. Horribly sadly. 'So don't worry. You won't have to feel awful for too long.'

There was no malice in his voice, but, even so, as he walked out of the office she had to bite her lip to stop herself calling after him, taking him to task about what exactly he meant. *She* hadn't done anything wrong. *He* had. So how come his words made her feel so guilty? Hope felt her whole body slump in her chair. She didn't want to be part of so much hurt. It hurt her, too. She sat for several minutes with her face in her hands, and felt utterly wretched and alone. It didn't matter how much she told herself it wasn't her fault, that this wasn't her doing, there was still someone out there wretched and unhappy and suffering and the cause was irrefutably herself. It felt like an impossible weight to have to carry, and she didn't feel up to the job.

She didn't mean for Jack Valentine to be in her head again. She just wanted someone to give her a cuddle. Was that so much to ask out of life?

Chapter 26

She'd known the day was coming, of course. It was written in her diary. He'd even phoned the office yesterday, to re-confirm the time. Yet when Hope first entered the conference room she had to steady herself against the door frame to stop herself fleeing the place and jumping on a bus to Land's End. There was no question of trying to fight it. Here he was and she was utterly, hopelessly in love with him. But she didn't know what to do about it, because she wasn't joining any queues.

She plastered what she hoped was a friendly, workaday smile on her face and took her place next to Mr Babbage at the table. Jack, who had evidently slipped in with Madeleine while she'd gone off to photocopy an extra agenda, was sitting opposite her and smiled back with similar urbanity. Yet there was something unreadable in his expression. She busied herself with her notes.

The meeting – which was to be their last before the day itself – soon stilled her frantic pulse. There was just so much to do. Still the warm-up aerobic session to be finalised, the St John's Ambulance stand to be organised, a consignment of cereal bars for the goody bags to chase up and a new batch of race numbers to get printed. And the timings, of course. Item five.

'So,' Madeleine was saying, 'my feeling would be for us to convene at the main gazebo at five-thirty, latest, you think? By then we should have assembled and warmed up the runners, and it'll give us time – sorry, *Jack* time, to –'

'Hang on,' said Jack, flipping through the pages of a bulky black diary he had on the table in front of him. 'It was starting at seven, wasn't it?'

'No, six,' said Madeleine equably.

Jack consulted a page and glanced across the table at her. 'I have seven here.'

'You do?' said Madeleine. 'Oh.'

'That's the old time,' said Hope. 'Remember?'

Jack turned, still smiling nicely. 'Oh? Remember what?'

He was looking straight at her.

'We had to change it, didn't we? The police.'

'What about the police?'

'There's a concert at the CIA that night. They won't close the roads after seven. It was all in the email.'

Jack's eyes hadn't left her face. 'What email?'

She felt her face fall. 'The email we sent you about the time change.'

'Doh,' said Mr Babbage, cheerily. 'I thought things were going too well!' He picked up a fruit shortcake and started munching on it.

'Is it a problem?' asked Madeleine.

'*What* email?' Jack said again.

'The email I sent you,' said Hope, becoming flustered, riffling through her memories. She *had* sent him the email. And followed it up.

But he was shaking his head. 'I definitely didn't get an email from you.'

'Well I certainly sent one. I did ask you to confirm, but when I spoke to your secretary –'

'I don't have a secretary.'

'Whoever she was, then.'

Madeleine looked from one to the other. Then back at Hope, somewhat pointedly, the 'whoever she was, then' hanging between them all like the breasts of a lap dancer at a tea party. 'Is it going to be a problem, Jack?' she asked again.

He closed the diary and pinched his fingers together over the bridge of his nose. He looked tired.

'Well, yes it is, frankly. I'm in London that day. I had planned on getting back for six-thirty.'

'Oh dear,' said Mr Babbage, reaching for a second biscuit. Jack shot him an irritable look. Hope had never seen Jack look irritable before.

Madeleine switched on her brightest and most apologetic smile. 'I'm so sorry, Jack,' she said smoothly. 'It's entirely our fault. We should have followed it up more carefully. Bit hectic round here right now, as you can imagine.' She glanced at Hope, waiting for her to follow suit with platitudes and kittenish smiles of appeasement. Which Hope dutifully did. Madeleine clasped her hands in front of her. 'I'm sure we can work around it. Your

224

contribution is very valuable, Jack, but I know you're a busy man. If the worst comes to the worst, we can always have someone else start the race and you can come in and do a big closing speech or something instead.'

Jack was shaking his head. 'No, no,' he said. 'Hold off for the moment. I'll see what I can do first, OK?'

'Well, that's very kind of you, Jack,' said Madeleine warmly. She batted her lashes at him. 'Are we forgiven?'

'Forgiven,' agreed Jack, and Hope could feel his eyes on her. She kept her own trained on the biscuits.

'Look,' he said, once the room had emptied and Madeleine, who was rolling her eyes at Hope behind Jack's back, had pulled the door shut behind her. 'I'm sorry about that. I didn't mean to upset you.'

'You didn't upset me.'

'I think I did.'

Hope shrugged. 'OK, then, yes. You did upset me.'

She knew she sounded haughty, but she just didn't know how to *be* with him any more. She wished she didn't have to see him at all. He was grinning at her now. 'Secretary, eh? Chance would be a fine thing.'

Hope began gathering up the agendas. 'Look, I *did* email you. And I also spoke to a woman, and I expressly asked her to get you to call me if there was any problem with the new time, OK? And you didn't.'

'Well, of course I didn't. I didn't get the message, did I?'

'Fine.'

'Fine.' But his look said otherwise, and for a fraction of a moment she wondered if he was going to say something about her own track record of not getting messages, but he didn't. She blushed, nevertheless. She felt suddenly tearful. He picked up the last of the agendas and handed it across the table to her. 'When was this, anyway?'

'When I was there doing the interview last week.'

'So why didn't you just come and ask me?'

Hope slipped the pieces of paper between the covers of her file, and closed it with a snap. 'I tried to. But you were off out having lunch with someone, I believe.'

She hadn't realised there would be anything so pointed in her voice when she started to say this, but it had come along for the ride. He'd clearly heard it. He narrowed his eyes.

'"*Off* out"?'

'Off out.'

He looked irritable again. 'Oh. Right. Which makes it my fault you didn't get the message to me then, does it?'

'Look, I left a message in the confident expectation that it would reach you. Because I was told it would. But it didn't. That's hardly my fault.'

'Which makes it my fault?'

'No! But that doesn't mean it was *my* fault, OK?'

How was this happening? How was she standing here feeling so cross with him? It wasn't his fault any more than it was her fault, but it *wasn't* her fault. And now she'd evidently rattled him.

'Look,' he said, his habitual good humour gone, it seemed, for good. She'd never seen him so short-tempered. 'You left a message telling me to get back to you *only* if there was a problem, right? Which, I'm sorry, but is frankly a cock up waiting to happen. If you'd left a message asking me to confirm either way, then this wouldn't have happened. That's all.'

His eyes flashed turquoise darts at her.

'Don't patronise me,' she said.

He rolled his eyes. Then pushed both hands across his forehead and up over the top of his head.

'Right,' he said coldly. 'My cue to leave, I think.' He raised one eyebrow fractionally then nodded again.'Tell Madeleine I'll call her.'

And he left.

Damn her, damn her, damn her, he thought, as he nosed out into the late-afternoon traffic. He had been so looking forward to seeing her. It didn't matter that he'd already as good as cocked it up with her. Didn't matter that she hadn't been in touch. He knew that if he could just see her face-to-face that he'd be able to tell straight away how things really were. See beyond her pronouncements that she didn't want to see him. Get some hint of whether there might be any point in – Jesus! He slammed his palms against the steering wheel. Was this God's doing, or something? God's way of punishing him? But for what? Just what had he done to deserve all this crap? He felt seriously fed up. More than that, he felt justified in being seriously fed up. Which was novel. Forget the endless pep talk he kept giving himself. He should just let himself feel fed up and be done with it, and stop pretending he was happy when he wasn't. A red Fiesta cut him up at the Gabalfa roundabout, and then proceeded to get in his way.

'Fuck you too!' he roared. Which should have made him feel better. But as he drew level he could see the driver was an elderly lady, so he only felt worse.

He checked the time. He was supposed to be collecting Ollie from Lydia at six-thirty, to take him to a friendly over in Grangetown. It wasn't much past four. There was nothing to rush home for. He had purposefully left an end-of-the-day window in his diary in case there'd been a chance with Hope, but now it was fit for little other than jumping out of. Decided, he signalled right instead of left at the next junction, and headed back to the studios.

It wasn't so much the fact of the administrative cock-up, but her being so riled about it. Off out to lunch, eh? Shit. It was so obvious. It spoke volumes. He tried to recall which day it was that she'd been in to do the PM show, but failed. All he knew was that he'd heard about it after the event, and been pathetically upset that he'd missed her. Perhaps he should have called her then. Kicked his precious pride into touch. But hell, was he really up to another bloody knock-back? Didn't he have enough on his plate right now?

But how the hell had he not picked up her email?

He slipped into the office to a chorus of the usual derisory cheers.

'Good grief, Jack? Is it Christmas?' someone quipped. Helen. The bloody junior. He ignored her and went over to his sometime desk. There was the usual plethora of junk on it, plus the junk from the desk beside it which had spilled across. He sat down and went through the pile methodically. Two weeks back was pre-historic in BBC paperwork terms. Nothing. He turned his attention to his out-tray. There was plenty in there – there always was. He often wondered what happened to all those endless bits of paper he signed. Nothing again. And then he saw something pink at the edge of another document. A Groovy Chick post it, which was some stupid researcher's idea of getting in touch with her inner child. What was it with women that they had to adorn every desktop with cuddly toys and Snoopy Mugs and Bob the Builder bloody stationery? He peeled it off and turned it over, already knowing what it said.

Please call Hope Shepherd @ heartbeat if any probs with 6pm start.

Well, damn, frankly. Damn and blast it. Why the hell didn't these people realise that writing a message on the back of another message was just plain stupid? Stupider still when it was on a bloody post-it and the message was on the side with the glue. It was stuck, ironically, on the back of a memo about emotional intelligence at bloody work.

But that didn't explain about the email.

He switched on his terminal and scowled at his reflection. There were umpteen emails, of course, which he scrolled through irritably, right back to the middle of January. But nothing from Heartbeat. And then something occurred to him, and he clicked on his address book. Scrolled through it. Heartbeat's email address wasn't listed. Of course. When he'd emailed the publicity jpeg he'd done it from Hil's terminal. Of *course*. Because she had all the mug shots on hers. Different screen name.

Different email address.

'Look, I'm sorry, I'm sorry, I'm sorry, OK?'

The phone had rung nine times before Hope had picked it up. He'd almost put it back down. She sounded out of breath.

'I beg your pardon?' she said.

'You were right and I was wrong and I'm sorry. I went back to the office. I found the note. I found the email. I found –'

'You did all that?'

He couldn't gauge anything from the tone of her voice. 'Yes. I did all that,' he said.

There was a very long silence. 'You didn't have to do that, Jack,' she said eventually.

'*And* I re-jigged my meeting in London. *And* I re-booked my train. *And* I will be there for five-thirty. And I'm sorry, Hope.'

'Oh, God, you don't need to be,' she said. Her voice, all of a sudden, sounded animated. 'It *was* my fault. You were absolutely right. I should have double checked. I should have done it the way

228

you said, and I shouldn't have got so bloody uppity about it. And I certainly shouldn't have told you not to patronise me. You weren't patronising me at all, and I wish I hadn't said that.'

He cursed himself for having been so short.

'I really hate that I upset you, Hope.'

Another silence. Was she taking notes or something? He couldn't fathom her. He heard her exhale. 'You didn't upset me, Jack. Really you didn't. It's just that it's been such a hard couple of weeks and there's just too much to do, and my sister-in-law has been in hospital and my mum's staying there at the moment, so I've got the most God-awful logistical difficulties with the children right now, and I don't know whether I'm coming or going, and I've just been so – so –'

She stopped speaking. Abruptly. And breathed heavily out instead. 'Oh dear,' he said, wanting to kiss it all better for her. 'Is she OK?'

He heard another long sigh at the other end of the phone. He wondered what she was doing right now. He wanted, he realised, to stay on the phone and listen to her forever.

'Oh, she'll be fine. But, really Jack, you don't want to know. Believe me, you do *not* want to know. Anyway,' she seemed to be winding herself up to tell him anyway, but no. 'Jack,' she said suddenly. '*I'm* the one who should be apologising. You go out of your way to fit us in and all I do is bitch and grouse and… ' She laughed a shy little laugh. 'And send you stomping off in a huff.'

'I wasn't in a huff.'

'You were in a serious huff. You had every right to be. Has it been a big hassle? I mean, you have so much on, and –'

'It wasn't a big hassle.'

'You're sure?'

'I'm sure. Did you get much grief at work?'

'Not at all,' said Hope firmly. 'Maddie's a friend.'

'Only I was worried that – well, I was a teeny bit cross, wasn't I?'

'You were a bit cross.' She laughed now. Properly. This was better.

'But you're sure.'

She laughed again. 'I'm sure I'm sure.'

'And I'm sorry, Hope.'

'Doh! You said that already.'

A thought occurred to him. Suddenly. Hearing her laugh.

'Hope, what day were you born?'

'Twelfth of August. Why?'

'No, not the date. What day of the week?'

'Oh. I see. A Sunday. Why?'

He'd known without doubt that she would be. That she could never be anything else.

'Because you're sounding very bonny and blithe and all that stuff,' he answered. 'So does that mean I'm forgiven?'

He waited for her to laugh again, but she didn't. The silence lengthened. 'Hmm. What's London?' she asked eventually. 'Anything exciting?'

As 'exciting' was one adjective he didn't think h'd be using in relation to his work for some time, her question brought him up short. He wondered if he should tell her about it but couldn't seem to find the right words. I've lost my job. I didn't get my new one. I'm a failure. He couldn't find the right thoughts for it, let alone the right words, with which to tell her he was none of the things she thought he was, but simply an ordinary man with few prospects and whose father was dying and who was needy and sad. He knew he wouldn't feel like this forever. But right now it was like being impotent all over again, except worse. The sense of emasculation was so total. No. He wouldn't tell her. He didn't think he could cope with her feeling sorry for him. Besides, she sounded like she had more than enough on her plate.

'Oh, nothing exciting,' he said, breezily. 'Just have to see a man about a job.'

'Oh,' she said. 'In London?'

'Uh-huh.'

'Oh. Right. Is this something to do with the television thing?'

'Er... nope. Something else.'

'Oh.'

'Hope?'

'Yes?'

'You know how sorry I said I was?'

'Yes.'

'Well, I still feel bad, you know.'

'Jack don't be. I told you.'

'I know, but I'd feel a whole lot better about it if you'd let me say sorry properly. You know. Like with a glass of wine? Or dinner? Or... '

'Oh, *Jack*... '

'Oh Jack, what?'

'I just... oh, God. There's Iain for the children. Look. I'd better go.'

'You didn't answer my question yet.'

'I know. I just... look, can I call you back, maybe?'

He could hear her doorbell ringing.

'No. Not until you've said yes.'

But she hadn't said yes. She'd only said maybe. And refused to elaborate. She'd said she couldn't do Saturday, but might manage Sunday. Though wasn't sure. He'd have to call her back on Sunday. Then she'd bundled him off the phone.

He'd said he'd call her Sunday. It would just have to do.

The flat felt airless and gloomy when he put the phone down. As if it was not part of the real world but suspended in some sort of plasma bubble, with him trapped inside. It pressed in on him. He went into the kitchen and peered without much hope in the fridge. Nothing to eat and he couldn't stomach another take-away. There was no point in trying to cross Cardiff yet to get to the hospice. Perhaps he'd better do that thing normal people did and pop down to Sainsbury's to get some supplies. Yes. He grabbed his jacket from the hook and escaped.

Jack wondered how he would feel if his dad were not dying, but instead suffering from some chronic though not immediately life-threatening illness. Like mild angina (Lydia's mother) or perhaps arthritis (Danny's) or just the general wear and tear of ageing. The inevitable role-reversal that had offspring talking to their elderly relatives in loud voices and taking round flagons of soup.

He felt, sometimes, that he'd been cheated out of a stage. He would hear Hil in the office, railing endlessly about picking up her mother's laundry, or collecting her prescriptions or taking her to see a stupefying stream of doctors, podiatrists, dentists and nutritionists. Sorting out her pension payments, having someone in to do her hair. Before the divorce, before his father's diagnosis, before everything that had gone wrong in his life, he had blithely assumed that this would be his cross to bear too. Had he minded? He didn't think so. He realised he'd sort of taken it for granted that Lydia would deal with the lion's share of it, and that he'd have only a small but well-defined role. Picking his dad up to come for Sunday lunch with them, maybe. Helping in the garden – God forbid. Things like that.

But with his father's diagnosis had come the realisation that, no, he probably wouldn't be doing any of those things, and he didn't know how to feel at all any more.

And then Lydia had divorced him and with that had come another realisation, that, as things stood – and, he felt at the time, were likely to remain – he would have no cause to feel aggrieved and irritable, because he'd have no-one to look after at all. No five-hour round trips to Llandrindod Wells like Hil had, no-one to be tetchy with. No-one to resent. He knew he should feel this was in some way compensation for the loss of both his parents, but it hadn't felt so at the time. It didn't feel so now. In fact, the sense of loss was growing ever more acute. He missed Ollie so much. Missed polishing his school shoes for him. Missed fixing his bike. Being alone was about feeling you had no-one to look after you, certainly, but that was only half the story. He wanted someone to look after. He *needed* someone to look after. Did that make him peculiar? He really wasn't sure. But as he drifted around Sainsbury's, his eyes fixed on and held a woman of about his own age, plucking apples from their spongy blue nests under the watchful eye of a largely critical pensioner in a wheelchair, and it made him feel empty at heart.

He avoided the confectionery aisle with great deliberation and bought a 'Taste the Difference' *Duck à l'orange* for his dinner. Lonely. That was all he was. Nothing more dramatic or less ordinary than that. He picked up a blackcurrant cold remedy, too. He was coming down with something as well.

Chapter 27

It wouldn't do, Hope kept telling herself, to get too excited. It wouldn't do to get excited at all, in fact. Whatever her heart was telling her – and boy, had it been clamouring – it was her head she needed to listen to. And her head was telling her simply not to go there. Here was someone with a busy life, a big career – perhaps a job in London, even – and, most importantly, a man with a queue. A queue that was growing, perhaps, even now. The pity was that she couldn't help it. It had become chronic. Like asthma. Or a tendency to boils.

'You're looking chirpy,' her mother remarked, as she opened the front door to let her in.

'I am?'

'Most definitely. Stress obviously suits you.' She sighed a rare sigh. 'I wish it suited me. It's good to see you, love.'

Hope had come to visit Suze. They'd kept her in hospital overnight when she was first admitted, and she hadn't wanted to see anyone the first week. But the children would be coming home at the weekend, when everything would be back to normal. Everything bar the still potent unreality of it all, together with the fact that her mother was still staying with Suze, and the nightmare it had been organising her own children as a consequence.

But it had worked out OK. In some ways better. She'd been thinking long and hard since Suze's 'episode' (which was what her mum had taken to calling it, so she supposed she should too). Yes, it had been a shock. How could it not have? But it had also been good for her. It was quite empowering to be sorting things out on her own at last. She'd spent too long since Iain had left, she realised, meekly accepting both help and advice: taking the easy option of letting her mother take charge of the children, of letting her new life be managed and cushioned, of letting Suze tell her what was best for all of them.

Her dependence, she could see, had been holding her up. She needed to take charge of her own life now. The childcare was tricky, and would remain so a while yet, but Maddie had been great about it, and she knew she would cope. The best thing was that she was beginning to feel stirrings of confidence again. She could make her own decisions regarding her children. She could make her own decisions regarding herself.

Hope had brought Suze a big bunch of tulips and, tiny though the action was, just the arranging of them in Suze's kitchen, in a vase and in a manner of entirely her own choosing, was pleasing in a way that surprised her. 'There,' she said now, to her mother. 'What do you think?'

'Lovely, dear. Lovely. They'll cheer her up no end. Shall I make some tea? While you go on up?'

It was strange to see Suze in bed. Hope tried, and failed, to recall a time when she had ever seen her sister-in-law anything other than fully dressed. There'd been a rare (and never repeated) Christmas when they'd stayed at Paul's, ten years back, but even then, when they had surfaced at around five, Suze was already showered and dressed before broaching the lounge.

Yet here she was, her pale features naked of make-up, hair hanging loose, in jersey pyjamas, and with an expression of un-Suze-like vulnerability on her face.

'How are you?' Hope asked her, because that's what you did.

Suze stroked the duvet. 'Oh, I'm fine,' she replied. Hope placed the tulips on the chest of drawers in the window. There were two men in the garden kneeling over mole-mounds. It looked a bit like an Easter egg hunt, she decided. She said nothing. Best not stir the waters further. 'Actually I'm not, of course,' Suze said suddenly. 'I feel like I've been hit by a truck. I feel like crying all the time. I feel useless and a nuisance and like I really have no business putting everyone to so much bother.'

'You won't feel like that for long,' said Hope. 'You'll see. You'll feel better.'

Suze clasped her hands together and laced the fingers in her lap. 'Ah, but that's such a relative term, isn't it? Feeling better. Rather depends on what you're feeling better *than*.'

Hope considered this a moment, smiling to herself. Yes, she knew that. But she had no idea what to say in response to it. They were all living with such questions just now, weren't they? And there weren't any answers. It would ever be thus. She could see

234

that now. She perched herself on the edge of the bed and nodded. 'I know.'

'But I'm feeling better than I was yesterday, so, yes, you're right. It's progress of a sort. I'm going to start seeing someone, you know. A psychologist. She sounds nice. How about that, eh? Bit of a turn-up, don't you think?'

The old Suze surfaced briefly, and a confrontational expression visited her face. But it was only for a second. Merely an echo. As if she'd suddenly remembered she didn't need to do that any more. Hope could still find nothing useful to say. An affirmative would seem patronising. A denial even more so. This was new and strange territory. 'I wish I'd known, Suze,' she said instead. 'I wish – I mean I always thought you had everything so sorted. If I'd the slightest idea you'd been – well, I wish I'd been able to support you better, that's all.'

Suze looked at her more intently now. 'You know, Hope, it really wouldn't have made any difference. Not to anything. What's wrong with me isn't something someone else can fix – it wouldn't have made any difference.' She shook her head. 'No, that's not even true, is it? It probably would have made it worse.'

'I don't see how that can be.'

'Because it would. Because it would have made *me* feel worse. Everyone knowing. Even my mother doesn't, you know.'

'Your *mother*?'

Suze shook her head. 'It wouldn't help. She's so like me, you see. It would make her ill. I know it would. I'm her success story. I'm her reason for feeling OK about herself. She thinks I have everything. I *do* have everything, don't I?'

Hope had only met Suze's mother a handful of times. She'd seemed brisk, capable. A lot like Suze. 'I don't know,' she said. 'I guess most people would think so. I guess I would. But then I'm not you, am I? It depends what you want. Do *you* think you have everything?'

'Indisputably.' She raised a hand and fanned her fingers. 'I have a lovely caring husband, two beautiful children, a perfect home, nice friends, good health. I have no business being like this, Hope. Really I don't.' She dropped her hand. 'I've just never seemed to be able to help it.'

Hope wanted to offer platitudes. Sound encouraging. Tell Suze it didn't matter. That they'd all rally round. But even as she thought it, she knew that would be wrong. She should say something else.

'You shouldn't be so hard on yourself, you know. You've made a fine job of coping. Bringing up the kids. Supporting Paul...'

'Ah. Yes. I'm very good at that. Getting on. Papering over all the little cracks. Pretending. But that's all it is, Hope. A pretence. I'm not like you. I wish I could be like you. But I'm not.'

Hope smiled at her. 'Me? I'm not much of a role model.'

'Ah, it's not for you to say.'

'I'm sure you wouldn't want my life. It's *all* cracks with me right now, believe me.'

Suze lifted her hand again and waved it dismissively. 'I don't want your *life*. God knows, you've had such a tough time of it, Hope. That's exactly it. Don't you see? I just want your way of living it. Your indomitable spirit. To feel optimistic and jolly and spontaneous and energetic. To get on. To not fuss about things that don't matter all the time.'

'I'm not sure you've quite got me right there, Suze.'

'Oh, but I *have*, Hope. I have. You just don't see it at the moment, that's all.'

Hope could hear her mother clattering up the stairs with the tea tray. Suze glanced at the open door, then clasped Hope's hand tightly. 'You know what I *really* want, Hope? I just want to be the sort of person who wakes up in the morning and feels happy for no reason. Like you do.'

It was this, more than anything, that lodged in Hope's mind when she woke up on Sunday morning. Suze was right. That *was* her. That *was* what she was like. She'd just forgotten, that was all. Got sidetracked, and lost sight of who she was, because she'd been stumbling around in the dark for so long. So much so that when the first chink of light had appeared she'd been too fearful to let herself step into it. The dark seemed so much darker when you came in from the light.

Well, she'd had enough of the dark now. She smiled at herself in her dressing table mirror. Suze was right. She did have an

236

indomitable spirit. She was still here, wasn't she? She'd made it through worse, hadn't she? So sod it. She *would* go out with him. Just for a drink. Once she'd got the kids settled and given them tea, she would get Emma round and go and have a drink with him. Why not? She had nothing to lose that she hadn't lost already. She needn't feel scared. Yes. That's what she would do. And she would take it from there.

It was in this spirit of emotional courageousness that Hope now pressed the play button on her answer-phone. She'd only been out half an hour or so, to get food in for when the children came home. Which they'd just done. They'd all clattered in together. She'd even shouted a cheery greeting to Iain. Stopped and said hello. Asked him about work.

But her valour was redundant.

'It's Jack.' Yes, she knew that. *'I'm really sorry to have missed you. Look, about us going out this evening. Something's come up Er.... look, I'm really sorry, but I don't know how long I'm going to be, so... well, I'll try and call you again later, OK?'*

'Who's that man?' asked Chloe.

'Jack Valentine,' said Tom.

'Jack who?'

'Jack Valentine. The man off the radio.'

She sloughed off her backpack. 'What does *he* want?'

'I dunno.'

'What's he want, Mum?'

Hope stabbed at the delete button. 'Oh, nothing,' she said lightly. 'We're just sorting something about the fun run, that's all.'

'Oh. What's for tea, anyway? I'm starving. Dad made us walk miles. I hate going for walks. Why do we have to go for walks all the time?'

'Because –'

Tom put on a silly voice. 'Because that's what *Rhiannon* likes to do.'

'Well, she's stupid,' Chloe sniffed.

'Don't we know it. Hey, Mum?'

Oh, how quickly the gloss had worn off. She wasn't sure if she was pleased or dismayed. She could see trouble brewing, but she could also go 'hah!' Except that she wouldn't, because she didn't much feel like it. 'What?'

'You know next time?'

'Next what?'

'Doh! Next time we go to Dad's, of course.'

'What about it?'

'Well, do I have to, like, stay the *whole* weekend?'

'Of course you do.'

'But it's so boring.'

'You think you'd be any less bored here? Besides, he takes you to football. You love that.'

'I know. But couldn't you pick me up Sunday morning or something? I never get to see my mates any more.'

'Hardly, Tom,' Hope said. 'You get to see them plenty. Besides, you have to. He looks forward to you going.'

'No, he doesn't! Well, OK, I suppose he does. But he still spends half his time holding hands with *her* and expecting us to run about finding acorns and stuff, like we're babies or something. And I got mud all over my trainers.'

Hope knew this would be a circumstance of some gravity, and felt for him. 'Well, I don't know about that,' she said levelly. 'But I do know your father does look forward to seeing you. Very much. He –'

'Yeah, yeah. But couldn't you just ask him if we could come home Sunday lunchtime? Tell him I've got homework or something?'

'I don't know, Tom. I –'

Chloe put her hands on her hips and pouted. 'That's not fair! If Tom doesn't have to stay all weekend I shouldn't have to stay all weekend!'

'Yeah, you should. You're nine.'

'So what?'

'So you have to do as you're told. Doesn't she, Mum?'

'But that's –'

'Enough!' declared Hope. 'No more debates. I'll think about it, Tom, OK? Right. How about the three of us go out for a pizza or something?'

'What about Jack Valentine?'

'What about him?'

Tom pointed to the phone. 'Aren't you supposed to be doing something this evening?'

'No. No, we're not. And I'm starved as well. Now. Dirty washing in the kitchen please and school bags for the morning. We leave in twenty minutes, OK?'

It felt so wrong not to be bringing wine gums. Jack felt naked as he stepped into the hallway of the hospice and accepted the pats and the sympathetic looks that everyone gave him. That were all part of the process of preparing for death. He'd done this before, of course but this was so different. He'd done it last time *with* his father. As a child and parent conjoined in mutual devastation and support.

They'd called him at four. You might want to come, they'd said. Nothing more. So he'd called Ollie, whose mobile had been switched off, and then Lydia, who explained that he'd gone round to a friend's house. Jack hated to be told that Ollie had gone to 'a friend's house'. He wished she wouldn't say that. It felt all wrong. He'd wanted to pick him up, but Lydia told him to go on to the hospice. That she'd collect Ollie from the friend's house and bring him over herself.

And then he'd called Hope, but she wasn't at home, and his heart had sunk to his boots.

Even though it was Sunday tea-time and therefore rush-hour in terms of visitors, the hospice was a place of almost palpable stillness. There were paintings on the walls of nymphs and snowy mountains. There were flowers – he idly wondered who came in and arranged them – low tables, and chairs, the latter naked of cushions, and Jack wondered, seeing them, just exactly who might sit on them. There were no magazines because the waiting to be done here was full-on, one-on-one, not social at all. Everyone holed up in their own private quarters, playing out their own private tragedies.

His dad, as was usual now, was dozy from the morphine, but stable again, they told him. Jack had come to regard the drugs they gave his father not as medicine but as Valkyries, caressing him while pulling him inexorably further away. His father responded to his touch, squeezed Jack's hand in his own, and yet the effort of speaking was obviously all too much. Jack wondered if consciousness wasn't a little like a cork bobbing on quicksand. So often, it seemed, his father would clamber free of it, make some lucid comment, and then sink into its embrace again.

239

Jack talked to him anyway. He didn't know what else to do. He was reminded of being with his mother when she'd died. How his dad had just sat there, hour upon hour, and talked to her, softly and entirely unselfconsciously, about the weather, the news, sundry anecdotes about Ollie. A ceaseless monologue about all the minutiae of their lives. Jack had only been able to look on, paralysed with embarrassment.

But there'd been one time, when his father had gone to speak with the doctor, when Jack had been left alone with her. He'd tried to talk. Don't worry, Mum. We're here. Don't worry. But the words, proper words, proper thoughts wouldn't flow. Then a nurse had come up.

'Why don't you tidy up her hair for her, lovely?' She'd handed him a comb and slipped silently away.

The nurse couldn't have been more than twenty-one or twenty-two, and Jack, at the time, had so resented the ease with which she dealt with death. But she'd been right. He had combed his mother's hair, and it had helped.

He combed his father's hair now, and wiped his mouth with a tissue. Then took another and cleared the small plug of mucus that was lodged in his nose. It wasn't difficult now. He was practised at death beds. He could clean and wipe and stroke and pat. There was still an ever-present part of him that wanted to pluck his father from his sheet-shroud and scream 'I love you! I need you! Dad, you can't leave me yet!' but he could suppress it; just as long as he kept doing these little things for him. Just as long as he didn't give himself enough space to think.

There were new cards since yesterday. Someone called Brian, from his father's bowls club, and a short letter from the woman who used to come and do his ironing after Jack's mother had died. He read these to his father slowly, enunciating carefully, peppering them with anecdotes and comments of his own. Then he pinned them to the cork board that was fixed on the wall for the purpose, knowing even as he did it that these cards, which he himself would take down and take away with him, would soon be consigned to a box somewhere and never seen again. Their purpose was not to be cried over in perpetuity, but simple connection. The paper chain of his father's roots.

A nurse came up. Placed a cool hand on his shoulder.

240

'Trolley's coming,' she said. 'Shall I get you some tea?'

Jack smiled and nodded. It was something to do, this strange ritual. He'd accept it and get up and walk across to her station and they'd talk in hushed voices about the weather and the telly, and she'd mention some aspect of his show she'd enjoyed. They'd laugh, even. It didn't feel wrong. It was all right to laugh a little. It would make his Dad smile.

Ollie was smiling when Jack went out to meet him and Lydia. She, however, was looking pinched and uncomfortable, as if ill-at-ease with her new status. That this was something she no longer had a right to share.

He watched his son re-configure his expression as he approached, and it saddened him. He'd spent altogether too little time here with Ollie. Insufficient for them to feel easy together with it. But the loss of a grandparent, however painful it might be, was a world away from the loss of a parent. And however much he'd like to have been able to share his grief with Ollie, it wouldn't have been fair on him.

He met Ollie's frown with a wide smile and a hug.

'Three nil!'

'Three nil!'

Jack raised his hand. 'Gimme five!'

Ollie did. The moment was righted again.

'You coming in for a while?' he asked Lydia. She nodded.

'If I may,' she said quietly. 'You know –' Her voice wobbled. 'To… well, you know, to say my goodbyes.'

She had, and it had been gruesome to watch. Lydia had never been the quiet stoical type, but Jack, for some reason, had thought that today she would hold herself together. That was all he asked of her. For Ollie's sake. For his sake, even, damn it. But she hadn't. She'd sobbed, spilling enough self-indulgent tears for the three of them. He knew he was being hard on her (well, tough – he wasn't feeling charitable right now) and he also knew she did care for his father. Did, in some ways, have a right to be here. But he also knew how much of her distress wasn't actually about that. It was really about guilt and remorse and forgiveness, *Jack's* forgiveness more than anything else. She'd clutched at him, before making her

241

grand exit, and whispered, 'I'm here for you, Jack, you do know that, don't you?' and so agitated was she, so desperate for absolution, that he relented and accepted her hugs. He had more than enough guilt to carry through life with him. The least he could do was acknowledge hers.

By the time Lydia had gone, Oliver was ashen, and, anxious to lighten the load that was etched so clearly on his son's face, Jack got the paper out and had Ollie read out the football scores for his Grandad. He did the premier league, the first division, the second division and the Scottish premier league too, then Jack had him read out the *Times'* sports column from yesterday. That always made his dad laugh.

Then he told his father all about how Ollie had scored a magnificent goal yesterday morning, and how the Cougars, as a result, were now second in the league.

'We can win it, you know,' he told Ollie.

'We can,' agreed Ollie, managing a smile. 'And we will. Hear that Grandad? We will!'

A whole two hours had passed somehow, and when the nurse came over to let them know she was going off shift, Jack could feel his joints creaking.

'And I need to get you home, mate,' he told Ollie. 'School in the morning.'

He stood up and stretched. His muscles ached, too. He leaned across and gave his father a kiss on his forehead. Ollie stood, and, following his lead, gave his grandad a kiss also and spoke a whispered goodbye. Jack's throat tightened. Would this really be the last time?

The nurse touched his arm.

'Why don't you get off home as well,' she said softly. 'You look dreadful. We can call you if we need to.' She glanced over at the tissue-filled waste bin and grimaced. 'And frankly, we can do without your germs.'

He should go home. Of course he should. Except here was his father and here his only child. His only real home, right now, was where they were.

Ollie was silent as they made their way through the hospice to the car park, and Jack felt such a powerful need to clasp his son to him that he had to stuff his hands into his pockets to stop himself. It wasn't that they weren't still physical with each other, but, out here, with visitors and nurses scurrying around, he knew he mustn't. He could so keenly recapture the fifteen-year-old him. Ollie's pride, his composure, would be all.

'A bit grim, eh?' he said as they climbed into the car.

Ollie nodded, his face pale. 'I can't believe Grandad's going to die.'

Jack pushed the key into the ignition but didn't switch on the engine. He rested the back of his head against the headrest.

'Nor can I, son,' he said. It was the truth.

'That tube. The one in his wrist. What goes in there, then?'

'Morphine.'

'Oh.'

'He's not in pain, Ollie. It'll be just like going to sleep.'

'Only forever.'

Jack nodded. 'I know. But he's had a good life. And a long one. If he were sitting here now he'd be waggling his finger in our faces and telling us just that.'

He turned to face his son, and could see him fighting tears. His eyes were brimming and his chin was quivering, and he looked, right then, just as he'd done as a toddler if he got into trouble or grazed his knee. Jack hadn't seen Ollie cry for years. Not even on the day he and Lydia had told him about the divorce. He'd just sat, nodding minutely, as if being given instructions. Looking old and sagacious and calm.

For a moment, Jack thought he'd say nothing. Do nothing. Let Ollie get a hold of himself and hang on to his dignity. But there was so much love inside him that he felt he might burst.

Ollie sniffed and brushed angrily at his eyes. 'I don't want you to die, Dad. I don't think I could bear it.'

'I'm not going to, Ollie. Not for a long, long time. Don't think about that.'

'But how can *you* bear it?'

Jack twisted in his seat so he could meet his son's eye. 'I can't. But I have to. We all have to one day.' Ollie's chin was still trembling. Jack could see he couldn't speak now.

'It's all right,' he said softly. 'It's all right to cry, son.'

He reached over and took him in his arms.

243

There'd been lots of painful times in Jack's life. There'd be lots more ahead. But dropping Ollie back at his mother's that evening the pain hit him suddenly, physically and completely unexpectedly. Watching his son's hunched form, his teenage swaggering-but-self-conscious gait as he headed up the path, made Jack feel so sad he could almost taste it on his tongue. He waited till Ollie had let himself in, then drove off into the night, fighting tears. He let them flow for a moment, then shook himself mentally. This was not useful.

One thing, all at once, became blindingly obvious. He could no more take the producer's job Graham had offered him, than he could contemplate taking a job on the moon. Apart from his Junior league round-up – no more than an hour or two's writing – he could take no job that interfered with his weekends. He should not and would not. Forget his career. He'd find a new one, a better one. There were plenty out there for someone with his skills. You just had to look. Perhaps go the way of Lydia and train for a different one. Would there ever be a better time to do it? In the meantime, he still had plenty of freelance work. He still had his columns. Still had all sorts of sports one-offs coming up. He could manage. Sure he'd be poorer. He could forget Cardiff Bay. But life would be so very much poorer if he lost his precious time with Ollie every week. That was finite and irreplaceable. The most important gift he could give him.

Having made the decision, Jack felt better. Mainly, he knew, because it had at last sunk in that what mattered in his life was not, after all, being some cheesy TV star or sports pundit, but being a father. Ollie's father. That was who he was.

He was feeling much better by the time he'd got home. There was still the dead weight of the expectation of getting *that* phone call, but, that ordeal notwithstanding, he felt as in control as he'd felt about anything in the last two years. And it still wasn't late. He could even still see Hope, maybe.

Everything about her manner when they'd spoken seemed to be signalling that he should not be without hope, and, whatever doubts had been simmering about commitment, they too, like the job, now felt far less important than going with his instincts and following his heart. He rolled his eyes at his reflection in the car window as he locked it. Following his *heart*? Was he hearing himself right?

He was certainly hearing his answer-phone right. There was a message from Hope, in response to his own one. '*No problem*,' she'd trilled in a rather spiky falsetto. '*I know you're a busy man, Jack, so call me whenever. No rush. Goodbye.*' And that – bloody hell, bloody *hell* – had been that.

Jack had winced at the 'Jack'. It sounded so cold. Couldn't have felt more so if she'd just said 'you bastard'. He picked up the phone and dialled her number from memory. It rang eleven times and then a woman's voice kicked in. But it wasn't Hope's voice. It was the telecom woman. He didn't leave a message this time.

Chapter 28

She was getting good, Hope decided, at dealing with disappointment. Good at things not working out. It wasn't your successes that defined you as a person, it was the way you dealt with life's blows. Well, she'd certainly had lots of practice on the blows front over the years. And life was just one big series of them right now, so perhaps when things eased up and something good happened she'd appreciate it all the more. She looked around carefully at the fun run people surrounding her. Here recognising a face, there a whole family. Many of them here, she reminded herself sternly, had altogether less mundane tales than her own. Tales of disappointment, and heartbreak, and loss. She was no big deal, with her small time heartache and her insignificant longings. Just another human being, serving time.

She mounted the podium to scan the field again. She was, at least, proud of all they'd achieved here today. It was no small thing they'd done. She could take her disappointment and tuck it somewhere less visible. She was all right before she'd met him, she'd be all right once she got over him. What did she expect? To have it all laid out on a plate for her? Love and happiness and bloody roses round the door?

More to the point though, where *was* he?

The start point, now demarcated by means of a large pink banner, was a little to the north of the field. Thanks to the unexpected clemency of the weather, the turn-out was staggering. Even now there were crocodiles of enthusiastic runners, lycra-clad and sinewy, waiting to get their numbers, their limbs fluid. All anxious to make their mark. To achieve their own personal nirvana today.

'Well over a thousand is my guess,' said Mr Babbage. Hope decided, having never really thought about it before, that she was really rather fond of Mr Babbage. He was here. He'd been persuaded out of running, but he'd still made the effort. He wasn't just after publicity. No-one important knew he was here. His logo was already in place on all the banners, his firm's name above the number on everyone's front. And yet he'd come anyway. Yes, he was a fine man.

Madeleine flipped her sunglasses down from hairdo to nose. 'One thousand, one hundred and twenty-eight,' she said. 'WOW. Can you believe it?'

Madeleine wasn't running, either. Her back, she explained, with a wink and a grin. Hope was pleased for her. Two months and counting with this one. Perhaps she'd hang up her lucky thong at long last. But Simon had shown up and was down with the front runners, bobbing from foot to foot and cycling his arms. He was wearing a plain white T-shirt and a baseball cap. Hope felt a stab of relief to see him. She had so expected him not to come. She looked at the start clock. Five forty-two. Where *was* Jack? He surely wouldn't let them down now.

Patti, who had pitched in at the last minute to help with the warm-up, was now jogging across the grass towards them. She'd gone back to her car to try to get Jack on her mobile.

'Has he showed yet?' she asked.

Hope shook her head.

'Well, I've tried his mobile again. It's still on divert.'

'We'll give it five minutes,' Madeleine decided. 'And then we'll go with plan B.'

She turned to Hope. 'You'd better get down there, hadn't you?' Hope had difficulty hearing her above the noise of the PA. She shook her head.

'There's no rush. I'll stay here a bit longer.'

'There's a thought,' said Madeleine. 'Can you stick around too, Patti? If Jack doesn't show would you mind starting the race for us?'

Patti shrugged. 'Sure. If you'd like me to. Hey – result! Does this mean I get to get out of the race?' Hope was still scanning the sea of heads anxiously. He couldn't let them down. He couldn't.

'Did you try the office again?' she asked her. 'I mean he might have had trouble getting through here. What with the noise and everything.'

Patti looked at her watch.

'Tell you what,' she said. 'I'll run across and get my bag. If I'm not running I might as well anyway. Not running, hurrah!' And she was off.

When she came back she was waving her arms. She climbed up to the podium.

'He's not coming.' She waggled the mobile. 'He's left a message on my voicemail.'

Hope felt her stomach hit her boots. 'What did he say?'

'Not a lot. Just that he was sorry but that something had come up and he wouldn't be able to make it.' She opened a bottle of water and drank from it.

'That was all?'

'That was all.'

Madeleine, by now, was in full flow at the microphone, trying to chivvy the massed runners into some sort of order. Hope passed the news on and turned back to Patti.

'D'you know where he was calling from?'

'Well, his mobile, of course.' She frowned. 'He sounded a bit odd. I hope he's OK.' She looked genuinely concerned.

'OK?' asked Hope, anxious now. 'Why shouldn't he be?'

Patti looked at her for a good long moment, then upturned the Evian bottle to her lips again. Then she frowned. 'Well, you know. What with the job and everything.'

'The job in London?'

'London?'

'The job he was going to see about today.'

Patti looked confused.

'Job? What job was that?'

Hope shrugged. 'I don't know. I thought he was going to see someone about a job in London.'

Patti shook her head. 'Oh, you mean the 'Five Live' thing? Oh, I get you. I thought you meant a job *in* London. No, that's just an OB thing he's doing for the European Cup. No, I mean the show.'

'What, *his* show?'

Patti was studying her more carefully now. She looked cagey all of a sudden. 'Look, I'm not sure it's my place to… Look, I'm sure he'd have made it if he could.'

Hope placed her hand on Patti's arm. 'No, please tell me. What about his show? Is this something to do with the television thing? He told me about a television thing. Is it something to do with that?'

248

'You mean the HTV thing?'

'I don't know. All I know is that he told me about something in the pipeline to do with a television show. What happened?'

Patti looked at Hope quizzically. Then she narrowed her eyes and grinned.

'Oh, I get it,' she said smoothly. 'Well, well, well. He's a dark horse, and then some. Are you two, like –'

She raised her eyebrows in enquiry.

'No. Not… Well, maybe.' Hope could feel herself colouring. 'Well… but what's happened about his show?'

Patti seemed to consider for a moment. 'Well, I guess it's going to be common knowledge any time now anyway,' she said eventually. 'It's been axed, that's all. And I –'

'Axed? You mean they're not going to do it any more?' It suddenly felt as if she'd been felled by a punch.

'Well, not as such. I mean there's still going to be a show. It's just that Jack won't be presenting it any more –'

'But that's awful!'

Patti narrowed her eyes.

'Hey, not *so* awful. It's kind of par for the course. It's been running four years now, you know. Which is a pretty good innings. It's not like it wasn't on the cards or anything.'

'Oh, but poor Jack! Was he very upset?'

Patti shrugged. 'I don't know. Yes, I'm sure he was. I mean, I don't think it was any kind of surprise, you know? It's just that he's had such a shit year, what with the divorce and everything, and what with the HTV thing not happening… he was so excited about that.' She stopped speaking and seemed suddenly lost in thought. 'And I feel bad, of course. I mean I know it's not like I pushed him out or anything, but we're mates, you know? I'm sure it must have been hard for him to swallow.'

Hope blinked at her. 'You mean *you're* the one who's taking over?'

Patti nodded. Then she sighed.

'So it's kind of tough on him, you know?' She spread her hands. 'But what can I do? I have a career to think about too. And you know what it's like. These opportunities don't come up that often.'

Hope didn't, but she also didn't doubt that was true. Poor Jack. No wonder he'd seemed so irritable and tired. But Patti was right. 'I know,' she agreed.

'I mean, that's life, isn't it? When an opportunity like that comes up, you don't sit around thinking about it too long, you know? You just have to go out there and grab it with both hands. One life. No read-throughs. You know?'

Hope rather thought Patti might have been saying that to herself a lot just lately. But she was probably right. It *was* too good an opportunity to miss. But poor Jack.

'Poor Jack,' she said. Patti agreed. Then suddenly slapped the palm of her hand against her forehead and groaned.

'Shit. I just had a thought!'

'What?'

'Of course! Oh, shit. His father!'

'What about his father?'

'God – of *course*. That might be it. I bet that's it. I remember him telling Hil about it the other day.'

'*What?*'

'That they'd had to move him to the hospice. Perhaps his Dad's –' Her brows creased. 'Shit, now that would be a bitch. On top of everything else.'

Hope touched her arm. 'Hospice? Which hospice?'

'Christ, don't ask me. He doesn't tell me stuff like that.'

Madeleine was waving from the podium at them. Hope looked up at the time clock. Only a couple of minutes to six now.

Patti waved back at her and started moving towards the podium. 'I'd better get up there and strut my stuff, eh?'

'But who *would* know?'

Patti said she didn't know. Hope mounted the steps with her.

'But someone must.'

Patti looked down at her, obviously bemused at her insistence. 'Hadn't you better get down to the start line?'

'*Someone* must,' she persisted. Patti thought a moment.

'I guess Danny might.'

'Danny?' That name again.

'His mate. He's –'

'Do you have his number?'

'Yeah, but –'

Madeleine was introducing Patti over the loudspeaker now. Hope could hear the words 'Valentine's Day' booming out of the speaker behind her. Poor Jack. What a day *he* was having. What a life he was having. Decided, and exhilarated, she grabbed Patti's arm.

'Look. Can I borrow your phone a minute?'

'Sure, but –'

'So I can get the number.' Madeleine was beckoning Patti to come across to the microphone now, while the runners bobbed and cheered beneath. 'In here, right? What's his surname?'

Patti smiled. 'You'll find him under D. For "dickhead". Bless.'

'Hi Pats, how's it hanging?'

Hope had walked a little way from the speakers, but the noise was still deafening, and the voice at the other end of the phone was low.

She explained who she was, and why she was calling on Patti's phone, pressing the flat of her hand against her ear.

'It's just that Jack was supposed to be here starting the race, and no-one can get hold of him and Patti said she thought he might have had to go to the hospice?'

'Shit, what a bitch,' he said. She heard him sigh. 'Yes. She's probably right. I know things were pretty bad yesterday. Who did you say this was again?'

'Hope,' she said. 'Hope Shepherd.'

'*Ah*,' he said slowly. 'Got you.'

Another telling tone of voice. She didn't care. She ignored it. 'And she thought you might know which one it was.'

There was a short exhalation. 'Look, I hardly think he's going to be thrilled to be bothered by you guys right now, you know?'

'No, no,' said Hope quickly. 'I've no intention of bothering him. I just wanted to... well... just ring and make sure he's OK. Let him know we're thinking of him.' She felt a complete fool, but the rush of exhilaration was still moving through her limbs.

'Well, OK, I guess. It's the – damn, what was it called? Something Court. In Penarth. That's it. It's –'

'Holly Court?'

'You got it. I'm sure it's in the phone book. It's –'

'That's OK, thanks. I know the one.'

Knowing all the hospices was, of course, all part of the service. Hope had them in a box on her desk. But that wasn't much use right now. She called directory enquiries and had them text their number to Patti's phone. It took only seconds, and within a few more the phone was ringing. Yes, he was there, they said, and did she want them to go and fetch him?

'No, no,' she said quickly. 'Don't worry. Could you just give him a message? Let him know that we're all thinking of him? That's all.'

It wasn't all, of course. It was very far from all.

She'd just disconnected when Patti and Madeleine came down from the podium. The race was underway. She could make out the front runners as a mass of primary colours and bobbing heads, streaming, as one, beneath the start line banner.

'I can't believe it!' said Maddie. 'All that training and you're not even running! What's happened, Shepherd? You worried Simon'll put you to shame?'

Hope shook her head and handed the phone back to Patti.

'Thanks for that.' She felt liberated. Energised. Alive.

'Any joy?'

She nodded. No. Not liberated exactly. Just like a new her had finally surfaced from the dark. Someone else, someone braver, was in the driving seat now.

Patti picked up her backpack and slipped the phone back inside. 'I'd better go and get changed,' she said, glancing at the clock. 'Before someone spots me and drags me along for the ride. Look, if you do manage to get through to him, will you give him my love?'

Hope agreed that she would, and Patti jogged off once again across the grass.

'Right then,' said Madeleine, who was looking at her more carefully now. 'Get through to who exactly? Jack?'

'Yes,' she said. 'But not get through to exactly. Look, Maddie, I need to ask you a really big favour.'

'That sounds ominous,' said Madeleine.

She told Maddie about the show and the TV thing and Jack's father, and how she'd left such a cool message on his answer machine, and that ridiculous and mad though it probably sounded,

252

she wanted to drive down to the hospice right now and see Jack face to face.

'What, *now*? Like it's that urgent?'

'I know, I know. But I was thinking about what Patti said about opportunities. I'm all done with sitting around thinking about this one while it flies out of the window without me. I've got to *go* there. I mean I'll come straight back, if, you know, if there's nothing I can do. But I've got to go there. We're all sorted here, aren't we? There's plenty of volunteers to help with the goody bags and everything, and I already fixed up where the photographer needs to be, and –'

Madeleine waved her to a stop. 'You don't need to convince me,' she said. 'You've done enough work for ten of us already. But are you sure that's such a good idea? I mean, his Dad might – well, supposing he's already popped his clogs and you come bursting in on the grieving family like the Lone Ranger in Lycra? Suppose all that sort of stuff?'

Hope was shaking her head.

'There won't be. I just *know* there won't be. He hasn't *got* any family. Just his son. And I just – Oh, God, I don't know. I just want to see him, Maddie. I just want to get there before I can think myself out of it. Look, have you ever got that feeling that someone you cared about really, really needed a hug? Maddie, I've got to go there.'

Maddie lifted her arms and hugged Hope herself then.

'You know what? You're right. You're mad but you're right. Go on. Get off there. Go give him his hug.'

Hope grabbed her bag and a bottle of water. There'd be a whole lot more hurdles for her to jump – she knew that. But she'd just jumped the biggest and it filled her with hope. She jogged across the field, and leapt the boundary fence too.

Then she sprinted all the way to her car.

Chapter 29

Jack couldn't quite believe his eyes, and for a moment he thought he shouldn't. Perhaps this was a mirage in a desert. Or a wish wished almost hard enough. He hadn't known he'd been wishing exactly, but now she was standing here it was so obvious he had.

'I hope you don't think this is an outrageous imposition on your privacy,' she said softly. 'I can go again. I just thought – well, I only just heard. Oh, Jack, I'm so sorry.'

Her chest was rising and falling steadily. She was real. Alive. *Here*. He leapt up from the bench he'd been sitting on.

'No,' he said. 'Not at all. I couldn't be more happy to see you.' He wanted to pick her up and hug her, just to check she *was* real. But instead he cast his eyes over her and then pointed to her feet. 'Look,' he said. 'You're even wearing your trainers, Cinderella.'

She nodded. 'So I am.' She looked uncomfortable. 'I wish you'd told me, Jack. This is where you were on Sunday, wasn't it?'

Jack nodded.

'Why didn't you tell me? If I'd known, I could have – well, I wouldn't have –'

He shook his head. 'I've been trying to make a conscious effort not to offload my problems on other people.' He smiled wryly at her. 'You know how it is.'

'Yes,' she said. He could see that she meant it. 'Yes. You're right. I *do* know how it is. Jack, is it – has he –'

Jack patted the bench and sat down on it again himself.

'He's hanging in there. I just came out to stretch my legs for a while. It gets a bit grim.' He shook his head. 'But it's OK. He's still hanging in there.'

She didn't say 'good', or anything. She just nodded and sat down. Her slender brown knees were shiny beside his. He still couldn't quite believe she was here.

He shifted to face her properly. 'I'm sorry about the race.'

'Oh, for God's sake, don't even think about that. The race is carrying on perfectly well without you.'

'But what about *you*?'

'*And* without me.' She hooked a clump of hair behind her ear. She was wearing it in a pony tail, but lots of it had escaped. It made her look very young. It made him want to hold her. So much. 'Anyway, I really wouldn't care if it didn't,' she said firmly. 'I'm so sorry, Jack. I'm so sorry about *everything*.'

And then, suddenly, and almost as if the granting of Jack's wishes was her very reason for being, she gathered him into her arms and held him very tightly, while a scatter of late starlings took flight above them.

Jack let himself be held by her, happy to be still. Tucked into her embrace, breathing her in. Feeling the warmth in her limbs creep in through his shirt. He hadn't realised how chilly it had become. Hadn't realised how utterly alone he'd been feeling, and how much he didn't want to be alone any more. How much her being here, holding him, meant to him.

'Don't be,' he said at length. 'Really, Hope, don't be.'

She lowered her arms and spread her hands in front of her. 'But your job!'

'Is just a job. I have several. There'll be others.'

'But the TV thing! What happened?'

Jack shrugged. 'It didn't happen. They often don't.' Jack, to his relief, found he could say these things with a detachment he never thought he'd be able to feel. He *could* have a different future. It *would* all work out. Now was the time to re-think, make new plans. He only hoped that, in some way, his dad would know too. Hope was looking out over the slope of the hospice gardens to the sliver of Bristol Channel beyond. He could tell by the way her head was angled. The curve of her chin. All at once so familiar.

'But what will you do?' she asked, turning to him now and searching his face. He shrugged again. He was chock full of ideas but maybe now wasn't the time. There would be time enough soon. 'I'm sorry,' she said. 'Stupid, stupid question. That's got to be about the very last thing on your mind right now.'

He took her hand and squeezed it, and the silence grew and eddied around them, broken only by the irritable cawing of the birds.

'It isn't,' he said at length. 'As it happens, it isn't. But it's funny, you know. It actually doesn't matter. All that really matters is – well, *this*.' He glanced at her. 'I was just thinking about something. You know, when you got here? When I was small – I don't know how old exactly. Definitely no more than four – I won a football in a raffle. My mum and dad used to go to these dinner dances, and they'd always buy a raffle ticket for me. Anyway, this time, I won a football. It was one of those charity ones they do – you know? You probably do. Signed by the whole 1966 World Cup team. You can imagine how pleased my dad was. But I wanted to play with it, of course. I was four and I gave them merry hell. I mean, why couldn't I kick it? It was mine and it was a football and I wanted to play with it!' He laughed. 'Anyway, in the end, he caved in. I got my football and I kicked merry hell out of that as well, and it wasn't long before all the autographs on it had vanished. And eventually, of course, I lost it. Kicked it over a wall, or something. I don't even remember. But that was that. And I guess I didn't really think about it until I was a teenager – another World Cup, probably – and I would have so loved to have a football like that. And then, out of the blue, on the day of my twenty-first birthday party, my dad made this little speech and presented me with my football. As new and perfect as the day he'd won it for me. He said he thought I was just about grown up enough not to attack it with my right foot.' He smiled at the memory. 'He hadn't ever given it to me at all, you see. He'd been out and bought another just like it, and painstakingly written all the signatures on it, plus his own, or so he told me – though I never twigged.' Hope remained silent, her eyes shining. '*That* was my dad,' he said. 'That was him all over. So the football's still here, and it'll pass down to Ollie. Probably worth a small fortune by now. I'm going to give it to him on *his* twenty-first.' He sighed. 'But you know what?'

'What?'

'I really wish I had that other ball right now.'

He fell silent again and Hope took his hand in hers. 'Your poor father. Was it sudden?'

Jack shook his head. 'No. Not at all. He's been ill for a long time. Prostate cancer. We thought – well, *I* thought – that he was going to be OK. But then, well, he got secondaries. And... No. I've known for a long time. But when they said he was going to... that there was nothing more they could do for him –' His tongue felt thick in his mouth. He swallowed. 'Well, you're never really prepared for it, are you? You tell yourself you will be, but you never really feel… ' He sighed. 'I don't know. Ready. You know?'

'I know,' she said softly. 'It's tough, isn't it? The waiting. I remember it when my dad died. As if it was yesterday.'

'When did he die?'

'A long time ago now. I was twenty-five. I was pregnant with Tom. I wish he'd seen him. He so wanted to.'

She looked at Jack for a long moment.

'But he's still *with* me,' she said. 'I think of him all the time. Sort of check in with him.' She smiled. 'He would have liked you.'

He swallowed again. Let the silence lengthen. Then took a tissue from his pocket and blew his nose hard. Hope squeezed his hand again.

'I know,' she said. 'I know.'

He smiled wanly at her.

'I have a very bad cold.'

'Oh, poor you!' she cried. 'On top of everything!' She twisted her head. 'Can I get you something? I have some paracetamol in my car. And water.'

The amber in her eyes was turning gold in the light of the setting sun. He shook his head, then reached over and placed his other hand over hers.

'You have, you know,' he said at last.

She met his gaze, her brows furrowed in confusion. ' Have what?'

'Been on my mind. All the time, Hope. Ever since I first met you. I've been such an idiot. I so nearly called you. Many times. But you made it so clear that you didn't want to see me, and… '

'I *did*, Jack. I just… well, I was just scared, that's all.'

'Of me?'

'Of… well… ' She stopped speaking and looked out across the water again. 'No, Jack. Far from it. Of letting myself fall in love with someone like you.'

Jack thought he'd never in his life felt such a physical effect from a state of mind. It was as if a mushroom cloud of happiness was right there inside him, growing palpably. Almost, *almost* within reach. He gripped her hands tighter. 'God, Hope, believe me. I'm really not the person you think I am. I'm not the person *I* thought I was. I wish I could explain to you. I'm just… ' But she shook her head and motioned him to stop. She released her hands and placed two of his fingers on the soft skin of her forearm.

'Feel this?' she said.

'What?'

Her eyes were fixed on his now.

'Red squashy thing. Pumps blood. A little worse for wear, you'll notice. But it's OK, Jack. It's OK now.' She lifted both arms towards him. And he folded her gratefully in his.

'I *know*,' she said again. 'So you don't have to explain. You don't have to say anything at all.'

She lifted her face and touched her lips gently against his own. And so they sat, saying nothing, while the sun met the water. Because, suddenly, with her here, with her head on his shoulder, there was nothing else he needed to say.

They heard the nurse before they saw her. A steady click-clack of feet on the footpath. Jack swivelled his head and she smiled at him, her eyes full of professional compassion. Oh, God. Was this it? But she raised her hand.

'It's all right,' she said. 'It's just that there's been some changes in his breathing. We thought you might want to come in and… well… '

This was the language of death, Jack knew. All those unfinished sentences. Changes in his breathing. A form of shorthand. Or longhand, perhaps. It meant it wouldn't be long.

He raised his own hand and stood.

'Thank you.'

The nurse tilted her head and turned back towards the buildings. Hope, getting to her own feet beside him, found his hand again and gave it a squeeze.

'I'll go now.'

He nodded, letting her hand drop from his own and feeling the hollowness rise within him again. They turned and began walking back up the path, the nurse a few steps ahead of them, her low heels still clicking as she walked. The sky was dark now, the birds all flown.

'I'll call you, shall I?'

She looked shyly at him. 'That would be good. But… well, you know. Whenever.'

They'd reached a junction, where the path diverged around a big circular bed. Cream roses, in bud still. Massed and almost ready, thrusting towards the heavens. But frozen in time. For his father, at least.

'Or – Jack?' She stopped on the path and put her hand on his forearm. Looked up into his eyes. 'Jack, shall I stay?'

He shook his head. 'Hope, I'm sure you don't want to be –'

'Jack, I *mean* it. Would you like me to stay? I have nothing to get back for. The children are with my mother. I can stay. I can be here, and… well. If you'd like me to. If you think it would help.'

Jack couldn't trust himself to speak. But then he saw himself reflected in the mirror of her eyes and it gave him a strength he didn't know he possessed. He found a wry smile. 'I told my dad about you, you know,' he said. 'He wanted to meet you.' It was the most ludicrous thing to say, and yet, suddenly, it felt like the most important thing in the world. That she should meet him. *See* him. Connect with him in some way. Jack didn't know why, but he knew it was what he wanted her to do. It didn't matter that his father would know nothing about it. It was simply the connection with his past that mattered. Continuity. He traced a finger across her forehead and tucked a wisp of hair behind her ear. 'Would you? Would you do that?'

'I'd love to,' she said.

'I mean, he's not conscious. It's not –'

'Jack, I know that.'

'I mean, he's dying, Hope. It's not pretty. It's –'

They had reached the edge of the gardens, and the building itself loomed expectantly ahead. The language of death had now utterly engulfed him. But she nodded and touched his arm again and he could see from her expression that she'd already been here. That she knew what to expect. That she wanted to be here. That it was right that she was.

'I *know*,' she said again.

God, how he loved her.

He swallowed. 'Thank you. I'd like that, Hope. Yes.'

She slipped her warm hand into his and they walked back in together. It would be OK now. He was ready.

Other titles coming soon from Lynne Barrett-Lee...

Straight On Till Morning

Is our destiny written in the stars?

*'It was then that it struck me, with terrifying clarity. I was going to die. I was going to die at any moment. I was going to die, moreover, in a pair of tartan pyjamas and a grubby black cardigan. For whatever was attached to the headlights in front of me was actually driving on **my side of the road**...'*

So begins Sally Matthews' date with destiny. She doesn't actually believe in destiny, of course – she's way too busy looking after her husband, arranging her step-daughter's wedding, and humouring her mum-on-a-mission (which currently involves Tony Blair). No surprise, then, that she's out late at night, with nothing but a dog and a cricket bat for company. In short, Sally hasn't time for a near-death experience. However handsome the man who's about to run her off the road...

ISBN: 1905170394 (9781905170395)   Price:£6.99

Julia Gets a Life

A hilarious and romantic thirty-something novel about a woman who leaves her philandering husband to embark on a very alternative voyage of self-discovery.

When Julia's husband has an affair with local siren Rhiannon de Laney, she feels as if her world is falling apart. Once the arguments have abated, and her husband has moved out, Julia realises she's well and truly on her own, a single parent with two teenage children, a bad haircut and no idea of what to do or where to go next.

Gradually, however, Julia begins to recognise the benefits of being single: it's the chance to meet new people and make new friends, change her hairstyle, throw out her old clothes, experiment with a new image, resurrect her photography career, travel the country with a boy band and, in short, rediscover herself outside the context of loyal wife and dutiful mother. She also rediscovers the joys of dating.

After a few false starts, she finds herself learning more about the talents, musical and otherwise, of the lead singer of Britain's most famous band. Julia's certainly got herself a life; you wonder whether it is the kind of existence she wants to live permanently, or whether her ailing marriage is worth saving. Light-hearted, humorous and at times surprising, Julia's battles with this age-old dilemma prove instantly recognisable yet highly entertaining, with a twist in the tale that may surprise or perplex.

ISBN: 1905170408 (9781905170401)   Price: £6.99

One Glass Is Never Enough

Jane Wenham-Jones

"Delightfully sparkling, like champagne,
with the deep undertones of a fine claret."

Three women, one bar and three different reasons for buying it. Single mother Sarah needs a home for her children; Claire's an ambitious business woman. For wealthy Gaynor, Greens Wine Bar is just one more amusement. Or is it?

On the surface, Gaynor has it all – money, looks, a beautiful home in the picturesque seaside town of Broadstairs, and Victor – her generous, successful husband. But while Sarah longs for love and Claire is making money, Gaynor wants answers. Why is Victor behaving strangely and who does he see on his frequent trips away? What's behind the threatening phone-calls? As the bar takes off, Gaynor's life starts to fall apart.

Into her turmoil comes Sam – strong and silent with a hidden past. Theirs is an unlikely friendship but then nobody is quite what they seem in this tale of love, loss and betrayal set against the middle-class dream of owning a wine bar. As Gaynor's confusion grows, events unfold that will change all of their lives forever…

ISBN: 1905170106   Price: £6.99

Passing Shadows

Della Galton

"Della Galton is always worth reading!"
Take A Break

"Della Galton is one of our best loved and most talented
serial writers. I am delighted to see her first novel in print"
Gaynor Davies, Fiction Editor, *Woman's Weekly*

"Della's writing is stylish, moving, original and fun : a
wonderfully satisfying journey to a destination you can
eagerly anticipate without ever guessing."
Liz Smith, Fiction Editor, *My Weekly*

How do you choose between friendship and love?
Maggie faces an impossible dilemma when she discovers that
Finn, the man she loves, is also the father of her best friend's
child. Should Maggie betray her best friend, who never
wanted him to know? Or lie to Finn, the first man she's ever
trusted enough to love? The decision is complicated by the
shadows of her past.

ISBN: 1905170238   Price: £6.99

The Boy I love

Marion Husband

"Compelling & sensual. Well written..."

Set in the aftermath of World War One. Paul Harris, still frail from shellshock, returns to his father's home and to the arms of his secret lover, Adam. He discovers that Margot, the fiancée of his dead brother, is pregnant and marries her through a sense of loyalty. Through Adam he finds work as a schoolteacher; while setting up a home with Margot he continues to see Adam.

Pat Morgan who was a sergeant in Paul's platoon, runs a butcher's shop in town and cares for his twin brother, Mick who lost both legs in the war. Pat yearns for the closeness he experienced with Paul in the trenches.

Set in a time when homosexuality was 'the love that dare not speak its name' the story develops against the backdrop of the strict moral code of the period. Paul has to decide where his loyalty and his heart lies as all the characters search hungrily for the love and security denied them during the war.

ISBN 1905170009   Price £6.99

Paper Moon

Marion Husband

"This is an extraordinary novel. Beautifully controlled pacy prose carefully orchestrates the relationships of many well drawn characters and elegantly captures the atmosphere of England in 1946...This novel is perfect." Margaret Wilkinson, Novelist

The passionate love affair between Spitfire pilot Bobby Harris and photographer's model Nina Tate lasts through the turmoil of World War Two, but is tested when his plane is shot down. Disfigured and wanting to hide from the world, Bobby retreats from Bohemian Soho to the empty house his grandfather has left him, a house haunted by the secrets of Bobby's childhood, where the mysteries of his past are gradually unravelled.

Following on from The Boy I Love, Marion Husband's highly acclaimed debut novel, Paper Moon explores the complexities of love and loyalty against a backdrop of a world transformed by war.

ISBN 1905170149   Price £6.99